"Before you go, just have to do,"

She released a weary sigh. "W"

"This."

He framed her face in his palms and covered her mouth with his before she had time to issue a protest. She knew she should pull away, but as it had always been, she was completely captive to the softness of his lips, the gentle stroke of his tongue, his absolute skill. No one had ever measured up to him when it came to kissing. She suspected no one ever would.

Once they parted, Austin tipped his forehead against hers. "Man, I've missed this."

"We're not children anymore, Austin. We can't go back to the way it was."

He took an abrupt step back. "I'm not suggesting we do that. But we can go forward, see where it goes."

"It won't go anywhere because you'll never be able to give me what I want."

"What do you want, Georgie?"

"More."

* * *

An Heir for the Texan

AN HEIR FOR
THE TEXAN

BY
KRISTI GOLD

MILLS
BOON
&

First Published in Great Britain 2017
By Mills & Boon, an imprint of HarperCollins*Publishers*
1 London Bridge Street, London, SE1 9GF

© 2017 Kristi Goldberg

ISBN: 978-0-263-92804-4

51-0117

Our policy is to use papers that are natural, renewable and recyclable products and made from wood grown in sustainable forests. The logging and manufacturing processes conform to the legal environmental regulations of the country of origin.

Printed and bound in Spain
by CPI, Barcelona

Kristi Gold has a fondness for beaches, baseball and bridal reality shows. She firmly believes that love has remarkable healing powers, and she feels very fortunate to be able to weave stories of love and commitment. As a bestselling author, a National Readers' Choice Award winner and a three-time Romance Writers of America RITA® Award finalist, Kristi has learned that although accolades are wonderful, the most cherished rewards come from networking with readers. She can be reached through her website at www.kristigold.com, or through Facebook.

To my former farrier and dear friend Stephanie S., and her fantastic mother-in-law, Florence, for all the support they've shown me throughout the years.

Love ya both.

One

If Austin Calloway had to hang one more damn holiday light, he'd book a flight to the Bahamas to ring in the New Year.

For the past six Decembers, the D Bar C Ranch—his home, both past and present—had morphed from a South Texas ranch into a fake winter wonderland, all in the name of community involvement. Next week, the chaos would begin with cars lining up to bask in the holiday glow and deliver toys for underprivileged children. As much as he appreciated the cause, he didn't particularly care for the effort involved in transforming the place, especially while being supervised by two nitpicky female relatives.

After draping the last string on the barbed wire, Austin hopped off the fence flanking the entry and climbed onto the ATV, taking off through the main gate toward temporary freedom. He passed by the family homestead, where his sister-in-law, Paris, sat on the front porch, hands resting on her pregnant belly. He raised his hand in a wave, and grinned when he noticed his brother, Dallas, struggling to set up the inflatable Santa beneath the massive oak while his blond-haired bride cheered him on. But his smile faded fast when he thought about his own failed marriage, and the loneliness that plagued him during the holidays.

Shaking off the self-pity, Austin picked up speed before someone chased him down, namely one of the two self-proclaimed elves now hanging angels on the manicured hedges. As much as he appreciated Maria, the former nanny who'd become his much loved stepmom after the death of his birth mother, and Jenny, the surprise stepmom they'd only learned about six years ago during the reading of his father's will, he was more than done with the decorating demands.

Once he rounded the corner and reached his own cedar-and-rock house, he pulled into the driveway, shut down the ATV, then slid into the cab of his dual-wheel truck. He backed out and retraced the path he had taken, not bothering to acknowledge the family members standing on the lawn, shooting dagger looks in his direction. He continued toward the safety of the highway as he headed to an atmosphere where he could feel more macho.

A few miles down the road, Austin pulled into the gravel parking lot at the outdoor arena and claimed a spot among all the stock trailers, plagued by past memories of the life he'd left behind. He'd said goodbye to the rodeo circuit several years ago to enter the cutthroat world of car dealerships. Actually, several truck dealerships spanning three states, thanks to the help of his winnings and inheritance. At least he'd succeeded at that endeavor, even if he had failed at his marriage.

Shaking off the regrets, he walked through the entry, nodding at several cowboys, some who had been his competition. He immediately noticed all the young bucks crowded round the catch pens, eyeing him with awe like he was some sort of rodeo god. Those glory days were long gone and only remnants of the memories remained. But at least he'd left some sort of positive legacy to some kids since he'd probably never have any of his own.

He climbed the steps two at a time and slid onto a wooden bench as a spectator, not a participant. That's when he spotted her rounding the arena—a great-looking filly he knew all too well. A literal blast from his past. She was as flighty as a springtime moth, and as stubborn as a rusty gate. She could bring a man down with the swish of her tail. Austin should know. She'd brought him to his knees on more than one occasion. And even though several years had passed since he'd last seen her, he fondly recalled how she'd always given him a damn good ride.

He shifted slightly as he watched her weave in and out of traffic, black mane flowing behind her in the breeze. She hadn't lost her spirit, or her skill, or her ability to completely captivate him.

Austin tensed when he noticed a gelding coming toward her, trying his best to buck off the cowboy on his back. If the filly didn't slow down, move over, an equine wreck was imminent.

No sooner than he'd thought it, it happened. The filly in question went one way, the mare she was riding went the other, and Georgie Romero, his black-maned, flighty, spirited first real girlfriend, ended up on the ground in a heap.

A distant memory from his early childhood shot through Austin's mind in response. The recollection of his own mother falling from her horse when he'd been too young to comprehend the consequences, or the impending loss. When he'd been too little to understand.

That alone sent him on a sprint toward the arena in an effort to come to *this* woman's rescue. He damn sure didn't want to relive that tragedy.

He hoped like hell this time he wasn't too late.

When Georgia May Romero opened her eyes, she sensed a gathering crowd, but a pair of brown boots earned her immediate focus. She then noticed jean-encased legs and two large masculine hands resting casually on bent knees. And next—one very impressive, extremely big…belt buckle.

Clearly she had died and gone to Cowboy Heaven.

Her gaze traveled upward to take in the blue plaid shirt rolled up at the sleeves, revealing arms threaded with masculine veins and, above that, an open collar showing a slight hint of chest hair. She then visually journeyed to a whisker-shaded jaw surrounding a stellar mouth and an average nose with a slight indentation on the bridge. But there was nothing average about the midnight blue eyes. Devilish eyes. Familiar eyes. Surely not.

"You okay, Georgie?"

No, she'd died and gone to Cowgirl Hell.

Shaking off her stupor, Georgie sat up and scrambled to her feet, silently cursing her bad luck and the man standing before her. The only man who could shake her to the core with only a smile. The man who'd changed her life six years ago, and he didn't even know it. "Where's my horse?"

He pointed toward the outside of the arena. "Over there, tied to the rail. She's a little bit shaken but she's physically fine."

Only then did she venture another glance at her walking past, Austin Calloway. "Thanks," she muttered. "She's a two-year-old and still a little green. I brought her out to get used to the crowds. Obviously she's not ready for competition."

He had the gall to grin. "I figured that much when she tossed you on your head. You fell pretty hard."

Oh, but she had…for him. Ancient history, one she didn't dare repeat despite this chance meeting.

Chance.

She did a frantic search for the dark-haired, hazel-eyed boy who'd been the love of her life for the past five years, and thankfully spotted him still seated in the stands, holding cowboy court with a host of familiar men laughing at his antics. Andy Acosta, the middle-aged father of five, and horse trainer extraordinaire, sat at Chance's side. Not only had Andy been a longtime hand on her family's ranch, he happened to be one of the few people she trusted with her son.

"Are you sure you're okay, Georgie? No headache or double vision? Broken bones?"

Just a pain in her keister. "I'm fine," she said as she tore her gaze from her son to Austin and tried to appear calm. Having him learn of her own child's existence, and the risk of prodding questions, was the last thing she needed at the moment. When she'd made the decision to move back to town to establish her veterinarian practice, she'd known she would have to tell him eventually, but she wanted to prolong that revelation until she'd had more time to prepare. Until she could gauge how he might react. Standing in a busy arena wasn't an appropriate venue to deliver that bombshell.

"You don't look fine," he said. "In fact, you look a little out of it."

She swept the dirt from her butt with her palms and frowned. "I assure you I'm okay. It's not the first time I've been bucked off."

He took off his tan felt hat, forked a hand through his golden brown hair, then set it back on his head. "True. I remember that summer you broke your arm when you tried to ride your dad's stallion."

Leave it to him to bring that up. "I remember when you broke your nose getting into a fight with Ralphie Jones over Hannah Alvarez."

He smiled again, throwing her for a mental loop. "Hey, he started it. Besides, I didn't really like her all that much, and I was young and pretty stupid."

She'd been the same way at that time, and the price for her naivety had been high—losing her virginity to him. "Look, it's been nice seeing you again, but I have to go."

He inclined his head and frowned. "How long are you going to be in town?"

She considered lying but realized he would eventually learn the truth. At least one truth. "Indefinitely."

He looked shocked, to say the least. "You're living here now?"

"Yes."

"How long have you been back?"

She wasn't in the mood for a barrage of questions, although she did have one of her own. "A couple of weeks. Dallas didn't tell you?"

He scowled. "No. Dallas doesn't tell me a damn thing. When did you see him?"

"Actually, he called me after he learned I've taken over Doc Gordon's practice. He asked me if I'd be the vet for the D Bar C, and this new venture you have in the works, although he didn't exactly explain what that entails other than it involves livestock."

"We're calling it Texas Extreme," he said. "We're starting a business that caters to people who want the whole cowboy experience. Roping and bull riding and all things rodeo, plus we're considering a good old-fashioned trail ride."

Just what the Calloways needed—another business that would pad their pockets even more. "Interesting. I don't think the ranch house is large enough to accommodate guests and your brothers, so I assume you're going to put them in the bunkhouse."

"We're in the process of building a lodge. And since you've been away awhile, you probably don't know that we've all built our own houses. Or at least Dallas, Houston, Tyler, Worth and me. Fort won't step foot on the place. He basically hates the entire family."

She recalled how upset Austin had been when he'd learned he had twin brothers, Forth and Worth, and a stepmother in Louisiana, thanks to a bigamist father who'd revealed all after his death. She also remembered how Austin had turned to her following the reading of the will, and his distress that had led to her providing comfort. If only she could forget that night, but she'd been left with a constant, precious reminder.

Georgie sent a sideways glance toward her son, who fortunately didn't seem interested in her whereabouts. But if she didn't get away soon, he might notice her and flag her down. Worse still, call her "Mama." Then she'd have to explain everything. Almost everything. She backed up a couple of steps and hooked a thumb over her shoulder. "I guess I better go now."

"You aren't competing in the barrel racing with a more seasoned horse?" he asked.

She shook her head. "Not today."

He favored her with another sexy grin. "Guess I'll be heading out, too."

"But you just got here." And she'd just given herself away.

His smile faded into a confused look. "How do you know that?"

She studied the dirt at her feet before raising her gaze to his. "I saw you take a seat in the stands." The distraction had resulted in her lack of concentration in the arena, and the fact that he'd come to her rescue still stunned her.

He hooked both thumbs in his pockets, causing her to glimpse a place no self-respecting mother should notice, and it wasn't his buckle. "I was only here to escape all the holiday decorating at the ranch," he said. "If I don't get back, my stepmom is bound to send out a posse."

She forced herself to look at his face. "How is Maria?"

"Feisty as ever. How are your folks?"

Georgie didn't care to broach that topic in detail, and preferred to let Austin assume she still lived at home. That would guarantee he wouldn't come calling, considering the long-standing feud between both their families, compliments of their competitive fathers. Only one time had a Calloway son entered their abode. Through her bedroom window. She had given Austin everything that night eighteen years ago, including her heart. "Mom and Papa are doing fine," she said, banishing the bittersweet memories from her mind.

"I'm sure they're glad to have you back from school. I bet Old George is strutting around like a rooster over his only kid becoming a veterinarian."

Not so much. Her father was still shamed over having a daughter who'd had a baby out of wedlock, information her family had kept away from the public eye. In fact, she hadn't spoken to her dad to any degree in years. Luckily her mother hadn't passed judgment and still supported her when she'd stayed away from the small town and the prospect of gossip. She purposefully lost touch with friends, and now that she'd returned, she'd fortunately been able to find a remote place of her own, even if it was only a rental. But eventually everyone would know about her son because she couldn't hide out forever, nor did she want to.

When Chance waved, Georgie tried for a third departure. "Well, I better load up and leave before the competition begins."

A slight span of silence passed before Austin spoke again. "You look real good, Georgie girl."

So did he. Too good. Otherwise she might scold him for calling her by his pet name. "Thanks. I'll see you around."

"You most definitely will."

Georgie disregarded the comment, turned away and then walked through the gate to retrieve her mare. She lingered there for a few moments and watched Austin leave the arena before seeking out her son. "Let's go, Chance," she called as she untied the horse and started down the aisle.

Chance scampered down from the bleachers and came to her side, his face and baseball cap smeared with dirt. "Who was that man, Mama?"

Oh, heavens. She had so hoped he hadn't noticed. "Austin Calloway."

"Who is he?"

She kept right on walking as she considered how she should answer. She settled on a partial truth instead of full disclosure as she walked toward her trailer, her baby boy at her side.

"He's an old friend, sweetie."

An old friend who'd been her first lover. Her first love. Her one and only heartbreak. But most important, the father of her child.

If or when Austin Calloway learned that she'd been withholding that secret, she could only imagine how he would react—and it wouldn't be good.

Austin stormed into the main house to seek out the source of his anger. He found him in the parlor where they'd grown up, his pregnant wife seated in his lap. "I've got a bone to pick with you, Dallas."

Both Dallas and Paris stared at him like he'd grown a third eye, then exchanged a look. "I think I'll go see if Maria and Jenny need help with dinner," Paris said as she came to her feet.

Dallas patted her bottom. "Good idea. I can't feel my legs."

She frowned and pointed down at her belly. "Hush. This is all your fault, so complaining is not allowed."

"You sure didn't complain when I got you that way," Dallas added with a grin as his wife headed toward the kitchen.

Watching his brother and sister-in-law's banter didn't sit well with Austin. "If you're done mooning over your bride, we need to talk."

Dallas leaned back on the blue floral sofa that Jenny had brought with her, draped an arm over the back and crossed his boots at his ankles. "Have a seat and say what's on your mind."

Austin eyed the brown leather chair but decided he was too restless to claim it. "I don't want to have a seat."

"Then stand, dammit. Just get on with it."

He remained planted in the same spot even though he wanted to pace. "Why the hell didn't you tell me Georgia Romero was back in town?"

"Georgia's back in town?" came from the opening to his right.

Austin turned his attention to Maria, his stepmother, mentor and crusader for the truth, and sometimes intruder into conversations. "So he didn't tell you, either?"

Dallas's jaw tightened and his eyes narrowed. "I'd forgotten I'd talked to her day before yesterday. Besides, it's not that big a deal. A drought is a big deal."

"It's a big deal to your little brother, *mijo*," Maria said as she tightened the band at the end of her long braid. "Austin and Georgia have a special relationship."

Obviously the family was intent on throwing the past up in his face like prairie dirt. "*Had* a relationship. That was a long time ago."

Dallas smirked. "You'd take her back as your girl-friend in a New York minute."

"You have a girlfriend, sugar?"

Enter the blonde, bouncy second stepmom. The woman Austin's dad had married without divorcing Maria. Jenny was a good-hearted gossip and that alone made him want to walk right back out the door. Doing so would only prolong the conversation, unfortunately. "No, Jen, I don't have a girlfriend."

"He used to have a girlfriend," Maria added. "Georgia and Austin were real close in high school."

Jenny laid a dramatic palm on her chest below the string of pearls. "I just love Georgia. Atlanta in the springtime is..."

"Focus, woman," Maria scolded. "We're talkin' about a girl, not a state."

Jenny lifted her chin. "I know that, Maria. You're telling me about Austin being joined at the hip to his high school sweetheart, who happens to be named Georgia."

Dallas chuckled. "You've got that 'joined at the hip' thing right, Jen, but Austin chased her for years before that *joining*."

Austin needed to set this part of the record straight. "I damn sure didn't chase her." Much. "She hung around all of us when we were kids. I never paid her any mind back then."

"Not until she came back from camp that summer after she turned fourteen," Dallas said.

Man, he hadn't thought about that in years. She'd returned with a lot of curves that would make many a hormone-ridden guy stand up and take notice. Every part of him. She still had a body that wouldn't quit, something he'd noticed earlier. Something he wouldn't soon forget. "Yep, she'd definitely blossomed that summer."

"You mean she got her boobies," Jenny chimed in. "Mine came in at twelve. That's when the boys started chasing me like Louisiana mosquitoes."

Maria waved a dismissive hand at Jen. "No one wants to know when you reached puberty and how many times you got a love bite."

Austin didn't want to continue this bizarre conversation. Luckily Paris showed up to end the weird exchange. "Dinner will be ready in about five minutes."

Jenny turned her attention to Austin. "Maybe you should invite your special friend to dinner."

Of all of the stupid ideas—subjecting Georgie to an ongoing conversation about puberty. Then again, he wouldn't mind sitting across a table from her. He wouldn't mind her sitting in his lap, either. "It's late and I'm sure she's busy."

Paris perked up like a hound coming upon a rabbit's scent. "She? So that's what you were discussing in my absence."

Dallas pushed off the sofa. "Yeah, and boobies and mosquitoes."

"Don't ask, Paris," Maria stated. "Now you boys wash up while we put the food on the table."

No way would he subject himself to more talk about his history with Georgie. "I'm not staying for dinner."

"Suit yourself," Dallas said. "But you'll be missing out on Jen's chicken-fried steak."

Any other time he would reconsider, but not today. "I'm sure it'll be great. Before I take off, Dallas, we need to finish our conversation."

His brother shrugged. "I'm listening."

When Austin noticed the women still hovering, he added, "In private. Outside."

Dallas sighed. "Fine. Just make it quick. I'm starving."

He had every intention of making it quick while getting his point across.

After they walked out the door onto the porch, Austin faced his brother. "Look, I would've appreciated you consulting all the brothers before you hired Georgie as the ranch vet."

Dallas streaked a hand over his jaw. "Actually, I did. Houston doesn't have a problem with it, and neither does Tyler. Worth doesn't know about it but he trusts my judgment, unlike you."

Austin's ire returned with the force of a tornado. "You consulted them but you didn't bother to ask me?"

"Majority rules, and I figured you weren't going to be too keen on the idea after the way you two ended it."

"What the hell does it matter what happened when we were in high school?"

"I meant six years ago, after the reading of Dad's will."

"How did you know we hooked up then?"

"Georgie called me a few months later and asked how she could get in touch with you. By that time you'd already married Abby. When I told her about that, she was upset. In other words, you broke her heart. Again."

Yeah, he probably had, and he'd never been proud of it. "It was just one night, Dallas, and I didn't marry Abby until four months later, so I wasn't cheating on either Georgie or Abby. Besides, I married Abby on a whim."

"A whim involving a woman you barely knew."

Only a partial truth. "Not so. I'd known Abby for years. I just didn't date her on a regular basis."

"But you did date Georgie at one time, and she's not the kind of woman to take sex lightly."

He was inclined to agree but decided not to give Dallas the pleasure of knowing he was right. "Georgie and I agreed no promises, no expectations, the last time we were together."

"Maybe you didn't have any expectations, but I suspect she did. She's always loved you, brother. I wouldn't be surprised if she still did, although I don't get why she would after the way you've treated her."

He didn't welcome his brother's counsel or condemnation. "You're a fine one to talk, Dallas. You left a trail of broken hearts all over the country."

"Yeah, but it only took one woman to set me straight."

"A woman you married because you wanted to keep control of the ranch."

Dallas leaned against the porch railing. "In the beginning, that was true. But it didn't take me long to realize Paris could put an end to my wicked ways."

He'd thought that about Abby, too, but his ex-wife hadn't been as sure. In the end, they realized they'd had no choice but to go their separate ways after rushing into a marriage that should never have taken place. "I'm glad for your good fortune, Dallas. But I don't think that woman exists for me."

Dallas's expression turned suddenly serious. "If you open your eyes, you might just see you've already found her. In fact, you ran into her today."

With that, Dallas went back inside, leaving Austin

to ponder his words. True, he'd always had a thing for Georgie, but he'd chalked that up to chemistry. And she'd always been a beautiful woman, even during her tomboy phase. But he couldn't see himself with her permanently. See himself with anyone for that matter.

He'd already wrecked one marriage and he wasn't going to wreck another. He refused to fail again.

That said, if he and Georgie decided to mutually enjoy each other's company down the road, he wouldn't hate it. As long as she understood that he wasn't in the market for a future.

When it came to Georgia May Romero—and his ever-present attraction to her—keeping his hands to himself would be easier said than done.

"How's your first day as the Calloway vet going, Georgie girl?"

Fine…until he'd walked into the main barn dressed in chambray and denim, looking like every gullible girl's dream. Yet when she decided to accept Dallas's job offer, she'd known seeing Austin would be a strong possibility. In fact, that had been part of her reasoning to sign on as the resident veterinarian—to size him up, but only when it came to his life, not his looks. However, she was still a bit shaken over their encounter yesterday, and she was bent on ignoring him today.

For that reason, and many more, she continued putting away her equipment in the duffel without looking at him. "I was just vaccinating the pregnant mares."

"At least we only have four this year, not ten like in years past."

"True." Georgie straightened and patted the bay's muzzle protruding through the rail. "I remember when this one was born, and that had to be fifteen years ago. We're both getting on up there in age, aren't we, Rosie? They should really give you a break from the babies."

Georgie sensed Austin moving toward her before he said, "She keeps churning out prime cattle horses, but hopefully Dallas will decide to retire her from the breeding program after this year."

"Good, although I'm sure she'll have no trouble foaling this year. Dallas did ask me to be here when Sunny foals since she's a maiden mare. I told him I'd try, although horses have given birth without help for centuries. Of course, I expect to have to pull a few calves in the future."

When he didn't respond to her rambling, she faced him and met his grin. "Do you find some sort of warped humor in that?"

He braced his hand on the wooden frame and leaned into it, leaving little distance between them. "No. It's just strange to see you doing your animal doctor thing."

Boy, did he smell good, like manly soap, as if he'd just walked out of the shower. She imagined him in the shower...with her. Slick, wet bodies and roving hands and... Good grief. "Are you worried I'm not qualified?"

His come-hither expression melted into a frown. "I have no reason to believe you're not qualified since you went to the best vet college in the country. I guess I'm just used to you riding horses, not giving them shots. It's going to take a while to adjust to the new you."

"I'm the same old me, Austin." And that had never been more apparent than when she continued to react to him on a very carnal level. "Only now I have a career that I've talked about since we were climbing trees together."

He reached out and tucked one side of her hair behind her ear. "Do you remember that one time we were in the tree near the pond on your property? You were twelve at the time, I believe."

What girl didn't remember her first kiss, even if it had been innocent and brief? "If you're referring to that day when you tried to put me in a lip-lock, I definitely recall what happened next."

His grin returned. "You slugged me."

"I barely patted your cheek."

"I almost toppled out of the tree. You didn't know your own strength."

He hadn't known how much she had wanted him to kiss her, or how scared she had been to let him. "That kind of thing was not at the top of my to-do list at that time."

"Maybe, but I found out kissing had moved to number one on the list that summer after you came back from camp."

She felt her face flush. "I was fourteen and you were fifteen and a walking case of hormones."

He inched a little closer. "You had hormones, too. They were in high gear that first night we made out behind the gym after the football game."

She shivered over the recollection. "Big deal. So you managed to get to first base."

His blue eyes seemed to darken to a color this side of midnight. "Darlin', I got to second base."

"Your fumbling attempts weren't exactly newsworthy."

Oddly, he didn't seem at all offended. "Maybe I was a little green that first time, but I got better as time went on."

Her mind whirled back to that evening full of out-of-control chemistry. She didn't want to acknowledge how vulnerable she'd been that particular night, and many nights after that when they'd met in secret. How completely lost she had been for three whole years, and she hadn't been able to tell one solitary soul. "We were so reckless and stupid and darn lucky. If my father would have ever found out I was with a Calloway boy—"

"He would've shot first and asked questions later. He'd probably do that now."

Time to turn the subject in a different direction. "I'd hoped that after J.D. died, my father would've buried the hatchet and been more neighborly to you and the brothers."

"Ain't gonna happen," Austin said. "Last month he called the sheriff when one of our heifers ended up on his property. He blamed us for not maintaining the shared fence line when it's his responsibility, too."

"That doesn't surprise me."

"I'm surprised he approves of you working for the enemy."

"Actually, he doesn't know because I haven't told him." Just one more secret in her arsenal.

Austin pushed away from the wall, giving her a little more room to breathe. "That's probably wise. It's not fun to suffer the wrath of George Romero. But he's bound to find out eventually."

She shrugged. "Yes, but it really doesn't matter. I'm all grown up now and I make my own decisions, not him."

He winked. "Yep, you're all grown up for sure."

Her heart executed a little-pitter patter in her chest. "I need to get back to work now."

"Me, too. If I don't get busy soon, I'm going to suffer the wrath of Dallas."

If she didn't leave soon, she might be subjected to another journey into their shared past, including their sex life. *Former* sex life. "I've got a very busy day ahead of me, so I'll see you later."

He moved closer, as if he didn't want her to leave. "Then business is good?"

"So far." Yet she wouldn't be tending to livestock for the remaining hours. She would be sending her son off on a trip without her for the first time since his birth.

"I'm glad you've returned, Georgie," he said as he finally stepped back. "And by the way, if you're not busy this evening, Maria wants you to have dinner with us. All the usual suspects will be there. Have you met Worth or his mom, Jenny?"

"No. I haven't had the opportunity yet."

"All the more reason for you to come."

But being close to Austin was the best reason to decline. "I'm not sure I'll be finished with everything before dinnertime."

"We don't usually eat until around seven. If you decide to join us, and we really hope you will, just show up. We'll set a place for you."

If she agreed, she would have to spend even more time with him, all the while trying to conceal her true feelings. If she didn't, she would insult Maria. "I'll think about it."

He grinned, started away then said without turning around, "I'll see you tonight."

His confidence drove her crazy. *He* drove her crazy. But right then she had only one immediate concern... Her son's impending departure.

Two

Georgie climbed into her truck and headed home to face what would probably prove to be one of the most difficult times of her life. After she pulled into the drive and slid from the cab, Chance rushed out of the door and ran to her as fast as his little legs would let him. He wrapped his arms around her waist and stared up at her, his grin showing the space where he'd just lost his first tooth. "Mama, did you see the rolling house?"

Georgie glanced to her right to find the massive RV parked on the dirt road leading to the barn. "I see that, baby. It's huge."

Chance let her go and rocked back and forth on his heels, as if he was too excited to stand still. "Aunt Debbie said I could ride up front with Uncle Ben and she could stay in the back and play cards with Grandma."

No doubt the wily pair would be engaging in poker. "That sounds like a plan. Are you packed?"

He nodded vigorously. "Uh-huh. I gotta get some toys." He grabbed her by the hand and jerked her forward with his usual exuberance. "Come on, Mama."

"All right, already. Just hold your horses."

Chance released his grasp on her and threw open the front screen door. Georgie followed him inside to find her mother's sister, Debbie, decked out in a blue floral sundress and an inordinate amount of jewelry, and her Uncle Ben wearing a yellow polo and white shorts that revealed his usual golf tan that ran from the top of his bald head to his beefy legs. Not exactly December attire, but luckily the region had yet to experience any significant cold weather. But that was all about to change in the next two days, according to the forecast.

"Georgia May!" Debbie said as she crossed the room and drew Georgie into a hug. "You are still as pretty as ever."

Georgie stepped back and smiled. "You look great, too, Aunt Debbie. I love the blond hair."

Debbie patted her neatly coifed bob. "Glad you like it. I just wish I could say the same for my husband. When I got it done, he didn't say a word. I don't think he's even noticed."

"I noticed, woman." Uncle Ben crossed the room, picked Georgie up off her feet, hugged her hard and then put her back down. "You're still no bigger than a peanut, Georgie. And don't listen to Deb. She knows I'm jealous because she still has all her hair."

"So how are you enjoying retirement?" Georgie asked.

"Love it," Ben said. "We just drove all the way from California."

Debbie smiled. "Los Angeles was so wonderful and warm, but the traffic was horrible."

Chance tugged on Georgie's hand to garner her attention. "Can we go now, Mama?"

Georgie swallowed around an annoying lump in her throat when she thought about watching him leave without her. "Don't you need to pick out some toys?"

"Oh, yeah."

"Don't bring too many things, Chance." Her directive was lost on her child as he sprinted out of the room.

"Your place is really precious, Georgie," Debbie said as she surveyed the area. "And it's been so well done."

Quite the change from when Georgie had first seen it—a basic two-bedroom, one-bath rental with outdated everything. But the appeal had been in the ten surrounding acres, complete privacy and the four-stall red barn. "You can thank Mom for the restoration. She had the hardwoods refinished, put new carpet in the bedrooms, remodeled the kitchen, including appliances, and redid the entire bathroom before I moved in. As much as I appreciated the effort, I do think it was overkill for a house I don't own."

Right on cue, Lila Romero breezed into the room, her silver hair pulled back in a low bun, her peach slacks and white blouse heralding her classic taste in clothing. "I couldn't let you live in squalor, dear daughter."

Leave it to Lila to overexaggerate. "It wasn't that bad, Mom."

"It wasn't that good, either." Lila turned to her sister and sighed. "Georgie is such a nervous Nellie, I'm surprised she's actually allowing my grandson to go with us to Florida."

Ben turned to Georgie. "He'll be fine, pumpkin. I used to fly big jets holding hundreds of passengers, so rest assured, I can handle a forty-five-foot motor home."

Georgie took some comfort in knowing her son would be on the ground in good hands, not in midair. "I trust you, Uncle Ben. I'm more worried that Chance will drive you insane with all his energy."

Aunt Debbie patted her cheek. "Honey, we have eight grandchildren. We're used to high energy. We'll be stopping along the way and—"

"If he acts up, we'll lock him in the toilet." Uncle Ben topped off the comment with a teasing grin.

Chance ran back into the room, his arms full of stuffed animals, miniature trucks and his special blue pillow. "I'm ready. Can we go now?"

Georgie fought back the surge of panic. "Can I at least have a hug, baby boy?"

As if she sensed her daughter's distress, Lila took the toys from her grandson's grasp. "I'll put these in the RV while you tell your mama goodbye."

In that moment, Georgie appreciated her mother more than she could express. "Thanks, Mom."

"You're welcome, honey. Take your time."

After her family filed out the exit, Georgie knelt down on Chance's level and brushed a dark lock from his forehead. "You'll be a good boy, right?"

"I'll be good. I'll brush my teeth and go to bed on time. And I'll mind Grandma."

"Are you going to miss me?"

He rolled his eyes. "Yeah, Mama."

She drew him into her arms. "I'm going to miss you something awful, too. I love you, sweetie."

"I love you, Mama."

Georgie held him tightly until he began to wriggle away. "I gotta go now, okay?" he said, his hazel eyes flashing with excitement.

"Okay." She kissed his cheek and straightened. "Eat some vegetables while you're gone."

He wrinkled his nose. "Do I hafta?"

"Just a little. That's better than nothing."

After taking him by the hand, Georgie led her son to the RV where she earned one more hug, one more kiss and an understanding smile from her aunt. Chance scurried up the stairs with Debbie following behind him, and once he had disappeared, Georgie turned to her mother. "You'll call me later, right?"

Lila raised her hand as if taking an oath. "I swear I will report back to you on a regular basis. And I also swear I will not sell my grandson for gas money."

Georgie felt a little foolish. "I'm sorry, Mom, but this is the first time we've been away from each other for any length of time. He'll be gone for two weeks."

"Two weeks' worth of amusement parks that he'll dearly love." She laid a palm on Georgie's cheek. "I know it's hard, honey, yet there comes a time when you have to let go a little. I learned that the hard way with you."

"I know, Mom. It's just so difficult."

"It is for both myself and your father, even if he doesn't show it."

"I wouldn't know since he's clearly still refusing to speak to me, much less see me or Chance."

"He'll come around, and that reminds me…" Her mother hesitated a moment, which gave Georgie pause. "Speaking of fathers and their children, have you given any more consideration to telling Chance's father about him?"

She'd been considering it nonstop. "I'm still on the fence about that. The hows and the whens and whether or not it would serve any purpose at this point in time."

"Honey, it would serve a major purpose. It would give your son the opportunity to know his dad. They deserve to know each other."

With that, Lila climbed on board and closed the door without awaiting her daughter's response.

As Georgie watched the RV drive away in a cloud of dust, she felt more alone than she had since she'd realized she would be raising a child on her own.

She could stay at home this evening, missing her baby boy. Or she could go to the Calloways for dinner. Then again, that would mean facing Austin while reuniting with his family. Several years had passed since she had seen Maria and the boys, and the thought of eating a frozen dinner held little appeal.

Decision made. Wise or not, she would go.

"She's not coming." That reality had become apparent to Austin with every passing moment.

Dallas stopped rocking the back porch glider and shot him a hard look in response to the comment. "You don't know that, Austin. Dinner isn't even on the table yet."

Austin pushed off the wooden chair and stared out at the fence row lined with mesquites. "Georgie is never late. If she'd decided to be here, she would've already shown up."

"For a man who claimed five minutes ago, twice,

that he didn't care if she stepped foot through the door, you sure seem concerned."

He spun on his brother and glared at him. "I just don't like people to go back on their word."

Dallas leaned forward and rested his arms on his knees. "So she told you she'd be here for sure?"

He had him there. "Maybe not in so many words, but she did seem open to the idea."

"That's a stretch from saying yes."

Austin muttered a few curses as he collapsed back into the chair. "Doesn't matter one way or the other. I was just being nice when I asked her."

"You were wishful thinking, Austin. You can protest all you want but you've always had a thing for her. You still do."

Time for a subject change. "Tyler mentioned that Fort called you earlier today. What did he want?"

Dallas sighed. "A part of the proceeds from Texas Extreme."

Austin couldn't believe his stepbrother's nerve. "He's never even stepped foot on this place. Why the hell does he think he's entitled to any profit aside from what the will stated?"

"Because he's a greedy jackass, and that's what I pretty much told him."

"I just hope he doesn't make this into some legal issue."

"That's why we have attorneys on retainer." Dallas checked his watch. "Looks like it's dinnertime, and that means your girlfriend probably isn't coming."

"No big deal."

Dallas smirked. "Yeah, right. That's why you look so damn disappointed."

He'd obviously been too transparent. "You're full of it, Dallas."

"You're foolin' yourself, baby brother."

"Am not."

"Are, too."

His frustration began to build. "I really don't care if she shows up or not."

When the bell rang, Austin shot off the chair, strode through the hallway leading to the den, then stopped short before going any farther. Truth was, he had no idea who might be at the door. Probably one of the hands. Maybe even a neighbor. Or a brother.

"Georgia, it's so good to see you!"

Okay, so Maria confirmed it was her. No need for him to rush into the room and have her thinking he was anxious to see her again. Even if he was.

On that thought, he took his time as he headed toward the front of the house to the sounds of excited voices. He stopped off in the kitchen, grabbed and uncapped a beer from the fridge, then continued on through the dining room where the food had been laid out like a banquet. He paused at the arched opening to take a drink and watch the women circling Georgie, bombarding her with compliments and questions. He wouldn't blame her if she backed out the door and left for the sake of her sanity.

Jenny glanced over her shoulder and smiled at him. "Oh, Austin, sugar, she is just precious," she said, like she'd been presented a puppy.

Then the feminine wall parted, revealing a full view of the revered guest dressed in a pale blue sweater and jeans tucked into knee-high boots. Her long, black hair, gathered up on top and secured in a clip, fell around her shoulders in soft curls.

Precious wasn't the description that came to Austin's mind. *Sexy* was much more like it. She might be small in stature, but she had an abundance of curves that would kill a lesser man. He'd had the good fortune to explore that territory on more than one occasion. He'd like to do a little exploring tonight. Slowly. With his mouth.

He felt the stirrings down south, thanks to his sinful thoughts, and realized if he didn't get a grip, he'd have to step outside.

Austin took another swig of beer and moved forward. "Glad you could come."

She sent him an overly sweet smile. "I wouldn't have missed good home cooking for the world."

Maria hooked an arm through Georgie's. "*Mija*, you are welcome anytime. Now let's go have a seat."

"Let's," Jenny said. "We don't want the food to get cold."

Austin didn't want to sit through the upcoming interrogation, but it was too late to turn back now. After all, Georgie might need a protector. Nah. She could hold her own better than most.

"I'll go get Dallas," Paris said as they wandered toward the dining room.

Austin trailed behind the threesome, all the while watching the sway of Georgie's hips. She had a butt that wouldn't quit, and he better quit thinking about that butt or he'd have to stay at the table long after dinner was done.

Jenny gestured toward the place at the head of the

table. "Georgie, you sit here since you're the guest of honor."

Georgie looked a little flustered. "That's not necessary. I've sat at this table many times before."

Maria pulled out the chair. "Tonight it's necessary, *mija*. Like Jenny said, you're a special guest, even if you are practically family. We're all about hospitality around here."

"So true," Jenny said. "I came here for a weekend to let Fort meet his brothers, and I haven't gone back to Louisiana since."

"No matter how many times I've asked her to go," Maria muttered.

Jenny frowned. "Hush up, Maria. You know you like me being here to help out with the place."

"She likes your mint juleps," Austin added.

Maria hinted at a smile. "Bad as I hate to admit it, those would be hard to give up."

Following a spattering of laughter, Georgie took a seat while Maria and Jenny claimed the chairs on either side of her. Austin held back until Paris and Dallas came in and chose the two of the three remaining spots, leaving him the space at the opposite end of the table from Georgie.

He settled in, set his beer aside and eventually passed his plate to Jenny, who took great pleasure in serving the masses every night. She heaped enough food on it to feed the entire town and handed it back to him. "Do you need another beer, sugar?"

"No, thanks. I'm fine." Actually, he wouldn't be fine unless he downed a bottle of whiskey, or poured a bucket of ice down his jeans.

Georgie took a bite and just watching that ordinary gesture sparked Austin's imagination. After she dabbed at her mouth with a napkin, she asked, "I'm sorry Houston and Tyler aren't here tonight."

"They're at a rodeo in Waco," Dallas said. "Houston's determined to get one more national championship, and Tyler's there to pick up the pieces."

"Hush, *mijo*," Maria cautioned. "You'll curse your brother with such talk."

"He's already cursed," Austin added. "And if he gets one more concussion—"

"Boys," Jenny began, "you're upsetting your mothers. Now let's talk about something more pleasant." She turned her smile on Georgie. "I heard at the beauty salon that you're living at the McGregor place."

She glanced at Austin before returning her attention to Jenny. "Yes, I am. The family was nice enough to lease it to me after Liam went into the nursing home. They're not quite ready to sell the place."

Austin had a hard time believing she hadn't moved back into the Romero homestead. He figured there had to be a story behind it. "Did your mom and dad turn your room into a gym while you were gone?"

She took a drink of iced tea and set the glass down a little harder than necessary. "No. I'm an adult and I prefer to be on my own."

Jenny reached over and touched her hand. "Of course you do, but it's good to keep family close."

"As long as it's not too close," Dallas muttered, earning him a dirty look from his wife. "Speaking of family, where is Worthless?"

Jenny scowled at Dallas. "He's heading back from South Padre Island so he's running a little late. And would you please stop calling him that?" She smiled at Georgie. "You would just love Worth, sugar. How old are you?"

"Did you leave your filter in the kitchen, Jenny?" Maria asked.

"It's okay," Georgie said. "I'm thirty-four."

"Worth is twenty-nine, but five year's difference isn't bad," Jenny added. "I think it's okay for you two to date."

"It's not okay with me," Austin blurted without thought. When everyone stared at him, he had to dig himself out of the hole he'd created. "I mean, Georgie's a nice woman. Worth likes to chase nice women, but he's not the settling down kind."

Georgie lifted her chin. "Just to clarify, I'm not in the market for marriage at this point in time. Actually, I'm really too busy to date. But thanks for the offer, Jenny. I still look forward to meeting him."

"You might want to wear full-body armor," Austin muttered.

Maria stood, plate in hand. "Who wants peach cobbler?"

"I definitely do," Georgie said as she came to her feet. "I'll help you bring it in."

The pair left the kitchen and when they returned, Georgie approached Austin and set the dessert in front of him, inadvertently brushing his arm in the process. That simple touch made him shift in his seat, especially when he got a whiff of her subtle perfume. He remembered that lavender scent well. He also remembered how her hair felt brushing across his chest and lower...

Damn, damn, damn.

After everyone was served, the conversation turned

casual, while Austin kept his focus on Georgie and the way her mouth caressed the fork.

Caressed the fork?

Man, he needed to get a grip. He needed some kind of distraction. Something to take his mind off Georgie.

"Hey, folks, what did I miss?"

Worth showing up was not what Austin had in mind. He glanced at Georgie, who stared at him, midbite. He could imagine what she was thinking—where did this overly buff, tanned blond guy fit into the family tree?"

"You missed dinner, Surfer Worth," Paris said. "How's the yacht?"

He walked behind Jenny's chair, leaned over and kissed her cheek. "The *Jenny Belle* is fine. How is baby Calloway?"

Paris patted her belly. "Growing like a pasture weed."

"I see that." Worth slapped Dallas on the back. "Looks like the lodge is almost finished. I'm champing at the bit to see it in its finished state."

"We still have a couple of months before that happens," Paris said.

Austin held his breath while hoping Worth made a hasty exit before he noticed Georgie.

Jenny scooted back from the table and stood. "Sugar, we have someone we'd like you to meet," she said, shattering Austin's hopes. "This is Georgie, a longtime family friend."

Worth leveled his gaze on Georgie, grinned and eyed her like she was a prize heifer. "Where have you been hiding out?"

"College Station," Georgie answered. "Going to college."

"Veterinarian school," Dallas added. "She's going to be taking care of our livestock."

Worth moved closer to Georgie. Too close for Austin's comfort. "Then I guess I'll be seeing a lot more of you."

The veiled innuendo sent Austin from his seat. "Cut it out, Worth."

The man had the nerve to look shocked. "Cut what out?"

"Treating Georgie like she's one of your conquests."

Worth streaked a hand over his jaw. "Relax, brother. I'm just being hospitable."

Jenny patted his cheek. "Just like his mama taught him."

Maria rose and began gathering the empty plates. "Before the brawl starts, I need to clear out your Grandma Calloway's good china."

Dallas and Paris stood at the same time. "There won't be any brawl," Dallas said. "We're going to go outside and act like civil humans, not animals."

Georgie pushed back from the table and grabbed her glass. "I'll clean up."

"Or the boys could clean up," Paris began, "and we'll go out on the porch."

Maria shook her head. "We tried that one time. Their idea of a clean kitchen leaves a lot to be desired. It took me a good hour to get the grease off the stove and rewash the pots and pans. If we all help, we'll get it done faster."

"You two mothers should join the boys," Paris said. "Georgie and I will take care of this. That gives us a chance to get to know each other better."

"I don't believe the boys need a chaperone," Jenny added.

"They might need a referee." Maria rounded the table and came to Austin's side. "Come on, Jenny. We could use the break and we also need to discuss some ranch business."

Austin wasn't in the mood to discuss business with his brothers and mothers. That would mean leaving Georgie alone with his sister-in-law to most likely discuss him. But if he protested, he would wind up catching hell from everyone over his presumed *attraction* to Georgie. Okay, real attraction to Georgie. He'd go along with the plan for now, but later, he had other plans for the lady...provided she was game.

Who the hell was he trying to fool? If he laid one hand on her, she'd probably throw a right hook. Not that the prospect of getting punched would keep him from trying. First, he had to get this little family meeting over with, and then he would put the Georgie plan into action.

"Do you have plans for the upcoming weekend, Georgie?"

She took the last plate from Paris and put it in the dishwasher. "Maybe I'll unpack a box or two." Or maybe she'd just sit around with a glass of wine and mope.

Paris wiped her hands on the dish towel, hung it on the rack near the sink, then leaned back against the marble countertop. "You should come here for the festival."

"Festival?"

"I'm surprised Austin didn't mention it."

He hadn't mentioned anything other than old memories. "We haven't been together that long." And that sounded suspect. "*Together* as in the same room, not *together* together."

Paris smiled. "No need to explain. I already know you and Austin were an item in high school."

More like idiots. "Yes, we were. Now what about this festival?"

"Well, Jenny came up with the concept when she decided to leave Louisiana behind and move here. We decorate the entire place and open the ranch to the public from the second to the last week in December. It's family entertainment and it's affordable."

"How much?"

"Free."

Very surprising. The Calloways she'd always known were in the business of making money, not giving the goods away. "Seriously?"

"Seriously. Admission is the price of a toy, but that's voluntary. No one is turned away."

"That's very generous. And it includes a festival?"

"Actually, the festival is invitation-only and all the proceeds from ticket sales go to shelters in the region. We have a lot of the local ranchers attending, and several rodeo champions, along with a few San Antonio VIPs with big bucks. The food is complimentary, but we have a cash bar for safety reasons."

"Good idea. Free booze and rowdy cowboys is a surefire recipe for disaster."

"Hunky cowboys," Paris said with a smile. "I'd like to claim I haven't noticed a few in town, but I've discovered pregnancy does not render you blind. It does mess with your hormones. Just ask my husband. He told me the other night I was wearing him out."

Georgie did recall the hormone rush, and no place to go to take care of them. "I suppose you could say the D Bar C has its share of hunks."

"True, and I suspect we'll see several other sexy men this weekend from all walks of life. So if you're available, please come. And you don't have to worry about buying the ticket. It's my treat. I could use all the support I can get."

Georgie could use a night out, and since her son wouldn't be returning until three days before Christmas, she had no prior engagements. Yet she had to consider the Austin element… "I'll definitely think about attending, as long as something work-related doesn't come up."

"I'll send good thoughts that no emergencies arise." Paris laid her palm on her abdomen. "However, if I get any bigger between now and then, I'm going to need a wide-load sign to wear with my maternity cocktail dress."

Georgie smiled, remembering how she had felt that same way during her own pregnancy. "Stop it. You look great. When are you due?"

"Mid-January, as best we can tell from the ultrasound. I'm not exactly sure when I got pregnant. I found out the morning Dallas and I married the second time."

"Second time?"

Paris laughed. "It's a rather strange tale. The first time we married for all the wrong reasons. I needed a job and Dallas needed a wife before his birthday to keep control of the ranch, thanks to J.D.'s stipulation in the will. As it turned out, my ex-husband lied to me about my divorce being finalized. Dallas threatened him, I quit my position as designer for the new lodge and then he realized he couldn't live without me, so we married in earnest. End of story."

And quite a story it was. "I'm glad it worked out for you both."

"So am I." Paris flinched. "I swear, Junior here is playing soccer with my rib cage. Dallas is always asking me if the baby's kicking so he can feel it."

"Do you mind if I do?"

"Not at all, and thanks for asking. I've had complete strangers coming up to me in the store and patting my belly like a pet without my permission."

Georgie laid her palm over the place Paris had indicated, and received a tap as a reward. "Wow," she said after she moved her hand away. "Definitely a strong little guy. Or girl. Do you know the gender yet?"

Paris shook her head. "We've decided to be surprised."

"Any names picked out?"

"If it's a girl, Carlie. And if it's a boy, Luke."

"Please tell me that Luke isn't the short version of Luckenbach to carry on the tradition of naming the kids after Texas cities."

Paris grinned. "Funny you should mention that. Dallas thought it would be clever to name him Luckenbach, which I immediately nixed since it would be difficult for a child to spell it. Of course, he then came up with a whole alternate list, including Midland, Odessa, Arlington and the crowning glory, Texarkana."

"Glad you decided on Luke and Carlie."

They exchanged a laugh followed by Paris pressing her palms in her lower back. "These spasms are not fun."

"I remember that pain and pressure. It makes it very hard to sleep, especially when it's coupled with having to go to the bathroom five times a..." Her words trailed off when she realized she'd completely given herself away.

Paris raised a brow. "Sounds to me like you've had some experience with pregnancy."

She saw no reason to lie to Paris at this point, at least about her child's existence. "Actually, I have a five-year-old son."

Paris's eyes went wide. "I didn't know that."

"Aside from my mother and father, no one around here knows."

"Not even the Calloways?"

"Not yet." But if all went as planned, they would eventually know... As soon as she figured out how to tell the father.

"What about your son's dad?" Paris lowered her gaze. "I'm sorry. I'm being too nosy."

"It's okay. I appreciate having someone to talk to. He hasn't been in the picture."

"I'm so sorry, Georgie. I hate it when a man doesn't take responsibility for his child."

"He doesn't know."

Once more, Paris looked stunned. "Why?"

"It's complicated." More than anyone would ever know.

Paris sent her a sympathetic look. "I can do complicated, but only if you want to talk about it."

Although she'd only known Paris for an hour, Georgie sensed she could be objective, and nonjudgmental.

Not to mention she'd kept the truth bottled up far too long. "When I found out I was pregnant, I tried to contact him and discovered he'd recently married. I didn't want to rock that boat."

"Is he someone you met in college?"

"No. He's from around here. That's one of the reasons I decided to return here to set up my practice. I needed to be close to my family, as well."

"Then you plan to involve him in your son's life."

She hadn't even planned how she would tell him. "Whether or not that's an option would solely be dependent on his attitude. He's not going to be thrilled that I've kept him in the dark for so long."

Paris remained silent for a few seconds, as if she needed time to digest the information. "Georgie," she began, "do the Calloways know this mystery man?"

She hesitated a moment to mull over how she would answer, and how much she would reveal. "Everyone knows everybody around here."

Paris turned and began to fold a dish towel. "Okay. It's not Dallas, is it?"

"Heavens no." Georgie realized the comment was borderline rude. "Don't get me wrong, Dallas is an attractive man, but he's always treated me like a kid sister."

Paris laid a palm on Georgie's arm. "I wasn't exactly serious. I can tell there's nothing between you two. Which leads me to another question. It's your decision whether to answer or not."

Georgie braced for the query. "Ask away."

Paris leaned back against the counter and studied her straight on. "Is it Austin?"

Georgie studied the toe of her boot. "Well…uh… I…"

"I know you two have been involved before," Paris continued. "And I can tell you still care about him by the way you look at him."

If Paris had noticed, what about the rest of the Calloways? What about Austin? Had she really been that obvious? "Yes, I cared about him a lot a long time ago, and in some ways I still do. Unfortunately I made the fatal mistake of letting those feelings get in the way of logic six years ago."

"Then if you do still care about him, Georgie, you should tell him you have a child together."

"I never actually said he's the father."

"You haven't denied it, either."

Georgie resigned herself to the fact that she couldn't get out of this predicament without digging a deeper deception hole. "All right. Austin is Chance's father. We got together the night after the reading of his father's will. He was upset when he learned about J.D.'s double life, and I wanted so badly to comfort him. That's how we conceived our son."

Paris sent her a sympathetic look. "Austin is a good man. He'll understand why you felt you couldn't tell him at that point in time."

If only she could believe that theory. "I had every intention of telling him, but when I found out he was married, I didn't have the heart to mess up his life. At the time it seemed like the right thing to do. But when I learned he was divorced right before I finished vet school, I realized maybe I'd been wrong. Now he's going to hate me for not telling him sooner."

"He's going to be angry, but I doubt he'll hate you.

And I know he won't hate having a son. That's why I believe you should let him know, unless you plan to keep your son hidden until he's an adult."

She needed more time to think. She needed to get home before her mom called.

With that in mind, Georgie turned to Paris and attempted a small smile. "I'm going to take everything you've said into serious consideration. In the meantime, if you don't mind—"

"Not saying anything to anyone?" Paris returned her smile. "I promise I won't mention it, and after you've told Austin, I'll pretend to be as surprised as everyone else."

"After you've told me what, Georgie?"

Three

Georgie startled at the sound of Austin's voice, so much so she physically jumped. "We were talking about...uh... We were playing a game."

He tossed the beer can in the recycle bin and frowned. "What kind of game?"

"A guessing game," Paris said. "Georgie tells me a story from your childhood, and I have to guess which brother did what."

Georgie thanked her lucky stars Paris had such a sharp mind. "That's right. I just mentioned the time someone was doing donuts in the Parkers' pasture. I told her everyone thought it was Dallas, when it was really you, and she thought I should tell you to confess to Dallas to clear the air." And that had to be the lamest fabrication ever to leave her mouth.

He strolled farther into the kitchen and frowned.

"Yep, that was me doing the donuts on the night after I found out I got accepted into college. And FYI, Dallas already knows. He took the blame because he knew Dad would come down harder on me."

Georgie recalled that fateful day when Austin had informed her about his college acceptance, and she had assumed he would be out of her life forever. Now just the opposite would be true, if she told him about Chance.

She did a quick check of her watch and saw an excuse to escape both Austin's and Paris's questions. "It's time for me to go. I have to be up very early in the morning to make my rounds."

"I'll walk you out," Austin said.

"Thanks, but I can make it to the truck on my own. Finish your visit with the family."

"I see the family almost every day and Mom would skin me alive if I wasn't gentlemanly." Austin turned around and headed away. "I'll wait for you on the porch."

Great. Just great. The man was as persistent as a gnat on a banana.

Paris drew Georgie into a brief hug. "I've enjoyed our talk. Let's do it again very soon."

Georgie didn't have to ask what they would be discussing. "That sounds like a plan. Maybe we can have lunch."

"Lunch would be great. And I know you're going to do the right thing and eventually clear the air, once and for all."

That's exactly what Georgie intended to do. She simply wasn't sure when, where or, most important, how.

Now was not the time. Georgie recognized that reality the moment she stepped onto the porch and met a swarm of Calloways bombarding her with goodbyes.

Jenny gave her the first hug. "Please come again soon, sugar. I'll make my juleps."

"You'll make her drunk," Maria said as she gave Georgie a quick embrace, as well. "It's been good to see you, *mija*."

"Don't be a stranger," Dallas added as he patted her back like the brother he'd always been to her.

Worth stepped forward, kissed her hand and grinned. "Call me sometime and we'll hang out."

"When he's not hanging ten on a surfboard," Jenny said.

"Or hanging out in town, trying to pick up women," Dallas remarked.

"Yeah, all three of them," Worth said.

The comment earned some laughter from everyone but the man leaning back against the railing, arms folded across his chest, his blue eyes boring into Georgie. She waited until the crowd reentered the house before she moved forward, seeking a quick getaway.

Unfortunately Austin had other ideas, she realized when he clasped her arm before she made it down the first step. "Where are you going so fast?"

She turned a serious gaze on him and he relinquished his grasp on her. "I'm heading home. It's getting late."

"Are you sure you don't want to hang around a little longer and tell me what's going on with you?"

Hey, I had a baby over five years ago and he happens to be yours. Just thought you might like to know. "Nothing's going on, Austin, other than I'm tired. As I said earlier, I have to be up at dawn."

He pushed off the rail and moved close enough to almost shatter her composure. "You're as nervous as a colt in a corral full of cows. I can't help but think it has something to do with me."

He would be right. "Check your ego at the door, Austin. Not everything has to do with you. Now if you don't mind, I'm leaving."

She sprinted down the remaining steps and quickened her pace as she headed down the walkway without looking back. When she reached her silver truck, she grasped the handle only to have a large hand prevent her from opening the door.

Frustrated, she turned around and practically bumped into Austin's chest. "What is it now?"

"Before you run off, I wanted to ask you something."

"Okay, but make it quick."

"We're having a party here this weekend and—"

"Paris invited me."

"Are you going to come?"

With the cowboy in such close proximity, his palm planted above her head on the door, she could barely think, much less make a decision. "I'm not sure. It depends on my schedule."

His grin arrived as slow as honey and just as sweet, with a hint of deviousness. "It's been a long time since we've danced together."

"True, and I've probably forgotten how."

He took a lock of her hair and began to slowly twist it around his finger, as he had done so many times before. "Do you remember that barn dance back when we were in high school? Specifically, what happened afterward?"

Here we go again... "I recall several dances back in the day."

"The one right before my graduation, when we fogged up all the windows in my truck while we were parked down by the creek."

He seemed determined to yank her back down memory mile. "It wasn't all that monumental, Austin. Only some minor teenage petting."

"Minor? You were so hot you took my hand and put it right between your legs."

"I don't exactly remember it that way." One whopper of a lie.

"Do you remember that you didn't stop me from undoing your pants and slipping my hand inside? I sure as hell haven't forgotten, even if you have."

A woman never forgot her first climax. "Your point?"

"I definitely had a *point* below my belt buckle," he said, his voice low and grainy. "I went home with it that night, and several times after that until the night before I left for college."

Ah, yes, another enchanted evening...and one colossal mistake. "That should never have happened, Austin. I didn't plan to give you my virginity as a high school graduation gift."

"But what a gift it was." He leaned over and brushed a kiss across her cheek. "I liked the sports socks, but not as much."

"Not funny," she said as she unsuccessfully tried to repress a smile.

"Seriously, Georgie girl, don't you ever believe I didn't appreciate what that night meant to you, and me. I've never wanted you to think I took it for granted."

Over the past few years, she'd managed to suppress those particular recollections. But now, they came rushing back on a tide of unforgettable moments. "I know you didn't, Austin. You apologized to me a million times, not to mention you were so gentle. When it comes right down to it, I'm glad it was you, and not some jerk bent on bragging to all his friends that he nailed the school wallflower."

"Wallflower?" He released a low, rough laugh. "Georgie, you were anything but a wallflower. Every girl wanted to be just like you, every guy in high school lusted after you and because you wouldn't give those guys the time of day, that made you all the more attractive."

Like she really believed that. "I highly doubt anyone was lusting after me, and even if they did, I was too busy maintaining a secret relationship with you."

"We still had some good times, didn't we?"

"Yes, we did." Something suddenly occurred to her. "Did you ever tell anyone about us?"

He glanced away before returning his gaze to her. "Dallas knew. He told me several times we were playing with fire and we were going to get burned if either of our dads found out. Did you tell anyone?"

She shook her head. "No." Not until she'd found out she was pregnant, and then she'd only revealed the secret to her mother. "I didn't dare."

Georgie's cell phone began to vibrate and after she fished it from her pocket, she discovered Lila on the line, as if she'd channeled her mom. "I need to take this, so I better go."

Austin pushed away from the truck but didn't budge. "I'll wait."

She couldn't have a conversation with her son while Austin stood by, staring at her. That became a moot point when she noticed the call had already ended. "It's just my mom checking in from Florida. I'll get back to her when I'm home."

"Good. I've enjoyed talking to you again, just like old times."

Fortunately talking hadn't turned into something more, just like old times. "I've enjoyed it, too, but I really do need to go."

"Before you go, there's something I just have to do."

She pointed at him. "Don't even think about it."

He had the nerve to look innocent. "Think about what?"

"You know what."

"No, I don't. I was going to give you my cell number, in case you need anything."

Feeling a little foolish, she opened the contacts list and handed him her phone. "Fine. Plug it in there. But hurry."

He typed in his number, then handed the cell back. She laughed when she noticed he'd labeled himself "Studly," the name she jokingly used to call him. "Very clever."

"Can I have your number?"

"I'll text it to you."

"Can I have one more thing?"

She released a weary sigh. "What now?"

"This."

He framed her face in his palms and covered her mouth with his before she had time to issue a protest. She knew she should pull away, but as it had always been, she was completely captive to the softness of his lips, the gentle stroke of his tongue, his absolute skill. No one had ever measured up to him when it came to kissing. She suspected no one ever would.

Once they parted, Austin tipped his forehead against hers. "Man, I've missed this."

Sadly so had she. "We're not children anymore, Austin. We can't go back to the way it was."

He took an abrupt step back. "I'm not suggesting we do that. But we can go forward, see where it goes."

"It won't go anywhere because you'll never be able to give me what I want."

"What do you want, Georgie?"

"More."

"How much more?"

"I want it all. Marriage, a home and family."

"I've gone the marriage route, and I blew it. I don't want to travel that path again."

She turned and opened her truck door. "Then it's probably best that we stay away from each other."

"Is that what you really want?"

Her head said yes, while her heart said no. "Right now I want to go to bed."

He grinned like the cad he could be. "Mine's just down the road a bit. A big king-size bed with a top-grade mattress made of memory foam. A good place to make a few more memories."

She tossed her phone on the passenger seat, withdrew the key from her pocket and started the truck. "Good night, Austin."

"Night, Georgie. And if you change your mind about us exploring our options, just let me know."

"Don't count on it."

When she tried to close the door, he stopped her

again. "Just one more question. Are you still worried about what your folks would think if they knew we were together?"

In many ways, she was. "If we started seeing each other again, and I'm not saying that will happen, I'm sure my father would go ballistic. I'm fairly certain my mother wouldn't care what we do together."

"Georgia May, have you taken leave of your senses?"

Georgie collapsed onto the bed and sighed. "I went there to see the family, Mom. Just because you've never cared for the Calloways because of that stupid dispute between J.D. and Dad, doesn't mean I don't like them. They've always been nice to me."

"I assume Austin was there."

"Yes, he was."

"You didn't tell him about Chance, did you?"

The panic in her mother's voice wasn't lost on Georgie. "No, not yet."

"I don't think you should tell him."

Georgie couldn't be more confused. "But you told me right before the trip that you thought I should tell him."

"I've changed my mind. Your father agrees with me."

A strong sense of trepidation passed through her. "Dad knows Austin is Chance's father?"

"Not exactly, but he has his suspicions. Regardless, we think it's better if you remain silent to avoid any disappointment for both you and Chance."

They'd been having this back-and-forth conversation since she'd told her mother about the baby. "Mom, we've been through this a thousand times. I'm going to do what's best for my child, not to mention Dad has no say-so in the decision. He refuses to even acknowledge he has a grandson. He's barely spoken to me for the past six years."

"I know, sweetie, but—"

"Where are you now?" she said in an effort to move off the subject.

"Alabama for the night. We'll be in Florida tomorrow afternoon."

"Is Chance doing okay?"

"He's been an angel. Right now he's outside with Ben and Deb hooking up the RV. He's so inquisitive."

Georgie wouldn't debate that, and her son's curiosity about his father had begun to increase by leaps and bounds with every passing year. "Do you mind putting him on the phone? It's getting late."

"All right. Hold on a minute."

"Mom, before you go, I just wanted to say how much I've appreciated your support. I couldn't have raised my baby boy without your guidance. I love you for it."

"I love you, too, dear, and I only want what's best for you and Chance. If that means you decide that telling Austin he's a father is best, then so be it."

She was simply too befuddled to make any serious decisions right now.

A few moments later, she heard the muffled patter of footsteps, followed by, "Hi, Mom. I have my own bed and we have a kitchen. Uncle Ben showed me how to plug in the 'lectricity and roll down that big thing over the door so we don't get sunburned. It's so cool."

She could imagine her son rocking back and forth on his heels, his hazel eyes wide with wonderment. "It sounds great, baby. It's way past your bedtime. You must be tired."

"Nope. We're gonna roast marshmallows."

Lovely. Her child was being exposed to electricity and fire. "Be very careful, Chance. I don't want you to hurt yourself."

"Aw, Mom, I'm not a baby."

No, he wasn't. "You're still my baby. I love you, ya know."

"Love ya, too, you know. Gotta go now."

"Don't stay up too late and—"

When the call cut off, Georgie's heart sank. How would she survive the next two weeks without him? By keeping herself occupied with work. By having lunch with Paris. Maybe she would even attend the Calloways' party.

And perhaps she would finally get off the fence and tell Austin he had a son. She worried he already suspected something was up.

As sure as the sun would rise in the east, Austin sensed Georgie was hiding something. Then again, she'd always been one to hold back.

He strode into the den, grabbed the remote and started to watch a replay of his last national championship roping. But the thought of revisiting that part of his past didn't seem all that appealing. He'd rather relive another part.

On that thought, he pulled down the yearbook, dropped into the brown leather chair by the fireplace and flipped through the pages until he reached the class photo of Georgie. She'd been a junior, he'd been a senior, and they'd been secretly hot and heavy that whole year.

Funny, she hadn't changed all that much. Her hair was still as long, her face still as beautiful, her brown eyes still as enticing. She could never see what everyone had seen in her—a perfect blend of her Spanish/Scottish heritage.

She hadn't been a cheerleader or a drill team member. She'd been a rodeo girl through and through, friends with many, and more popular than she'd realized until she'd been elected homecoming queen her senior year. And class president. And eventually, prom queen. During all those milestone moments, he'd been away at college, never serving as her escort, never revealing they had been an item in high school. He should've been horsewhipped for not standing and shouting it from the rooftop when he'd had the chance, their fathers and distance be damned. He should have been there for her.

Too late now, he thought as he closed the book and set it aside on the mahogany end table. He couldn't help but think his life might have been different if he'd stayed home six years ago instead of moving back to Vegas.

He recalled that last night with Georgie, when her touch had temporarily eased his anger over learning about his father's deceit. They'd made love until dawn, then parted ways. And then he'd met Abby, married in a matter of months and ended it without much thought. Not that it could have been any other way. Not when Georgia May Romero still weighed on his mind on a regular basis. Abby hadn't known about her, but she'd always claimed she'd never had all of his heart. She would have been right.

Now he found himself reunited with Georgie. Together again, to quote an old country song. Nope, not exactly together. If Georgie had her way, he'd fall off the face of the earth, or go back to Nevada. But damn, she had kissed him back. And damn, he wanted to kiss her again. Maybe that wouldn't be fair in light of their opposing goals—he wanted to stay single, she wanted to be a wife.

If he had any sense, he'd grow up, get with the program and open himself to all the possibilities. But the thought of failing Georgie, not being the man she needed, battered him with doubts.

But the thought of having her so close, and not being with her again, didn't sit well with him. He would just keep his options open whenever he saw her again. And he damn sure planned to see her again.

Four

When she maneuvered through the D Bar C's iron gate, Georgie pulled behind several slow-moving, white limos as they traveled down the lane leading to the party site. She marveled at the complete transformation of the Calloway ranch.

The lawn of the main house to her left had been laden with various decorations depicting holidays from around the world. Every tree and hedgerow had been draped with twinkling lights, and laser beams in rotating colors sparkled across its facade. Several cartoon characters and giant candy canes lined the curbs on either side of the street, enhancing the fairy-tale quality.

Georgie passed by three more massive houses set back from the road, all adorned like the first, and she wondered if one of the cedar-and-rock houses belonged to Austin. She hadn't bothered to ask him the other night for fear he might get the wrong idea, but she couldn't deny her curiosity.

She also couldn't deny her building excitement as the caravan turned to the right to reveal a large silvery tent set out at the end of the road, a two-story residence, bigger than any she'd seen to this point, serving as its backdrop.

Georgie came to a complete stop when a parking attendant, dressed in a tuxedo and cowboy hat, approached her. She shut off the ignition, grabbed her silver clutch that complemented her sleeveless black dress, draped her silk wrap around her shoulders and slid out of the cab.

The valet offered her a long once-over and a somewhat lecherous grin. "What's a beautiful little thing like you driving a big ol' truck like this? You belong in a limo."

You belong back at college, frat boy. "My big ol' boyfriend owns this big ol' truck."

He looked unfazed by the threatening lie. "He's an idiot for letting you attend this little get-together all by your lonesome."

"He had to work."

"Oh, yeah? What does he do?"

She handed him her keys, a ten-dollar tip and another tall tale. "He's a professional wrestler. Take good care of his truck."

With that, she turned on her spiky black heels and carefully made her way to the party. Once inside the tent, she navigated the milling crowd, past tables filled with sophisticated finger foods and prissy desserts, searching for a familiar face among the strangers. Luckily she spotted two familiar faces positioned near the makeshift dance floor. With Paris wearing a flowing green empire-waist dress barely showing her belly, her blond hair cascading in soft curls around her bare shoulders, and Dallas decked out in a black suit, complete with red tie and dark cowboy hat, they looked as if they belonged on the cover of a trendy fashion magazine…or a bridal cake. A fortysomething man with a hint of gray at his temples stood across from the couple. Most women would label him debonair. From the looks of the expensive suit and high-dollar watch, Georgie would label him wealthy.

After Paris waved her over, Georgie wandered toward them, hoping she hadn't inadvertently interrupted some sort of business deal.

Paris immediately left her husband's side and greeted Georgie with a hug. "You look beautiful, Georgie."

She nervously tugged at the dress's crisscross halter neck that felt a bit like a noose. "Thanks. I haven't worn anything like this since my college senior spring formal a dozen years ago."

Paris looked surprised. "You're thirty-three?"

"Actually, thirty-four."

"I swear you could go to a high school dance right now and blend right in. And that is not a bad thing."

Unless I tried to purchase a glass of wine without being asked for my ID. "That's nice of you to say, but the only thing that might help me pass for a student happens to be my height. My dad used to call me 'Peanut.'" And now he wouldn't even acknowledge her as his daughter. The thought dampened her mood.

"Don't discount your beauty," Paris said. "Every

man in the room, from twenty-one to eighty-one, would like to take you home."

Yeah, sure. "I'm flattered, but I don't believe it."

"Hello. I'm Rich Adler. Who are you?"

Georgie turned her attention to the man behind the introduction. The same man who'd been conversing with Dallas. She found his name both ironic and appropriate. "Georgia Romero," she said as she took his offered hand for a brief shake.

Dallas moved forward as if running interference. "Rich is an attorney. He also owns a quarter horse operation outside San Antonio."

The lawyer sent her a somewhat seedy smile. "I'm into breeding."

She resisted rolling her eyes. "I'm sure that keeps you busy."

"Not as busy as I'd like," he said. "Dallas tells me you're a veterinarian."

"Yes, I am."

He winked. "I could use a good vet."

She could use a quick exit. "I'm sure you have several options in the city."

"Not any who look as good as you. Have you ever been to Italy?"

She sent him an overly sweet and somewhat sarcastic smile. "Oh, yes. That nice little town right outside Hillsboro. I passed by it once on the interstate on my way to Oklahoma."

Now he looked perplexed. "I'm referring to the country, not the town in Texas."

She started to mention she was kidding, but she suspected his arrogance trumped any true sense of humor. "'Fraid not."

He had the gall to move closer. "You would enjoy it there. Extraordinary cuisine and superior wine. The Amalfi coast is a great place to don your bikini and sunbathe. Do you have a passport?"

She had a strong urge to back up and run. "Passport, yes. Bikini, no. I do have a very busy practice to run. No time for vacations." Even if she did, she had no desire to travel with him.

Dallas cleared his throat and slapped randy Rich on the back. "Let me buy you a drink, Adler, and we'll leave the ladies to talk about us."

Georgie planned to do just that, and she would have nothing flattering to say about the lecherous lawyer. "Nice to meet you, Mr. Adler." Not.

"It's Rich." He pulled a card and pen from his inside pocket, jotted something down, then handed it to her. "If you need a job, here's my info."

She wouldn't work for him if he happened to be the last employer on earth. "Have a good night."

He leaned over and murmured, "Call me. For business or pleasure."

Oh, she'd like to call him…several names that wouldn't be fit to utter in this atmosphere.

As soon as the men left the area, Paris turned to Georgie. "I'm so, so sorry. That guy is a first-class jerk."

As far as Georgie was concerned, that was a colossal understatement. "A jerk and a creep."

"A married, creepy jerk."

Georgie wadded up the card and tossed it into a nearby waste bin. "Figures."

"He's on his fourth wife."

"What a shocker. I could have gone all night without meeting the likes of him."

When a roving waiter passed by, Paris snatched a crystal tumbler from his tray and offered it to Georgie. "Drink this. It might help erase the memory."

Georgie took the glass and held it up. "What is this?"

"It's Jenny's infamous mint julep. She made several gallons' worth to go with the champagne."

She eyed the dark gold liquid for a moment. "Does she use a lot of bourbon?"

"Yes, and a splash of rum and she adds tequila for a little extra kick."

"Interesting." Georgie took a sip and found it to be surprisingly palatable, albeit extremely strong. "Wow. This will wake you up today and give you a headache tomorrow."

Paris leaned over, lowered her voice and said, "Take some advice. Sip it slowly, and don't have more than one, unless you have a designated driver."

"Believe me, I won't."

For the first time since her arrival, Georgie scanned the room to study the attendees…and spotted Austin standing nearby, dressed in a navy jacket, white shirt and dark jeans with a dark cowboy hat to complete the look. He had a bevy of woman hanging on his every word and wore a grin that could melt the icing off the red velvet cupcakes lined up on the stand behind him.

As bad luck would have it, he caught her looking, and when he winked, Georgie downed a little more of the julep than she should. "Still the cowboy cad," she muttered, the taste of tequila and jealousy on her tongue.

Paris frowned. "Who are you referring to?"

"Your brother-in-law. The one who's named after

the capital of Texas." She nodded to her left. "He's over there, draped in women."

She followed Georgie's gaze to where Austin was surrounded by several young females who were probably quite willing to be at his beck and call. "He came here alone," Paris said. "In fact, I haven't known him to date anyone since we met."

Georgie took another ill-advised gulp. "Austin doesn't date. He passes through a girl's life, shows her a good time, then blows away like a tumbleweed."

"He dated you, didn't he?"

"Using today's teenage vernacular, we basically hooked up."

Paris remained silent for a moment before she spoke again. "Have you talked to him yet about…the issue?"

Issue as in their child. "I've been busy, and I'm waiting for the right time."

"Maybe you'll have the opportunity to speak to him tonight."

She glanced Austin's way to find his admirers had disappeared and he was now leaning back against the bar, his gaze trained on her. "Maybe I will." Maybe not.

Paris hooked her arm through Georgie's. "You'll know when the time is right. And by the way, I have a doctor's appointment Tuesday morning. After that, I'm free for the day. Why don't you and I have lunch in San Antonio?"

Georgie could use the break and the camaraderie. "Most of my appointments are in the morning. I can probably rearrange my schedule and clear the afternoon."

"Good." Paris looked a bit distracted before she returned her attention to Georgie. "I need to go rescue my husband from the creepy jerk. I'd invite you over but—"

"No offense, but no thanks. I've had enough exposure to Rich. I'll just mingle a bit and we can catch up later."

"Sounds like a plan." Paris started away then turned around again. "Be careful with that drink."

What was left of the drink. "I will."

After her friend departed, Georgie milled around the tent, greeting a few people she'd known a while back and nodding at several strangers. She could see Austin from the corner of her eye, basically tracking her path like a cougar stalking his prey, yet keeping his distance. She felt like a walking bundle of nervous energy, and that led her to finish the drink and take another from the waiter as he walked by. She planned to only hold this one, not drink it. But when the cat-and-mouse game with Austin continued and he smiled at her, she took another sip. And then another, even with Paris's warning going off in her head like a fire alarm.

After she noticed Austin approaching her, she began to survey the silent auction offerings laid out on a lengthy table. If she ignored him, maybe he'd just go away—and that was like believing the temperature wouldn't reach one hundred degrees in South Texas next summer.

"Georgie girl, I'm going to bid on that six-horse trailer with the sleeping quarters."

The feel of his warm breath playing over her neck and the sultry sound of his voice caused her to tighten the wrap around her arms against the pleasant chills. If she turned around, she would be much too close to him, so she continued to peruse the items until she regained some composure. "The spa day looks intriguing."

"I've never had a massage for two. I'm game if you are."

She disregarded the comment and sidestepped to the next offering displayed beneath a small glass case—an exquisite oval diamond ring encircled by a multitude of sparkling rubies. "Now this is quite nice." She then noted the shocking top bid on the sheet. "Surely I'm not reading this right."

Austin leaned over her shoulder, causing her to shiver slightly and take another sip of the drink. "Yep, you are. It's twenty-thousand dollars' worth of nice. You should go for it."

She regarded him over one shoulder. "I don't believe wearing this while inoculating cattle would be practical."

"All work and no play makes for a boring life."

"As beautiful as it is, it's not me." She noticed another, less gaudy ring to her left. A simple silver setting with a round sapphire surrounded by petite diamonds. "Now that's more me, but ten thousand dollars still isn't in my budget."

"Maybe Santa will bring it to you."

Against better judgment, she pivoted around and confronted Austin head-on. "If Santa Claus, Mrs. Claus, the elves and the tooth fairy pooled their funds, I still doubt they can afford this ring."

"Then let me bid on it for you."

He'd clearly lost his mind. "Don't you dare."

He sent her a sexy, sultry grin. "I have something better to give you."

She could only guess what that entailed. "We're not going there, either, Austin."

He frowned. "Get your mind out of the gutter, Georgie. I want to give you a dance."

That took her aback. "What?"

"The band's playing a slow song. Dance with me."

"As I told you recently, I highly doubt I remember how."

"I highly doubt you could ever forget. Now put down that drink and that bag you've been hanging on to like a lifeline, and follow me onto the floor."

She scraped her mind for some excuse to prevent her from falling into his sensual trap. "I can't just leave my purse unattended."

"What's in it?"

"My phone, driver's license, a five-dollar bill and lipstick."

"Credit cards?"

"No, but—"

"I guarantee no one in this crowd is going to steal that dinky bag, and if someone does, I'll replace your phone and the cash. You're on your own when it comes to the lipstick and driver's license."

Against better judgment, she finished off the last of the julep. "I'm holding you responsible if my *dinky* bag turns up missing."

Austin took the purse from her grasp and handed the glass off to a waiter. He then set the clutch on a table and used her wrap to cover it. "No one will even know it's there."

No one would know how needy she felt at the moment when Austin clasped her hand, either.

Unable to fight his persistence, Georgie allowed

Austin to lead her onto the floor and, once there, he took her right hand into his left, wrapped his arm around her waist and pulled her close.

The slow country song spoke of lost love and long-ago memories, a fitting tribute to their past. Georgie felt a bit light-headed, and she wasn't sure if it was because of the booze, or her partner. She pressed her cheek against his chest, closed her eyes and relaxed against him. She relished the feel of his palm roving over her back, his quiet strength, his skill. The first song gave way to another, then another, and still they continued to move to the music, as if they didn't have a care in the world.

When Austin tipped her chin up, forcing her to look into those magnetic cobalt eyes, she sensed he wanted to say something. Instead, he kissed her softly, deeply, taking her breath and composure. After they parted, Georgie could only imagine what the attendees were thinking, particularly Paris and Dallas, who were standing not far away, staring at them. She also noticed the couple had been joined by a crowd of Calloways. Mothers Jenny and Maria seemed pleased, the two dark-haired brothers, Houston and Tyler, looked annoyed, and the only blond sibling, Worth, evidently found the whole scene amusing, considering his grin.

Georgie tipped her forehead against his chest. "We're going to be the talk of the town."

"So?"

She looked up at him. "So if my father finds out I was canoodling with a man in public, and that man happens to be a Calloway, it won't be good for either of us."

Austin stopped and escorted her into a secluded

corner. "Georgie, it's high time you stop caring what your dad thinks. And when it comes down to it, we weren't making out on the dance floor. I just gave you a simple kiss."

A kiss that curled her toes in her stilettos. "Some would deem it inappropriate."

"*Some* can kiss my ass."

Georgie suddenly felt very warm and a tad bit dizzy. "I need some air."

Taking her by the arm, Austin guided Georgie outside the tent and set her on a wooden bench. "Better?" he asked.

She pinched the bridge of her nose and closed her eyes. "It's the drinks."

"Drinks? You had more than one of those mint juleps?"

"I know. Paris warned me, but I was…thirsty."

"You could've gotten water or a soda at the bar."

She frowned up at him. "I don't need a lecture. I need to go home."

"You're not fit to drive, Georgie."

She wouldn't debate that. "I know. Do you mind driving me home?"

"You can stay at my house."

She wasn't *that* tipsy. "Not a good idea."

"I have four bedrooms and four bathrooms. You can take your pick."

She found that odd. "Why so many?"

He shrugged. "The builder told me it was better for resale, not that anyone would buy a house in the Cowboy Commune."

Georgie giggled like a schoolgirl. "Is that what you're calling it these days?"

"That's what people around these parts have labeled it."

"I suppose it does fit."

He took both her hands and pulled her up. "Let's get your things and get you to bed."

She gave him a quelling look. "Austin Calloway—"

"A bed in a guestroom." He wrapped his arm around her waist and traveled toward the tent. "Of course, my bed is probably the best."

"Hush."

He favored her with a grin. "Okay. I'll be good."

Georgie knew how good he could be when he was being bad. For that reason, she should demand he drive her home. But all her wisdom went the way of the cool wind when he paused and gave her another kiss, and this one wasn't simple at all.

She wasn't too mentally fuzzy to know that if she didn't keep her wits about her, she would end up in Austin Calloway's bed.

"Here's the bedroom." Austin opened the door and stepped aside to allow Georgie some space to move past him. When she brushed against his belly, he realized he should've stood at the end of the hall. Or outside on the front porch.

He could hear his stepmom telling him to be a man about it and leave her be. Unfortunately, that seemed to be his problem. What man wouldn't want to sweep this woman up and make love to her until dawn?

Don't even think about it, Calloway.

But that was all he could think about when Georgie wandered into the room, perched on the edge of the bed and ran her palm over the teal-colored comforter like she was stroking a pet. "This is a really nice room. Has anyone stayed in here before me?"

He moved into the doorway but didn't dare go farther. "Nope. You're the first. Jenny's the one who decorated the place. That's why it's so frilly."

"It's pretty. I like peacock colors." She hid a yawn behind her hand. "I want to apologize for my behavior. I didn't plan to get drunk."

"I wouldn't qualify you as drunk. In fact, in all the time I've known you, I've never even seen you have a beer."

She crossed her legs, causing the dress to shift higher, revealing some mighty nice thighs. "I've only done it once. On my twenty-first birthday, a group of my college girlfriends and I hired a limo and went bar hopping. I had several cosmopolitans and a hangover to beat all hangovers the next day. It was awful."

"We've all been there before."

She leaned back and braced herself on her elbows. "I prefer not to go there again. Do you have a spare toothbrush?"

"Yep." He pointed at the sliding door across the room. "In the bathroom. That's Jenny's doing, too. She stocked the place with everything any guest would need, male or female."

"She didn't happen to put a gown in there, did she?"

"I don't think so."

"Then can I borrow one of your T-shirts? Otherwise I won't have a thing to wear."

Damn. Just when he'd gotten his mind off seeing her naked. "Sure. I'll be right back."

He took off down the hall at a fast clip and, when he reached his bedroom closet, tugged a faded blue rodeo T-shirt off the hanger. On the way back, he gave himself a mental pep talk on the virtues of keeping his hands to himself and his mind on honor.

Georgie sent him a sleepy smile when he reentered the guestroom. "That was fast. Hand it here."

Austin almost froze in his tracks when Georgie began to fiddle with the collar at the back of her neck. Honor and virtue went down the drain when he imagined the front of the dress dropping to her waist. Maria's cautions went unheeded when he fantasized about putting his hands on her. And to make matters worse, she came to her feet and turned around, giving him a bird's-eye view of her butt. "Can you help me with this?"

Man, he'd love to, but probably not in the way she'd meant. "Help you with what?"

She held her hair up with one hand. "This bow thingie. It's in a knot."

His *gut* was in a knot, and that would be the least of his problems if he came anywhere near her.

He could do this. He could help her with the kink in her collar and ignore the one building below his belt buckle. Good thing she didn't have eyes in the back of her head.

After tossing the T-shirt on the bed, he studied the twisted bow and worried over what would happen if he managed to get it untied. "Just hang on to the dress."

"Of course I will," she said, her tone hinting at irritation.

He'd been known for his steady hands, but he actually fumbled with the tie for a time before he had it undone. "There you go. All set."

Without warning, Georgie spun around and somehow managed to whack him in the jaw with her elbow. He hadn't been at all prepared for the accidental blow, nor had he expected his inadvertent attacker to frame his face in her palms. "I'm so sorry, Austin. Did I hurt you?"

Oh, yeah, he was hurting, but it wasn't from getting smacked. Right there, in his field of vision, a man's biggest fantasy, and in his case, worst nightmare—a pair of bare breasts. Tempting, round breasts close enough to touch. He'd seen breasts before. He'd seen hers before, several times, although they looked a bit fuller than he recalled. He'd touched them before, with his hands and his mouth. Damn if he didn't want to do that now.

"Austin?"

He forced his gaze back to her face. "You forgot something."

She glanced down, then back up and her eyes went wide. "Oops."

The next oops came when he noticed *that* look, the one she'd always given him when she'd wanted a kiss. But maybe that's only what he wanted to see. Regardless, he had to maintain some control. Be a true gentleman. Hang tight to his honor.

And that plan went right out the window when she pulled him down to her lips. That's when caution gave way to chemistry. She started walking backward, taking him with her. and before he knew it, they were on the bed, facing each other with their legs twined together. He managed to remove his jacket while they continued to kiss like there was no tomorrow. She worked the buttons on his shirt and slipped her hand inside. He slid his palm slowly up the back of her thigh and continued on until he contacted a skimpy pair of silk panties.

Completely caught up in his need, Austin planted

kisses down Georgie's neck and traveled to her breasts. He circled his tongue around one nipple before taking it into his mouth, using the pull of his lips to tempt her. She answered by running her hands though his hair and moving restlessly against him.

He wanted more from her. He wanted it all. But he couldn't have it unless he knew she wanted the same. On that thought, he raised his head and sought her eyes. "Before this goes any further, convince me you know what you're doing."

Unfortunately the interlude ended as quickly as it started when Georgie broke away, scrambled to her feet and pulled the top of her dress back into place. "Apparently I don't know what I'm doing since I swore this wouldn't happen again," she said, clear frustration in her voice.

Austin rolled to his back, draped an arm over his closed eyes and tried to catch his breath. "You started it."

"You didn't seem to be complaining."

"I couldn't complain with our tongues in each other's mouths."

When he heard the sound of a slamming door, Austin opened his eyes, expecting to discover Georgie had left the premises, if not the house. Instead, he noticed the bedroom door was still open, but the one leading into the bathroom had been closed.

Austin sat up and rubbed both hands over his face in a futile effort to erase the memories of their encounter. He figured he might as well leave now since he doubted she'd come out unless he made a quick exit. Obviously he'd been wrong, he realized when she walked back into the room wearing only his T-shirt and no smile.

She folded her arms around her middle and leaned back against the wall next to the door. "I'm sorry. You're not to blame for my behavior."

Regardless of blame, the damage to his libido had already been done. "I need to apologize to you. After two of Jenny's drinks, I should've realized you're not in charge of your faculties."

She crossed her arms around her middle and raised her chin. "I wasn't drunk."

"Okay. Tipsy."

"Maybe, but I'm quite sober now."

And he was still so jacked up he could pull that too-big shirt up over her ruffled hair and take her up against the wall. "And I'm betting you're tired. Have a good night. See you in the morning."

He turned on his heels and almost made it to the door before she asked, "Where are you going?"

Straight to hell if he faced her again. "To bed."

"I thought we could talk awhile."

He didn't want to talk. He wanted to get back down to business. "I'm pretty worn out," he said without moving.

"Come on, Austin. You're a night owl just like me."

He'd be hooting up a storm—or howling like a coyote—if he got anywhere near her again. "Georgie, I'm fairly sure if I stay, I wouldn't want to use my mouth to talk, especially since you're half-dressed."

She laughed. "You've seen me in a bikini. Actually, you've seen me wearing nothing."

If she kept talking that way, she'd see the evidence of what those memories did to him. What she'd done to him a few minutes ago. He had one hell of an erection and no place to go. "I think it might be better if I go to my own room."

"Man up, Calloway. You're not a teenager anymore. You can have an adult conversation with a woman without any other expectations."

Under normal circumstance, that was a given. But with her...

Dammit, he was up for the challenge, *up* being the operative word. Still, he vowed to prove to her he could be mature in spite of the noticeable bulge below his belt buckle. In an effort to calm down, he ran through a mental laundry list of a few times he'd been in pain. His first broken rib during one rodeo. When Maria made him eat spinach. The day Abby had him served with divorce papers.

That did it, or so he thought until he faced Georgie again. The T-shirt hit her well above the knee and hung off one shoulder. He could see the outline of her breasts and that's exactly where his gaze landed again, and his imagination kicked into overdrive.

"Austin."

He finally tore his attention away from her attributes and came in contact with her scowl. "What?"

She pointed two fingers at her eyes. "Up here."

"Sorry," he muttered, although in some ways he wasn't.

Georgie dropped down onto the bed and patted the space beside her. "Sit for a few minutes."

She really expected him to remain upright after their recent make-out session? Yeah, she did, and so would his stepmothers. With that in mind, he perched on the edge of the mattress, keeping a decent berth between them. "So what's on your mind?"

"Us," she said as she stretched the hem of the shirt to her knees. "Everything we've been through over the years."

He smiled. "We have been through quite a bit."

"And during all that time," she continued, "our friendship always meant the most to me."

Now he got it. She was about to deliver the "let's be friends" speech. "Yeah, we've always had a good friendship, and some really friendly foreplay in the bed of my truck."

She playfully slapped at his arm. "You know what I mean. I'm referring to all those instances when we were there for each other, like the time I made an A minus in Mr. Haverty's class."

"Oh, yeah. You nearly had a nervous breakdown over that one. What about the time you helped me pass calculus?"

"And biology and world geography and, I believe, algebra one."

"You never had to help me with athletics."

"True enough."

They paused to share a smile before Austin said, "Now that we've established we've been friends for a long, long time, is there another point to this conversation?"

She studied her hands and twisted the silver ring round and round her little finger. "That's what I want from you right now, Austin. That's what I need from you."

Damn. "Fine. You've got it."

She leveled her gaze on his. "Problem is, I'm not sure you're capable of being only my friend."

Anger sent him off the bed to face her. "You're being

freakin' unfair, Georgie. We were friends long before we were lovers."

"I just don't know if you're willing to go back to that. I'm not sure you can."

He might be willing, but that didn't take away the wanting. "I damn sure could be only your friend, and I'll prove it."

"How do you propose to do that?"

Hell if he knew. "From now on, when I see you, I'll only shake your hand."

That earned him her smirk. "If you say so."

"I say so." Starting now. He stuck out his hand. "Hope you sleep well."

Ignoring the gesture, she rose from the bed and damned if she didn't draw him into a hug. She then stepped back and smiled. "See there? You managed to accept a friendly show of affection and you didn't even try to cop a feel. Maybe I've underestimated you."

Yeah, she had, because it had taken all his fortitude not to grab her up and toss her back onto the bed. "I'm a lot stronger than you think, Georgie."

"Only time will tell, Austin. And I hope you get a good night's sleep, too."

"Not hardly," he muttered as he headed out the door and down the hall.

Being only friends with Georgia May Romero could be the biggest mountain he'd ever had to climb, but he was determined to do it. He would find some way to show her he could be the man she wanted him to be, even if it might do him in during the process.

To postpone the inevitable test of his mettle, he hoped that when he woke up in the morning, he'd find her gone.

Five

Before she went home, Georgie sought out an energy boost and the means to wake up after a restless night. She padded into the deserted upscale kitchen on bare feet, wearing Austin's oversize T-shirt and suffering from a mild hangover. She retrieved a cup from the gray cabinet and located the canister of dark roast on the white-quartz countertop, right next to the fancy coffeemaker that looked as if it might require a barista degree to operate it.

After two attempts, she finally figured out the formula and waited for the stainless carafe to fill before she poured the brew into the mug. Normally she preferred cream and sugar, but black coffee seemed more appropriate under the circumstance.

She leaned back against the center island, clutching the cup and worrying over her behavior after stupidly finishing off two high-powered cocktails the night before. But she couldn't blame her complete lack of control on the booze. Not when the situation involved a sexy cowboy.

How could Austin still affect her so strongly? How could she forget how he'd flitted in and out of her life without a second thought? More important, how could she disregard that he'd fathered her child and still didn't know it?

She had to tell him soon. When and where remained a mystery yet to be solved.

"Mornin'."

Georgie glanced to her right to see Austin trudging into the room, his hair slightly damp and his jaw blanketed with whiskers. He hadn't bothered to put on a shirt, but at least he'd had the wherewithal to put on a pair of faded jeans that rested a little too low on his hips to be deemed decent. She didn't need to see the slight shading of hair centered into his broad chest or the flat plane of his belly or that other stream of hair that disappeared into his waistband. She definitely didn't need to look any longer, but she did.

Bad Georgie. Bad, bad Georgie.

Austin seemed oblivious to her blatant perusal of his body and continued toward the coffeemaker to pour a cup. He briefly brushed against her shoulder and gave her a good whiff of manly soap as he turned to face her. "I thought you'd be gone by now, or at least dressed." He topped off the comment by raking his gaze down her body and back up again, slowly.

She experienced a sensual electric shock down to the bottom of her soles. "I just needed to wake up a bit before I drove. I'll be leaving very soon."

He sent her a sleepy grin. "Don't go on my account, unless you have appointments."

She took a sip of coffee before setting the cup on the counter. "Only emergencies on Saturday and so far I haven't had any."

"I could always put you to work in the barn."

He could do a lot to her in the barn that had more to do with pleasure. He already had. "I still have some boxes I need to unpack and some things to put away. I didn't have a lot of time to do that in the past two weeks since I dove right into work."

"Do you need help?"

If he stepped through her doorway, she'd be too distracted to get anything done. Not to mention he would notice all the signs pointing to a child in residence. "I'll manage, and I really need to get out of here."

Austin leaned a hip against the counter. "Before you leave, I have a proposition."

Oh, brother. "I believe we established there would be no more of that last night."

He looked highly incensed. "It's not *that* kind of proposition. I'm talking about my second favorite pastime—a trail ride on open land. Just you and me and total freedom."

She didn't dare ask about his first favorite pastime, although she suspected it was a toss-up between calf-roping and carnal endeavors. "Does that include prancing naked on the prairie?"

He released a low, sexy laugh. "No prancing on my end, and since it's going to be in the forties, naked won't be happening for the sake of my dignity."

Georgie suddenly longed for summer. "It's been a while since I've ridden for pleasure." When he smirked and opened his mouth to speak, she pointed at him. "Before you make some suggestive comment, I'm referring to horseback riding."

"I didn't have one dirty thought rolling around in my brain."

"Yeah, sure."

He winked and smiled. "Just so you know, it's been a while since I've ridden just for the heck of it. We could have a good time. As friends."

The friend part still concerned her. "When do you propose we take this ride?"

He forked a hand through his dark hair. "We'd leave out this afternoon and come back tomorrow."

She raised both hands, palms forward. "Wait a minute. You're talking about an overnight trip?"

"Yeah. We're gearing up for the opening of Texas Extreme, so I thought I'd map out the best course for the trail ride for beginners."

"You can't do that in an afternoon?"

"We're going to be taking the guests on an old-fashioned campout, complete with a chuck wagon. We might even herd a few cows."

As much as Georgie would enjoy the getaway, warning bells rang out in her head. "Couldn't you ask Dallas to go with you?"

"Nope. Dallas is freaking out over the baby coming in less than a month. He barely leaves Paris's side."

That made sense, but still… "What about Houston or Worth?"

"Houston's busy chasing the dream and Worth, well, he's busy chasing women."

She was down to her last option. "That still leaves Tyler."

"He left this morning to check out a couple more pack mules for the trail ride and I'm not sure when he'll be back."

Georgie narrowed her eyes. "If you expect me to ride a mule, my answer is definitely no."

His grin arrived, slow as sunrise. "Do you have a problem with my ass?"

She slapped at his arm. "You're so comical this morning."

"Thanks, and for the record, I don't expect you to board a mule."

"Good to know, but my mare isn't ready for a trail ride. She's still pretty skittish."

"I know," he said. "I saw her dump you on your butt last week, remember?"

She wished she could forget. "I guess that settles it then. I don't have an adequate ride, so you're on your own."

"I still have the dynamic duo."

She was blasted back into the past to a wonderful time when they'd set out on horseback in secret. "You mean Junior and Bubba?"

"Yep. They're still going strong at the ripe old age of fifteen."

"I loved Junior."

"He probably feels the same about you. Only one way to find out. Come with me on the ride."

She turned the idea over and over and couldn't quite pull the trigger on a definitive decision. "I'm still not too keen on the overnight idea."

He rubbed a hand over his jaw. "Tell you what. If you agree to go, and you decide you don't want to spend the night with me, we'll ride back."

That she could live with, but she still had responsibilities. "I'll see what I can get done before noon and I'll let you know."

"Fair enough," he said. "But don't take too long. I want to get started right after lunch."

"If I do agree, what do you propose we have for dinner? Or do you plan to play hunter and gatherer and catch our meal in the creek?"

He winked. "Leave that up to me. I promise you won't be disappointed."

He'd never disappointed her when it had come to showing her a good time. He *had* let her down during those two mornings when he'd disappeared out of her life to pursue his interests. Yet Chance had become the most important person in her life, and maybe this journey would present a prime opportunity to have a heart-to-heart with Austin.

On that thought, Georgie walked to the sink, rinsed out her cup then turned to find Austin staring at her. "Where and when do you want me to meet you?"

He looked mildly surprised. "Around one p.m., at the main barn. Be sure to bring a coat. The temperature's going to be dropping this afternoon when the cold front comes in."

She might be better served by wearing several layers of clothing for protection, both from the elements and her escort. "Okay. Right now I better get dressed and retrieve my truck."

He hooked a thumb behind him. "Your truck's in the driveway. Feel free to wear my T-shirt home."

Oh, sure. "With my high heels?"

He streaked a palm over his face. "Get out of here, Georgie, before I..."

She couldn't hold back a smile. "Before what?"

"Before I forget we're just friends."

Georgie needed to remember the friend pact, too, no matter what Austin Calloway might throw at her. But if their past behavior predicted future deeds, that would darn sure prove to be difficult.

"Where in the hell are you going?"

Austin ignored Dallas's question and continued to secure the bedrolls to Bubba's saddle. "I'm going to chart out the trail ride for Extreme."

Worth wandered into the barn and eyed the bay gelding. "Seems a little early to be worrying about that. The lodge isn't going to be finished for a couple of months and we haven't even started building the new catch pens yet."

Austin moved across the aisle to Junior and tightened the jet-black gelding's girth strap. "I'll be busy with the dealerships after the first of the year. I figure now's as good a time as any."

Tyler suddenly made an appearance to add to the unwelcome audience. "Since you have two horses saddled, I'm guessing you want one of us to go with you."

He began to shorten the stirrups without looking back. "Nope."

"You're going to take both horses?" Dallas asked.

Austin finished and finally turned around. "Yep."

Worth pulled a piece of straw from his pocket and started chewing on it. "You must be planning to cross the border if you're taking both horses."

He really wished they'd all leave before Georgie arrived. The odds of that happening were slim to none, he realized, after he heard the sound of approaching footsteps. Austin braced for the fallout until Jenny—not Georgie—breezed into the barn, wearing a crazy red Christmas sweater and matching slacks.

She strode over and offered him a small square blue cooler and a plastic sack. "Here you go, sugar."

Austin took the containers, strode to Bubba and draped the straps over the saddle horn. "I appreciate it, Jen. Hope you didn't go to too much trouble."

When he faced Jenny again, she patted his cheek. "No trouble at all. Oh, and I just talked to Georgie. She said she had to make a phone call and then she'll be heading this way. Ten minutes tops."

Damn. The companion cat was out of the bag, and no doubt he'd have hell to pay. "Thanks for letting me know."

The look Dallas sent him wasn't lost on Austin. "Georgie, huh?"

He figured he should just fake indifference and hope for the best. "Yeah, Georgie. She wasn't busy this afternoon so we decided to do it together."

Worth chuckled. "Doing it together is a lot more fun than doing it alone."

Jenny sent her son a frown. "Hush, Worth Calloway. A man can go for a ride with a woman without anything disreputable going on." She turned her attention back to Austin. "Your supper should be set. I put in all the fixings for a wiener roast."

When the boys began to chuckle, Austin balled his fists at his sides, itching to throw a punch. Jenny's weapon of choice involved a stern look aimed at the brothers before she turned to him again. "I added marshmallows and I wasn't sure what Georgie liked on her hot dog, so just to be safe, I included several condiments."

"If you're really worried about safety, Mom," Worth began, "you might want to pack some condoms with the condiments."

Jenny laid a dramatic hand over her heart. "My dear, sweet child, don't be so crass. You're acting like an oversexed heathen."

Like a bunch of junior high jocks, the brothers' chuckles turned into full-fledged laughter. "Come on, guys," Austin said. "Get your minds out of the sewer and have some respect for Jen."

Jenny propped her hands on her hips. "Austin is absolutely right. You boys have apparently forgotten your raising."

"Sorry, Mom," Worth muttered, followed by Dallas's and Tyler's apologies.

Jenny gave Austin a quick hug. "I'll see you tomorrow, and, you two, be careful."

"We will," Austin said. "And thanks again for everything."

After Jen strode out of the barn, Tyler said, "I personally think Worth had a good idea about the condoms. Do you have one in your wallet that's not from your high school years?"

Austin had about enough. "Look, Georgie is just a friend. That's all. We're not doing anything we haven't been doing for years."

Dallas took on a serious expression. "That's what worries me. I've already warned you about—"

"Dammit, I know, Dallas." Austin drew in a calming breath and let it out slowly. "You're just going to have to trust me on this one. We're not the same stupid kids we used to be."

Tyler came up and slapped Austin on the back. "Good luck, bud. Wide-open spaces and a beautiful woman can equal a lack of control. If you can resist her, you're a better man than me."

"Or crazy," Worth added. "But if you only want to be friends with her, I'll be glad to pick up where you leave off."

Austin sent him a menacing glare. "Not every woman is interested in you, Worth."

Dallas stepped forward. "We're not trying to get into your business. We just don't want you leading Georgie on."

Same song, fiftieth verse. Austin understood where his brothers were coming from, but he was up for the challenge. He could have a platonic relationship with a woman, even one he'd slept with before. Even one he'd wanted to sleep with last night, minus the sleeping…

"Sorry I'm late."

His focus went straight to Georgie strolling down the aisle, her hair pulled up high into a ponytail. She wore a heavy flannel shirt over a white T-shirt, a pair of faded jeans and worn brown boots. With every move she made, every smile she gave the boys who now stood, hats in hands, staring at her, Austin's confidence began to slide.

He cleared the uncomfortable hitch from his throat. "No problem. I'm just now finishing up with the supplies."

She held up the small nylon duffel. "Do you have room for this?"

"What's in it?"

She glanced over her shoulder at the brothers, who continued to stand there like statues, eavesdropping. "Just a few essentials in case we lay over. Toothbrush, toothpaste, that sort of thing."

Too bad she hadn't said a sexy nightgown, but he supposed that wouldn't be practical. Fantastic, yeah, practical, no. "Hang it over the saddle horn."

"Good idea." After she complied, she brought her attention to the brothers. "Are you guys going, too?"

Dallas shook his head. "Nope. I'm hanging out with the wife."

Tyler scowled. "I'm hanging out with the mothers."

"I'm hanging out at the local dance hall," Worth began, "but I'd be glad to change my plans and accompany you."

Georgie smiled at him sweetly. "I wouldn't feel right leaving all those local women without a dance partner."

Worth returned her smile. "You and me, we could take a stroll in the moonlight while Austin roasts a few marshmallows."

Austin pointed at the door. "Out. Now. All of you."

While the crew trudged away, Tyler muttered, "Fifty dollars says he'll need the condiments."

"I'll see your bet and raise you fifty," Worth added as they walked out the barn, laughing all the way.

Georgie frowned. "What was that all about?"

He checked to see if both bedrolls were secure beneath the saddles' cantles. "Nothing. They're just mouthing off like usual."

"It sounded like they were making some kind of bet on me."

Austin ventured at glance at Georgie to find she looked a little put out. "It has more to do with me. I told them this was a friendly trip, and they don't believe I can be only friends with you without getting too friendly."

"Can you?"

He was going to do his best. "Sure. Are you ready to roll?"

"I guess so."

He sensed her hesitation, and felt the need to reassure her. "Georgie, I promise to be a gentleman, just like Maria taught me to be. And if I slip up, Junior knows his way back to the barn."

She patted the black gelding's neck and received a nuzzle in return. "Yes, he does, and he's still as gorgeous as ever."

So was she. "Yep, he's in good shape. He also recognizes you."

She pulled the headstall from the hanger and began to remove the horse's halter. "We all had some unforgettable times."

Austin recalled one great time that had occurred not so far away in the tack room. Some hot and heavy kisses, taboo touches and a moment when they'd almost gone all the way. His focus went straight to her body and it took all his strength not to grab her up and carry her back in the cramped room to refresh her memory. "Are you ready to go?"

She sent him a look over her shoulder. "Do you plan to ride Bubba without a bit?"

Keep your mind on your business and not her butt, Calloway. "I probably could, but I guess it's best I don't."

After they were all tacked up, Georgie mounted Junior with ease and Austin followed suit on Bubba. "Let's get this adventure started," he said as he guided the gelding down the aisle with Georgie and Junior tagging along behind them.

Once they emerged into daylight, they rode through the gate, side by side, and into open pastureland. A strong gust of wind kicked up some dust, and Austin wondered if Georgie had on enough clothes to keep warm. He could keep her warm. Give her his heat in ways she wouldn't forget...

"I've forgotten how wonderful this feels," she said, interrupting his suspect train of thought.

"Yeah. Nothing better than wide-open spaces." *Wide-open spaces and a beautiful woman can equal a lack of control.* Austin erased Tyler's warnings from his mind as they continued down the path leading to the creek.

They rode in silence for a long time before Georgie spoke again. "Any ideas on your route?"

He had some ideas, but none having to do with routes. "I thought I'd follow along the fence line for a couple of miles."

She sent him a fast glance. "That means you'll be bordering the road leading to my dad's ranch. Nothing will ruin an Old West fantasy more than a delivery truck."

He couldn't argue that point. "Hadn't thought about that. Then I guess we'll head south and ride toward the far end of the creek."

She looked straight ahead and smiled. "Ah, the creek. I can remember spending a lot of summers at the place."

So could he. "The rope is still there, but the water isn't as deep as it used to be. I wouldn't suggest using it."

That earned him a sour look. "It's a little too cool to be swimming today, don't you think?"

He adjusted his hat on his head with one hand. "Probably so."

She favored him with a smile right out of a dirty dream. "Wanna race?"

He wanted to pull her off the horse and into his arms. He wanted her. Real bad. "No need to ask me twice."

He cued Bubba into a lope and Georgie didn't miss a beat. When he picked up speed, so did she, smiling all the way. And she became that girl again, the one who'd spurred his adolescent fantasies. A more mature version, but still as pretty. Still as spirited.

They ran headlong past the places where they used to meet in secret, sometimes at midnight, sometimes in broad daylight if they were feeling more daring, avoiding detection by their fathers and caught up in the thrill of trying not to get caught. They'd engaged in long conversations, when they hadn't been engaging in experimentation.

So many ghosts on this land. Good times mixed with the not so good. Most had been good, except for one in particular, the old windmill on the horizon serving as a reminder. The place where he'd planned to tell her goodbye before he'd left for college, but she hadn't shown up.

As they slowed their pace, Georgie's laughter echoed over the plains and, in that moment, he couldn't want her more. But he had to remember the friendship pact, and adhere to it. He had to take hold of some serious honor and not act on his desires.

If he could manage that accomplishment, then he expected to encounter a few flying pigs before the end of the day.

Six

Before the end of this trip, Georgie planned to fully disclose her secret to Austin. If only she could find the appropriate place, appropriate time and, most important, the appropriate words. Right then those words escaped her.

As they neared the familiar creek, she noticed gray clouds gathering on the horizon, completely concealing the sun. They'd been riding for a little over two hours when she sensed now would be a good time to take a break and assess the weather.

"Let's stop for a while," Austin said before she could get the suggestion out of her mouth.

They trotted to the tree line and, after they dismounted, led the horses to the shallow brook for a drink. Austin then took the reins from her hands and guided the geldings to the pasture to turn them loose.

"Shouldn't we tie them up?" she asked as soon as he returned to her side.

"Nah. They'll hang around here and if they don't, they'll find their way back to the barn."

Great. "And that would leave us stranded in the middle of nowhere on foot."

Without responding, Austin put both pinkies in his mouth and blew out a loud whistle, bringing the equine boys back in record time. He grinned at Georgie as he patted the geldings' necks. "They don't have any intention of going anywhere without me."

Georgie had felt the same way about him at one point in time. "They've always been well trained."

Austin rummaged around one of the saddlebags, withdrew two carrot chunks, laid them in his flattened palms and offered them to Junior and Bubba. "They know who feeds them." He waved them away. "Now you two go back to the grass for a bit."

As if they understood every word, the geldings turned around and hurried back to the pasture to graze. "You missed your calling, Austin. You should've been a lion tamer in the circus."

"Maybe so. I pretty much grew up in a circus." He wandered over to the bank and sat down on a rock. "Come over here and take a load off."

"I've been sitting for almost two hours."

"Then suit yourself and stand."

In reality, her legs felt a little shaky from the long ride, but the thought of sitting next to him didn't help matters. Still, this could be an opportunity to open up the lines of communication before she lowered the baby boom.

Georgie strolled over to Austin, lowered down onto the dirt slope and hugged her knees to her chest. "Looks like it might rain."

"The forecast says tomorrow midday."

She sent him a sideways glance. "This is Texas and when Mother Nature comes for a visit, she doesn't always listen to meteorologists."

"True."

A brief span of silence passed before Georgie spoke again. "I'm still amazed at Bubba's and Junior's obedience. Way back when, they were both pretty wild, especially Junior."

"But he pretty much taught you how to rope."

"With a little assistance from you."

He sighed. "Yeah. It's hard to believe how long they've been in my life. But so have you."

Yes, she had. A very long time full of happiness and heartache. She snatched up a stick and began tracing random circles in the soil. "How long did you know your wife?"

"For a while," he said. "We ran into each other on the circuit on a regular basis during my rodeo years before we got hitched."

A possibility burned into Georgie's mind, and it wasn't good. She shifted slightly to gauge his reaction to the impending question. "Were you dating her when your dad passed away?"

He studied her for a moment before reality dawned in his expression. "If you're asking if we were together when I was with you, the answer is not only no, but hell no. I can't believe you'd even think such a thing."

"What did you expect, Austin? I found out you'd married her four months after that night."

He lowered his gaze to the ground. "I guess that's a reasonable assumption under normal circumstances, but it shouldn't be with us. Not with our history."

A lot of their history hadn't exactly been hearts and flowers, or complete honesty. "When I didn't hear from you after that last night we spent together, I assumed you'd moved on again. I just didn't know you'd moved on into a marriage."

"More like a huge mistake."

For some reason the declaration pleased her. "Surely it wasn't all bad."

He ventured a quick glance in her direction. "Not all of it. Not in the beginning. But sex alone can't sustain a relationship."

She cringed at the thought of him with another woman, even though she'd never had any real claim on him. "Did it ever occur to you that maybe you two should have tried living together before tying the knot?"

Austin sent her a cynical grin. "The whole wedding was spontaneous, and stupid. Too much beer and too much time on our hands and a Vegas chapel at our disposal."

At least that explained the hasty nuptials. "Never in a million years would I have believed you'd be a drunken Vegas wedding cliché, Austin."

"Well, believe it. I tried to make it work but Abby wasn't willing. In fact, to this day, I'm still not sure what I did."

"Maybe it wasn't what you did, but what you didn't do."

He frowned. "What do you mean?"

He was such a guy. "Were you attentive? Romantic? Did you tell her you loved her more than once in a blue moon?"

He almost looked ashamed. "None of the above, and I'm not sure we were in love. I mean, I cared about her, but I knew the marriage idea was wrong when I finally signed the divorce papers and I didn't feel anything but relief."

"Yet you hung in there for quite some time, right?"

"Three years, but it was pretty much over in the first six months."

"Wow. I'm surprised you didn't end it sooner."

"I didn't want to admit to the failure."

Nothing new there. "You can't shoulder that burden alone. It takes two to make or break a solid marriage."

"Maybe you're right, but there was one thing she wanted that I wasn't willing to give her."

"What was that?"

"A kid. I told her several times I didn't want any, but she started making noise about two months into the marriage. I reminded her that wasn't in my immediate future."

His assertions gave Georgie pause. "Then you're not completely ruling it out."

He shrugged. "I'm not sure. I only know I'm not going to be ready for that responsibility for a long, long time."

Georgie swallowed hard around the swell of disappointment mixed with panic. She had to acknowledge one serious reality—Austin might never accept their son. "I guess I always saw you as the fatherly type. You did a good job keeping your younger brothers on the straight and narrow."

He picked up a pebble and tossed it into the creek.

"But if they screwed up, it was ultimately my folks' responsibility. And maybe I got my belly full keeping them in line while my dad was off doing whatever he was doing aside from work."

Meaning marrying another woman and birthing two more boys without telling anyone. Essentially she had done something similar by not telling him about their child, although her reasoning had seemed honorable at the time. "Did his deception influence your attitude about having children at all?"

"Nah. That would be Dallas, although he obviously changed his mind." He stared off into space for a moment before presenting a surprising smile. "Do you think it's still here?"

He'd always been a master at changing the subject when it got too hot in the emotion kitchen. Admittedly she could use a break, too. "What is still here?"

"The tree."

She'd known it was still around from the moment they'd ridden up to the creek. "To my right, about three oaks down."

He slapped his palms on his thighs and stood. "Let's go look at it before we head out."

"Why?"

He took her hand and pulled her to her feet. "I could use a good memory about now."

Georgie had to admit that secret meeting site did hold more than a few fond recollections. "Oh, all right. Lead the way."

She followed behind Austin along the bank, weaving in and out of foliage, until they reached the memorial tree sporting a pair of initials. She ran her palm over the carvings. "I wonder if anyone ever saw this."

Austin came to her side and grinned. "If they did, I'm sure they're still trying to figure out the identity of R and J."

She returned his smile. "Randy and Jill?"

"Ralph and Julie."

"Ronald and Jessie."

"Wasn't that a real couple from high school?" he asked.

"Possibly, but I guarantee we didn't know any Romeos or Juliets." And that had been the inside joke— star-crossed lovers caught between feuding fathers. She turned and leaned back against the trunk. "At least no one packed any daggers or poison."

He braced his palm on the tree, right above her head. "But the first time I kissed you here, that really packed a punch."

A kiss that had almost sent her to her knees. "I suppose."

"Suppose?" He leaned forward and ran a fingertip along her jaw. "Maybe I should refresh your memory."

As he leaned forward and rested his other hand on her waist, Georgie fought that same old magnetic pull. She decided to verbally push back. "Why do you continue to do this?"

"Do what?"

"Test my strength."

He traced her lips with a fingertip. "Maybe I'm testing mine."

"Friends, Austin," she muttered without much conviction.

"Good friends, Georgie girl."

When Austin traced the shell of her ear with his tongue, Georgie released a ragged breath and shivered.

And when he centered his gaze on her eyes, she tried to prepare for what would predictably come next...a kiss that she couldn't resist.

Then he stepped back and winked. "Guess I'm stronger than we both thought."

Georgie gritted her teeth and spoke through them. "You're a tease."

To the sound of Austin's laughter, she stormed away through the trees, half tempted to ride back in the direction of the ranch. She then realized she had no horse, and whistled at the geldings the way Austin had. They didn't budge, at least not for her. After Austin summoned them, they came running back, looking for a handout from their master.

Georgie didn't afford Austin a glance, didn't say a word, as they mounted their respective horses. Frustration kept her and Junior in the same spot as Austin headed away, leaving her behind. Frustration over his actions, and her typical feminine response.

A few moments passed before he glanced back and pulled Bubba to a stop, then turned the gelding to face her. "Do you have a problem?"

"Yes. You."

He released a low, grainy laugh. "Obviously you traded in your sense of humor to get that vet degree."

"I don't exactly find your determination to play with me very funny."

"Sweetheart, if I'd seriously played with you, you'd be moaning, not complaining."

Now why did that make her want to twitch in the saddle? "Look, before I agree to continue this little trip, you have to promise you won't tease me again."

He narrowed his eyes and studied her straight on.

"Best I recall, you used to like to be teased, especially when I had my hand in your—"

"Austin," she cautioned, despite the damp heat gathering between her thighs.

He raised both hands, as if surrendering. "Okay. I'm sorry. Old habits die hard."

Old memories clearly never died. "Apology accepted, as long as you don't pull anything like that again."

"Okay. But keeping my hands off you isn't going to be easy. Keeping my mouth off you is going to be really tough."

A very detailed sexual image filtered into Georgie's mind, bringing about a blanket of goose bumps. The girl she'd once been might have begged him to end her misery, but she wasn't that girl anymore. She was a woman. A vital woman who hadn't been with a man in six years. A woman who desperately needed his touch, his kisses, but recognized that the cost of intimacy with this man could be too high. "Where are we heading now?"

"The old cabin."

Just one more monument to the past, she thought as she cued Junior forward. She'd been at the ramshackle cabin before, but not to fool around with Austin. She'd met him there on his late mother's birthday at his request, an unusual appeal, but he'd been uncharacteristically sentimental. Those moments hadn't been about teenage hormones and unbridled lust. They'd been about comfort and communication. Buried regrets and obvious pain. Emotional exposure. Friendship at its finest.

Yes, she had been at that cabin, and during that fateful encounter, Georgie had quietly, completely fallen in love with Austin Calloway. Sadly, she still was, proving some things never changed.

The place hadn't changed a bit. Austin realized that when they arrived at the rickety structure that had somehow weathered at least a hundred years' worth of Texas heat. The windows were still boarded up, and he found that funny considering anyone could probably knock the door open with the swing of a rope. But his dad had always been a stickler when it came to security, even if it involved a one-room house that was barely hanging on. At least the front porch still appeared to be intact, and that might be a good thing if it rained.

He looked to his left to find Georgie staring at the cabin like she'd never seen it before. "It's exactly how I remembered it," she finally said. "Old and probably moldy."

Austin climbed off the saddle and guided Bubba to the pole barn adjacent to the cabin. "I imagine it's pretty dusty inside. Maybe even a critter or two hanging out."

Georgie dismounted and joined him. "Lovely. Nothing like stumbling upon a skunk."

"Skunks come out in the spring. Same with snakes. In fact, most of the animals are hibernating. Come to think of it, the last time I was here, I didn't see one living creature except maybe a spider or two."

"Bugs don't hibernate."

"That's true, but I don't see any reason why we'd have to go inside."

She studied the dreary sky. "A storm comes to mind."

"We'll worry about that if it happens." He needed to ask a question before they settled in for dinner. "Do you want to go back to the ranch?"

She sighed. "After sitting for the better part of six hours, I'd rather just relax for a while. We'll play the overnight plan by ear."

He couldn't deny his disappointment if she didn't spend the night with him, not that he expected anything to come of it aside from companionship. But that was okay. It was high time he relearned how to be her friend, although he figured he'd be fumbling his way through it. He also envisioned sitting on his hands and keeping his mouth shut when he wasn't talking. "All right then," he said. "Let's get these guys unsaddled. I'll turn them out with some hay, then I'll build a fire for dinner."

After they'd accomplished that goal, Austin retrieved the supplies, tossed them onto the porch and searched the yard for a few rocks to fashion a makeshift fire ring. He placed them in a circle in front of the house then went about gathering kindling from fallen limbs on the side of the house. He returned to find Georgie sitting on the top porch step, elbows resting on her knees, palms supporting her jaw, a smile on her pretty face.

He dropped the wood into the middle of the circle and faced her. "You look amused."

"You look cute, all dressed in your red flannel shirt, getting ready to cook dinner. A cross between Paul Bunyan and Betty Crocker."

"I'm not sure how I feel about that description."

She straightened and pushed her hair back from her shoulders. "I didn't mean to insult your manhood. Actually, I'm impressed you're going to be playing chef tonight."

"Don't be too impressed." He leaned over and pulled two of the straightest limbs from the pile. "Here's our utensils."

She laughed. "We're having hot dogs?"

"Yep."

"Darn. I was hoping for filet mignon."

"Sorry to disappoint you."

"I'm not disappointed at all, Austin. I'm looking forward to it because I'm starving. So come on, baby, light that fire."

He'd like to have his fire lit by her. Ignoring the dirty thoughts, Austin pulled an old book of matches from his back pocket. "Keep your fingers crossed this doesn't take more than a few tries. I don't have too many of these things."

Georgie came to her feet and brushed off her bottom. "We can always rub two sticks together."

Why the hell did hearing the word *rub* suddenly threaten his dignity? "Yeah, sure. You get going on that."

Turning his attention back to the fire pit, Austin struck the first match and watched it fizzle out. The second try didn't turn out any better. Now down to his last two, he wondered if they might have to return to the ranch for a decent meal. If that happened, he'd be sorely disappointed.

"Look what I found, Calloway."

Austin turned toward the porch where Georgie stood, holding a red-and-black barbecue lighter. "Where did you find that?"

She hooked a thumb over her shoulder. "In the sack

back there. I also found marshmallows and a lot of little packets of condiments."

That reminded him of the previous condiment and condom conversation with the brothers. Funny thing was, he always carried a condom with him. Not that he had a snowball's chance in the desert to use it this trip. "That's Jenny for you. She hoards those things."

"They do come in handy."

After Georgie sprinted down the steps and gave him the lighter, Austin had little trouble getting the fire going, in spite of the steady breeze. Seated on the ground, they ate their hot dogs, roasted marshmallows, reminisced and laughed a lot. The whole time Austin kept his attention on Georgie's mouth, imagining another kiss. Imagining was all he could do, unless she gave him some sign she wanted it, too. Not a whole lot of chance that would happen.

By the time they were done with dinner, the only light that illuminated the area came from the dwindling fire. Austin found more wood to stoke the blaze, then returned to the porch to retrieve the one thing that would give him an excuse to have her in his arms. He set the radio on the wooden slats and tuned in to a country music station.

"Oh, my gosh," Georgie said from behind him. "You still have that relic?"

He turned to find she was real close. "Yeah, and it still works."

"If I'd known you wanted music, I would've brought my MP3 player and speakers."

He reached over and tucked one side of her hair behind her ear, revealing a pair of diamond heart studs. They looked a lot like the same earrings he'd given her for her sixteenth birthday. He'd worked overtime at the feed store to earn enough money to buy them for her, and it had been worth it when she'd been so damned pleased. "I enjoy having the past around now and then."

She smiled. "So do I."

On cue, the radio went from a commercial break to a country ballad. "Care to dance with me again?"

"Twice in one week? That's so daring."

And kind of dangerous if he didn't control his hands and mouth. "You've never shied away from risky behavior."

"That was before..." Both her gaze and words trailed off.

"Before what?"

"Before I became an adult with adult responsibilities. However, I wouldn't refuse a dance with the consummate cowboy."

"Good to know."

After taking Georgie's hand, he led her down the steps and close to the fire where he put his arms around her. She laid her head on his shoulder and he placed his palm lightly against her back. As the song continued, he found his hand drifting lower, like he didn't have control of his appendages. He managed to stop the progress before he lost the wager that he could ignore his libido. But if she made one encouraging move, all bets were off.

They remained that way for a time as the wind picked up steam, and then came the deluge. Georgie pulled back and did something Austin would have never predicted. She laughed. Just the sound of it caused him to laugh, too. They continued to stand there, drenched to the bone and behaving like preschoolers who didn't have the good sense to come out of the rain.

When he noticed she was shivering, he led her to the porch, drew her against him and held her close. Then she did something else he didn't expect—brushed her lips across his neck.

He bent his head and took her mouth with a vengeance, sliding his tongue against hers slowly, deliberately, and she responded with a little action of her own. They stayed that way through one more song, making out like they had as kids. But the man in him backed her against the wooden wall, grabbed her butt and pressed against her, seeking relief but finding none. And what he was about to do wouldn't help a damn bit, but he wanted to do it. Had to do it.

He shoved her shirt off one shoulder then slid the strap to the tank she wore underneath down her arm partway. Now that he'd gained access, he broke away and took her breast into his mouth, circling her nipple with the tip of his tongue. She answered by undressing enough to reveal her other breast and framed his head in her hands. The small sexual sound she made drove him to the brink of insanity, pushed him toward forbidden territory. Right then, right there, he could take her down to the ground just to be inside her. Instead, he decided he would make this about her, but only if she agreed.

With that goal in mind, Austin released the button on her jeans and paused for a protest. When that didn't happen, he slid the zipper down and whispered, "Do you want me to stop?"

"I..." She let out a long, broken breath. "No. Don't stop."

That was all he needed to hear. He worked his hand into her jeans, where he rimmed the edge of her panties. She gave no indication she'd changed her mind, which drove him to keep going, keep searching beneath the silk for that very sweet spot. She was warm and wet and definitely ready for the attention. He gave it to her with slow strokes before he quickened the pace. She gripped his shoulders tightly, moved her hips rhythmically in time with his touch.

After she tensed, he raised his head from her breasts and brought his mouth to her ear. "It's okay, babe. Just let go."

And she did, with a rush of dampness and a low, ragged moan. He didn't let up until he knew he had milked every last pulse of her climax and she collapsed against him. He kissed her again, softly this time, as he pulled her clothes back into place. He turned away and rested his palms on the railing to regain some scrap of composure.

"Austin, are you okay?"

As okay as he could be with a flaming erection and no place to go to douse it. "I'm fine."

"Well, I'm not."

He prepared for a lecture that no doubt would arrive soon, swift and sure. And since he'd gone back on his word, tossed the friendship pact to the wind, he damn sure deserved it.

Seven

Georgie truly wanted to scold him, but this wasn't all his fault. He had asked if she wanted to stop, and she'd told him no. She wasn't some weak wilting flower with no free will. Truth was, she had wanted him so much she hadn't been able to control the familiar underlying chemistry. They were combustible together. They always had been. She'd known that when she'd agreed to come with him. Deep down she knew this would likely happen. And in all honesty, she didn't care, even if she should.

She stood there, shivering, her damp shirt and jeans only adding to her overall discomfort. "I'm freezing."

He pushed away from the banister and faced her. "Understandable. You're soaked to the skin."

"So are you."

"Sweetheart, that's the least of my concerns at the moment."

She sent a pointed look at his distended fly, somewhat surprised that he didn't invite her to finish what they'd started.

"Take your clothes off, Georgie."

Apparently she'd been mistaken. "Excuse me?"

He bent over, snatched one of the blankets from the floor and tossed it to her. "Don't look so worried. I'm not going to ravish you."

"You just did."

His patent slow grin came out of hiding. "Yeah, I did, and I don't regret it because obviously you really needed it."

Boy, had she. "It's been a while."

"Same here."

She had a hard time believing that. "Try six years."

Shock passed over his expression. "You mean—"

"The last time you and I were together was the last time for me. Now turn around so I can get these clothes off."

He started unbuttoning his shirt. "I've seen you naked before."

"Maybe, but I'd rather that not happen now."

"Fine, but if I turn around, you're going to see my bare ass."

"Not if I don't look." Maybe she'd take just a little peek. Or a long gander.

"Alrighty then."

Georgie made quick work of shedding her clothes, socks and boots, while Austin took his sweet time. She was already wrapped securely in the blanket by the time he shoved down his pants. She remained glued in place, holding the blanket closed with one hand and her wet clothes in the other. She studied all the planes in his broad back, the buns of steel, the strong thighs and calves dusted with hair, and decided she couldn't speak if her life depended on it. Then he did something completely off-the-wall—laced his hands behind his neck and flexed his muscles, then did some crazy thrust reminiscent of a male-stripper movie she'd seen a while back.

A chuckle bubbled up in her throat and came out in a full-fledged laugh when he looked over one shoulder and grinned. "Stop it," she said when she'd recovered her voice. "And cover up."

"You didn't like my moves?"

Oh, yeah. "Please put something on before you catch a good case of pneumonia."

"Fine, but just let me know if you want some more cheap entertainment."

She averted her gaze when he leaned over and snatched the blanket from the porch slats. When she ventured another look, fortunately she found him covered from the waist down. Of course, that left his stellar chest in full view.

In order to distract herself, Georgie draped her shirt, jeans and pink panties over the railing while he came to her side to do the same. Once that was done, she faced him with a frown. "What now?"

"I guess we could go to bed."

"We don't have a bed."

"We have a couple more blankets and a dry floor in the cabin, unless you want to sleep out here."

A sudden clap of thunder and subsequent bolt of lightning told her that wouldn't be wise. "The cabin it is. Did you bring a flashlight?"

"Yep. It's in that bag behind you."

"Then get it."

"You're closer."

She muttered a few mild oaths as she bent down, opened the canvas duffel and rifled through the contents. "You brought clothes."

"An old shirt and a few rags. Keep going."

Of course the flashlight happened to be on the bottom. She straightened and handed it to him. "You're going in first."

"I wouldn't have it any other way."

Austin opened the door and shone the beam into the vacant cabin. Georgie followed him inside and couldn't see much of anything aside from the pine floor and barren walls, but she didn't spot any wildlife, either. Then suddenly he spun around and headed out the open door, leaving her all alone, in the dark.

"Austin Calloway, where are you going?"

"Don't panic," he said as he returned with the light. "I just grabbed the rest of the bedding so we can tolerate the bare floor."

"I'm not sure I'll get much sleep with the threat of vermin hanging over me."

"I'll protect you," he said. "Here, hold this so I can see what I'm doing."

She aimed the beam on her half-naked bed buddy while he spread out two more blankets, one on top of the other. Once that was done, he rolled what appeared to be the aged shirt and the aforementioned rags into two pillows.

"Your accommodations are ready, ma'am," he said.

"Not exactly a five-star hotel, but it will do."

Austin dropped down onto the pallet and patted the blanket. "Soft as a mattress."

"Maybe a concrete mattress." Georgie lowered herself beside him and scanned the room with the narrow beam, thankful she didn't see any animal eyes staring back at her.

"Hand it over, Georgie."

"Why?"

He stretched out on the pallet, easy as you please, not leaving a lot of space between them. "I don't want to wake up with a light shining in my eyes because you heard a noise. Worse still, I don't want you whacking me with it when you mistake me for a raccoon."

She reluctantly relinquished the flashlight and laid back, making sure the blanket was secure around her. Still, she didn't find much comfort in the limited covers, the floor beneath her or his close proximity. "I wonder how long this storm is going to last. If it doesn't end soon, our clothes won't be dry."

"You brought an extra pair of panties."

She paused until the shock subsided. "How do you know that?"

"I peeked inside your bag."

"That makes you a snoop, don't you think?"

"Yeah, you're right. Sorry. Sometimes I'm just a little curious."

A little too familiar with her, she decided, as she rolled to face him. "Extra panties or not, they're not going to do me much good when we head back to the ranch."

"You wouldn't be the first woman to ride naked as a jaybird through town on a horse."

"Very funny."

He turned the light on her. "I'd buy tickets to that, and so would every man in a thirty-mile radius."

She refused to honor him with a response. "Turn that thing off, please. I'm half-blind."

"You got it."

After he snapped off the flashlight, silence hung over them for a few moments before he spoke again. "How many boyfriends have you had in the past six years?"

None. Zero. Nada. "There you go again, being intrusive."

"Hey, I told you about my marriage. Turnabout is fair play, right?"

He did have a point. "If you must know, I was too busy to date."

"You're saying you didn't have one man in your life?"

Only her little man. "No, I did not, and I assumed you would figure that out when I told you how long it's been since I've had sex. And for your information, women don't have to have a man to be happy. I had school and now I have my career, and that's all I need."

"All signs pointed to the contrary on the porch a little while ago."

Darn his insistence on reminding her of her vulnerability. "I had a moment of weakness."

"You had one hell of an orgasm. Do you want another one?"

Oh, yes… "No, thanks. That should last me another six years."

He chuckled. "Sweetheart, I don't believe for a minute that's true. And if it is, you're a lot stronger than me."

"I don't know about that. You didn't ask for a thing in return after our interlude."

"Interlude? Is that sophisticated talk for foreplay?"

"Go to sleep, Austin."

"Whatever you say, Georgie girl. And FYI, I apologize in advance for the tent I'll be pitching in the morning underneath this blanket."

That sent all sorts of naughty visions running amok in Georgie's mind. But the heat those fantasies generated did little to rid her of the sudden cold when a breeze blew through the ancient cabin. She pulled the blanket closer and tried hard to control her shivering body and chattering teeth, to no avail.

"Roll over, Georgie."

"I beg your pardon?"

"I'm going to put my arms around you because you're cold."

"We're also naked."

"All the better."

"No way."

"We'll keep the blankets between us."

She wanted to rebuff his request, but her chilled state wouldn't let her.

After Georgie shifted to her side, away from him, he scooted flush against her and wrapped her up in his strong arms. She had the strongest urge to rub her hands over that masculine terrain but realized it would be in her best interest to remain cocooned in the blanket, maintaining some semblance of separation. "Try to make sure we don't have any skin-to-skin contact."

"Darlin', we already have several times in the past."

"But this is the present. We don't need to stir up something again."

"Too late."

Infuriatingly sexy man. "Good night, Austin."

"Good night, sweetheart."

Georgie closed her eyes, but sleep wouldn't come. She thought about her schedule for the following week, a spattering of Monday appointments, lunch with Paris on Tuesday, her son's arrival home on Thursday.

Her son. *Their son*. She had very few hours to tell Austin the truth if she stuck to her original plan. She had so many qualms about doing that very thing after his previous statement about not wanting to be a father for a long time.

He *was* a father. But could he transition into being a dad to a little boy who needed one so desperately?

As soon as she finally confessed, only then would she know for sure. And that confession would need to come in twenty-four hours or less.

Austin woke up with an erection as hard as a hammer and a sexy woman beside him. He rolled to his side, bent his elbow and supported his jaw with his palm to do a little studying of that woman.

At some point during the night, Georgie had flipped onto her belly, the blanket draped low to expose her dark hair trailing down her back, her eyes closed tightly against the morning light. He took a visual trip down what he could see of her body and paused where he glimpsed the curve of her bottom.

He wanted to uncover her completely, make love to her until noon. Maybe even later. Then suddenly she caught him off guard when she shifted to her side and draped her arm over his bare hip underneath the covers. Worse still, she buried her face into his chest, right below his sternum, and he could feel the warmth of her lips pressed against his skin.

Oh, man, what was he going to do now? He knew what he'd like to do, but since he saw no real signs she was fully awake, he remained in the same position, rigid as an anvil. All of him.

Refusing to take advantage of a woman in a sleep-induced coma, Austin considered all the ways he could bring her around and a kiss came to mind. Or a touch. Or the sound of a honking horn outside the cabin.

Startled, Georgie popped up and looked around like she needed to gain her bearings. "What was that?"

Unfortunately for Austin, those thick locks of hair concealed her breasts. "I think someone's here."

"Who?"

"I'm not sure, but I'll find out." And he planned to give them a piece of what was left of his mind.

He came to his bare feet, taking the blanket with him and tucking it around his waist to hide the result of his sinful thoughts. He then strode to the window and swiped the dust from the panes to discover one familiar black truck and two equally familiar men leaned back against it. "It's Dallas and Houston."

"Oh, no. What are they doing here?"

"I have no idea, but I'm damn sure going to find out."

Austin swept open the door and closed it behind him after he stepped onto the porch. He immediately noticed his brothers eyeing the discarded clothes draped over the rail.

"Nice panties," Houston said. "I wouldn't have pegged you for a pink kind of guy."

He'd just stepped on his last nerve. "What in the hell do you two want?"

Dallas held up his hands. "Simmer down, Austin. We thought you might be needing a ride."

Likely story. "We've got two perfectly good geldings as transportation, so thanks but no thanks."

"Two geldings that showed up at the barn this morning," Houston added. "They must not have taken too kindly to the storm."

Damn. "Maybe we'll just walk back."

Dallas smirked. "You might want to ask Georgie if she's up for a six-mile hike."

Houston rubbed his stubbled chin. "Georgie, huh? Glad that explains the panties on the porch. I was worried about you, bro."

He didn't appreciate their kidding, or their laughter or the fact that they'd just shown up, unannounced. "You guys could've called. I have my cell with me."

Dallas exchanged a look with Houston before regarding Austin again. "Actually, Jen called and when she didn't get a hold of you, she called me to check on you two."

Austin realized he hadn't taken the phone from the bag, and he hadn't checked the battery. "Fine. Give us a few minutes and we'll head back with the two of you. And you better be on your best behavior around Georgie."

"Before you go inside," Houston said, "I have a question."

That was the last thing he needed, more stupid questions. "Make it quick."

"Could you not have waited until you got in the house before you started taking off your clothes?"

He'd had too little sleep and not enough sex to deal

with this. "Not that it's any of your concern, but we both got wet."

Dallas chuckled. "I just bet you did."

Austin pointed at the truck. "Go start up the rig and we'll be out as soon as we're finished."

"Finished with what?" Houston asked, looking way too amused.

Austin ignored the question, grabbed all the clothes, both pairs of boots and headed into the cabin without looking back. "Get dressed," he said as he tossed Georgie her things. "The horses went back to the barn so Dallas and Houston are taking us back."

She shimmied her panties into place beneath the blanket, sparking Austin's fantasies. "I can only imagine how this looks to them," she said as she worked the tank top over her head, giving him a glimpse of her nipple. "I'm sure they think something wicked happened between us last night."

He'd like to try out a little wicked right now, to hell with his brothers. "They do think something happened, and actually, it did."

She sent him a harsh look as she put on both her shirts and then tossed the blanket back to wriggle into her jeans. "I prefer not to be reminded of my few moments of weakness."

He dropped the blanket without regard to his naked state. "Darlin', if it was that forgettable, then I'm not doing my job."

She stared below where his belt would be, then brought her gaze up to his eyes. "If you decide to return to the ranch like that, then we'll definitely be the talk of the D Bar C, if not the nearest town."

He grinned when he noticed her attention drifting

downward again. "As soon as you're done looking, I'll put my pants on."

"I'm not looking," she said as she scrambled to her feet. "Now please get dressed."

"Yes, ma'am."

While Georgie pulled on her boots, Austin managed to get into his clothes in record time. He helped her gather the bedding and walked out the door to meet the verbal firing squad, thankful to find they were both seated in the truck's cab. After tossing the supplies into the bed of the truck, Austin opened the back door for Georgie and they climbed inside.

"Good to see you, Houston," she said in a meek voice. "How's it going on the circuit?"

"Good to see you, too, Georgie," he replied. "I'm doing fairly well so far this year."

When Austin draped his arm over the back of the seat, Georgie shifted closer to the door and asked, "How's Paris, Dallas?"

"She's cranky," he answered. "She told me to tell you she's looking forward to your lunch together in San Antonio on Tuesday."

Austin wouldn't be surprised if he ended up being the primary topic of conversation during that meeting. "You're off on Tuesday?"

She clutched her shirt closed, like she thought he might actually make a pass at her in the backseat. If they were alone, he would. "I don't have any appointments that afternoon, although everything is slowing down with the holidays fast approaching."

Austin hadn't experienced much of the Christmas spirit in spite of the fact that he'd been surrounded by excessive decorations for the past few weeks. He hadn't bought any gifts, except for one, and he'd been saving that for the right time. That right time might not come until spring, at this rate.

All conversation died during the ride back, and after Dallas dropped them off in the driveway of his house, Austin turned to Georgie before she had a chance to climb into her truck and escape. "Do you want to come in and take a shower?"

After fishing the keys from her pocket, she tossed her bag into the passenger seat, closed the door and faced him. "First of all, I don't have any extra clothes aside from the damp ones I'm wearing. Second, I live only five minutes away. And lastly, I prefer to shower alone."

Not what he wanted to hear. He began his own countdown to counter hers. "First, I have a pair of sweats and a T-shirt you could wear. Second, you look cold and miserable and even five minutes will feel like five hours in those wet jeans. Third, I didn't say you had to shower with me, although I'm never opposed to saving water." When she just stood there, arms folded beneath her breasts, he decided to sweeten the deal. "I'll even cook you breakfast."

"You don't cook, Austin."

True that. "I can make scrambled eggs and bacon. I can have a pot of coffee on in a few minutes."

"Maybe some other time."

He really didn't have a clue as to why he was so desperate to keep her there. Why he couldn't just let her go and get on with his day? "Tell you what. Why don't you come here for lunch? It's Maria's turn to cook and she's most likely going to make her famous enchiladas."

She hesitated a moment before asking, "What time?"

"Usually around one."

"Okay."

That was way too easy. "You're going to accept, just like that."

"Yes. And afterward, we need to talk."

"About?"

"I'll see you at one, Austin."

He followed her as she rounded the hood and slid into the driver's side. "Can you give me a hint?" he asked before she closed the door on him.

"Sorry. You'll just have to wait until I'm clean and coherent."

Austin watched her drive away, wondering what he'd done this time that would warrant a serious conversation. He suspected it had to do with his continual pursuit of her affections. Maybe she'd decided she didn't want to be friends. Maybe she wanted nothing else to do with him.

He could drive himself crazy trying to figure it out, or he could go inside, shower and grab some coffee. After that, he'd distract himself with chores, and prepare for anything that might come out of Georgia May Romero's sweet mouth.

"Hello, baby boy."

"Hi, Mama."

Georgie held the phone tightly, wishing she was holding her son. "Are you having fun?"

"Uh-huh. We rode the rides and played some little golf and we even saw Santa and I got to ask him for presents!"

Georgie chuckled over the usage of "little" instead

of "miniature" golf comment, but she didn't dare correct him. "That's great, sweetie. What did you tell him you wanted?"

"A fire truck and some games and a pony."

She'd been working on the last wish. "That's some list, Chance."

"I asked him for one more thing."

"What?"

"My daddy, but I don't think he can bring me him."

Her heart broke over the sadness in his voice, and cemented her goal to work on that, too, though she feared the outcome. "Tell you what, sweetie. When you get home, we're going to make cookies together and go pick out a real Christmas tree. How does that sound?"

"Okay, I guess. I gotta go. We're going to go see some sharks."

"That sounds wonderful, Chance. Now put your grandmother…"

The line went dead before her son could answer her request. She would call her mother later, when she returned from Austin's house, because that might be the time when she'd need her most.

On that thought, Georgie postponed the shower and opted to take care of the horses, all the while rehearsing what she would say to the father of her child.

Hey, Austin, guess what? You have a kid. Hey, Austin, a funny thing happened the last time we were together. I gave you comfort and you gave me a child. Hey, Austin, this little boy needs you, and so do I.

She truly didn't want to need him, but she did, and so did Chance.

After tending to the livestock, she returned to the house, bathed and laid across the bed to take a brief nap before the moment of truth arrived. She decided to be positive, let herself imagine they could live as one big, happy family. Let herself dream that Austin loved her, too, and he would love their son equally. That he would forgive her for waiting so long to tell him. Yet deep in her soul, she knew that would probably prove to be only a pipe dream.

Georgie soon drifted off into fitful sleep, and woke with a start when she realized she hadn't set an alarm. She glanced at the clock to discover the digital number displaying five past noon and shot out of the bed to get ready. She dried her hair, put on a little makeup, tried on three different outfits before settling on black slacks and a red silk button-down blouse covered by a black cardigan. She even chose to wear real shoes—a pair of simple black flats.

After putting on a pair of simple silver hoops, she ran a brush through her hair, took one last look in the mirror as well as a few deep breaths, then grabbed her keys, sent a text to Austin letting him know she was on her way and dropped the phone into her black purse.

On the way to the D Bar C, she said a little prayer, recited a few wishes, hoped for a miracle and grew more anxious as she approached the ranch's entrance. By the time she pulled into Austin's driveway, she was a twisted bundle of nerves.

She exited the truck, silently chanting, *It's time, it's time*, all the way to the front door. But when Austin greeted her wearing a black shirt and hat, crisp jeans and a winning smile, she wondered if she would be strong enough to say what she needed to say. He gestured her inside, then closed the door behind them, and as they stood there in silence, studying each other, the tension was palpable.

"Is something wrong?" she asked when he continued to stare.

"Lunch won't be ready for another hour. Something about Jen burning the tortillas."

"Oh. It happens. I guess we could go to the house and visit with everyone."

"Or we could stay here." Austin moved closer, searched her eyes and touched her cheek. "You are so damn beautiful."

She began to feel light-headed, vulnerable, fearful that she might not be strong enough to resist him. "You know what they say about beauty, Austin."

"It's in the eye of the beer holder?"

Did he have to be so darn cute? "Something like that."

"I'm not holding any beer. Besides, you're also smart, honest and sexy as hell."

She could certainly debate the honesty, considering what she'd been holding back. She also knew what would happen next if she didn't keep her wits about her. But common sense was no match for that continuous spark, or the sensual words the irresistible cowboy whispered in her ear, followed by a deep, provocative kiss.

"I need you, Georgie. I swear you've been all I've thought about since we met up again in the arena."

He'd never been far from her thoughts for years. "I need you, too, Austin, but if we keep giving in, where does that leave us?"

"As far as I'm concerned, we're two consenting adults who enjoy each other's company. We always have. I don't want to be only your friend, Georgie."

"What does that mean?"

"I want to spend time with you, out in the open, without worrying about what anyone thinks."

For years Georgie had longed to hear him say that, but she also recognized he might change his mind once he learned the truth. "Austin, there's something I need to say."

He pressed a fingertip against her lips to silence her. "We can talk later. Right now, I just want to be with you. I want *all* of you."

That *It's time* chant that had been running through Georgie's mind suddenly became *Later. Much later.* Maybe she was simply stalling. Maybe she'd grown weary of fighting the attraction. Maybe she just needed to be with the man she had always loved, perhaps for one final time. "Then, cowboy, take me away."

When Austin literally swept her off her feet and into his arms, Georgie surrendered to her needs, to this strong, handsome man, as she had so many times in the past. As she had last night, when he'd required nothing more than giving her pleasure. Now it was her turn to reciprocate.

Lunch, and the all-important talk, would simply have to wait.

Eight

Georgie closed her eyes as Austin carried her into his room and laid her across the bed. When she opened them, he pulled her up, removed her cardigan and paused with his hand on the top button of her blouse, indecision in his blue eyes.

"I want to make love to you, sweetheart, but only if you want it, too."

She swept one hand through her hair. "I do want it, even if I probably shouldn't."

"But—"

"Let's not talk it to death, okay?"

"That's all I needed to hear."

Everything happened in a rush then. She kicked off her shoes, he toed out of his boots. He unbuttoned her blouse, she undid his shirt. Together they pulled off their pants, leaving them clad in only their underwear. Austin slowed down the pace when he removed her bra, then stood by the bed and shoved down his boxer briefs, leaving no doubt he was primed and ready. After he leaned over and slid her panties away, she expected him to join her, yet he surprised her by sending soft kisses down her torso.

Georgie knew where he was heading, and the thought made her hot as blazes and damp with anticipation.

He stopped below her navel and smiled up at her. "Remember the first time I did this?"

As if it had happened yesterday. "In my bedroom, right before you left for college."

He rubbed his knuckles along the inside of her legs, coaxing them apart. "I wasn't sure you trusted me enough, but you proved me wrong."

Funny, she'd trusted him enough to allow him to do anything, even when they were teens. "I admit I was a little scared, but it turned out to be one of the most memorable experiences I've ever had."

"One you want to repeat?"

"Yes," came out of her mouth in a breathy sigh.

After Austin bent her knees and moved between her legs, Georgie understood the futility in trying to talk. She struggled to stay still when he feathered kisses down the insides of both her thighs. She stifled a moan as he worked his way up and his mouth hit home. She involuntarily lifted her hips toward him, demonstrating how much she needed his attention, and where.

He knew exactly how to use his tongue in slow, deliberate strokes, driving her to the brink. He knew how to let up before she let go, then start again until the pressure began to build. He kept the pace for a few more moments, a sensual tug-of-war until she was prepared to lose the battle. And then he used the pull of his lips to completely shoot her over the edge into an orgasm so intense, she literally cried out.

Georgie clutched the sheet in her fists as she continued to ride the waves of the climax, only remotely aware that Austin had left the bed, and extremely aware when he returned, condom in hand. "Are we ready for this?" he asked as he held up the silver packet.

She glanced at his impressive erection. "You definitely are."

He tore into the package like a dog with a ham bone. "That I am."

Feeling a bit daring, and somewhat impatient, Georgie held out her hand. "Let me do it."

He favored her with a grin as he answered her request. "My pleasure."

"It will be."

And she made sure to focus on that pleasure when he fell back onto the bed. After tossing the condom aside, she swept her hair back with one hand and kissed her way down his belly, the same as he had done to her. She had a few tricks of her own, lessons learned from him, and put them in play, sliding her tongue down the length of him, then back up again.

"Damn, sweetheart," he muttered. "If you keep doing that, this is going to be one short ride."

"We can't have that," she said as she sat up, retrieved the condom and rolled it in place.

He clasped her arm and pulled her atop his chest. "Do we go traditional or your favorite position?"

She was both pleased and surprised he remembered. "What do you think?"

"Your favorite it is. Turn to your side."

Georgie rolled away from him and waited for that first sensation, that sense of completion. Luckily she didn't have to wait long as Austin draped her leg over his, then eased inside her. The last time she'd been in this position, little had she known they'd made a baby. He still didn't know, but he would in the near future.

All thoughts of sins and secrets faded away as Austin kissed her neck and placed his hand between her legs to again tenderly manipulate her.

"Austin, I don't think I can."

"You can. You will. I promise."

He made good on that vow in a matter of seconds with deep thrusts and deliberate caresses. She wanted so badly to see his face so she'd know when he reached his own climax, but her choice dictated that wasn't to be. She simply relied on the unsteady cadence of his breathing, the strength of his thrusts, the tension in his entire body and the one crude word that slipped out of his mouth.

Austin held her tightly then, his face buried in the back of her neck. She wanted to remain this way indefinitely. She wanted to shut out the world and the burden of truth, but that wasn't logical.

After Austin slid out of her body, Georgie shifted to face him. "It's probably past time for lunch."

He pressed his lips against her forehead. "I'm not that hungry right now."

She released a laugh. "Oh, come on, Austin. You're always starving after sex."

He gave her a slow grin. "Only when I'm finished having sex."

"You're kidding, right?"

"Nope. I have to have some time to recover, so I'm thinking we should put my big ol' shower to good use."

She liked that idea, but… "What about Maria and Jenny? They're not going to be happy if we don't make an appearance."

"I'll call them and tell them we got tied up." He gave her a quick kiss. "Better still, I'll send a text. That way, I won't have to explain anything in detail."

Thank goodness for small favors, and modern technology. "Good plan."

Austin grabbed his phone from the nightstand, typed in the message, then smiled. "First one in the shower gets to set the temperature."

Georgie was in the bathroom and standing at the shower before Austin even made it to the door. Unfortunately she could only stare at a panel of illuminated blue lights, completely perplexed. "How do you work this?"

Austin reached around her and pushed a button, then keyed in a number, sending several spray heads into action. "It's not rocket science."

She glanced back at him. "It's a little too high-tech for me. What happened to just turning a knob?"

He leaned over and kissed her neck. "If you really want to turn one—"

"I already have."

His rough, sexy laugh gave her more than a few pleasant chills. "Yes, ma'am, you sure did. And it was mighty fine."

Georgie yanked open the glass door and stepped inside the spa-like shower, decorated in brown stone and trimmed in copper mosaic, then attempted to avoid the overhead spray. "I don't want to get my hair wet," she said when Austin joined her.

Without regard to her wishes, Austin pulled her beneath the jet, soaking every inch of her.

She gave him a mock frown. "Not fair."

He kissed her softly, touched her gently, stoking the fire again. "Everything's fair in love and water wars."

"Clever," she said as she reached for the shower gel clearly made for men. "Turn around and I'll wash your back."

"If I don't turn around, what will you wash?"

Cowboy cad. "Hold your horses, Calloway. I'll get to that."

"Lookin' forward to it."

Austin finally turned around, leaving Georgie with an up close view of his broad back and undeniably tight butt. She lathered her hands, then set out to search the terrain with her palms, taking her time investigating every plane, angle and dip at her disposal. Yet Austin disturbed her exploration when he turned around and grabbed the gel from the built-in soap dish.

"Wait a minute," she protested. "I'm not done yet."

He squeezed a few drops into his palm. "Yeah, you are, and I don't want you turning around."

"Interesting. I am going to smell like a guy."

His hands immediately went to her breasts. "You sure as hell don't look like one, and you don't feel like one, either."

No, she felt like a truly desirable woman. A naughty nymph. A needy female when the water play turned into more foreplay. The kisses were hot, the touches deliberate—both his and hers—and in a matter of moments, he had her in the throes of another strong climax. Then, before Georgie realized what was happening, Austin backed her against the tile, dangerously close to throwing caution out the window.

She braced her hands on his face to garner his attention. "Austin, we can't. We don't have any birth control."

He stepped back, went to her side and braced both hands on the wall. "Damn. I know better. Not once have I ever forgotten a condom."

"Yes, you did." And he was still ignorant of the outcome of that mistake.

He straightened and gave her a confused look before reality showed in his expression. "The last night we were together. We were damn lucky."

Oh, but they hadn't been, although despite the consequences, she wouldn't take anything for the time she'd spent with their child. Now would be the perfect time to tell him, she decided, until he wrapped her in a huge towel, picked her up and returned to the bedroom to lay her across the tangled sheets. When Georgie opened her mouth to speak, he kissed her again. Passion precluded any admissions and, after Austin had the condom in place, the lovemaking began again.

This time Austin moved atop her, guided himself inside her and moved in a tempered rhythm. Georgie ran her hands over his damp back, held on close and listened to the sound of his labored breaths.

Oh, how she cherished the moments right before he climaxed. Oh, how much she cherished him. And when he tensed with his release, the words clamored out of her mouth. "I love you, Austin."

He stilled against her for a moment, then rolled onto

his back. She waited for a response, and the one she received was extremely unexpected.

"It was always you, Georgie."

She shifted to her side. "Meaning?"

"The demise of my marriage. Abby never measured up to you. No woman ever has. I've known that for a long time, but I didn't want to admit that you have that much control over me. Call it stupid pride or male ego or however you want to label it. I'm over it now."

Georgie couldn't recall a time when she'd felt so optimistic, yet so fearful when she considered the impending declaration. "You've always been the only man for me. Actually, you've been the only man I've made love with."

He lifted his head and frowned. "Seriously?"

"Seriously."

He slid his arm beneath her and brought her against his chest. "I'm honored, Georgie. And dammit, I love you, too."

She laid a palm over his beating heart, the first hint of tears welling in her eyes. "Seriously?"

"More than my best roping horse. More than my money or all my material wealth. More than I realized until now."

Georgie began to silently rehearse how she would tell him about Chance and her explanation as to why she had withheld the truth for so long. Feeling as ready as she would ever be, she lifted to her head and whispered, "Austin."

He didn't open his eyes, didn't stir a bit. From the rise and fall of his chest, she determined he'd fallen asleep.

Georgie laid her cheek back on his chest, her emotions a blend of relief and regret that she hadn't spoken when she'd had the chance. But she would still have the opportunity once he finally awoke. In the meantime, she would join him in a nap and hope that when the revelations finally came, he would find it in his heart to forgive her, and embrace fathering their son.

An annoying sound jarred Austin out of sleep for the second time in twenty-four hours, only this time it was a buzzer, not a horn. He worked his arm from beneath Georgie, kissed her cheek then went into the bathroom to clean up. He grabbed a T-shirt and jeans from the closet, got dressed quickly and entered the bedroom where Georgie was sitting up against the leather headboard, clutching the sheet to her chin.

"Where are you going?" she asked as he headed toward the door.

The bell rang again, letting him know that the unknown intruder hadn't left. "I'm going to see who's at the door and send them on their way."

"Okay. Hurry back."

Exactly what he planned to do. He strode through the great room and once he reached the entry, he peered out the peephole. Jenny stood on the porch with a paper sack in hand, looking determined as ever. He doubted she would leave anytime soon, which drove him to yank open the door and scowl. "What's up?"

She patted her big blond hair and smiled. "Well, sugar, since you and Georgie didn't come for lunch, lunch is coming to you."

He felt the need to preserve Georgie's reputation. "What makes you think I'm not alone?"

She nodded toward the driveway. "Because that's

her truck, sweetie. And don't worry. I'll just hand this over and be on my way."

Austin took the bag and worked up some gratitude. "Thanks. I appreciate the hospitality."

Jenny centered her gaze on his bare feet before focusing on his face. "And I'm sure Georgie appreciates your hospitality, as well. You two enjoy the rest of your afternoon. If you're in the mood for a drink, you know where to find me."

After Jen spun on her heels and stepped off the porch, Austin waited until she'd climbed onto the golf cart and drove away toward the main house. He shut and locked the door, then walked toward the kitchen to drop off the care package before returning to the bedroom. He discovered Georgie seated at the island, dressed in the only robe he owned—a heavy blue flannel that hung off her like a scarecrow.

He set the sack down at the end of the quartz counter and claimed the stool beside her. "Guess you figured out the identity of our guests."

She tightened the sash at her waist. "I kind of heard Jen's voice."

No shock there. "She brought food. Are you hungry?"

She ran a fingertip along the edge of the island. "Not at the moment, but feel free to go ahead."

He sensed something was bugging her. Maybe he'd said too much in the moment. "Are you okay, Georgie?"

When she lifted her gaze to his, he saw a few tears welling in her eyes. "Actually, I'm not okay. I have something I need to tell you. Something I should have told you long before now."

A laundry list of possibilities bombarded his brain.

One horrible conclusion came home to roost. "Are you sick?"

She shook her head. "No, that's not it. Not even close."

"Then what is it?"

"Just promise me you won't be too angry."

"I'll try, but that depends on what you're about to tell me."

She fidgeted in the seat, a sure sign of her nervousness. After a deep breath, she said, "Okay. Here goes. I have a five-year-old son."

Austin didn't know what to say or how to react. He did recall with absolute clarity what she'd said to him earlier.

...you've been the only man I've made love with...

The mental impact hit Austin like a grenade, sending him off the stool to pace. Shock gave way to confusion then melted into blinding anger. He turned around to confront her head-on, grasping the last shred of his composure. He had a burning question to ask, although he suspected he already knew the answer. "Who's his father, Georgie?"

Her tears flowed freely now, and she looked away before returning her attention to him. "You are, Austin."

Georgie held her breath and waited, wanting so badly to plead with him to give her a chance to explain. Instead, she remained silent and watchful as he braced his elbows on the table, lowered his eyes and forked both hands through his hair.

"Why the hell didn't you tell me sooner?" he asked without looking up.

"I tried, Austin."

"Obviously not too damn hard, Georgie."

She deserved his scorn, but she wouldn't stop attempting to make him understand. "When I found out I was pregnant, I was pretty much in denial for a couple of months until I finally confirmed it. Then I called your cell phone and some woman answered. I thought I had the wrong number, so I got in touch with Dallas. He told me you'd just married. I was so in shock over the baby, and learning you'd found someone else, I didn't know what to do."

He straightened and leveled a stern stare on her. "You should've called back. You should've told me immediately."

"I considered that, but when I decided not to give Chance up for adoption, I realized that if I told you, I might ruin your relationship."

"And you thought it was okay just to leave me in the dark?"

"Believe me, I've questioned my actions since the day he was born."

"You damn sure should have," he said, barely concealed venom in his tone. "And no matter what excuse you try to hand me, you had no right to keep this a secret."

"I know." She paused a moment to gather her thoughts. "He's an incredible little boy, and so much like you. He loves the horses and he's so smart. If you'll get to know him, I'm sure—"

"You need to leave, Georgie."

So much for that strategy. "I'm not leaving until we discuss this further."

"I don't want to discuss anything right now. I'm too damned angry. Just put on your clothes and go home."

She would grant him this latitude for the time being. "Fine," she said as she came to her feet. "I'll go for now, and I'll wait to hear from you. And if I don't, have a nice life. Chance and I have done fine without you. We'll continue to do the same."

Georgie rushed past him and into the bedroom, holding fast to her sadness until she returned to the safety of her home. After she dressed, she returned to the kitchen, but Austin was nowhere to be found. She didn't bother to seek him out, or attempt to convince him that his little boy needed him. He would have to come to that conclusion on his own.

She would give Austin more time, pray he came around and learn to accept that he might not. She only hoped that she could grant her son's wish, and he'd finally have a daddy for Christmas. If not, she would continue to love him enough for the both of them.

Nine

"I'm so sorry I'm late."

Georgie looked up from the menu at Paris, who was struggling to be seated in the booth of the small San Antonio bistro. "That's okay. How did the appointment go?"

Paris set her bag aside and tightened the band securing her low ponytail. "That's why I'm late. The doctor decided to do a last-minute ultrasound."

"Is everything all right?"

"Yes, aside from the fact that if I reach my due date, the baby will weigh at least eight pounds. No wonder I'm so huge."

"You look great, especially in that dress. Green is definitely your color."

"I look like a giant jalapeno pepper." Paris leaned over and studied her. "You look like you're exhausted."

She was, mentally and physically. "I haven't been sleeping."

"But you have been crying. A lot."

Clearly her reddened eyes had given her away. "I didn't know it was that obvious."

Paris leaned over and touched her arm. "Tell me what's wrong."

Georgie didn't want to burden a very pregnant woman, but she could certainly use a friend. "It's Austin."

"You told him."

"I did, and it didn't go well." She hadn't heard a word from him since.

Leaning back, Paris rested her arm across her rounded belly. "That explains it."

"Explains what?"

"Austin took off yesterday morning for heaven knows where and he didn't come back last night. When Dallas sent him a text, he replied that he was okay, and that's it. And you haven't heard from him, either?"

"I sent him a text to ask if he was okay," Georgie said. "He responded 'no,' and I decided to leave him alone."

Paris seemed surprised. "You didn't try calling him?"

She'd thought about it, several times. "In all the years I've known Austin, I've learned you don't back him into a corner. Usually after he thinks things over, he comes around."

"That's good," Paris stated. "I'm sure he'll be back in touch soon."

If only Georgie could believe that. "He might not this time. He's angry and he's hurt and I have to accept that he could reject the prospect of being a father to Chance."

"Austin is a good man, Georgie. I can't imagine him abandoning his own flesh and blood."

"I hope that's true, but you didn't see the look on his face when I told him. He was furious, understandably so."

"You honestly don't believe he'll get over it?"

She thought back through the years and couldn't recall a time when he'd been so irate. "When we were kids, and he got mad at me for some reason, he wouldn't leave until we worked it out. He'd make self-deprecating comments about his ignorance and a few bad jokes, and before I knew it, I was laughing and all was forgiven."

"The Calloway brothers must share the brooding gene," Paris said. "That's exactly what Dallas did when he learned, as did I, that I wasn't officially divorced and he stood to lose control of the ranch to Fort because our marriage wasn't real. Fortunately, Jenny saved the day on that count."

Her interest piqued, Georgie rested her elbow on the table and supported her cheek on her palm. "So how did you manage to convince Dallas to come back to you?"

Paris laughed. "It wasn't me. The family gave him a swift kick in the jeans and booted him to right here, in San Antonio, to beg my forgiveness. The rest, as they say, is history. Now I'm happily married to the love of my life, for the second time, and about to give birth to a baby apparently the size of a moose."

Georgie smiled for the first time in two days. "Hopefully the doctor is wrong about the baby's weight."

"And hopefully you're wrong about Austin. I wouldn't be surprised if he reaches out to you soon."

Georgie sat back and sighed. "I would love it if that happens before Sunday."

"Then you could all be a family on Christmas," Paris said in a wistful tone.

"And I could answer a little boy's wish. Chance asked Santa if he would bring him a daddy."

Paris's expression turned somber. "Oh, Georgie. That must have broken your heart. How much does he know about Austin?"

Georgie shrugged. "Very little. He didn't ask a whole lot until about a year ago, and I attribute that to being in preschool and noticing everyone else has a father. I've only mentioned that his dad lives far away, which I thought he did at the time, and that he travels a lot because he's a cowboy."

"Does he know his name?"

"He asked right before he left for Florida, and then he became distracted by something on TV. I'm sure he'll ask again when he gets home." Georgie had given Lila specific instructions to direct Chance to her with any queries, and she had no reason to believe her mother wouldn't comply.

"And you'll know what to do if and when that happens." Paris began to scan the menu. "I'm starving. What are you having?"

A strong urge to call her mom and check on her baby boy. "Probably just a Cobb salad. I'm not very hungry."

Paris closed the menu and set it aside. "I'm going to have the spinach enchilada plate and eat every last bite. And after that, I might even eat dessert. Gotta feed the moose."

They joined in a laugh before the waiter arrived to take their orders. Once he left, Georgie regarded Paris. "As soon as we're finished with lunch, I'm going to go shopping. I haven't bought a thing for Chance, aside from a pony, and I can't put her under the tree."

Paris sipped at her glass of water. "Where did you get a pony?"

"The Carter ranch right outside Cotulla. She's fifteen years old and her name is Butterball, which fits her well. She'll be a good teaching horse for Chance, although I'm sure he'll want to graduate to something bigger very soon."

"That's great, and I could pick up a few more holiday gifts. I could also use a stroll on the River Walk to burn a few calories."

"Great. We'll make an afternoon of it."

Paris sent her a soft smile. "And with your permission, I'll see what I can do about Austin on my end."

Georgie saw more than a few problems with that scenario. "He'll be furious if he knows I told you about Chance before I told him."

"That's too bad. Besides, I'll let him assume you told me today. If he's going to pout like a child, then I'll just sic Dallas on him. Better still, I'll involve Maria, as long as you're okay with it."

She wasn't sure she was, but then again, what other options did she have? If the Calloways could convince Austin to step up to the plate, then maybe that would be best for the sake of her son. No amount of cajoling on their part would change Austin's mind about what she'd done. "I assume you're referring to a family meeting."

"Exactly. Power in numbers."

Georgie imagined Austin encountering his stepmothers and brothers in a showdown. She would definitely buy tickets to that.

Austin walked through his front door to find Paris, Dallas, Jenny and Maria seated on his leather sectional in the great room. He should never have told them he was heading home. He should never have given out spare keys.

After tossing his duffel onto the floor, he gave them all a good glare. "Mind telling me what you're doing here?"

Maria patted the space between her and Jenny. "Come have a seat, *mijo*."

No way would he suffer maternal advice in stereo. "I'll stand, thank you."

Dallas rose from the sofa where he'd been positioned next to his wife. "Makes no difference to any of us whether you sit or stand. We're more concerned with your total lack of responsibility to your family."

His foul mood grew even fouler. "I didn't know building a house on our land came with a clause that states I can't come and go as I please."

"We were worried about you, sugar," Jenny said. "You've been gone four days with almost no communication. That's not like you."

And to think he'd worried someone had found out about his and Georgie's kid. "I wasn't intentionally ignoring you all. I just have another business to run. Several, in fact."

"We're referring to your responsibility to your son."

Damn if he hadn't had cause to worry and wonder

exactly how this all went down. "Did Georgie also tell you that she hid him from me for five years?"

"Georgie didn't talk to them," Paris piped up. "She talked to me, and I told Dallas. Dallas told everyone else."

His shortened fuse was about to blow. "When it comes right down to it, this isn't anyone's business."

Maria looked fit to be tied. "It is our business, Austin Calloway. Maybe I'm not your birth mother, son, but I'm the only mother you've had for thirty-two years. That means I consider that little boy my grandchild."

"Mine, too," Jenny said. "At least that's how I see him, even if we're not blood relatives, either. But I'd like to borrow him until Worth and Fort have children."

Maria sent her an acid glare. "As long as you give him back."

Jenny ignored the dig. "Regardless, that little boy deserves to know our family, sugar."

Austin had agonized over that since Georgie spilled the baby beans. He'd been torn between a permanent escape and meeting the child who didn't know him at all. "Look, I've got a lot to think about before we plan a family reunion."

"Georgie's a wreck, Austin," Paris added. "She's beginning to believe you don't want to have anything to do with Chance."

Just one more blow to his and Georgie's relationship. "I'll be sure to thank her for nominating me for jerk of the year."

Maria suddenly rose from the sofa. "Everyone, go about your business. I want to talk to Austin alone."

What Maria wanted, Maria got, and that was apparent by the way everyone stood and started milling toward the door. Everyone but Jenny.

His stepmom stared at the other stepmother for a moment. "That means everyone."

Jenny lifted her chin. "I'm not going anywhere until Austin asks me to leave."

He didn't care if the Pope made an appearance. "Fine by me if you stay. In fact, you can all hang around and crucify me."

Dallas pressed a palm against his wife's back. "We're going home to spend some alone time together. The phones will be turned off."

Paris blushed. "A little too much information, Dallas."

"Who cares?" Dallas said. "It's pretty obvious by looking at you, we've done it before."

Dallas and Paris rushed out the door, leaving Austin alone to face the mothers—Maria wearing her trademark braid and a long green flannel shirt over her jeans, and Jen sporting a red-checkered dress and a matching bow in her big blond hair. Nothing like a verbal beating from a hardscrabble rancher's wife and a throwback from a fifties sitcom. He'd rather eat Nueces River mud.

Austin claimed the cowhide chair across from the sofa, determined to make this little soiree short and sweet. "Speak your mind, then give me some peace."

Jenny sent him a sympathetic look. "I know you're torn up about this, sugar."

"I also know you're mad as hell at Georgie, too," Maria began, "and I don't think anyone blames you for that. But she's always been a good girl and from what I hear, a good mother. If I were you, I'd march to her house right now, meet your son and make amends with Georgie."

If only it was that easy. "Neither of you know what I've been going through since she told me. I kept thinking about the things I've missed, like his first steps and his first words. I could've already taught him how to ride. How to throw a rope. Georgie robbed me of those experiences."

"It's not too late to make memories now, Austin," Jenny said. "I don't care how good of a job Georgie's done raising him as a single mother, that little boy needs his daddy. And you need him and his mother, too."

Austin leaned forward and streaked both palms over his face. "I know you're both right, and I plan to be involved in his life, pay child support, that kind of thing. But I don't know if I can ever forgive Georgie."

Maria frowned. "Why not? She's forgiven you."

They seemed determined to make this all his fault. "What did I do?"

"It's not what you did, sugar," Jenny added. "It's what you didn't do."

He recalled Georgie saying the same thing. "I'm not following you, Jen."

"After playing slap and tickle with her all during high school, did you stay in touch with Georgie, sugar?"

"No, but—"

"After you made a baby while passing through town, did you ever call her?" Maria asked.

He recognized where this was going. "Georgie knew we weren't exclusive, and besides, I met Abby right after that."

"And married a woman you barely knew, totally ignoring the other woman who's loved you since you pulled her ponytail the first time," Maria said. "We all know how that turned out."

He'd always appreciated Maria's brutal honesty, until tonight. Being on the hot seat with all his faults laid bare wasn't his idea of a good time.

Jenny smoothed a palm over her skirt. "I truly believe we only have one love in our lives, and your father was mine and, I assume, Maria's. However, J.D.'s one true love happened to be your mother."

"She's right," Maria added, much to Austin's surprise. "Your dad kept searching to fill that hole in his soul from losing Carol. I'd bet my best spurs that Georgie is your soul mate, and you're going to spend a lot of useless years if you don't own up to it."

Austin wanted to reject their notions. "I can't believe the two of you can overlook the fact that he was married to both of you at the same time. Hell, he spread himself so thin he wasn't giving anyone the time they needed, including his six sons."

"You're absolutely right, sugar," Jenny said. "All the more reason for you to resolve the issues with Georgie and get busy spending time with your little boy."

His head had begun to spin from all the unwelcome advice. "I'll consider what you've said, but right now I have to take care of the horses. So if you two don't mind, I need to get on with my day."

"Okay." Maria came to her feet. "*Mijo*, you need to learn that if you really love someone, nothing they do or say is beyond forgiveness."

Jen rose from the sofa. "Sugar, the best holiday gift

you can give yourself is a happy New Year with a new family."

Without another word, the mothers walked out the door, blanketing the room in stark silence. Austin leaned back in the chair and felt compelled to revisit his past. He stood and walked to the shelves flanking the white stone fireplace, then withdrew his final high school yearbook. He returned to the sofa and once again flipped through the pages, finding various photos of Georgie scattered throughout. He appreciated the one of her holding the volleyball district MVP trophy when everyone had told her she was too short to play. The one when she'd been voted to represent the junior class in the homecoming court was really something else, but then so was she dressed in that blue shiny dress, her long hair curling over her shoulders. He also hated that Rory Mills had been on her arm during the halftime festivities, while he'd escorted the senior queen, Heather Daws, who was about as shallow as a dried-up lake.

It suddenly dawned on him that not once had they appeared in a picture together, all because of an ongoing family feud and his resistance to rocking the boat. If he'd only stood up to his father, and hers, things might have been different between them. Or not. Maybe they'd been destined to go their separate ways, choose their own paths, make their own lives. Maybe his failed marriage had taught him what he didn't want—a relationship that would never live up to what he'd had with Georgie. But did he really deserve her now?

When a knock came at the door, Austin set the book on the coffee table and shot to his feet, anxious to see if maybe Georgie had stopped by. He was sorely disappointed to find a sibling standing on the threshold.

"Did I miss it?" Worth asked.

"Miss what?"

"The family meeting."

Dallas obviously told every last Calloway about his plight. "Yep. It's over."

"Mind if I come in for a bit?"

"Why not?" He didn't have anything better to do except sit around, feeling sorry for himself.

Worth brushed past him, dropped down on the sofa and eyed the yearbook. "Looks like you've been reliving your glory days."

He hadn't found any glory in the experience. "Just feeling nostalgic."

"Mom tells me you were a jock. Something about all-district wide receiver."

Austin had never been comfortable talking about his accolades. "It wasn't a big deal. My high school was so small there wasn't a whole lot of competition."

Worth forked a hand through his blond hair. "I know what you mean. I went to a private school. We didn't even have a football team, but I did play basketball. Our team pretty much sucked most of the time."

Austin was growing increasingly irritated by the small talk. "It happens. Look, I hate to cut this conversation short, but I have some chores to tend to."

"No problem. But before I go, I just have one thing to say about your current situation."

Just what he needed, more sage advice from a self-proclaimed Louisiana rodeo cowboy surfer. "Shoot."

"I know you've had everyone coming at you with suggestions on how to handle this news, but I just want you to know that if you want to talk, feel free to find me. No advice. No judgment."

That nearly shocked Austin out of his boots. "I appreciate that."

"What are brothers for? Besides, you'll figure it out."

"I'm not so sure about that."

"You're a smart guy, Austin. In fact, intelligence is a Calloway trait, although some of us intentionally don't show it."

"You've got to be pretty smart to build a fleet of charter boats all down the coast, Worth."

"I've been lucky in business. I just thank my lucky stars I didn't head down my original career path."

"Rodeo?"

"Medical school."

Now he was downright stunned. "I didn't know that."

"Most people don't. I swore my mom to secrecy after she bragged I was accepted to every Ivy League school I applied to. She was damn disappointed when I decided to stay in Louisiana and went to Tulane. She was proud of my 4.0 GPA as a chemistry major."

Austin wasn't sure he could take any more revelations. "No offense, Worth, but I've never pegged you as a science geek."

Worth stood and grinned. "I figured out early on it's best to dumb it down a bit when it comes to courting women. Take care, bud."

Austin came to his feet. "You, too, Worth. Are you going to be around during the holidays?"

"Nope. I'm going to Maui. I'd invite you along but I figure you've got more pressing issues at the moment."

"You're right about that," Austin said as he followed his brother to the door.

Worth paused with his hand on the knob. "You know, Austin, we're not our dad. Not by a long shot. Except maybe Fort. As bad as he hated J.D., he's the most like him. Mom hopes he'll eventually come around, but I've given up on that ever happening."

So had the rest of the family. "Happy holidays and have a good trip."

"Same to you, and when I get back, I look forward to meeting my nephew."

He might have been mad at Worth for tossing in that veiled recommendation, but in all honesty, his half brother had been the most helpful.

Austin settled back on the sofa and rolled all his options around in his head. Truth was, he did love Georgie and probably always had. He wanted to know his son and to avoid all the mistakes his own father had made. He still wanted to marry the love of his life... but what if he failed?

That in itself was his greatest fear, but maybe the time had come to stop being a relationship coward. First he had to decide if, when and where he would present the plan to Georgie, and hope that he hadn't waited too long.

When Georgie pulled into the drive, she was thrilled to see her mother and Chance waiting for her on the front porch. She'd barely exited the truck before Chance ran to her and threw his arms around her waist.

He smiled up at her. "Hi, Mama."

She leaned down and hugged him hard. "Hi, sweetie.

I missed you so much! I think you grew two inches while you were gone."

His eyes went wide as he stepped out of her grasp. "Did I?"

"I believe you did." She looked around but didn't see the motor home. "Where're Uncle Ben and Aunt Debbie?"

Her mother approached and ruffled Chance's hair. "They took off for Arizona to see the grandkids. They told me to tell you bye and what a pleasure it was to have your son along for the trip."

"I'm sorry I wasn't here to thank them," Georgie said as Chance ran back into the house. "I didn't expect you for another hour or so, and I had an emergency at the Rileys' farm. I had to treat a colicky mare."

"That's okay. You can give them a call later."

"Do you need a ride home?"

"No. Your father should be here any minute now."

Georgie was quite surprised by the news. "You mean he's actually going to step foot on his daughter's property?"

"Yes, and he wants to talk to you."

After everything that had happened with Austin, Georgie didn't have the energy for a fight. "I'm not up to that right now."

"Well, I suppose you should get up for that because this conversation is long overdue."

Before Georgie could respond, the familiar ancient white truck headed up the gravel drive, signaling her patriarch had arrived. She experienced a case of butterflies in the pit of her stomach and her palms began to sweat, despite the fact that the cold front had arrived in earnest, bringing with it forty-degree temps.

She had no clue what she would say to the man who'd raised her, and ignored her for five years. A hard-nosed man who could be as stubborn as a mule. A man who had never even seen his own grandchild. At least she had an ally in his wife.

Her mother began to back away as soon as the truck came to a stop in front of the house. "I'll keep Chance occupied while you two chat."

"But Mom—"

"You'll be okay, honey. Just hear him out."

Lila turned around and started away, while Georgie held her breath and waited for George Romero to appear. And he did a few moments later, looking every bit the brown-eyed hulking cowboy, only his hair seemed a little grayer and his gait a little slower. He'd always been larger than life, her hero, and she'd always been his little girl, until she'd shamed him by having a child out of wedlock. Heaven only knew what he would've done had he known the identity of Chance's father.

"Dad," she said when he walked up to her.

"Georgie," he replied, tattered beige hat in hand.

So far, so good. "You look well. How's your back?"

"Stiff as usual, but it's nothing compared to the scare I had with the old ticker last month."

That was news to her, and very disconcerting. "Mom didn't say a word to me about you having heart problems."

"I told her not to say anything until I could tell you myself."

"Is it serious?"

"Just some minor blockage. They did one of those angioplasty procedures and stuck some sort of tube in my artery. Now I'm good as new."

"I'm so sorry." And she was. "I wish I would've known."

"The only thing you need to know is I had a wake-up call. I've been a fool and prideful and a sorry excuse for a father. That comes to an end today."

"I appreciate that, Daddy."

That earned her a grin. "Been a long time since you called me that. I love you, princess. And I'm done being an old stubborn goat. I'm ready to meet my grandboy."

That earned him a hug. "I'm so glad we have this behind us. Chance needs his grandfather a lot. He hasn't had a solid male influence for five years."

Her father's expression melted into a frown. "No surprise there. Austin Calloway is a no-account tail chaser, just like his dad."

Clearly Lila hadn't hidden Georgie's secrets. "How long have you known?"

"When your mother told me you were coming back to town. She has some crazy idea that you and Calloway are going to set up house and raise your son together."

Considering she hadn't heard a word from Austin, that was highly unlikely. "Did Mom also tell you that Austin was unaware that he had a child?"

He inclined his head and studied her straight on. "Was?"

"I told him about Chance a few days ago."

"Is the jackass here?"

She shook her head. "No, he's not here. He's still trying to get over the shock."

He sent her a skeptic's look. "If you believe that, then I've got some swampland to sell you."

After what her father had done to her, Georgie felt

the need to defend Austin. "You're wrong about him, Dad. He's a good man."

"He wasn't man enough to ask permission to date you when you two were in school. He just continued to sneak around behind my back."

Lila had evidently provided a wealth of knowledge. "Neither of us wanted to tell you or J.D. because you two were still acting like kindergarten rivals."

"That's because J.D. tried to…" Both his words and gaze faltered. "Never mind."

"Not fair, Dad. You apparently know about my life, now it's time you tell me more about yours. What did J.D. do to you aside from compete in the cattle business?"

"He dated your mother before me," he muttered.

Georgie couldn't hold back a laugh. "That's it? You two had an ongoing feud because J.D. went out with Mom? That's rich considering you married her. And best I can recall, he married Carol."

He shook out his hat and shoved it on his head. "I'm ready to get off this subject and get on with the business of meeting my grandson."

"I'm all for that."

Georgie led him to the house where he followed her through the front door. They came upon Chance hanging ornaments on the Christmas tree she'd purchased yesterday, a seven-foot fragrant pine that had been the last decent selection on the lot.

"Hey, little man," she said. "I have someone I want you to meet."

Chance hooked a red globe over one limb, turned around and stared in awe. "Are you my dad?"

Lila smiled. "No, sweetheart, but he's the next best thing. This is your grandpa."

"Grandpa George?" he asked without a hint of disappointment in his tone. "My grandma said you were gone a lot."

Her dad stepped forward and took off his hat. "Yep, I've been gone far too long. And you must be Chance."

Her son nodded his head and grinned. "Chance William Romero."

"Well, bud, looks like you've got my middle name," George said in an awed tone. "Do you like to go fishin'?"

"Haven't gone fishin' yet," Chance said.

Amazingly, the grandfather took his grandson's hand and led him to the sofa. "Let's sit a spell and I'll tell you all about how to cast a line…"

Georgie began to finish the decorating tasks, all the while counting her blessings over the scene playing out before her. She'd almost given up believing that her dad would accept his grandson, much less begin a precious relationship with him. And if any more time passed, she would be forced to give up on Austin.

She wondered if it might be too much to ask for one more holiday miracle.

Ten

It would take a miracle if Austin survived this visit without incurring Georgie's wrath. For the past five days, he'd developed a plan that could smooth over his disregard, if she didn't kick him off her rented ranch.

Before he could climb out of the truck, his cell sounded, and he didn't even have to look to see who might be calling. If he ignored it, he'd have hell to pay. If he answered, he would only be further delayed. He answered it anyway.

"Yeah, Jen?"

"Have you done it yet?"

"I just got here."

"Oh, good. If all goes well, Maria and I want you to invite everyone to dinner."

He might not even get in the front door. "You're jumping the gun a little there. I don't even know if Georgie will see me yet."

"She will, sugar. Best of luck and we'll see you, Georgie and the little guy soon."

Before he could debate that point, Jen, with her overblown optimism, hung up. Now he had to return to the starting line and begin the mental race to the finish.

Gathering all his courage, he exited the truck and sprinted up the steps to the porch. He checked his back pocket for the gift, rehearsed what he planned to say and then finally knocked.

He expected Georgie to open the door, but what he got was her mother. Not a good way to begin his groveling.

Lila laid a hand beneath her throat like she might start choking. "Oh, my. Hello, Austin."

He took off his hat and nodded. "Nice to see you ma'am. Is Georgie here?"

"Yes. It's Christmas morning."

Good going, Calloway. "Mind if I have a word with her?"

"Wait here and I'll go get her."

He wasn't exactly surprised that he hadn't been invited in, and that was probably best. If George Romero happened to be there, Austin would risk getting a right hook as a greeting.

He paced around the porch for a few minutes until he heard, "What are you doing here, Austin?"

When he turned around, Austin would swear his heart skipped several beats, and it had nothing to do with his giant case of the nerves. Just seeing Georgie again served to confirm he had done the right thing, even if the end result could include her rejection.

He decided to lay it all on the line, beginning with their child. "I did a lot of soul-searching over the past few days, and I've come to the conclusion that I've already missed too much time with our son."

She folded her arms across her middle. "I'm glad. He needs to get to know you before he's any older."

One issue resolved, several more to go. "I plan to start on that immediately, and you need to be aware that I'm going to be there to support him and not only financially. I want to be part of his life in every way, including school and whatever extracurricular activities he chooses to do, and I'm banking on teaching him to rope."

He saw a mix of happiness and disappointment in her eyes. "That all sounds wonderful, Austin. We can work together to give him a good life. You can count on me to be cooperative when it comes to visitation. We'll work out a schedule."

She didn't understand he didn't give a damn about a schedule, but she would. "I haven't covered the most important aspect of our arrangement."

"Then please, continue," she said in a frigid tone.

"First, I have a question. Is your dad in the house?"

She looked confused. "Yes, but—"

"Could you send him out here?"

"Are you sure you want to do that?"

Not really. "Yeah. I have to talk to him before we continue this conversation."

"All right, I'll try. But I can't guarantee he'll do it."

If Old George wanted to be pigheaded, he'd have to go in after him. Fortunately that didn't happen when Georgie went inside and returned with her dad in tow, looking none too pleased to be there.

"Merry Christmas, sir," Austin said, even though

he realized the man didn't look like he embraced the holiday spirit.

"What do you want, Calloway?" George asked, confirming Austin's theory.

"I have a question to ask you before I finish my talk with Georgie."

"Let me make this easy on you. No, I don't want you here, and yes, you should get in that fancy truck and head for the hills."

"Behave, Dad," Georgie scolded. "You can at least hear what he has to say before you send him packing."

"Fine," George said grudgingly. "But make it quick."

He drew in a breath and released it slowly. "Mr. Romero, I've screwed up a time or two in my life, but my biggest mistake was letting Georgie go without a fight, even if it meant going into battle against you and my dad. Hell, when she didn't meet me that day I left for college, I should have come looking for her."

Georgie touched his arm. "What are you talking about?"

"I went to your house and gave your mom a card that asked you to meet me at the old windmill. I planned to invite you to join me at school once you graduated."

"I never got that card," she said, anger in her tone. "I definitely have a bone to pick with Mom."

"I tore it up," George muttered, drawing both their attention.

Now Georgie looked furious. "Excuse me, Dad?"

"You heard me. I took it from your mother, read it and shredded it." He pointed at Austin. "You should be glad I didn't know you were taking her behind the shed."

That explained a lot, and fed Austin's resentment toward this man. But in the interest of keeping the peace, he tempered his anger. "As pissed off as I am over your actions, it really doesn't matter now. What's done is done. We can't go back." Although he wished they could.

"Yes, it does matter," Georgie said. "I've always blamed you for not saying goodbye before you took off for college. Why didn't you tell me this before now?"

Austin shrugged. "I thought you had your reasons, the main one being we were on different paths. I figured you decided our relationship had run its course."

"If I had known, I would have been there."

Austin wanted to kiss her, but he still had business to tend to. "Back to the question at hand." He turned to Georgie's dad. "Mr. Romero, I'm going to ask for your daughter's hand in marriage, and if she decides to accept my proposal, I hope we have your and Mrs. Romero's blessing."

Georgie stared and George glared, while Austin just stood there, waiting for someone to speak. Her dad came through first. "I'd like to tell you hell no, you're not going to get my blessing, but you're going to do what you want anyway, so go for it. As far as my wife is concerned, she had visions of the two of you hitched the minute Georgie came back to town. Now get your proposing out of the way before your boy wakes up and wonders if his mama ran off with Santa."

When the man returned inside, Austin decided to proceed as planned, even though he worried Georgie's continuing silence indicated she wasn't too keen on the idea. He'd find out real soon.

He pulled the box from his pocket and set it on the

railing, then withdrew the ring before turning to Georgie. "Darlin', there is no one else on this earth that I want to wake up to every morning and go to bed with every night. I've made my share of mistakes, but having you as my wife wouldn't be one of them. I'd be proud and honored if you would marry me."

"This marriage proposal isn't because of Chance, is it?" she asked, the first sign of tears in her eyes.

"No, sweetheart. I want to spend my life with you because I love you. Always have. Always will."

"And you're absolutely sure you want to do this marriage thing again?"

"Sure as sunrise."

"I can be a handful."

"So can I. But together, we're pretty damn perfect."

Finally, she smiled. "Then yes, Austin Calloway, I will marry you, with or without my father's blessing. I love you, too. Very much."

"That's all I need to hear." Smiling, he slid the sapphire-and-diamond ring on her finger and waited for her response to the surprise.

She studied it for a moment before recognition dawned in her expression and her gaze shot to his. "This is the ring from the silent auction. I had no idea you bid on it."

"I didn't. I had to hunt down the guy who won it and pay twice the amount to take it off his hands when I saw how much you wanted it that night. I may not have consciously believed it would be an engagement ring, but deep down I probably realized that it should be."

She threw her arms around his neck, then kissed him soundly. "You're too much. And this is too much."

The joy in her eyes said it all. "Darlin', nothing is

too much for my future bride. But before we make this official, I probably need to ask the little man's permission, too."

She placed a hand to her mouth. "I hadn't thought about Chance. I think we should probably ease him into the idea. Meeting you on Christmas morning is a lot for a five-year-old to handle."

His first lesson in fatherhood. "Let's just play it by ear."

She let him go and reached for the door. "Are you ready?"

"As ready as I'll ever be."

Austin followed Georgie inside and surveyed the room, only to discover George seated in a chair, watching some cartoon on the TV mounted over a fireplace decked out with stockings. The Christmas tree positioned in the corner had been decorated in red and green, and a slew of unopened presents reminded Austin of what he'd forgotten.

"I'll be right back," he said as he headed outside and sprinted to the truck, then returned with the first gift for his son. He planned to give him many more—the most important, his time.

When he heard voices, a woman's and a child's, he clutched the package and waited anxiously for the moment he laid his eyes on his son. He didn't have to wait long before a brown-haired, hazel-eyed boy wearing pajamas dotted with bucking broncos padded into the room. Austin's first reaction—he looked just like his mother. His second—he couldn't have imagined the impact on his emotions. He hadn't known he would feel so strongly. He couldn't be more proud to be his dad. He only hoped his son shared his feelings.

With Lila following behind him, Chance pulled up short the second he spotted Austin, then he grinned. "You're that guy we saw at the calf roping. Mama's friend."

Before Austin could respond, Georgie gestured Chance to her, turned him around and rested her hands on his shoulders. "This is Austin Calloway, Chance. Austin, meet Chance."

He hesitated a moment before he approached slowly and knelt at his child's level. "It's great to finally meet you, bud. This is for you."

Chance took the offered present and looked it over. "Can I open it now?"

Austin turned his attention to Georgie who nodded. "Go ahead."

The boy tore into the package in record time, then pulled out the baseball glove from the box. "Wow. I don't have one of these."

"My dad gave me that when I was about your age," Austin said. "I figure we can play a little catch someday soon."

Chance wrinkled his nose. "Won't your dad be mad 'cause you gave it to me?"

He didn't have the heart to tell his son that he wouldn't ever know his grandfather. "Nope," he said as he straightened. "He'd be pleased."

Georgie ruffled Chance's hair. "Sweetie, before we open the rest of your gifts, we need to have a little talk."

Chance glanced back at her. "Aw, Mom. Do we hafta?"

She smiled. "Yes, but this has to do with something you wanted from Santa."

"A pony?" he asked.

"We'll get to that later," Georgie said. "Mom, Dad, do you mind if we have a few minutes alone?"

"Come on, George," Lila said. "You can help me make breakfast for a change."

George stood and muttered under his breath as he followed his wife out of the living room.

Georgie swept her hand toward the navy-colored sofa. "Let's have a seat."

After they settled in with Chance between them, Austin regarded Georgie. "Do you want me to go first?"

"I think you should," she said, wariness in her tone.

Austin shifted slightly so he could gauge his son's reaction. "Chance, I've known your mom for a long time. We went to school together."

"Kindergarten?" he asked.

"Yep, and all the way through high school."

"We were boyfriend and girlfriend," Georgie added. "Do you know what that is?"

Chance sent them both a sour look. "Yeah. That means you kissed and stuff."

After she and Austin exchanged a smile, Georgie continued. "Austin and I cared about each other very much. We still do."

When Georgie went silent and looked at him, Austin figured that was his cue. "I'm not only your mama's friend, bud, I'm your dad."

Chance stared at him without speaking, then his smile came out of hiding. "Santa sent you to me?"

Austin chuckled. "I guess you could say that, seeing how it's Christmas morning. How do you feel about this?"

"Are you a real live cowboy?"

"I guess you could say that, too."

"He's a calf roping champion, Chance," Georgie chimed in. "He has lots of trophies."

"Can I see them?"

"Sure," Austin said. "I plan to teach you how to rope and ride."

Then his son did something so unexpected, it shot straight to his heart. Chance wrapped his arms around Austin, gave him a hug and said, "I'm glad you're my dad."

Austin swallowed around the lump in his throat. If someone would have told him a year ago that he would feel so much love for a child he'd just met, he would've called them crazy. "I'm glad you're my boy, too."

Chance climbed off the couch and faced them both. "Can we go to the barn and see my pony now?"

Georgie frowned. "What makes you think you have a pony?"

"Because if Santa can bring me my dad, he can bring me a horse."

Both Georgie and Austin laughed, sending Lila and George back into the room. "Everything settled?" Lila asked.

Chance pointed at Austin. "He's my daddy and he's going to teach me how to rope."

"Great," George groused. "Now you can traipse around the country chasing cows and women."

Lila elbowed her husband in the side. "Hush, George Romero. He can be anything he wants to be."

"I want to be a cowboy," Chance proclaimed. "And I want to see my horse."

Georgie pushed to her feet. "All right. Go get dressed and we'll go to the barn."

Chance hurried to the opening to the hall and paused to face them again. "Are you guys going to get married?"

"How would you feel about that if we do?" Georgie asked.

He shrugged. "Would we live here?"

Austin determined he should field this question. "Actually, I have a big house not far from here, with a barn and a room reserved just for you."

"Cool," he said. "Mama, you should marry my dad."

She smiled. "Then I guess it's official. We'll get married."

Seemingly satisfied, Chance took off and Austin grabbed the opportunity to take Georgie into his arms. "You heard our son. Let's get married."

"When do you propose we do this?" she asked.

"The sooner, the better. In fact, I'm thinking a New Year's Eve wedding would be good."

"That's less than a week away," Lila interjected. "We can't plan a wedding in a week."

"I don't need a fancy wedding, Mother," Georgie said. "Just family and friends and my dad to walk me down the aisle."

George stepped forward, looking less cranky than usual. "You can count on me to do that, princess."

"That's great, if we can actually find an aisle," Lila added. "Six days won't be enough time, not to mention it's a holiday."

A remedy to the time crunch entered Austin's mind. "We can have the ceremony at the ranch's main house. It's big enough to hold everyone, and I happen to know a woman who'd be glad to arrange everything, and she'll do it in record time."

"Do you mean Jenny?" Georgie asked.

"The one and only. If for some reason she can't get it done, then we'll just take a trip to the courthouse on Friday."

Lila looked mortified. "You can't marry for the first time at the courthouse."

"We did," George said. "And we're still married."

Lila scowled at him. "Don't press your luck, George Romero, if you really think you're going to force our daughter to marry in a county building."

Chance ran back into the room as fast as his boots would allow. "I'm ready to go."

Georgie slipped his hand into hers. "Then let's go."

To add to the joy of the day, Chance took Austin's hand and together they walked to the barn. They didn't talk about weddings, only the wonder of a boy's first horse, and plans for their future together. Austin executed his first duty as a father by helping Chance saddle up the pony, and keeping a watchful eye as his son rode the pen like a pro.

He draped his arm over Georgie's shoulder and pulled her close. "You've done a great job raising him, darlin'."

"It was easy. He's a great kid."

"You went to school and took care of him all by yourself. There had to be some hard times, and I'm sorry for that."

She pressed a kiss on his cheek. "The hard times are behind us. I love you, Austin Calloway."

"Let the good times begin, and I love you, too, Georgia May Romero."

"Are you serious about the wedding in a week?" she asked.

"Yep, I am. I think it's a good way to end the old year and welcome in the new."

"If we can get it together."

He kissed her in earnest then gave her a smile. "I'd bet my last buck that Jenny will find a way to pull it off."

Georgie couldn't believe Jenny had pulled it off. The downstairs parlor was fraught with floral arrangements, the food was ready for consumption by the guests and the mint juleps were chilling in the fridge. She was dressed in a short satin gown with a lace cutout in the back and a pair of three-inch matching heels that Paris had insisted Georgie wear because she couldn't. The last she'd heard, the groom was pacing nervously throughout the family homestead and her parents' appearance hadn't started another uncivil war. Everything seemed to be going as planned. Almost everything. The officiate was still missing.

Five minutes ago, Maria had announced that the local justice of the peace, Bucky Cheevers, had been detained by another duty for another hour. Georgie worried that if his reputation rang true, he might be holed up with a woman. That was okay, as long as he finally showed up, which he promised he would. She could think of far worse things to stall a wedding.

"My water broke."

She hadn't considered that one. Georgie turned to Paris, now standing in the doorway wearing a bathrobe, not her bridesmaid's dress. "Are you sure?"

She shuffled over to the bed and perched on the edge of the mattress. "Yes, I'm very sure. I started having some twinges yesterday afternoon, and now they're... Oh, lord, I think this baby is going to come very soon."

Georgie rushed over to her and said, "Lie down." She then hurried to the top of the stairs to sound the alarm. "Dallas, get up here now. Someone call 911 for Paris."

She returned to Paris and sat by her side. "Just take some deep breaths and try to relax, although that won't be easy under the circumstance."

Paris gave her an apologetic look. "I'm so sorry, Georgie. I'm ruining your wedding."

Georgie took her hand. "You don't need to apologize. Besides, Bucky isn't even here yet. We can always wait a couple of days. Your baby can't."

The sound of pounding footsteps echoed through the corridor, followed by Dallas bursting into the room. "What's wrong?"

Paris lifted her head from the pillow. "We're going to have a baby."

He looked somewhat relieved. "I know that."

"Today," Paris added.

Now Dallas looked panicked as he rounded the bed and claimed a spot next to his wife. "Can you hold off?"

Paris grimaced and laid her hand on her belly. "I'm trying, honey, but maybe you should propose that to your son or daughter."

Maria rushed in with Jenny trailing behind her. "The paramedics are on their way. They should be here in five minutes."

"Five minutes I can do…" Paris sucked in a ragged breath. "I think."

"Should I boil some water just in case?" Jenny asked.

"Sure," Maria answered. "And while you're in the kitchen, have a drink. Or two."

Georgie peered behind the mothers, half expecting to see her future husband. "Where's Austin?"

"He's downstairs with Chance," Maria said.

"I told him it was bad luck to see the bride before the wedding," Jenny added. "If there's going to be a wedding. What am I going to do with all that food?"

"We're going to eat it," Maria muttered. "Now is not the time to worry about the nuptials or the catering. Austin and Georgie can still get married, even if we have to hold it at midnight after Paris delivers."

From the pain crossing Paris's face, Georgie doubted the next Calloway grandchild would wait that long.

Sitting in a hospital waiting room for five hours was not a part of Austin's plan. But here he was, dressed in suit and tie, with his almost-bride by his side and his son leaning against his shoulder, fast asleep. Jenny played games on her cell phone across from them while Maria focused on an Old West rerun playing on the TV suspended from the ceiling in the corner. George kept nodding off and, when he snored, Lila periodically shook him awake. Instead of a wedding, they'd inadvertently created a scene straight out of a weird reality show.

Austin had a good mind to go after Bucky Cheevers. If the jerk would have showed up on time, the wedding would already be over. Instead, they were clock-watching and coming to attention every time the Labor and Delivery door opened.

"What a way to ring in the New Year," he whispered to avoid disturbing Chance, who'd just settled down.

"We still have twenty minutes before the New Year is here," Georgie whispered back. "I'm surprised the baby is taking this long. I thought for sure Paris would have delivered in the ambulance."

That would've saved them this waiting game.

As good luck would have it, two minutes later, Dallas came through the door, holding a blue bundle in his arm. "I'd like you to introduce you to Lucas James Calloway."

Everyone scurried out of their seats to catch a glimpse of the newest member of the Calloway family. Everyone but Austin. He didn't believe for a minute that his own son would care to be disturbed from sleep to meet his cousin. But as bad luck would have it, Chance stirred anyway, rubbed his eyes and asked, "Are we gettin' married now?"

"Not yet, bud," Austin told him. "That probably won't happen until tomorrow."

"Come see little Lucas, Chance," Georgie said. "He reminds me of you when you were born."

Chance looked like he'd rather eat dirt, although he grudgingly climbed off the couch to answer his mother's summons. Austin followed him over to Maria who was now holding the baby. Chance took a quick peek then frowned. "He's all wrinkly and his hair is sticking up."

Georgie smiled. "That's what babies look like when they're first born."

"Okay." Obviously disinterested, Chance returned to the couch, stretched out on his back and closed his eyes.

Georgie slid her arm around Austin's waist and regarded Dallas. "Is Paris okay?"

"She's not as tired as I thought she'd be," he said. "She is relieved it's over."

Jenny took the baby from Maria without asking.

"Oh my. He looks just like Worth did when he was a baby, minus the blond hair."

Austin leaned over to verify that. As far as he was concerned, the kid looked like every other kid at that stage. And he wasn't as good-looking as *his* kid. "I think he looks more like Grandpa Calloway before he got his dentures."

Georgie pinched his side. "Stop it."

"I'm sorry we blew the wedding," Dallas said.

So was Austin. "We'll figure something out in the next day or so."

Jenny handed the baby to Dallas and uttered, "I'll be right back," then pushed out the door and disappeared into the lobby.

"I better get this guy back to his mother," Dallas said. "She's going to think we left without her. She's a little disappointed he didn't arrive after the New Year so he could be the first one born."

"When can we see Paris?" Georgie asked.

Dallas glanced at the clock. "I'll check, but she should be ready for guests in a few minutes."

After Dallas walked out of the room, Jenny returned with a tall man in tow. "Georgie, Austin, this is Chaplain Griggs. He'll be glad to perform the wedding ceremony so you won't have to wait."

Austin exchanged a look with Georgie. "Do you really want to get married in a hospital waiting room?"

Georgie shook her head. "No, but I wouldn't mind getting married in Paris's hospital room, if she's up to it. That way we can all be together as planned."

"I can do that," the chaplain said. "As long as medical personnel clear it."

"And Paris," Maria added. "She might not be up to it."

Lila stepped forward. "Georgie, honey, this isn't much better than the courthouse."

Georgie patted Lila's cheek. "It's okay, Mom. It's unique, like all of us."

"I'll drink to that," George said. "Too bad I don't have a drink handy."

"Before we go any further," the chaplain began, "I need to find out if we're cleared to continue. I'll let you know in a few minutes."

After the clergyman left, Austin turned to Georgie to find out if she was in fact serious. "If you're sure about this, I have the license."

"I'm very sure, but I don't have a bouquet."

Jenny crossed the room to an end table, yanked the fake flowers from a crystal vase and handed them to Georgie. "Here you go. It's not perfect, but it should do. Hopefully they won't send you a bill."

Maria pulled her cell from the pocket of her plain blue dress. "I'll call the other boys, just in case."

Austin saw several problems with that. "Don't bother, Mom. Before we left the house, they told me they were going to have a few beers, and I don't see any one of them being a designated driver. Besides, if we're going to get this show on the road, we have ten minutes before midnight arrives. I'd like to stick to at least one of our original plans to be married before the New Year."

"You could also use the chapel, sugar," Jenny said. "If the room doesn't work out."

"It's going to work out fine." All eyes turned to the chaplain as he continued. "I have been instructed that we need to have a quick ceremony out of respect to the new mother. Now if you're ready, follow me."

Lila went over and nudged Chance. "Time for a wedding, baby boy."

Chance hopped off the couch and grinned. "About time."

Austin couldn't agree more.

As they wandered down the sterile corridor, their son between them, Austin took Georgie's hand and gave it a squeeze. When he imagined what they must look like to strangers, a bevy of guests dressed in their finest, he couldn't help but chuckle.

They arrived at Paris's room a few moments later, where George offered his arm to Georgie. "Son, I've waited a long time to give my daughter away, and even though we don't have an aisle, I'd like to at least walk her into the room."

He didn't dare argue with a man who had a grip on his future bride. "Not a problem, sir."

"Should I sing?" Jenny asked.

"Good heavens, no," Maria answered. "You'll wake every baby on the floor and every dog in the county."

They pushed through the door where the chaplain immediately claimed a spot near the window.

Paris was sitting up in the bed, holding the baby close, Dallas at her side. "I'm tickled pink you're doing this, you two," she said. "Just excuse my not-very-chic attire."

Georgie kissed her dad's cheek, walked over to Paris and gave her a hug. "I couldn't have a wedding without my maid of honor standing up for me. And don't worry about standing."

The chaplain cleared his throat. "Shall we begin?"

Austin checked the black clock on the wall. They had all of four minutes to get this done. "You bet."

He guided Georgie and Chance to the officiate, who started off by saying, "At times the best moments in life come in the face of a miracle. And it appears it took a miracle for you both to get to this point."

"Amen," George said from behind them, drawing more laughter.

"Would you like traditional vows, or do you plan to say your own?" the chaplain asked.

"Our own," Georgie replied before Austin could even think.

She turned to face him and smiled. "Austin, we've both traveled differing paths, but all my roads led to you. I feel blessed to have you as my husband, and the father of our child, for the rest of our life."

Austin could only come up with a few short and simple words to say. "Georgie, it's always been you. It will always be only you. Thank you for giving me our son, and the opportunity to make up for lost moments. I promise I will stay this time, forever. I love you."

She swiped at her eyes. "I love you, too."

"Do we have rings?" the chaplain asked.

"I do." Dallas stood, fished the bands from his pocket, then passed them off to Maria who handed them to the chaplain.

They slid the rings onto each other's fingers, sealing the deal, and Austin happily obliged the directive to kiss the bride. He responded to the tug on his hand with a grin aimed at his boy. "Are we married now?" Chance asked.

Austin scooped his son up into his arms. "Yeah, bud, we are. Now let's go home and get you to bed."

"To our home," Jenny said. "We still have all that food and drink."

George clasped Lila's hand. "I'm more than ready for that drink."

"I'm ready for sleep," Paris said. "Congratulations to both of you. We'll celebrate large when we come home."

After the marriage license was signed, and Austin paid the man who married them with a minute to spare, everyone said their goodbyes to the new mother and baby, then filed into the parking lot. Georgie settled Chance into his booster in the backseat then turned and slid her arms around Austin's waist. "Maria is going to put Chance to bed in your old room. That way, we can have our honeymoon at your house."

"Our house," he amended. "I believe we should forego the food and drink, unless you're hungry."

"Only for your attention," she said as she pinched his butt.

He faked a flinch. "You've got it. And you've got me from now on. Can you handle it?"

"I don't know. You can be pretty tough to take, but I'll manage." She studied his eyes, her expression surprisingly sober. "We have a lot of catching up to do, Austin, and it's going to take a lot of adjustments to our lives, raising Chance together."

He cupped her pretty face in his palms and brushed a kiss across her lips. "We can make it through anything together, sweetheart. Just look how far we've come to get to this point."

"And look at what we've got."

When they turned their attention to their sleeping son, a host of emotions ran through Austin. Awe.

Amazement. The fierce need to protect him. Above all, an unexpected, abiding love.

Yeah, he'd made more than a few mistakes, failed at a few endeavors, feared he might continue that pattern. But with his cherished Georgie by his side, Austin no longer worried if he would falter because he knew he would. And that was okay. For the first time in his life, he knew what it took to be a deserving husband and father, a real man, and it had nothing to do with how much money he made, or how many championships he'd won. It had everything to do with opening himself to love, and that much he had done. And damn if it didn't feel good.

A year ago, if anyone would've told him he'd be married and have a kid, he would've called them crazy. But now, he called himself blessed.

* * * * *

"I'm not sure I believe you when you said you didn't feel anything earlier today. When we kissed in front of the cameras."

Logan's voice was low, resonating throughout her body. It wasn't just the kiss that made her feel something. Everything about him made her feel, and that was a terrifying feeling. Leaving herself open to him eventually led to hurt. Always.

A heavy sigh escaped her lungs. "It was a kiss. It didn't change my world," she lied.

Logan reared back his head and brought their dance to a stop. "I don't believe you."

"It was hours ago. I hardly even remember it."

"Then let me refresh your memory."

He clutched her neck and lowered his lips to hers. His mouth drifted to her cheek, his stubble scratching her nose, then he traveled to her jaw and kissed her neck. She kept her eyes closed, luxuriating in every heavenly press of his lips, not wanting it to end.

"Tell me you don't feel anything," he whispered into her ear.

"I don't feel anything." The truth was that she was feeling everything right now. Her entire body was so alert she could probably stay awake for the next twenty-four hours.

"You said it yourself earlier today. You're a terrible liar."

THE BEST MAN'S BABY

BY
KAREN BOOTH

First Published in Great Britain 2017
By Mills & Boon, an imprint of HarperCollins*Publishers*
1 London Bridge Street, London, SE1 9GF

© 2017 Karen Booth

ISBN: 978-0-263-92804-4

51-0117

Our policy is to use papers that are natural, renewable and recyclable products and made from wood grown in sustainable forests. The logging and manufacturing processes conform to the legal environmental regulations of the country of origin.

Printed and bound in Spain
by CPI, Barcelona

Karen Booth is a Midwestern girl transplanted in the South, raised on '80s music, Judy Blume and the films of John Hughes. She writes sexy, big-city love stories. When she takes a break from the art of romance, she's teaching her kids about good music, honing her Southern cooking skills or sweet-talking her husband into whipping up a batch of cocktails. Find out more about Karen at www.karenbooth.net.

For Bryony Evens, my sweet and lovely friend.
May the handsome guy in the flower shop
always flirt with you.

One

Julia Keys ducked out of the cab in front of her childhood home amid a hailstorm of camera flashes and shouts from reporters.

Where's Derek, Julia? Is he flying in from LA for your sister's wedding?

Is it true you and Derek are shopping for a house together?

Any chance you and Derek will tie the knot?

Ludicrous questions, and yet they kept coming. She wouldn't date Derek, her current costar, if her life depended on it. The idea made her queasier than her first trimester morning sickness, and that was saying a lot.

Dodging reporters and lugging a week's worth of designer clothes in a roller bag, she marched up the walk, past the rhododendron that had been in full bloom at the beginning of summer, the last time she'd been back in Wilmington. That was also the last time Logan Brandt had stomped on her heart. The very last time. Or at least that was the plan.

Her father raced down the stairs of the wraparound porch and folded her into his arms. "Y'all need to learn some manners," he yelled to the media militia assembled at the curb.

At least the local press had enough respect to stay off private property. The same could not be said for the paparazzi in a big city like New York or Los Angeles. A film career spanning nearly a decade had left Julia a reluctant pro. Judging by the frantic phone call from her publicist that morning, when the story of her nonexistent romance first broke, the press would be arriving in waves over the next several hours.

"Sorry about that, Daddy. Don't talk to them. They'll go away if we don't say anything." She pressed a kiss to her father's clean-shaven face. It was framed by thick, chocolate-brown hair—the same color as Julia's, except his had gone salt-and-pepper at the temples. The few wrinkles he had showed deep concern. Of course he was worried—one daughter was getting married, and the other, according to the strangers still yammering at them, had questionable taste in men. When her real predicament—the one that would make her father a granddad—finally came to light, she could only hope he'd stay as relatively calm as he was now.

Her father ushered her inside, which was only about ten degrees cooler than the eighty-degree day. She knew better than to ask her dad to adjust the thermostat. As far as he was concerned, it was September, and therefore autumn, which meant air-conditioning was no longer needed. Never mind that summer in coastal North Carolina could stretch on until Halloween.

Her mother strolled into the living room wearing a pink

sleeveless blouse and white capri pants, auburn hair back in a ponytail, pearls completing the look, as always. She wiped her hands with a checkered kitchen towel. Julia's younger sister, Tracy, brought up the rear. Spitting image of their mother and the bride-to-be, Tracy was a fresh-faced vision in a turquoise sundress, staring down Julia as if she were evil incarnate. Julia was now liking her chances with the school of piranha masquerading as the media outside.

Mom offered a hug and a kiss. "It's good to see you, hon. I feel so spoiled having you home for the second time in three months."

Three months. Just enough time to get pregnant. "The high school reunion was one thing. It's not every day my baby sister gets married." Julia went in for a hug from her sister.

Tracy was having none of that, planting her hands on her hips. "How long are we going to pretend that Jules isn't ruining my wedding? If y'all are going to stand around and chitchat like nothing is wrong, I'm asking Carter to fix me a stiff drink."

It physically hurt to know that her arrival didn't warrant a hug, but Julia couldn't blame her sister. If the roles had been reversed, she'd be mad as a hornet about the frenzy in the front yard. "I'm sorry about the mess outside, but it's all a stupid lie. The press has been hinting at something between Derek and me since before we even started filming. Trust me, I'm not involved with him."

"I saw the photos. You're practically kissing him." Her mother's sweet drawl teetered on *practically*. "Are you denying it because you're not proud of the way he's behaved? They said he's been arrested for public intoxication seven times. Why would you want to be with a man like that?"

Julia shook her head, sweat already beading up on her skin. If the press could sell this contrivance of a story to her own mother, they could convince anyone. "Mom. Listen to me." She grasped her shoulders. "I swear there's nothing going on with Derek. Yes, it looks like a kiss. We were rehearsing a scene. I have zero interest in him. And he has no interest in me." *And he has the world's worst breath.*

"Then go outside and tell those buzzards precisely that." Julia's father teased back the drapes, peering outside. "We spent an awful lot of money on this wedding. I'm not about to see it ruined."

If only her father knew the lengths to which Julia was already going to *not* ruin her sister's wedding—namely keeping a pregnancy under her hat, which was absolutely killing her. Why couldn't things be normal? Just once? If her life were normal, she'd walk into this room and tell her parents she was pregnant. Her mother would probably burst with excitement, then sport the start of a nine-month-long smile and ask a million questions. Her father would sidle up to Julia's loving, handsome husband and congratulate him with a firm handshake and a clap on the back. But of course, things couldn't be normal. No husband had materialized in Julia's twenty-nine years on earth, and that was of little consequence compared to not knowing whether her ex or Logan Brandt was the baby's father. Oops.

"You have to trust me," Julia said. "If we say anything, they'll just ask more questions. We should ignore them and focus on Tracy." *Please. Anything so I can stop fixating on wanting to blurt out that I have a tiny top-secret bundle of joy in my belly.*

Tracy snorted and shook her head. "Focus on me." Plopping down on the end of the couch, she broadcast her anger by aggressively flipping through a bridal magazine. "That's rich coming from you right now." Tracy had never been much for mincing words. Why start now?

Their father sat in his wingback chair. "Jules, I know you think you know what you're doing, but I've had my own experience with the media." Julia's father had been a state senator for two decades. Twenty-one squeaky-clean, scandal-free years. "If they've fabricated this much, they'll speculate until the cows come home. Who knows what they'll come up with next."

A heavy sigh came from her mother. "I can't even think about this anymore. I need to keep myself busy in the kitchen. Maybe open a bottle of chardonnay."

"See? Now your mother is upset. I didn't pay all this money for a scandal and an unhappy wife."

"Is that all you care about?" Tracy blurted. "The money? What people will say?"

"I have a reelection campaign to run next year. My family should be an asset, not a political liability."

Tracy tossed the magazine aside. "I swear to God, it's like I'm not even getting married. Julia and money and Dad's job are obviously far more important."

"We've never had a family scandal before, Trace. I intend to keep it that way."

Family scandal. If only they knew. Julia took a deep breath, but it made her head swim. A smooth start to Tracy's wedding was out the window, and it was all her fault. The guilt of that alone was overwhelming. Tracy had played second fiddle in the Keys family for the last decade, simply because of Julia's success. People were always making a fuss, as much as Julia tried to deflect. It was time for her sister to have center stage. Then Julia could avoid the family microscope and find the perfect time to break the baby news, only after the wedding was over and the happy couple was on a cruise ship to the Bahamas.

Tracy's fiancé, Carter, came downstairs. "Logan just pulled up."

Logan. There was that to deal with as well. Her stomach sank, adding an entirely new and unpleasant aspect to pregnancy queasiness. His hundred-watt smile painfully flashed in her memory. Then came the visions from their last time together. They'd spent nearly the entire weekend in bed. His bare chest, naked shoulders…and other glorious stretches of his tawny brown skin were all that wanted to cycle through her mind. *Damn pregnancy hormones.* Her pulse raced, stirring emotion—anger over the way Logan had ended things after the reunion, frustration over once again being the girl who never managed to do anything the right way. In between all of that was a churning sea of uncertainty. And some churning of her stomach as well. She was going to be a mom. And Logan might be the father. Or he might not. Either way, she had no choice other than to tell him, deal with his reaction and move on. There was nothing more than moving on between them, and that was to be done as two separate parties. Logan had seen to that.

But first she had to find the right time to tell him. Maybe she'd take the approach her mother did when she had potentially upsetting news to break to her father— she'd tell him while he was driving. A man could only freak out so much with two hands on the wheel.

Parked on the narrow tree-lined street, several houses down from the grand Victorian the Keys family had lived in since he could remember, Logan Brandt bided his time in his rental car. Sunglasses on, flipping the keys on his finger, he studied the reporters milling about, consulting their phones. Waiting.

"What a mess," he mumbled. The buzz of activity was normal when it came to Julia. Even if she'd never become a box office hit or had her stunning face land on the cover of countless magazines, drama still would've found her. As to the cause, Logan was so tired of this scenario he could hardly see straight. Julia was once again romantically entangled with a disastrous guy. One of her projects, no doubt, as he referred to them.

His phone rang. Carter, the groom-to-be, his best friend from high school. "Hey," Logan answered. "I'm just now getting to the house."

"Liar. You're sitting in your rental car because you don't want to deal with Hurricane Julia."

"How'd you know it was me?"

"Nobody in Wilmington drives a car that expensive. Well, nobody but you."

Logan snickered. He did have an appetite for nice cars, especially if they were fast, and if anyone knew him well, it was Carter. He and Logan had met freshman year of high school at baseball tryouts. Logan landed a spot on varsity, a harbinger of things to come—full scholarship to UCLA, eight years as a major league pitcher. Record-breaking seasons. Record-breaking salaries. Then a World Series, a loss, and a career-ending injury. His trajectory had never suggested it'd all be over by the time he was thirty.

Julia was a loss of another kind, although it dogged him in much the same way. His high school sweetheart, the woman who understood him better than most, and yet she'd hurt and disappointed him countless times. He must be a glutton for punishment, because he was still wrestling with his need for Julia.

"You have to come inside and talk to Julia about getting rid of the press. Tracy is freaking out," Carter pleaded.

"I doubt she's going to listen to a thing I say after what happened after the reunion."

Julia and Logan saw each other every year at their high school reunion. The meeting had several time-honored traditions that only they were a part of. First came the downing of a cocktail, followed by merciless flirting— laughing, innocent touches, pointed glances, the flipping of hair from Julia. After the second drink came a spirited round of one-upmanship, including desperate attempts to convince the other how "happy" they were. Once full tipsiness was achieved, the painful stroll down memory lane could commence, usually ending with a heated make-out session. In those instances, one of them was to cut it short before things went too far. It was customary for the other person to stomp on the brakes the following year.

The last reunion had veered off course. They'd both walked in wounded—Logan hated his new career as a network commentator covering the sport he missed terribly, while Julia had just been offered a role playing a much older woman. She'd also made mention of having been dumped by another boyfriend, but Logan had tried to ignore that part. They'd needed each other that balmy June night, and that translated into two unforgettable days in bed, making love, laughing and talking for hours.

Unfortunately, Logan had been shaken back to reality when he got to the airport at the end of their weekend and saw a tabloid story saying there was romance brewing with her next costar—the hapless movie star named Derek. True or not, it was too powerful a reminder that Julia wasn't capable of settling down. She was too busy trying to save the world, too drawn to an endless string of loser guys. Logan refused to be one of her losers. He'd had no choice but to end things before she hurt him again.

"Sorry you had to find out about her new boyfriend like this," Carter said. "It's gotta be tough."

"I'm fine. I'd already seen the papers. I knew all about it." *Just like last time. And every other time.*

"Will you please get in here so I can offer you a beer

and not feel guilty about having one myself at four in the afternoon?"

"I'll be right there."

Logan did his duty as Carter's best man, strolling down the aged sidewalk to the Keyses' house. The reporters yelled after him—mostly requests to get Julia to come outside, although there was one question about life as an athlete-turned-sports commentator. Logan didn't reply; he just waved. He wasn't about to chime in if they asked about Julia and her new boyfriend.

Mrs. Keys opened the door, welcoming him with a smile and a hug. "Logan Brandt. If my eyes don't deceive me. I hope you and Julia can play nicely today. We have enough drama for a lifetime."

Logan nodded, stepping inside and keeping an eye peeled for Julia. "Don't you worry about us." *I'll do it for you.*

Carter waved on his way into the kitchen. "Two beers, coming up."

Tracy rose from the couch, but grabbed Logan's arms rather than taking the hug he offered. Her eyes were ringed in pink. "Will you talk to her? You might be the only person she'll listen to about getting the press to go away."

"I don't know that I have any sway with…" Her name was poised on his lips when Julia waltzed in from the kitchen. Midstride, she froze. He couldn't move, either. Their eyes locked, and he felt as though he was up to his knees in a concrete block of memories, the most recent ones the strongest—watching her sleep in the early morning as his hand followed the contour of her lower back and a smile broke across her face. When Julia was happy, the world was a beautiful place, and she gave in to it, heart and soul.

For an incoherent instant, he wished he could take back

the message he'd left for her. The one that ended everything. Her pull on him registered square in the center of his chest—a tightening that said two opposing things: he couldn't live without her, but he had to stick to his guns or he'd end up romantic roadkill. "Jules."

"Logan." Julia didn't come closer, which was a good thing, albeit disappointing. She crossed her arms, building a fortress around herself. Still, her vanilla scent found his nose and warmed him from head to toe.

"How are you?" he asked. If ever there was a loaded question, that was it. Stress radiated off her, but she was as stunning as ever. Her silky chestnut hair fell about her face in waves, effortlessly sexy. His hands twitched with the memory of what it was like to have his fingers buried in it. Her peachy skin had a summer glow he couldn't place—she usually avoided the sun. It suited her. Perfectly.

"I'm fine. I'm ready to start talking about the wedding and stop talking about me," she said.

I bet.

"That's a wonderful idea," Mrs. Keys said. "I have a special treat for Carter in the kitchen, and then we'll get started. Trace, why don't we go over the schedule and you can fill us all in on the jobs we need to do."

Tracy pulled out a binder and perched on the middle cushion of the couch. Carter handed Logan a bottle of pale ale and took a seat next to his bride-to-be, putting his arm around her and kissing her temple. Logan had given Carter plenty to envy over the years, but when it came to this, Carter had him beat. Aside from a temporary breakup, Carter and Tracy's love story was uncomplicated and sweet. Logan would've done anything to have that.

Mrs. Keys triumphantly presented a platter of her world-famous deviled eggs to her future son-in-law.

Carter lunged for one the instant they were on the coffee table. "Oh, man. Thank you. I love these things." He popped it into his mouth and moaned in ecstasy.

Julia made a wretched sound and pursed her lips, turning away.

"You okay?" Logan asked as Mrs. Keys took the remaining spot on the couch, next to Tracy.

Julia clamped her eyes shut and nodded. "Bad experience with deviled eggs on set a few weeks ago. I'm fine."

"Oh, honey. I didn't know," Mrs. Keys said, as her husband grabbed several of the offending eggs. "I can put them away if you like."

Julia shook her head. "Don't worry about me. I know how much everyone loves them."

Mr. Keys sat in his chair, leaving the love seat for Julia and Logan. Once again, their gazes connected, and he had to fight to make sense of what his body was saying to him. The problem was, whenever she was in a foul mood, he had a deep longing to kiss her out of it. He was practically wired to do it.

Logan offered her a seat. "Please. Ladies first."

Julia rolled her eyes. "Such a gentleman."

"I'm just being polite."

"It's a little late for polite."

"No fighting," Tracy barked. "Julia, I swear to God, you're going to kill me. I need the maid of honor and best man to get along. The reporters are bad enough. Not that you don't have the ability to make them go away."

Julia sat, snugging herself up against the arm of the love seat, preemptively distancing herself from him. "I can only say it so many times. The story is fake. I know you all think I have the world's worst taste in men, but don't worry. I did manage to avoid this one. And if we just ignore the press, they'll leave."

Relief washed over him, followed by surprise. No romance with Derek? Really? "Julia's probably right. They'll get bored if you don't talk to them." Feeling considerably more at ease, Logan joined Julia on the love seat. "We're getting along just fine. No fighting."

Tracy's eyes darted back and forth between them. She seemed unconvinced, but returned her focus to her binder. "Give me a minute to figure out what I want everyone to do. Mom, can you look at this?"

Mrs. Keys slid closer to her daughter and the two became immersed in conversation. That left Carter and Mr. Keys to feast on deviled eggs.

Logan was still computing the revelation about Julia's costar. If the story was fake, had it always been? "So, no love connection with Derek, huh?" he asked under his breath.

"No."

"Never?"

"No, Logan. Not ever," she snipped. "After that lovely message you left for me, I'm surprised you care."

Ouch. "I never want to see you with the wrong guy, Jules."

"Okay, everybody. Listen up." Tracy straightened in her seat and started rattling off orders about the florist and picking up wedding bands, the baker and final dress fittings, like a four-star general about to lead them into battle. That left no time for Logan to continue his conversation with Julia, although he wanted to. At least to smooth things over.

Julia was scribbling notes as fast as Tracy could talk. "Got it. I'm on florist and cake duty. Don't worry. I'll take care of it. The only hitch is that I didn't rent a car." She cleared her throat. "Logan, maybe you can drive me."

"You're at the same hotel. It only makes sense," Mrs. Keys chimed in.

True. It *did* make sense, but he couldn't escape the feeling that Julia had ulterior motives. Something in her voice told him that she did. Whatever her plan, hopefully it didn't include ripping his head off and sticking it on a stake in the front yard as payback for the post-reunion breakup. "Of course. Whatever Tracy and Carter need us to do to help make this the perfect wedding."

Two

Julia was sure there was no sound more unhinging than that of reporters politely, but incessantly, rapping on the windows of Logan's rental car, raising their voices as he tried to pull away.

"These people are ridiculous. Somebody's going to get hurt." Logan inched the car out of his parking space. The second he had a clear path, he gunned it.

Julia jerked back in her seat. Her stomach lurched along with it. "Logan. Cool it." She whipped around to look behind them. The reporters were climbing into their cars. "They're following us. Of course."

Logan watched via the rearview window. "We have to get out of here. Now."

He took a sharp turn and ducked down a side street. He knew the shortcuts like the back of his hand. They both did. They'd both learned to drive on these streets. The house Logan grew up in was only seven or eight blocks away.

Logan was intensely focused, eyes darting between the mirror and the road. He ran his hand over his close-cut ebony hair. Being so near him, it was hard not to fixate on what his stubble felt like against her cheek when he kissed her. Or the way his warm and manly smell, citrusy and clean, begged her to curl up in his arms. Everything about being around him again made her chest ache. Things were so much simpler three months ago, for that brief forty-eight hours when she could kiss him and lose herself in him without reservation. Before he ended it forever.

His hands gripped the steering wheel. With the sleeves of his deep blue dress shirt rolled to his elbows, she couldn't have ignored the flex of his solid forearms if she'd wanted to. His arms could make her feel as if she were made of feathers—light as air. Ready to be taken anywhere he wished to have her.

Logan cut over again, navigating the city grid. All while inducing an acute case of nausea.

Julia crossed her arms at her waist. Maybe she'd be too busy barfing to worry about telling Logan about the baby. "Can you take it easy? I'm feeling carsick."

"First the deviled eggs, now this? You're the girl who wanted to eat corn dogs and go on every upside-down ride imaginable at the state fair. Twice."

Logan had thrown down the gauntlet, only he didn't know it. Logan was a smart guy. She could only keep her secret from him for so long. As soon as she turned down a cocktail this weekend, he'd know something was up. His eyes were trained on the road. Time to put her mother's theory to the test.

"I need to know if you can keep a secret." She rummaged through her purse. It was better if they were both busy doing something that precluded a lot of eye contact.

"About what?"

"I can't tell you or you'll know the secret."

He shook his head, taking a left onto the main road to the hotel. "Fine. As long as it doesn't involve a murder, I can keep a secret." He stopped at a yellow light. Normally, Logan would've gunned it through the intersection, but there was a police car parked at the corner.

Why had her mother never briefed her on the protocol for stoplights? This was *not* the way this was supposed to go. Her heart raced, but the secret was going to suffocate her if she didn't tell him. She had to tell him. At least the first part. Then she'd reevaluate. "I'm pregnant."

The light turned green, but he didn't go. "You're what?"

Julia pointed ahead. "It's green."

"Oh." Logan had them again under way. "You're pregnant?"

"I am." She choked back her breath, unable to come out with the part that came next. *And you might be the father.*

"I take it nobody knows? Your family didn't say a thing about it."

"Nobody knows. I've only known for about three weeks and I didn't want to overshadow Tracy."

"You have to tell your family, Jules. They won't be happy you kept this from them."

Julia swallowed hard. *And how does the maybe-father feel about me keeping the secret?* "You saw how Tracy is. She's a wreck already. It wouldn't be fair."

Julia caught sight of the hotel. They'd be there any minute. That was bringing up a whole new set of feelings. If only her mother hadn't turned her old bedroom into an office. If only there was another good hotel close to home. If only she and Logan hadn't slept together the last time she was here. Then she wouldn't be suffering from vivid flashes of hot, bittersweet memories—his welcoming pecan-brown eyes, smoldering, telling her every sexy thing he wanted to do to her, all without a single word leaving his tempting lips. He was a man of action in the bedroom, not big for talk, but when he did speak, it was usually a doozy. *You're so damn sexy, Jules. You make me want to lock the door and throw away the key.*

He'd done such a number on her. She'd been stupidly hopeful when she was last here, foolish enough to think that finally she and Logan had gotten their act straight. Then hours after they parted, he left his message. *We'll never work. Let's just admit it. Once and for all.*

And of course, if they hadn't slept together, there was a very good chance she wouldn't be in the business of keeping secrets at all. She cupped her belly with her hand. However difficult, she wanted this. She wouldn't regret her time with Logan, however painfully it had ended, if it had brought her this baby. Her baby wasn't the problem.

Logan turned into the hotel drive. "I don't know why I bothered to try to outrun anybody. The bastards are already here." He pointed to a handful of news vans in the parking lot out front.

"There are only so many hotels between here and Wrightsville Beach. It wasn't going to take them long to figure out where we were."

They pulled up to the valet stand, reporters waiting, but no attendant in sight. Logan grabbed her arm. "Hold on one second. Let me come around to your side of the car. I don't want you out there on your own. You know what these guys are like, and we're on public property now. It's not like it was at your parents' house."

"I can handle myself."

"Look, Jules. Just cut a guy some slack and let me have my macho moment, okay?"

She cracked a smile. At least chivalry wasn't dead.

"I owned up to it, didn't I?"

"Yes. You did." She folded her hands in her lap to wait.

Logan climbed out of the car. The reporters shouted his name, swarming him like bees. He was at her door in a flash. "Take two steps back, everybody, and let Ms. Keys out of the car."

She put on her sunglasses and opened her door. At this point, nearly a dozen people with cameras and microphones had them surrounded. She hated this more than pretty much anything.

Julia, where's Derek?

Are you having an affair with Mr. Brandt?

The valet pushed his way through the crowd. "Oh. Wow. Mr. Brandt. Ms. Keys. I'm so sorry I wasn't out here when you pulled up."

Logan surrendered his keys and a ten. "If you could have our bags brought in, that would be great."

"You got it, Mr. Brandt. I'm a huge fan. A huge fan."

Logan smiled wide. He was always gracious with his fans. "I'll be sure to sign something for you before I check out." He held back the press with one arm while he put the other around Julia.

This probably wasn't the right message to send, not with the reporters here, but she liked feeling protected by Logan.

"Are you two a couple?" someone asked. If only they knew the extent to which they were *not* a couple, even if he could be the father of her unborn child.

Logan picked up their pace as they neared the door. Still, the throng crushed in on them. "Everybody, back off." His voice boomed above the incessant chatter. He swiped off his sunglasses and straightened, employing all six feet and several more inches of him as intimidation. His audience actually shut up for a moment. Hard to believe. "One step inside and I won't bother with hotel management. I'll call the police. Leave her alone and find some other story to chase." He took her hand, and they escaped through the revolving doors.

"Are you okay?" Logan asked, not letting go of her as they made their way through the lobby.

His touch sent tingles throughout her entire body—unrequited, one-way tingles that served no purpose other than to frustrate her. "Yes. I'm fine." She stepped up to the front desk. "Checking in. The reservation is under Brady."

"Marcia?" Logan chuckled.

"Jan Brady. I'm no Marcia," she mumbled under her breath.

The front desk clerk, who looked familiar, smiled and winked, seeming to enjoy the idea of being in on the joke of a celebrity using a false name. "But, Mr. Brandt. I see you have a reservation with us as well." Confusion washed over his face as he glanced back and forth between them.

It was then that Julia recognized the man—he'd been working the front desk when she and Logan had had their tryst. They'd ended up staying in Logan's room that time. Julia hadn't bothered to check in before the reunion, and by the time they'd arrived at the hotel, they were about to tear off each other's clothes in the lobby. Two rooms had seemed laughable.

But not anymore.

Room keys in hand, Logan and Julia filed into the elevator. An elderly couple had joined them. No one said a thing, and the quiet gave Logan's mind plenty of space to roam. Too much space. *She's pregnant? And it's a secret? Who in the hell is the dad?* He glanced over at her. *No baby bump yet. She's known for a few weeks. She can't be very far along. Wait a minute... How far along was she? Could he? No. Not that. But wait. Could he be? The dad?*

The elevator came to a stop. Logan held the door to afford the other passengers some time. He caught the uncertainty in Julia's eyes. There was more weighing on her. He could see it, and he had to know it all, even if it might hurt. They made it to the top floor—as Logan remembered it, the only floor with suites. Judging by their room numbers, they'd be across the hall from each other.

"We should talk some more," Julia said when they'd arrived at their doors. Her voice was ragged at the edges, an apt reflection of her nerves. Considering the pressure from the reporters, her family and having to keep her secret, she had to be exhausted.

"Yes. We should. I want to hear more about your, um, situation." He felt idiotic the minute he'd worded it that way, but at least he'd kept his promise to not say anything.

"I need food, too. I'm really hungry."

"Even after being carsick?"

"Yes. It's one of the weird things about...it. I feel queasy, but I'd give my right arm for fried chicken and a peach pie. The whole pie."

He was still getting used to the idea of Julia being pregnant. Talking about it wasn't helping. It was only making it more bizarre. "With the vultures outside, we probably shouldn't leave the hotel until we need to."

"Can we order room service and talk after I have a chance to change?"

The bellman came strolling down the hall with their two roller bags.

"Looks like your change of clothes is right on time. My room? A half hour?"

"Perfect."

Logan brought his suitcase inside and ordered food— grilled pork for himself, and with no fried chicken on the menu, he chose a steak for Julia, medium rare. Just the way she liked it, and she never turned down a steak. He then unpacked his suit for the rehearsal dinner Friday night, as well as the rest of his clothes, and changed into jeans and a T-shirt. He might as well get comfortable for whatever it was that Julia was going to spring on him tonight. One thing was for sure. She had a talent for catching him off guard.

Room service was wheeling in the cart when Julia came out of her room. "Sorry I'm a little late. I nodded off for a few minutes."

She *was* tired—enough to nod off. That was so unlike Julia, he could hardly wrap his brain around it. She never slowed down. There was always something brewing, always something to do, someone new to meet, some new adventure on which to embark. So this was her new adventure. A baby.

A sweet smile that was tinged with melancholy crossed her face as she stepped inside. It struck him as she padded past, leaving her soft and sensuous smell in her wake—she seemed smaller. Was it because she was as out on a limb as a person could be, all while trying to hide? Although she rarely allowed herself to be vulnerable, Julia was a very open person. Keeping this secret from her family must've been one of the most difficult things she'd ever decided she had to do.

She'd changed into a loose-fitting pink top and a pair of black yoga pants. Julia could work a fancy designer dress like nobody's business, but he really preferred her like this—relaxed. And he had to admire the rear view as he trailed behind her. "We can sit on the sofa and eat."

They started in on dinner, Julia confirming her claim that she was starving. She'd always been an enthusiastic eater, even when she was skinny as a rail in high school, but this was an impressive showing. "I've been craving red meat, too. So thank you. This is perfect."

He smiled and nodded, not really tasting his meal, still getting accustomed to the notion of the pregnancy. He'd already psyched himself up for her to tell him who the dad was, although he dreaded the answer—some hotshot CEO, a power-hungry producer or one of her toothy costars. And then there was the voice in his head asking if he might be part of the equation.

The moment was still fresh in his mind—back in his room after the reunion, peeling away her dress, drinking in the vision of her curves, it all hitting him in an avalanche—he'd waited for a very long time to be with her again. The way she moved told him that she was far more comfortable with her body than she'd ever been in high school. As she unbuckled his belt and kissed him softly, she'd said they wouldn't need a condom. She was on the pill. She'd also quipped, "When I remember to take it." Then his pants had slumped to the floor and further clarification of birth control was the last thing on his mind. That night alone they could have conceived a baby many times over, and it had been only the start of their weekend together.

"So. Pregnant. That's big. Really big." Why he suddenly had so little vocabulary was beyond him. He only knew that his palms were starting to get clammy.

"I know. It is." She gathered her napkin and placed it on the table. "I was surprised, to say the least."

"So this wasn't planned."

"No. It wasn't."

"How far along are you?"

"Three months."

Just say it. "And how is the dad feeling about all of this?"

She twisted her lips and turned to look at him with her

wide brown eyes. He'd never seen them so unsure. "I don't know, exactly. The truth is that I'm not completely certain who the father is."

His heart was thundering in his chest. He knew she had men falling at her feet, but was it really this extreme? "Oh."

"It's either my ex, the guy who dumped me right before the reunion, or…it's you."

His heart came to a complete stop. In fact, the only thing that gave him any indication the earth was still spinning was the bat of Julia's dark lashes. He sat forward and rested his elbows on his knees, nodding. Thinking. Processing. Once again, she'd surprised the hell out of him. He'd prepared for either answer. Not *both*. *I might be the dad? Or I might not?* He couldn't live long without knowing for sure. He sat back up. "We have to have a paternity test. Right away."

"I knew you were going to say that, but I don't really see the point. It's not going to change anything."

"It'll change a lot for me." His brain hurt from the suggestion that they not find out who the father was.

"It doesn't matter. Either way, I'm pregnant by a man who chooses not to be with me. Do you have any idea how terrible that feels? I need to focus on the good, for my own sake. I'm choosing to focus on the baby."

Logan still couldn't believe what she was saying. "I'm going to go insane sitting around for the next six months wondering whether or not I'm about to be a dad."

"I'm sorry, but that's just too bad. It's not going to change the fact that we aren't together. We'll have to wait until the baby arrives and then we'll know. It should be fairly obvious once the baby is born. I doubt we'll need a paternity test."

Ah. I see. "So the other guy isn't black?"

"He isn't."

Well, that certainly made that aspect of things convenient. But still the logistics made no sense. Was he supposed to sit in a waiting room with her ex and hope like hell that the baby came out with a skin tone closest to his own?

"I've thought about it, and the most sensible thing is to wait until then and you can decide how involved you want to be. We'll have to negotiate all of that. I'm hoping I can count on you to be sensible and flexible. I don't want to bring in lawyers," Julia said.

His head pounded. She was discussing this as if they were two multinational corporations preparing to merge. "What did the other guy have to say about all of this?" He winced at the thought of her having this conversation with any other man, even when he had no claim on her.

"He's out. Like all the way out. He wants nothing to do with me. He was pretty sure I made up the baby so I could get him back."

A low grumble left Logan's throat. What kind of scum would think a woman like Julia would make up a baby to get him back? And how did she end up with a guy like that? "He's out? What does that even mean? You get a woman pregnant, you accept responsibility. That's the first chapter of the book called *How to Be a Real Man*."

A tear rolled down her cheek. She wrapped her arms around herself and settled back against the couch. "Apparently he doesn't agree."

Logan had to fight back his rage. He sucked in a deep breath. If the baby was his, he'd take responsibility. "If it's mine, we have to get married."

A dismissive puff of air left her lips. "This is not the time for jokes."

"It's no joke. We're getting married if the baby is mine. You grew up with both parents. I…" His voice cracked, thinking about his father. "I grew up with both parents until we lost my dad. A kid needs both parents. I won't be able to live with it any other way."

"I'm not getting married to you. That's not happening."

"Yes. You are. Unlike this other guy you were with, I'm a man and I accept my responsibilities. We have to get married if the baby is mine." He wasn't even sure what was coming out of his mouth anymore. It seemed perfectly sensible in his head a few seconds earlier.

"And none of that matters, Logan. You don't love me. You want nothing to do with me romantically. Remember? You were very clear with your message after the reunion. Painfully clear. I can recite it if you want. It wasn't hard to commit it to memory."

He'd ended it definitively, there was no question about that. Clarity had been for the sake of them both. Of course, he'd never imagined she'd memorize his message. Had he been too cold? "What was I supposed to do? I get to the airport and you're on the cover of a magazine that says sparks were flying when you were auditioning with Derek. That was a week before the reunion and you'd just come off a breakup. That told me everything I needed to know about any future between us."

"There were no sparks with Derek. Why doesn't anyone believe me?"

"There's always some other guy around the corner, isn't there? Some mess of a guy who you can try to fix."

She shot him a final look of disgust before she bolted from the couch and stalked to the front door. "You can be such a jerk. Really. You have an uncanny ability to say the most hurtful things."

He rushed to follow her. "Wait a minute. We're still talking."

She squared her body to his and poked the center of his chest, hard, even though he had a good fifty pounds on her. Maybe more. "If you think the next six months are going to be difficult for you, how do you think the pregnant woman feels? How about the woman who got dumped by both of the men who might've knocked her up? Did you even take two seconds to think about that?"

"I asked you to marry me. I'm willing to play my part."

"You did not ask me to marry you. You were issuing a mandate. And that's not happening, anyway. I'm not marrying someone out of obligation, and certainly not a man who broke up with me. I'm done making mistakes when it comes to you." She opened the door and stormed out. It closed with a *thud* behind her.

Logan turned, his eyes wide open. No way he was getting any sleep tonight. Julia had given him more than enough to chew on.

His phone beeped with a text. *What now?* He wandered across the room and picked it up from the coffee table. It was from Julia.

We have to leave for the florist by ten.

Great. A whole day of wedding errands with the pregnant woman who drove him crazy, refused to marry him and might be carrying his baby.

Three

Logan had been a royal jerk last night—selfishly worrying how he'd survive the next six months of uncertainty, informing Julia that he expected her to marry him. That was *not* happening. She could do this all on her own. She didn't need help from Logan.

Although she didn't mind the view.

"Oh. Hey. Good morning." He flashed a sheepish smile, standing in the doorway of his room, nothing more than a towel wrapped around his waist, beads of water dotting his shoulder. "I was just getting the paper." Bending over to pick it up, he showed off his perfectly defined back.

Julia stood stuck. His velvety voice delivered a too-sexy memory of their last morning in this hotel—Logan's long, warm naked body pressed against her back in the wee hours, his giving lips on her neck as he slid his hand between her knees, lifted her leg and rocked her world with the most memorable wake-up call, well, ever.

"Jules? You okay?"

"Morning," she sputtered, pushing a room service cart out of her room and into the hall. "I ordered bacon with breakfast, but the smell was making me queasy. If you want the leftovers." *Sexy, Jules. Real sexy.*

He looked both ways, flipped the latch on his door and crossed the hall. He raised the stainless cloche from the plate, grabbing some bacon. "Just two. The camera adds ten pounds."

"You're fine." She stole a glimpse of his stomach, just as hard and muscled as ever. He might not be paid to be an elite athlete anymore, but he maintained his body like one. And to think she'd reaped the benefits—those strapping arms wrapped around her, keeping her close, making her feel for two whole days that she belonged nowhere else. The price of admission had been far more than she'd been willing to pay—every shred of her heart. A big chunk of her pride, too.

"Ready in fifteen?" She braced herself against her door. Being around nearly-naked Logan was making it impossible to stand up straight.

"Definitely. I called down to the valet. We can go out the side entrance. They'll have the car waiting for us."

"You don't think the press will be tipped off by the eighty-thousand-dollar gleaming black sports car you just had to rent?"

He shrugged. "I'm not about to drive anything less. You'll have to suffer through it, babe."

Babe. As if.

Julia retreated to her room and tried not to obsess over her makeup or hair, but it was hard not to, knowing she'd be spending her day with Logan. He deserved to be tortured by what he'd so solidly rejected. It would likely be her only measure of revenge. She dressed in a swishy navy blue skirt that showed off her legs, black ballet flats and a white sleeveless top with a cut that left her expanding bustline on full display. Boobs. At least she was getting *something* out of this whole single-and-pregnant thing, other than a baby, of course.

She met Logan in the hall, and he just *had* to be stunning. So effortlessly hot in jeans and a white button-down, sleeves rolled up just far enough to again mesmerize her with his inexplicably alluring forearms. He led her out through the side exit and to his rental car. His plan to remain incognito was working perfectly until he peeled out of the parking lot.

"Why did you do that?" Her vision darted back to the hotel entrance. Sure enough, reporters were racing to their cars. "They're following us now." She shook her head. He always had to have his manly moment.

"Don't worry. I'll lose them."

He tried to shake the media as he had the day before, but they got stuck at a red light and he was left to lead a dysfunctional caravan to the florist, with his fancy car front and center. They found their destination a few minutes later, and Julia dashed for the door while Logan took his chance to reprimand the reporters yet again and tell them to stay outside.

Julia swept her hair from her face as a red-haired woman came out of the back with an enormous bucket of flowers blocking her view. "Can I help you?" she asked in a lovely singsong British accent. She plopped her armful onto the checkout counter. "Blimey. You're...her."

Her. Yep. Julia smiled warmly. It was the only way to put people at ease and get them off the subject of who she was. "Hi. You're doing the flowers for my sister Tracy's wedding on Saturday. She asked me to come by and look over everything. She's more than a little picky and I want everything to be perfect for her."

The woman nodded. "Yes. I'm Bryony. And I remember your sister. Very well. Come with me."

The bell on the door jingled as Logan walked inside. With a nod, Julia motioned for him to follow her, and he trailed behind her into a back room. While Bryony pulled buckets of blooms from a cooler, Logan assumed what Julia called his jock-in-command stance—feet nearly shoulder-width apart, hands clasped behind his back, shoulders straight, chest out proud. This was his way of taking in the world. She'd first noticed him doing it their junior year of high school, eyeing him when they played softball in gym class. What a joke that had been—like sending in an Olympic broad jumper to play hopscotch. No one had ever beaned a softball as hard as Logan.

He'd been so far out of her league in school that it took her nearly a year to get up the guts to talk to him, and only after he accidentally showed up at a party at her parents' beach house. Imagine the horror when it dawned on her during that first conversation, as she drank in the mesmerizing beauty of his eyes up close, that he didn't actually know her name. She must have done something right, though…he was her boyfriend a week later.

And when it came to part a year after that, as they both went off to college at far-flung schools, she'd taken the initiative and broken up with him. It had been a bit of a preemptive strike and her attempt to be mature about something. She was terrified to leave home, but she was even more scared of how badly it would hurt when Logan called her from UCLA and said he'd met another girl. Or more likely, another fifty girls. It wouldn't have taken long. In the end, Logan became the guy in her past she couldn't have. That was all there was to it. Circumstances, fate or other women—there was always something standing between them.

Logan waited dutifully next to her while Julia checked the array of flowers set aside for her sister. Her mother's penchant for gardening had left Julia more knowledgeable than the average person. She checked each selection off the list her sister had given her. Hydrangea, snapdragons and roses in white. Pink was for tulips, more roses and... *Oh no.*

"These aren't peonies," Julia said.

"Our supplier was out," Bryony answered. "We had to substitute ranunculus."

Julia shook her head. "No. No. No. Peonies are Tracy's favorite flower. She'll pitch a royal fit if she doesn't have them."

Bryony shrugged. "I'm sorry. That's the best we could do. They aren't that dissimilar."

"Logan, don't you think Tracy's going to be mad about ranunculus?" Julia asked.

"I wouldn't know a ranunculus if it walked up to me and introduced itself." He flashed a wide and clever smile.

The florist tittered like a schoolgirl at Logan's comment. "I'm sorry, but I can't make pink peonies magically appear this time of year. I told your sister there might be a problem getting them."

"I have to fix this." Filled with dread, Julia pulled her phone out of her purse and dialed her assistant, Liz. If Tracy didn't have the right flowers, not only would she freak out, by the transitive property of sisterly blame, it'd be Julia's fault.

"Julia. Is everything okay?" Liz answered.

"Hey. I need you to do something for me. Can you call your flower guy and have four dozen stems of pale pink peonies overnighted to the florist in Wilmington?

We need a very pale pink. Not rosy. Not vibrant. Does that make sense?"

"Yes. Of course. I'm on it."

"I'll text you the address. And make sure he knows it's for my sister. I need this to go off without a hitch."

"Got it. Anything else?"

Julia felt as if it was now okay to exhale. "That's it for now."

"Is everything else going okay? The press is really hammering you on this Derek thing, aren't they? And I saw you're hanging out with Logan. How's that going?"

Liz had worked for Julia for years. She might've heard her complain and wax poetic about Logan a few dozen times. Or a few hundred. "Oh, um, it's been fine." She couldn't say more, not with Logan in such close proximity.

"You know, if you wanted the press to go away, you could tell them that you're with Logan," Liz said. "They'll run off and speculate about it for at least a day or two. Or they'll turn it into more of a spectacle. Hard to know, but my gut is they'll take pictures, write their stories and hound Derek with questions about being heartbroken."

Julia watched Logan as he chatted up Bryony, who was blushing like crazy. If any man knew how to make a woman feel good about herself, it was Logan. His presence alone—just breathing the same air he did—made a girl feel special. Precisely why it hurt so much when he took it away. "Well, that's one idea. I'll think about it. Thanks. You're the best."

Julia hung up and took the florist's business card, texting the address to Liz. "The peonies will be here tomorrow morning. Everything else looks great. Thanks for your help."

She turned to Logan. He had the funniest look on his face—both bewildered and amused. She loved that expression, although if she were honest, she loved everything about his face—full lips shaping his effortless smile, square chin with a tiny scar obscured by scruff, and eyes so warm and sincere it was hard to imagine him ever doing something hurtful.

"Your sister is really lucky she didn't put me in charge of this," he said. "I mean really lucky. Imagine how horrified she'd be if she ended up with ranun...you know. Those flowers."

Julia granted him a quiet laugh. "Ranunculus. And you know how much I love my sister. I'm just trying to make the mess I made a little better. Now let's go deal with the cake."

The throng of reporters outside had grown. Either Julia was losing her patience or they were getting pushier. Logan made sure she got into the car safely, making her truly thankful to have him there. On the way to the bakery, she stole a glimpse of his handsome profile, allowing herself to think about what would've happened last night if he'd proposed for real, because he loved her. If he'd never called it off. If the baby was his. They could hold hands, they could stay up late talking for hours, they could make *plans*. Perhaps that was why she was so dead-set on making everything perfect for her sister. If she couldn't have the fairy tale, at least her sister could.

Fifteen minutes later, they arrived at the bakery and again had to sprint for the door as reporters shouted at them. They seemed to be at the end of their rope. There was much speculation about the reasons why Julia was running around town with Logan Brandt and not Derek. Not good.

Inside, one of the bakers led them to the work space where all three cakes were being decorated—one for the rehearsal dinner, the groom's cake and of course, the

grand, three-tiered wedding cake. Julia took pictures with
her phone and sent them to her sister. She got a quick response that, to Julia's great relief, everything except one of
the shades of pink frosting passed muster. After straight-
ening that out, and double-checking the delivery times and
addresses, she crossed the bakery visit off the list.

She and Logan stood at the bakery window. The reporters were waiting, clogging the sidewalk out front. Logan
was finishing a cookie he'd talked out of the girl working
behind the counter.

"What happened to 'the camera adds ten pounds'?"
Julia asked as he wiped crumbs from the corner of his
mouth.

"I will always relax the rules for a chocolate chip cookie.
It's my one weakness." He cleared his throat. "Well, that,
and my desire to pop one of these reporters in the mouth."

"I don't even want to go out there." Julia hitched her
purse up onto her shoulder.

He rolled his neck to the side as if working out a kink.
"I don't know if I can take an entire weekend of this. I'm
tempted to just tell them I'm your boyfriend to get them
to go away."

Exactly what Liz suggested. "It might work," Julia muttered. Of course then she'd have to live with the story. And
the myriad ways in which her sister would pitch a connip-
tion. "I'd say we could go out through the alley, but we're
still going to have to walk right past them to get to the car."

He took her hand. "It'll be okay. I won't let anything
bad happen." He opened the door and out they went, back
into the belly of the beast.

They narrowly escaped the reporters outside the bakery
unscathed. One of them, a brutish man with a camera lens
so long that Logan wondered whether he was compensat-

ing for some shortcoming, had become particularly curt with his questions. It was clear he just wanted an answer. And Logan was inclined to agree, only because he himself had reached the boiling point.

Now they were being followed in the car again. "Maybe it's better if you just say something, Jules. The only thing you seem to be accomplishing is frustrating them."

"I wouldn't even know how to say it. You know me. Give me a script and I can deal with it. In front of cameras, with unfriendly faces barking at me, I get panicky. The next thing you know I'm tripping over my words and accidentally telling the press I'm pregnant. And I'll have to spill the beans then. I'm a terrible liar."

"That's probably an argument for just telling your parents about the baby before you mess up and the secret comes out."

"No way As long as you keep your end of the bargain and keep your mouth shut, it'll be fine."

"Personally, I don't think it's a risk worth taking. Just tell them. Then you can relax and enjoy the wedding."

Julia directed a piercing glare at him. "That's the most harebrained thing you've ever said. My plan is not only the best plan, it's the only plan. My baby. My plan."

Her plan. Jules was doing what she always did—putting her head down, forging ahead and ignoring what everyone else said. Like a beautiful steamroller. She was far better at handing out advice than taking it, which would make it impossible to change her mind. "And what exactly is the rest of your plan? What are you going to say to your parents about the baby's father?"

"I'm going to have to tell them the truth. You might be the dad. And you might not."

Hearing her say that didn't sting any less today than it had last night. "Have you taken the time to think about how they're going to react? Because there could be a lot of fall-out, and I'm sorry, but most of that is going to fall on me."

"You have to make everything about you, don't you?"

"No. I don't. I'm just thinking this through to its logical conclusion. Do you remember what your dad asked me the night I took you to senior prom?"

Her eyes narrowed. "What does that have to do with anything?"

"Just answer the question. Do you remember what he said?"

She reached into her bag, pulled out a lip balm and rolled it across her lips. Logan was thankful he was driving and only caught a glimpse of what she was doing. He had a soft spot for her mouth, especially for the things it could do to him.

"My dad asked you what your intentions were with his daughter. Doesn't every dad ask that?"

"Maybe in old movies, they do. My point is that your dad is an old-fashioned guy. And that's part of what I love about him. He's going to want to know if I'm accepting my responsibility. And I told you I'm willing to do that."

"Logan. You dumped me three months ago." She turned sideways in her seat and confronted him. "*Dumped* me."

He didn't want to feel remorseful about ending things with Julia, but he was starting to. Even though he was also certain that they wouldn't have made it through the summer. Julia would've gotten flighty. She would've started doing the things that made him question whether she wanted to be with him, and he never handled that well. "But that was before the baby."

"Precisely the reason this won't work. A baby is not a reason to be together. And I'm not going to be with some man who didn't want me three months ago, just because he's worried about what my dad might think."

"A child deserves two parents." It bothered him to hear his voice crack like that. A few words and the pain of losing his dad returned to the center of his chest, just as it had the night before. After all these years, it hadn't gotten easier; there were merely longer stretches of time when he could focus on other things. It was hard enough to think about how difficult it'd been on his mom to shoulder the responsibility of three boys, a mortgage and law school. It was even more difficult to recall the promise he'd made at the age of twelve, to his father, his hero, as he slipped away. *Don't worry. I'll be the man of the house. I'll take care of Mom and my brothers.* "I have to accept my responsibility. I owe you that much, and I won't allow your dad to think anything less."

Logan pulled up to the curb out in front of the Keyses' house. The reporters were parking their vans and cars. They'd be descending on them in no time. "We have to make a run for it, Jules. Now."

She gathered her things. Logan hopped out of the car and hurried around to Julia's side. They squeezed past the reporters, walking upstream against a rush of people coming at them. The obnoxious man with the big camera elbowed his way next to Julia, butting into her with his shoulder. The woman behind him pushed ahead. Too many people. On a narrow sidewalk flanked by parked cars and azalea bushes.

Julia stumbled. Her fingers splayed to brace her fall. Her purse flew out of her hand. Muscle memory took over. Logan lunged like an outfielder going for the ball. He curled his arm around Julia, pulling her into him. Everyone came to an abrupt stop.

"Are you okay?" he gasped. Adrenaline surged through his veins. That was too close. She could've been hurt. The baby could've been hurt.

She shook like a leaf, telling him exactly how rattled she was. "I'm okay."

"Don't move." He plucked her purse from the sidewalk and handed it to her. Turning back, he positioned himself directly between Julia and the reporters. He spread his arms wide. If they were going to come another step closer to her, they'd have to go through him. He set his sights on the reckless cameraman. "If you come within fifty feet of her again, you're going to be a very unhappy guy." *More like you're going to be in traction.*

The man puffed out his chest. "Are you threatening me? The sidewalk is a public right-of-way. We have the right to ask questions."

If only there weren't so many cameras trained on him. Two minutes and this guy would know not to get in Julia's face again. Reluctantly, Logan lowered his arms. He hated to do it, but he had to back down or this would escalate. He couldn't manage to unclench his balled fists, though. "Why don't you show some decorum? We're here for a wedding."

"Yesterday she was linked with one of the biggest stars in Hollywood, and now she's at her sister's wedding with her old boyfriend, one of the most successful athletes of the last decade. You can't blame us for wanting to know what's going on."

"Julia, just tell us if you dumped Derek for Logan and we'll leave you alone," one reporter shouted.

"Yeah. Just tell us," another voice chimed in. "Are you cheating on Derek? Is that why he's not with you for your sister's wedding?"

Oh hell no. Cheating? With him? Steam was about to pour out of Logan's ears. He turned back to Julia. The color had been sapped from her face. She looked so defenseless, not at all the self-assured woman he knew. All he could think about was the other helpless person in the middle of this—the baby. God, he'd been an ass last night. Julia was stuck at the center of two crises—Derek and the pregnancy—and he'd let his ego get in the way. The question of paternity was painful for him, but she had to live with much more. He did an abrupt about-face. "Julia and I are together. We're a couple. There's nothing with Derek."

For a second, everyone shut up. Then came a single question. "Is it serious?"

He had to act. And he had to say yes. What kind of man says he isn't serious about the woman he got pregnant? Once the baby news got out, that would be the media's logical assumption. "Yes. It's serious. Now leave us alone, please. Her sister is getting married and the family would like some peace."

"Give us a kiss for the cameras first," one of the reporters said. "So we know it's real."

"Don't push it," left Logan's lips before he realized what he was saying. He couldn't help it. Telling the press no was his gut instinct. And a kiss? As if his feelings weren't confused enough. Not that he didn't want to kiss her. He'd spent a good deal of time in her parents' living room yesterday wishing he could do exactly that. Before things got complicated. Again.

The reporters complained and grumbled. *Just a kiss and we're out of here.*

He was about to tell them to forget it when delicate fingers slipped into his hand. *Julia.* He turned. A sweet smile crossed her face. The color had returned to her cheeks. Although by the way she was now gripping his hand, he was fairly certain the flush was anger, not acquiescence.

"If you guys promise to let my sister get married in peace, you can have your kiss. But you have to promise." The words were for the reporters, but she directed them at

Logan. Her lips—the lips he'd fixated on so many times, were waiting right there for him. Pouty and plump.

We promise.

He didn't risk waiting another second, threading his arm around her waist. He witnessed the graceful closing of her eyes and took that as his cue to do the same, to shut out the press and tune out everything around them. When it was Julia and him, all alone, things could be right. It was the rest of the world that made things complicated. Her lips sweetly brushed his—a hint of warmth and sugar, enough to make the edges of his resolve melt and trickle away.

Pressing against her, he felt the newness between them. There was no visible baby bump yet, but there was undoubtedly something new there—a slight, firm protrusion of her belly. That hadn't been there at the beginning of the summer. New life. Was the baby his? Could it bring Julia back to him? Could it bring him back to Julia? Could he really get past that feeling that things would never be right between them?

Just like that, Julia ended the kiss and stepped away, turning toward the house. There was no sentiment, no moment of recognition for what had happened between them.

Logan cleared his throat, trying to conceal how disoriented he was. He was as thrown for a loop by her choice of tactics with the media as he was by his own. Julia, and that kiss, had turned his thinking upside down. "There you go, guys. I expect you to hold up your end of the deal." He turned to Julia and grasped her elbow to usher her ahead, but she stood frozen on the sidewalk. He caught the surprise on her face as she stared ahead at her parents' front porch. He followed her line of sight. The whole family was standing there—Mr. and Mrs. Keys, Tracy and Carter. Judging by their expressions, they'd heard—and seen—it all.

There were car doors closing and engines starting behind him. Probably the vultures on their way to the closest Wi-Fi hotspot to break the news. Or in reality, his little white lie.

"Tell me you didn't just start what I think you did," Julia muttered under her breath, smiling and waving at her parents.

Logan adopted the same phony grin and began walking up the sidewalk, squeezing Julia's hand.

"Tell me you didn't just do what I think *you* did. A kiss?"

"What about you? It's serious?"

His pulse was thumping, but he was sure he'd done the right thing. Mostly sure, at least. "I didn't have a choice," he mumbled. "Somebody was going to get hurt. You were going to get hurt. I had to make them go away. And you're worried about ruining your sister's wedding. That was going to ruin your sister's wedding."

Four

Tracy wasted no time letting her opinion be known. "Nice job making my big weekend all about you." She whipped around and stormed into the house.

Logan grimaced and shrugged, apparently at a loss for words. Julia wasn't doing much better. She was too busy trying to get her bearings after the kiss.

We're together?

This was a bad idea.

Fake romance or real, there would be no opening of those old wounds.

And yet here she was, holding Logan's hand, scaling the stairs to the wraparound porch and filing inside her parents' house. Logan closed the door after her, while her father clapped him on the shoulder.

The grin on her dad's face was as wide as the beach at low tide. "Sounds like I'll be marrying off a second daughter soon. Julia's mother and I had always hoped this day would come."

Married? Good God, what was it with the men in Julia's life assuming marriage was the next logical step? "Dad, isn't that a little presumptuous?"

"The man said serious. What else am I to presume?"

"We're so happy, Jules. We've always thought Logan was the only one for you." Her mother's ability to radiate warmth and happiness made everything worse. How would her parents feel when she told them her secret on Sunday? Would they only be happy for her if Logan was indeed the dad? Precisely the reason she didn't want a paternity test. She didn't want her baby to be judged because of who his or her father might be. It was such an old-fashioned fixation, anyway. She could be a mom on her own, with no need for a man. The baby was Julia's, and that was all anyone needed to know.

Julia sucked in a deep breath, not knowing what to say. Logan had put them in a horrible position. And admittedly, Julia had probably made it worse with the kiss, but the press had said they'd go away. She wanted that insurance. Still, playing fast and loose with the truth... Julia might be an actress, but she sucked at lying. "Logan and I aren't together. He just said that to make the press go away."

"I knew it!" Tracy exclaimed, breaking her momentary silence. "At least Logan cared enough about me to do something about the problem." She shot Julia a pointed stare. "Unlike my sister."

"What about the kiss? That's what really made them go away."

Logan nodded in agreement. "True. The kiss was definitely Julia's idea."

Don't remind me.

"The kiss was fake?" Her mother's voice was rife with distress, just as it had been the day before when this all started. "No. It couldn't have been. It was so sweet. It looked real."

I bet. Julia still felt that kiss all over every inch of her body. Damn Logan and his resolve-destroying lips. "It was just what they asked for. A kiss for the cameras. Nothing else. I am a halfway decent actress, you know."

Julia had thought she'd have to fake her way through it, that she was still too mad at Logan for the way he'd treated her. That wasn't the way it had gone at all. The second his lips fell on hers, her body cast aside any hurt feelings and went for it. Her traitorous mouth knew exactly what to do, and sought his warmth and touch, his impossibly tender kiss. Her body knew how perfectly they fit together, physically at least, and was all too eager to find a way for them to squeeze three months of lost time into a few short heartbeats.

Logan stepped forward. "Actually, it's not entirely true that Julia and I aren't together."

If Julia could've clamped her hand over Logan's mouth and make it look like an accident, she would have. Tracy threw up her hands, stomped once on the hardwood floor with her jeweled beachcomber sandal and began pacing the room. "Which is it? Will you two get your act together so we can go back to enjoying my wedding week?"

And to think that earlier today, Julia's big concern had been shades of pink frosting. Now she was far more worried about shades of red. Namely the various hues of crimson coloring her sister's face. Volcano Tracy was about to blow.

"I spent the last six months worrying about everything that could go wrong," Tracy continued, circling the room. "Would the church put us down for the wrong date? Would I find the perfect dress? Would the caterer serve fish instead of chicken? I never imagined that the person who would ruin it would be my own sister. You just can't let me have the spotlight. You *have* to create all of this drama. You can't live without it, can you?"

Julia's father stuffed his hands into the pockets of his flat-front khakis. "Now wait a minute, Trace. We're just having a conversation. Your mother and I would like to know what exactly is going on with Logan and Julia."

Yeah, Dad. Get in line.

"Julia and I had a long talk last night about…" Logan started, looking over to Julia as if he was waiting for her to say that now was a good time to come out with the baby news, which it absolutely was not.

Julia felt as though she was going to be sick. She tried to send him direct messages with her eyes. *One word and I'll never speak to you again.*

"Julia and I had a long talk about things," Logan finished, scratching his head. "No one should put the idea of Julia and me, together, out of the realm of possibility."

Julia would've let out a massive sigh of relief about the baby secret still being under wraps if she weren't so annoyed. The two of them together was out of all realms. She'd wasted enough of her life on men who didn't love her.

The smirk on Tracy's face showed zero amusement. She wagged her finger in the air. "Oh no. I'm calling BS on this. Jules, you told me you two were done. And with good reason, remember? I didn't spend all those hours on the phone listening to you cry for nothing."

Tracy had indeed clocked a lot of time listening to her sob into the phone. She knew Julia and Logan's long history, the one that had taken its first horrible turn when Julia broke up with Logan before they both went off to college. Tracy had listened to Julia complain year after year about the women Logan was linked to in the tabloids—always models, always stunning and perfect, one of them even becoming his fiancée for a short time. Even though his engagement hadn't lasted, it ate at Julia like crazy, and Tracy had to suffer right along with her sister. Tracy knew exactly how dysfunctional they were together.

"Tracy Jean. I don't know why you'd be so rude to your sister," their mother said.

"Come on, hon." Carter walked up behind Tracy and set his hands on her shoulders. "Why don't you and I go in the kitchen and get a nice, cold drink?"

Tracy shrugged her way out of Carter's grip. "Oh, please. I love you, but you don't see what's going on, and you're yet another person who thinks Logan can do no wrong. And Mom, don't even start with rude. All I'm saying is that Julia and Logan have zero business being together. That ship has sailed. I mean, seriously, Jules? After what happened after the reunion?"

Well, then. Was Tracy about to air Julia's dirty laundry in front of their parents? Julia's mind raced for diversion tactics. If only an earthquake could hit the coast of North Carolina right now. Or a hurricane, at least.

"Did I miss something?" Julia's father asked.

Logan cleared his throat and bugged his eyes at Julia. As if that was going to help her figure a way out of this mess. Or keep Tracy's mouth from running. Sweat dripped down Julia's back, part nervousness, part the iron fist her dad used to rule the thermostat. "Dad, can we please turn on the air-conditioning?"

"Julia and Logan slept together," Tracy blurted, not giving her dad a chance to answer. "And then he dumped her."

Julia braced for a gasp of disgrace from her mother or a disapproving grunt from her father.

"I'm sorry to hear that," Julia's mother said. "But couples have rough patches. You and Carter should know that better than anyone. You two broke up for an entire year before you got back together and got engaged."

"You're both smart. I'm sure you'll work everything out," their father said, easing into his wingback chair as casually as if they'd all been discussing where to go to dinner.

I'll be damned. That in itself was pure evidence of how much her parents adored Logan. Talk of premarital sex—words spoken out loud, in the living room of the scandal-free state senator from New Hanover County and his wife no less, and not a judgmental peep came from either of them.

"This really doesn't seem like a topic for polite conversation," Julia said. *Or even impolite conversation.* "Let's get back to focusing on the wedding. Logan got the press to go away. Let's be thankful for that."

Tracy arched her eyebrows and cracked a fake smile. "The only way it stays that way is if you two put on a convincing show. For everyone. The wedding guests, the people at your hotel. All of our friends and family. They can't all be in on your little lie, or it'll just get out and that will bring back the press with a vengeance."

Oh no. Julia's stomach sank. Tracy was right. They couldn't trust anyone beyond these four walls with the truth. Julia didn't even want to think about the return of those awful reporters, especially the guy with the big lens. They were going to have to put on a show. A convincing show of love and affection and romance. Great. Julia sighed. If that was what it would take, then fine. For now, she only wanted peace and calm. And somewhere to sit. And maybe a cheeseburger.

Her grandmother's antique cuckoo clock in the foyer chimed three o'clock, which really meant it was two thirty. The thing had never worked right. "The afternoon is wasting away. Trace, don't you and I have a date to decorate the beach house for the rehearsal dinner? It's our only real chance for sisterly bonding this weekend." *And I can un-ruffle a million feathers.*

"Honestly, Jules, you ruined it. I need a nap so I can calm down. I'm worried I might strangle you if we spend any time alone."

Julia swallowed, hard. That certainly clarified things. "Okay. I understand."

"Tell you what," Logan interjected. "Jules and I will take care of the decorating."

There he goes. Logan Brandt to the rescue.

"That would be wonderful," her mother said. "Plus, it sounds like it'll be good for you two to have some alone time."

Alone time. Good Lord.

"Happy to do it," Logan said.

"Yep." Julia nodded. Speaking as little as possible seemed like the only way to make a graceful exit from this house. Her entrance had been anything but.

After a quick trip to the bathroom, Julia joined Logan in the car, and they were on their way to perform their new wedding duties.

"I'm starving." Julia tore open the wrapper on a pro-tein bar she'd stuck in her purse. Her stomach rumbled, but gladly accepted the sustenance. "And this isn't going to be enough. I need real food."

Logan nodded, surveying the road ahead, a wide stretch of shopping plazas, gas stations and eateries. "Unless you want to find a sit-down restaurant, your options are chain fast food or biscuits."

Ooh. The dilapidated sign for Sunset Biscuit Kitchen was straight ahead. It'd been years since she'd eaten there. It wasn't exactly camera-friendly cuisine, but her pregnant appetite had her salivating at the thought of their fluffy, buttery pieces of heaven. "Biscuits."

"I was hoping you'd say that." Logan pulled into the parking lot of the restaurant, which was really more like a shack, with a battleship-gray exterior and a faded red roof. There was no drive-through or dining room—just a walk-up window and if memory served, lightning-fast service. "The usual? Fried chicken biscuit and a hash brown?"

"How do you remember this stuff?"

"I remember everything."

That was indeed her standard, very unhealthy order. But she wanted more than that. "Can you also get me a sausage and egg biscuit? And an extra biscuit with honey? You know. Just in case."

Logan nodded and smiled. "I like this whole pregnant and hungry thing. It's adorable."

"Adorable?"

"It's a nice change of pace. I spend entirely too much time with women who order side salads and nothing else."

As if Julia wanted or needed the vision of Logan's penchant for supermodels planted in her head. "Yeah, well, I'm going to have to spend every waking minute in the gym after this baby is born. But for now, I want to eat everything."

"I'm on it. One order of everything, coming up."

Logan hopped out of the car and strolled up to the ordering window. Maybe it was the aftershocks of the kiss, but she had to admire him as he walked away. How could she not? From a purely objective standpoint, one having nothing to do with hurt feelings or history, he was a spectacular specimen.

Luckily, the line wasn't long in the middle of the afternoon. Julia didn't think she could endure much of a wait. Logan was back in a few short minutes, white parchment bag, two bottles of water and a fat stack of paper napkins in hand.

He opted to drive and eat, and they went for an entire fifteen minutes without argument or conflict, Julia's stress level dropping with each artery-clogging but oh-so-delicious bite—crispy buttermilk fried chicken tucked inside a light-as-air biscuit. But then Logan finished his sandwich.

"I can't believe you couldn't keep our secret until we had a chance to talk about it. I had it all worked out and you ruined it."

"Our secret? Oh, no. That was your secret, not mine. You need to have your head examined. You made everything fifty times more complicated."

"I made the press go away, didn't I?"

"Yes. And apparently my parents would like to present you with a key to the city for doing so. In the meantime, they're going to be that much more confused on Sunday when I tell them about the baby. They're going to be asking themselves what exactly did all of that mean. Especially when you had to tell them that we talked about us last night."

"It doesn't have to be confusing, Jules. If you'd think about reality for a minute and realize that I'm your best shot at giving the baby a real father."

She knew for a fact he wasn't thinking straight. He was letting his macho brain run the show, and that never went well. He was relishing the idea of being her knight in shining armor, and although she appreciated the gesture, she knew how empty a promise it was. As soon as he realized the reality of what he was saying, of what he was getting into, he'd take it back. And then where would she be? Right where she was the last time he rejected her.

Plus, she knew Logan. He hated every guy who had

come along after him. Every last one. There was no way he would want to play Dad if it turned out that her ex was the father. She always stopped herself before she got much further in her thinking, wondering what that moment would be like. It was better for her to think of the baby only as hers—50 percent of her DNA, 100 percent of her heart. Julia wouldn't allow paternity to cloud her feelings for her child. Her future was the baby, making it work, finding happiness in what would become the new normal. Mother and child. Everyone else could worry about themselves.

"Right now, I'm focused on the only thing I can control, which is being a good mother. I can't afford to depend on anyone else, especially not a man."

"It's not a sign of weakness to count on someone."

"I'm not worried about how it might look if I agree with you. I'm worried about how bad it would feel if and when you changed your mind. Plus, let's not forget the most damning detail."

He stopped at the stoplight that T-boned into Lumina Avenue signaling for the left turn. It was as if they'd turned back the clock thirteen years and he remembered exactly where they were going. "Well? I'm waiting for the most damning detail."

Julia sighed quietly and looked out the car window, admiring the gorgeous shades of pink and purple that colored the edges of the darkening late-afternoon sky. So beautiful. So romantic. "We aren't in love, Logan."

Well, one of us isn't. The realization had been there in her head from the moment she saw him yesterday. Everything she'd convinced herself of over the summer was wrong. She wasn't over him at all. She was just going to have to try harder. It was a matter of survival. Of course, that wasn't going to be easy when they were keeping up their charade for the public and the array of guests at the wedding. She could see it now. Holding hands. Pet names. Kissing. Good God, kissing. How was she supposed to try harder to fall out of love with him at the same time they were expected to kiss? This would require her greatest acting skills. No doubt about that.

"Maybe we just need to figure out a way to fall back in love," he said, as if the statement was of little consequence.

The mere fact that he suggested they figure it out proved that he didn't love her. No one who was in love found it necessary to figure it out. "You can't force it. Either it's there or it isn't." Talk about a damning detail. If ever there was one, that was it.

Logan slowed down the car and pointed up ahead. "That's it, right?"

"Yep."

"I'm so used to finding it in the dark. I was worried I might not recognize it."

"Well, it just got a new paint job. My parents did some sprucing up for the wedding. I can't wait to see inside. This will be my first time."

Logan turned into the driveway of her parents' beach getaway, the one that had once belonged to her grandparents on her mom's side. The parking area was tucked underneath, the house up on stilts for the times when mid-Atlantic hurricanes lapped an extra twenty feet of water up over the dunes. She opened her car door and a waft of briny ocean, carried on a sticky breeze, hit her nose. It brought with it a wealth of memories, many starring Logan. He pulled plastic bins of party decorations from the trunk, and Julia led the way to the wood stairs up to the front door. Even with a fresh coat of butter yellow on the shaker siding of the house, every sensory cue shuffled images through her mind, like flipping through the pages of an old photo album. With the roar of the waves, the wind catching her hair and having him so near, distant moments felt like yesterday, the most palpable of which were the times when Logan had been her everything. And she had been his.

"You okay, Jules? Carsick again?" Logan was at her side as she paused at the front door with the key in the lock. His hand went to her lower back, true concern in his warm and gentle eyes.

It isn't even funny how not okay I am. She nodded. "Yeah. I'm good. We should probably go inside and get started, huh?"

"No time like the present."

Yes, it was now time to start, right where it all began.

Five

Logan followed Julia into the beach house, hardly believing his own eyes. Was this really the same place? Once dark, cramped quarters, the kitchen seemed nearly twice its original size. It was completely open to the living room thanks to the obliteration of an entire wall, the space crowned with high-beamed whitewashed ceilings. Where there had once been dark cabinets, wood paneling and avocado-green appliances sat their modern-day counterparts in white and stainless steel. "Your parents practically gutted the place. It looks incredible."

Julia nodded, appearing pleased as she admired the room. She ran her hand along the edge of the gleaming marble countertop on the center island, another new addition. "It does look great, doesn't it? I really hope Tracy's happy with it."

In Logan's estimation, Tracy was a complete brat if this didn't show her just how hard her family was trying to make her wedding as perfect as could be. "She'd better be happy. She'd better be thanking your parents for days."

Julia wandered into the living room, past a sprawling white sectional couch. Judging by the immaculate upholstery, it was brand-new. The old brick fireplace had undergone a makeover of stacked stone, topped with a distressed wood mantel hosting an array of framed family photos. He was oddly thankful for the considerable house renovation. It took an edge off the memories. It was difficult enough to be here with her, trying hard to keep from kicking up the dust of old memories, all while dealing with the issues of the present.

"How'd your parents afford to do this? There's no way a state senator makes a big salary, and your mom's a teacher." Logan joined her at the expanse of glass doors at the far side of the room that led to the sprawling deck. White rocking chairs pitched forward and back in the wind.

"They didn't afford it. When Tracy told me she wanted to get married here and that Mom and Dad were going to take out a second mortgage to spruce it up, I just sent a check. It seemed silly for them to be spending money on this."

"Wait a minute. I thought they were just doing the rehearsal dinner here. The ceremony's in town at the church down the street from the River Room, isn't it?"

"Yes. As soon as Tracy realized how hard it'd be to wear heels in the sand, she changed her mind about getting married on the beach."

"You spent tens of thousands of dollars so your sister could have a nice place for a rehearsal dinner and not have to worry about her shoes?"

"You haven't seen the shoes. They're really cute." She grinned and shrugged it off. "This is as much for my par-

ents as anything. They're so close to retirement. I wanted
to do something nice for them."

Julia wasn't one of the most generous people Logan had
ever met, she was *the* most generous. Logan had been on
the receiving end of her generosity many times, especially
when it came to advice and support. If you called Julia in
the middle of the night, she'd answer. And she'd listen, no
matter how long it might take to unravel a problem. It was
a wonderful quality, but it also meant people took advantage of her. Especially men.

Had Logan taken advantage in June? That night when
she was a damning mix of long legs and a laugh that was
like truth serum? That night when she was all open ears
and sympathy? That night when her touch electrified him
and reminded him that busted baseball career or not, he
was still alive? "That was awfully nice of you. You'd think
Tracy would lay off the extra-demanding routine considering all of that."

"It's her big day. I get it. It doesn't matter what I did last
week or last month to help out. Right now is what matters,
and she wants it to be perfect."

Julia stared off at the surf as if she were hypnotized.
Daylight was fading, coloring the sky with a swirl of pink
and orange that only made her more radiant. It wouldn't
be long until the moon would be making its appearance
on the horizon; night would be falling. They'd be all alone
in this beautiful house, no one expecting them anywhere,
all while his body persisted in sending potent reminders
of the kiss they'd shared mere hours ago.

He cleared his throat. If he thought for too long about
her lips on his, he might do something stupid—namely acting like they could kiss without hurting each other. "And
you want to give that to her."

"My sister and I fight, but we love each other a lot. We still talk almost every day."

Precisely the reason why Tracy knew what had happened at the reunion. "So I gathered by her reaction to the idea of you and me together."

She shook her head, seemingly bringing herself back to reality. Without so much as looking at him, she headed back to the kitchen island and began pulling party supplies out of the bins. "I had to tell somebody. I was pretty wrecked by the whole thing."

He'd been so certain at the time that it was the right call. Now, alone with her, part of him wanted somebody to smack him upside the head. Regardless of right or wrong, no matter if it had been smart to want to save himself, he'd messed up. "I'm sorry, Jules. Really, I am. It was never my intention to hurt you."

She shot him a look of pure skepticism, then unloaded strands of Christmas lights. "You knew it was going to hurt. I don't buy it for a minute that you didn't know that."

He *had* known that, but in the heat of the moment, angry that their frustrating past was repeating itself again, he hadn't worried about it much. "I figured you'd get over it pretty quickly. It's not like you don't have a million guys falling at your feet."

She chuckled, but it wasn't in fun. "Oh, please. Remind me to call you the next time I'm sitting around at home with absolutely zero guys at my feet. It happens all the time."

He had to stop himself from unleashing his own laugh. She was deluded about what she could have if she'd just settle on one person. "That's a choice you make and you know it. As soon as you finally decide you want to be with one person, you'll have no problem."

The look of hurt that crossed her face made him wish

he could take back his words, even though they had been the reality, and something she needed to hear. "That's hilarious coming from you. And I haven't decided anything. The men in my life have a real talent for making those decisions before I have a clue what's going on."

"Probably because they're the wrong men."

"Probably." She crossed her arms, pressing her lips together tightly, telling him without words that she considered him a member of the group of men labeled "wrong."

"Oh, come on. I'm not like those guys. It's not the same thing at all. What you and I had was different."

"Is it really that different? You think it's some special snowflake? Because the end result is the same. I'm on my own. Except this time I have a baby to worry about."

"You're just being stubborn about that. I told you I'd accept my responsibility."

Her jaw immediately tensed. Normally that might make him worry that he'd angered her, but the truth was it made her lower lip jut out in a very sexy way. So he'd take it. Her eyes blazed and she balled up her hands. That wasn't quite as sexy. She grabbed a roll of streamers and nailed a sofa cushion with it.

"Nice throw."

"I was imagining the couch was your face."

"Oh." He kneaded his forehead. He no longer had to wonder how mad he was making her.

She closed her eyes and took a breath so deep her shoulders rose to her ears. "Can we please talk about something else? After everything else today, I really don't want to get into this right now."

Logan stuffed his hands into his pants pockets, fighting his own brand of frustration. The circles he and Jules could talk in had worn a hole in his psyche. He didn't have the mettle to push her more tonight if it would only lead to an argument. "Fine."

"Let's focus on the wedding." She returned to rummaging through the box. "Make yourself useful and get the stepladder. I think it's in the laundry room."

"I'll be right back."

He wound his way down the hall past the bedrooms to the laundry room in the back corner of the house. This space hadn't seen much of a makeover aside from a fresh coat of white paint and what appeared to be a new washer and dryer.

Feeling nostalgic about a laundry room was odd for sure, but he and Jules had once had a pretty epic, albeit brief, make-out session in this exact place. He'd been invited over for a family cookout and bonfire a few weekends after they became boyfriend and girlfriend. Julia had spilled mustard on her top and was headed inside to change and treat the stain. After an exchange of pointed glances, Logan had gone with her, saying he needed to use the bathroom. With her parents watching their every move, they'd both known it was likely the only time alone they would get. She'd practically slammed the door shut once they were inside the laundry room. *I need to take my shirt off or this stain will never come out.* Logan had never before been thankful for an accidental condiment spill.

His hand had been up her shirt before then, but that moment had been different. He could finally see her—every beautiful vulnerability. They'd known they only had about five minutes before Julia's very observant father came looking for her. They'd made the most of it—frantic kisses against the door, tongues winding, hands everywhere. It took Logan hours to cool off that night, and he couldn't help but lie in bed when he got home and

think about Julia and how perfect she was and how lucky
he was that she was his girlfriend.

A few days later they had sex for the first time. Julia
had been a virgin, making him that much more nervous.
He hadn't been particularly experienced, either. After that,
their young love had grown so fast it was as if it had been
rushing to fill the corners of the universe. Every day was
magical, even when they fought, which was often. Even
so, they'd been incapable of getting enough of each other.
Never enough.

Just thinking about how all-consuming it had once been
was a little overwhelming, since it eventually led to unhappy memories. It had been such a shock to the system
when Julia ended it. The girl who had lifted him out of the
fog of losing his dad had removed herself from his life. Of
course he'd kept a stiff upper lip that day, playing it off,
agreeing that it was for the best. What else could he have
done? They were both going off to college. And everyone
had preached to them for months that high school sweet-
hearts never made it long-distance.

He took a deep breath, stopping himself from exploring this train of thought. The past was only clouding up
the here and now, and he only had a few days to convince
her they needed a solid plan. If the baby was his, he was
not about to be the guy negotiating weekends and joint
custody.

He found the stepladder in the corner storage closet and
brought it out to Julia. "You put on some music," he noted.

"You and I could use the distraction." Julia fanned a
piece of paper in the air. "Tracy drew up a schematic of
how she wants the room decorated."

"Wow." Logan studied the drawing, which had all the
specifics about where streamers and strands of lights were
to go. He hadn't seen such attention to detail since the team

manager laid out the team strategy for game seven of the World Series. "Seems like we could've paid someone to do all of this."

"This was supposed to be my quality time with my sister. And honestly, she's way too much of a control freak."

Runs in the family. "It's a lot of work for a cookout for the wedding party and family."

"Doesn't matter. As big sister and maid of honor, I'm obliged to carry out her wishes." Julia handed Logan the trail end of a string of lights. "As best man, you are similarly obliged. So let's get to work."

Logan followed orders, scooting the ladder all over the room, moving furniture when needed, and looping lights and streamers as instructed.

"How's the new job going?" Julia asked, carefully looking over his work. "I have to say the wardrobe department puts you in some pretty interesting ties."

He wasn't sure how he felt about the fact that all she'd noticed was what he was wearing. At least she'd tuned in. "Do you watch often?"

"Every now and then. If I'm flipping through the channels."

"So I'm not a destination so much as something you pass by." The irony of that statement wasn't lost on him.

"What about you? How many of my movies have you seen in recent history?"

Logan didn't watch Julia's movies. The reigning queen of romantic comedies, she almost always had at least one on-screen kiss and sometimes even a bedroom scene. He couldn't handle that. Pretend or not, even when she wasn't his, the idea of her with another man made him crazy. "You know me. I don't get to the movies."

"That's such a lousy excuse. They're all on TV. *Losing Mr. Wonderful* is practically on a continual cable loop."

She shook her head in dismay. "And you're just avoiding my question. Do you like your new job?"

Yes, Logan had deflected on this subject. It wasn't that he hated his job so much as it wasn't the same. It wasn't taking the field and playing. "I like it. It's a challenge. But I'm getting used to it."

Julia handed him another string of lights. "You don't have to try to convince me. I know you better than anyone."

He sucked in a deep breath and climbed a rung higher on the ladder. He didn't want to tell her the truth. It led to a place where she pitied him, and he hated that more than anything. "I don't want to talk about it."

"Logan, just tell me. You know I'm a good listener."

"I know you are. I don't need the advice right now. I'm fine." He glanced down to see a doubtful smirk cross her face.

"If you don't like your job, you should just quit. Go do something else."

Why had he even bothered to deflect? She wasn't about to let it go. "It's not that. It's that nothing is going to replace baseball. I can't do what I really want to do, and you already know that."

"You know what you should do? You should write a memoir. You've led this amazing life, and you've always been an excellent writer. I'm sure it would be a bestseller." She waltzed off to one of the bins and fished out more bundles of lights.

"See? You're trying to fix my problems. Maybe I don't need you to fix me. Maybe I'm just fine the way I am."

"Why is it so hard for you to accept a little encouragement from me? It's okay to stop being the big, strong man for a few minutes, you know."

"I could ask you the same thing. Why is it so hard for you to accept my help?"

"If you're referring to your offer to marry me, we should agree that it's best if we're just friends."

Friends. Yes. Could they ever get beyond that? Three months ago, his decision had been absolutely not. But that was before the baby. That was before she needed him. Finally, for once, she needed him. "Maybe we could make another try at more than friends." This was a different and softer approach than the one he'd taken last night, one that might actually work if she'd listen.

"Ummm. No." Julia crossed her arms over her chest, then gazed up at the ceiling, scrutinizing his work. "And no to that, too." She pointed at the spot where he'd just hung lights. "Redo that."

"What's wrong with it?"

"They're not looped at the same height as the other ones. It doesn't match."

Logan grumbled and hopped off the ladder to grab a drink of water, partly annoyed by being bossed around by his high school sweetheart about holiday lights. The other part of him bristled over her quick dismissal of the notion of being more than friends. "A few cocktails tomorrow night and no one's going to notice, you know."

"Well, I don't get to drink, so I'll notice." She stepped onto the ladder, grabbing the top rung and making it clear she was on her way up. "I'll do it."

He rushed over to her, not thinking, just reacting. One hand landed on the ladder, the other on her hip. "No, you don't. You are not climbing up there."

She turned in his arms, gorgeous locks of hair cascading around her face. "Oh, please. I'm fine."

He should've stepped back, let her get down from the single step she'd taken, but he didn't want to. His body wanted this. And this was the one part of their chemistry that Julia had a hard time resisting. So let her resist. Let her tell him that she didn't want to at least explore things when he had his arms around her. "You and the baby are not getting hurt. Not on my watch."

"Please promise me you won't accidentally say something like that out loud in front of my family."

"I'm serious, Jules. I'm not kidding around. You and the baby. It's a game changer for us. You can't deny that." He gripped her waist and carefully lifted her, lowering her to the safety of the floor. He didn't let go. The notion of game changers had him wondering how he could ever do the same to her mind. As if fate was trying to give them both a nudge, a song came over the radio that had powerful memories for them both.

Recognition crossed Julia's face and she smiled, pressing her hand to her chest. "This song. Oh my God. I love this song."

The arrival of this song was about as ill-timed as could be. It had been Logan and Julia's make-out song when they were in school. Only a few notes in and Julia was already melting, probably not a good idea considering whose arms she was in. And yet she wasn't really sure she cared that this was a bad idea. After twenty-four hours of painful truths and uncomfortable secrets, it was too easy to give in to the one thing that felt good—Logan's hand at her waist, carefully sliding to her back, as if he was hoping to do it undetected. This was comfortable. Familiar. And she wanted that now more than anything.

He took her hand and began swaying them both back and forth.

"Typically, a guy asks a girl to dance. He doesn't just

launch into it without an invitation." She felt the need to at least feign a protest.

He smiled, sending a trickle of electricity down her spine. "I'm not big on asking. And you'll just say no."

Forget the song—she had little defense for Logan when he was acting like this. Romantic. Slightly bossy. Sexy as all get-out. This was precisely the version of Logan she couldn't resist at the beginning of the summer. This was the Logan who could leave her undone with a single glance. Dancing was the least of her worries—all he had to do was look at her in the right way and she'd be clay in his very capable hands.

"I'm worried about what might happen if there's too much touching."

"It's just a dance. We're taking the room for a spin. Seems like part of our due diligence as best man and maid of honor. We wouldn't want Tracy to tell us tomorrow that something's wrong with the way the lights are strung."

"You're just saying that because I'm trying so hard to keep her happy."

"Okay, then. How about this? You and I have to convince a whole lot of people that we're a couple. Consider it practice."

She couldn't argue with him on that. And at least she felt like she had someone on her side, stuck in her proverbial boat. Where would she be right now if she didn't have Logan? Feeling even more alone than she already did. At least someone knew her secret. And someone understood how she felt about making her sister happy. It was merely an unfortunate coincidence that her ally in secret-keeping and wedding planning also happened to be the man who broke her heart.

Logan continued with the dance, committing to it with a more deliberate sway. He squeezed her hand and pressed into her back with his other hand. Julia admired the hand-some and cocky grin on his face as each musical note pulled her further under his spell. It was like his lips were sending her secret messages. *Just another kiss, Jules. You know you loved the one from earlier today.*

His eyes drifted lower, and she couldn't help but be amused by the way he unsubtly ogled her cleavage.

"My eyes are up here, mister."

A guilty smile crossed his lips. "What? It's impossible not to look. I mean, they're right there."

"They've always been right there."

He cocked an eyebrow. "Not like this, they haven't." He shook his head. "Never mind. Forget I said anything."

"No. What were you going to say?"

He pulled her closer, pressing their chests together, his mouth drifting to her ear. "I'm not saying another thing on the subject. I'll just get into trouble." The heat of his breath grazed her neck, sending a rush of warmth through her.

"Fine. Then dance with me." She gave in to the moment, settling her head against Logan's shoulder. He pulled her even closer and held her tight. Side to side, slow and steady, feet moving only slightly, their dance continued into a different song—less meaningful in terms of their shared history, but still laid-back and sexy. His warmth poured into her, wrapping her up in contentment.

"I was thinking about the parties you and Tracy used to have here. The ones your parents didn't know about," Logan said.

"They were fun, weren't they?" So many of her memories of this house were tied to those parties. After Julia had gotten her driver's license, she and Tracy used to sneak the keys to the beach house and invite friends over. Neither girl had been particularly wild, and Julia always insisted the guest list be small and they leave the house immaculate, but they certainly did things they shouldn't have been doing—drinking beer and kissing boys, mostly, although Tracy had far more luck in that department than Julia. That was until the night Logan showed up.

"Of course, I think the first one I came to was the most fun."

She had to smile. "It might have been the best night ever." It had been the best—a huge turning point for her. Emboldened by half a can of light beer, Julia finally had the guts to talk to Logan. She'd been pining for him for more than a year before that. "We talked forever that night."

"A lifetime."

Indeed, they'd had an hours-long conversation out on the dunes, Julia with her knees pulled up to her chin and Logan stretching his legs and digging his feet into the sand. She'd never listened to anyone so eagerly, hanging on every word as Logan told her about losing his dad, about trying to be the man of the family, about baseball. Summer wind swirled, whipping at the beach grass as the roar of the ocean swelled and receded over and over again. It was literally a dream come true... Logan Brandt, the most perfect guy she'd ever laid eyes on, had not only noticed her, he'd talked to her. He'd held her hand. And then, beneath that impossibly beautiful midnight-blue sky, he'd done the thing she'd worried no boy as amazing as Logan would ever want to do. He'd kissed her.

Logan cleared his throat and began trailing his fingers along her spine. It felt so good. Too good. "I know I rambled on and on that night. I was nervous about kissing you."

"I don't believe that for a second. You were so smooth. You've always been the smooth guy."

"Something about you made me question my kissing ability."

She laughed quietly. "You were perfect. Absolutely perfect." Julia could've sworn she floated on air for two days after that first kiss. Even if nothing else had ever happened between them, she could have lived off the memory for a lifetime. When he'd asked her a week later to be his girl-friend? She was so gone, up to her neck in her first love, the then-shy Julia didn't even bother with an answer. She'd thrown her arms around his neck and kissed him like her life depended on it. Was there any better feeling than that? Julia didn't think so, even now. That love had transformed her. It had made her believe that she was lovable. She'd never really been sure of it before that.

"I'm not sure I buy it when you say you felt nothing from our kiss in front of the cameras." Logan's voice was low, resonating throughout her body. It wasn't just the kiss that made her feel something. Everything about him made her feel, and that was a terrifying feeling. Leaving herself open to him eventually led to hurt. Always.

A heavy sigh escaped her lungs. "It was a kiss. It didn't change my world," she lied.

Logan reared back his head and brought their dance to a stop. "I don't believe you."

"They're my feelings. I think I know what I did and did not feel." She tried to avoid his gaze, but he followed her with his, as if he was pleading for a retraction. "Fine. It was a nice kiss. You've always been a good kisser. Is that what you want to hear?"

"I'm not fishing for compliments. I felt something, and I think you did, too. I think you're trying to convince your-self of something that isn't the way it actually happened."

She shrugged, but she didn't like dismissing it. The temptation to give in and tell him how much she'd loved it was too great. He was wearing down her resolve, and she had to put a stop to it. "It was hours ago. I hardly even remember it."

"Then let me refresh your memory."

He clutched her neck and lowered his lips to hers. His mouth was warm and soft. Giving. Like Logan had an unlimited supply of affection and he was going to hand it out like candy. He dictated the pace—languid and dizzying, suggesting they deserved to take their time, and for the moment, she believed they did. Here they were, all alone, in this big empty house, all the time in the world. His mouth drifted to her cheek, his stubble scratching her nose, then he traveled to her jaw and kissed her neck. She kept her eyes closed, luxuriating in every heavenly press of his lips to hers, not wanting it to end.

"Tell me you don't feel anything," he whispered into her ear.

"I don't feel anything." She reasoned that she was merely following orders, but she'd actually become a fountain of fibs. She was surprised her nose wasn't growing. The truth was that she was feeling everything right now. Her entire body was so alert she could probably stay awake for the next twenty-four hours.

"You said it yourself earlier today. You're a terrible liar."

And you're a ridiculously good kisser. "I know what I said. You don't have to remind me."

Six

The ride back to the hotel was long. And quiet. Part of Julia was glad she'd had the sense to lie to him and pull them back from the precipice before bodies slipped out of clothes. And her sense slipped out of her brain. The other part of her, the hormonal part, was downright annoyed. She'd been in the arms of an eager Logan and she'd said she felt nothing. She'd lied and denied herself sex, all in the same breath. They could've christened the brand-new sofa. Regret was starting to needle her.

Focus on the baby. That was her key to keeping Logan where he belonged—in the strangest friend zone she could imagine. She had to keep her life in order for the sake of the baby. A child needed stability and normalcy. Allowing herself to be tangled up with yet another man who didn't love her was a recipe for anything but what she wanted to give her baby.

Logan pulled up in front of the hotel, and thankfully

the press had kept their promise. They'd stayed away. Finally, Tracy could be happy.

"Oh my God," Julia blurted. "Tracy."

"What now?" Logan asked, turning off the ignition.

"We can't stay in different rooms. Everyone thinks we're a couple. You saw the way that guy at the front desk looked at us when we checked in. He thought it was weird, and it was, because we stayed in the same room last time. If anyone is likely to tip off the press about something out of the ordinary, it's the guy working the front desk."

The valet approached. They were about to lose what bit of privacy they had. Julia's mind was whirring. She'd been psyching herself up for holding hands at the wedding reception and ignoring her feelings while doing it, not preparing for a roommate.

"Pardon me if I find this weird coming from the person who just told me she didn't feel anything when she kissed me."

"And I'm also the person worried about her sister's wedding. The press comes back and I'm sunk. But I have no clue how we're supposed to explain this to the people at the front desk."

He rubbed the side of his face as if he couldn't possibly stand another minute of thinking about this. "Don't worry about it. I'll come up with something."

Easy enough for Logan to say. Right now, Julia was worried about everything, especially the realization that she and Logan were about to share a room.

Logan turned the keys over to the valet and they went inside. The man with the familiar face was again manning the front desk.

"Yes. Hi," Logan started, clearly stalling. So much for coming up with something. "I need to check out of my room. I had a cold when we arrived, and I didn't want Ms. Keys to get sick when she's…"

Julia kicked Logan's foot. "He didn't want me to get sick right before my sister's wedding. It would be a disaster."

The desk clerk hesitated, looking back and forth between them, the moments ticking by at half speed. "Of course, Mr. Brandt. I'll send a bellman up to your room to move your belongings for you." He tapped away at his keyboard while Julia silently let out a sigh of relief.

"No need for that. I'll manage fine on my own."

"Let me know if you change your mind." The clerk swiped a room card. "And here's your extra key." The look he gave them said that he was in no way fooled, but Julia figured this guy had probably seen it all at this point.

They proceeded to the elevator. Today's second kiss seemed even more ill-advised now that she and Logan would be staying in the same room. Why did everything with Logan have to exist on such a slippery slope? She'd dipped her toes into those warm, inviting waters, and now it felt like she was up to her waist in trouble.

Logan went to collect his things while Julia quickly changed into pajama pants and a tank top. Apparently he was a light packer—he was opening her door minutes later, just as she was downing the second of the chocolates the maid had left on the pillows. She put her hands behind her back and crumpled the wrapper. Logan didn't need to know she wasn't just eating for two, she was eating chocolate for two.

"Hey, roomie," he quipped, flashing that beguiling smile of his and breezing into the room.

"Roomie is right. Platonic roommates. I don't want you getting any ideas." She discreetly dropped the evidence of her clandestine candy-eating into the trash.

"Getting ideas. You make me sound like a horny teenager. Don't worry about me. You made it pretty clear where you stand when you told me you didn't feel anything after our kiss." He wheeled his roller bag next to the bureau. "Which was a little odd considering how much you were actually participating in it."

"I plead hormonal insanity."

He toted his garment bag to the closet. "Where exactly do you expect me to hang my suit? You have enough clothes in here for a week."

"Oh, please. You're exaggerating." She walked over and began sliding hangers across the rod, cramming her clothes together. She took his suit from him and squeezed it in at the end.

"If it gets wrinkled, you're ironing it."

"Whatever it takes to appease you, Mr. Brandt." She turned and he was right there, peering down at her breasts. "You have got to stop staring at my chest."

"I'm sorry, but when it's just the two of us, it's really hard not to look." A sly grin crossed his face, and he looped his finger in the direction of her chest. "They're spectacular. And it's hard not to think about the reason why they look like that. It's surprisingly sexy."

Julia's head was swimming. She hadn't been prepared for that. Did he really feel that way? Pregnancy had made her feel anything but sexy—tired and starving most of the time, although she had to admit that being around Logan had a way of helping her find her more alluring side. "Thank you. I just wish they didn't hurt so much."

"Hurt?" Logan traipsed across to the other side of his room and kicked off his shoes.

"Yes. They're sore. You blow more air into a balloon, it stretches. Same principle."

"You paint a lovely picture." He turned and began unbuttoning his pants. "You're totally taking the fun out of the idea of you with larger breasts, though."

Before she knew what was happening, he'd shucked his jeans and was folding them neatly. In black boxer briefs that showed off his long, lean legs, he was doing far too efficient a job of helping her feel sexy. Probably because she couldn't have him. He was forbidden fruit, the shiny apple she wasn't allowed to take a bite out of, no matter how tempting he was, all because she'd promised herself she wouldn't. And now Mr. Temptation was unbuttoning his shirt.

"Will you please go change in the bathroom?" she sputtered, clamping her eyes shut out of self-preservation.

"You can't be serious. I'm getting ready for bed. It's late and I'm wiped out. Drama makes me tired."

"So put on your pajamas already."

"These are my pajamas."

"You can't just sleep in your boxers. You have to put on something else." Every breath out of her was coming way too fast. Her heart was hammering.

"I didn't pack anything else. And it's not like you haven't seen me in way less than this."

Holy crap. His voice was so close. Much closer than it had been a moment ago. She sensed him moving closer. She could feel the warmth radiating from his body. She was too scared to open her eyes. She already knew how amazing he looked half-naked.

"If you aren't nice, I'll just sleep in the nude."

She wrestled with the threat—be mean and have him take his clothes off. Dangerous, but not the worst deal in the world. "Fine. I'll be nice."

"Then open your eyes. I promise you'll live through it."

Yeah, right. She opened her eyes all right, but just as quickly whipped around to avoid the sight of him. That meant she was now confronted with the image of a king-size expanse of luxury linens atop what she already knew was a very comfortable mattress.

Guilt ate at her, about a lot of things—bogarting the chocolate, not telling him the truth about the kiss and knowing she'd be in the bed while Logan was stuck on the couch. "I got the extra blanket out of the closet for you. You can take one of my pillows."

"What are you talking about? There are plenty of blankets." Logan pulled back the duvet, slipping under the covers. Well, his legs were blanketed. His stomach and chest weren't. No, those parts of him were too busy building their torment in her body. Judging by the way her body temperature was spiking, they'd built an entire torment city. He patted her side of the bed. "Doesn't the mom-to-be need to get some rest?"

"Oh, no. You're sleeping on the couch."

"No way. Have you seen how short that thing is? It wouldn't fit a guy who's six feet tall, and we both know I'm a lot taller than that."

This was not happening. She could see it now—in bed with Logan, fast asleep, somebody's hand wanders, somebody starts spooning, one body part finds another body part and the next thing they know, the baby-making parade is under way again. "Fine. Then I'll sleep on it."

He bolted upright in bed. "I'm not letting a pregnant woman sleep on that couch. Stop being ridiculous. We're capable of staying in the same bed and things not turning to…you know. Sex."

"Why would you think that? We've never slept in the same bed without it turning to sex. Ever."

"That can't be right."

She nodded and dared to step closer to the bed, even though she was being dogged by memories of the last time they were sharing a room in this hotel. Everything she saw—the bedside tables, the lamps and of course half-naked Logan—brought her back to that magical weekend. "Think about it. Never. Ever."

He reclined against the pillows, placing his hands behind his head. Good God, now it was like he was posing for the cover of a men's fitness magazine. And she had to act as if she wasn't fazed, even when her eyes were drawn to his well-defined chest, his abs, that narrow trail of dark hair beneath his belly button. Deep down, she was anything but ambivalent—she wanted to read every square inch of his body like she was studying braille. *Deep breaths. Enjoy the view. You're fine.*

Stupid straight and narrow. Of course she wasn't fine.

He pursed his lips and nodded slowly. "Huh. Maybe you're right. Well, first time for everything, right? Unless you'd rather fully immerse yourself in the role of my fake, serious girlfriend and seduce me." He rolled to his side and propped up his head with his hand.

"I have plenty of roles to play right now, thank you. Let's just get some sleep, okay? We have a long day ahead of us and I'm exhausted." She gingerly climbed beneath the covers. That one movement caused goose bumps to pepper her arms. Why her body had this unrelenting reaction to Logan was a mystery. She only knew it was a constant, and even after all the years of ups and downs, showed no sign of abating.

She flipped off the lamp, plunging them into darkness and quiet. She rolled to her side, away from him. He shifted in the bed, but he did what he always did, which was more of a flop than a gentle roll. She tried to ignore it. Tried to pay no attention to what her body was telling her, to snug herself up to him, let him envelop her in those arms, keep her warm, make her feel safe.

He shifted in the bed again, except this time she heard his slow and measured breaths. He'd dozed off already. He'd always been like that. His body seemed to have little trouble finding sleep.

She turned to her other side, which was far more comfortable. That put her close enough to touch him, to feel his soft breath against her face. It was hard not to continue to cling to an alternate version of what had happened after the reunion. Thoughts of what this moment might be like if things had been different, if he hadn't called things off. If they'd kept it together all summer. If he'd just believed that they belonged together. The same way she did, however much it pained her to acknowledge it.

Reaching over, she pulled the covers up over his arm. She'd always care for him. That wasn't going anywhere. She knew that much. And he might be the father of her child. That wasn't going anywhere, either. Her mind leaped ahead to the end of the weekend, to that moment when she would tell her parents. Maybe she should've had the DNA test. But then again, if she had, and the baby wasn't his, Logan would remove himself from her life forever.

She placed her hand on her lower belly. If she was being completely honest with herself, there were far too many moments when she really wished that Logan was the dad. She wouldn't treat the baby any differently if he wasn't the father, but her heart really wanted it to be Logan. At least there had been love between them at some point. And despite their problems, they were friends. If there was a problem, she'd be able to call him, and she knew with certainty that he would help her. He would play the role of dad beautifully if that was what he became. As to the question of the role of husband and whether that day would come with her, the answer was no. She was too certain that friendship and attraction were not enough to sustain them. She needed him to love her.

Seven

"Ow! Ow!"

Logan opened one eye to darkness.

"Ow!" Jules yelped again. The bed shook.

He flipped on the lamp, wincing at the light, but alert. He hadn't really been asleep. Just dozing and replaying the kiss, along with her insistence that she'd felt nothing. "Are you okay? What's wrong?"

"Sorry. It's my leg. A cramp." She tossed back the covers and practically folded herself in half.

Scrambling out from under the comforter, he raced around to the other side of the bed. "Give me your leg." He grabbed her ankle, using both hands to flex her foot.

"Ow!" She reached for him, her face scrunched up in agony.

"Just lie back and try to relax." He gently raised her foot and planted it against his chest, massaging the calf muscle to unwind it from its painful contraction.

Julia knocked her head back on the bed and rocked it back and forth, a smile breaking across her face. "Oh, thank God. It's going away."

Logan pressed on her foot a little harder with his shoulder to get the full stretch while caressing her leg. Her skin was impossibly soft, conjuring so many pleasurable memories, accompanied right now by enticing visuals. Her pajama leg had slipped down to the middle of her thigh, revealing the part of her that he most loved wrapped around him. His hand spanned the back of her leg, rubbing from ankle to knee, up and down, the feel of her velvety skin slowly driving him mad, and yet there was no way he was about to let go. "Better?"

"Much. I keep getting charley horses in my sleep. It's a pregnancy thing. I'm sorry I woke you up."

"You didn't really. I was basically awake."

"I hope I wasn't snoring."

He laughed quietly. "You weren't. I was thinking about last night."

Several heartbeats of silence played out. "Last night?"

"The kiss. I don't want to give you a hard time about it, but am I crazy? Was there really nothing there?"

She chewed on her lower lip. Something of substance was running around in that beautiful head of hers, and he really hoped it wasn't the endless loop of denial. She sighed and looked him in the eye. "There was something there. There's always something there. Can't we leave it at that?"

Back and forth, he continued rubbing her leg. She was perfectly fine now. Her cramp was gone. He could walk away. Except that he couldn't, especially not after she'd finally told the truth. There in the soft, early-morning light, he couldn't get past how gorgeous she was. Rich brown hair splayed out against the white of the sheets, pleased grin on her face as she gave in to his touch, and then there were the sounds coming from her mouth. He kneaded her leg a little deeper with his fingers.

"That feels so good." Her voice was a sweet purr, uttering words he'd heard her say many times over their reunion weekend. She arched her back, then settled into the bed. Through the thin fabric of her tank top, he couldn't help but notice that her nipples had responded in a positive way. It took everything not to reach out and touch them. Not to lower himself to the bed and slip those skinny straps from her shoulders, cup her voluptuous breasts in his hands. Kiss her. Make her admit again that she felt something.

"Good. I'm glad. I like making you feel good." He couldn't have cared less that his words dripped with innuendo. All of the troubles and rough spots between them seemed so inconsequential right now. With the morning hours stretching out before them, all he wanted was to make love to her. He'd not only satisfy the thirst for her that never went away, he was certain that he'd know how she felt. He was tired of trying to interpret everything she said and did. The two rarely matched up.

With each pass of his hands, he made his journey a bit longer. He reached her slender ankle at the top of the pass, and now he was venturing beyond the back of her knee, lower and lower on her thigh.

"I could just stay like this all day." She put her hands behind her head and smiled. "My legs were killing me after all of that running around and standing all day yesterday."

"We don't need to be anywhere until your dress fitting, right?" That was at noon. He glanced at the clock, rubbing her leg, never losing contact. It was only a few minutes past seven. They had time. Oh boy did they have time. Everything in his body tensed at the idea, blood now fiercely coursing through him. Breathing became tougher, nearly

forced. Thinking wasn't much easier. Would his way back
in really be this simple?

"Yes. But don't talk about the wedding. It'll ruin the
mood." She closed her eyes, her full mouth relaxed, a look
of near-bliss on her face.

The mood. There was no mistaking that phrasing. He
slowed the pace of his hand, dipping below her knee, inch-
ing lower along her thigh. All he could hear was his own
heartbeat thumping in his ears and a breathy hum from
Julia. He knew that hum, and it meant only one thing. His
hand kept going, inches beyond previous passes. She didn't
flinch. Her eyes remained closed. His body reacted with
an abrupt stiffening in his chest, warmth creeping down
his torso and below his waist, the most primal of responses
to the beautiful creature in his clutches. Was this going
to happen? Or was he still asleep, and stuck in a dream?

Whatever Julia could say about Logan and the ways in
which he made her mad or hurt her, the man had amazing hands—one might go so far as to say he was gifted.
And then there was his incredibly firm chest. With her
foot planted against the muscular plane, she appreciated
how solid it was.

His hands might have started as givers of therapeutic
massage, but there was no mistaking their new role as tools
of seduction. She had zero inclination to fight it. She didn't
care to think about it. It was too good to be bad. Maybe
this was what they needed to figure things out—work out
their problems in bed.

He dipped his hand lower, his grip on the back of her leg
just strong enough to tell her his intentions. Or at least what
she surmised as his intentions. She begged the universe—
please don't let this be another time when she'd managed
to read him wrong. Her body was becoming far too accus-

tomed to the idea of what could be coming next—Logan's sleeping attire on the floor, followed quickly by her own.

His thumb rode along the inside of her thigh, his other fingers clamped around the outside of her leg, his palm creating heat and friction. Slow and rhythmic, his movements brought about a trancelike state, one in which she didn't care about repercussions or what might happen to her stupid heart if she let Logan back in. She only knew that she wanted him in. Inside. Her.

She opened her eyes, one at a time, nervous she'd built this all in her head, and all she'd see was a disinterested Logan. Her truth-seeking brought a rich reward—his eyelids heavy with desire. How she loved seeing that expression on his face. It was the sexiest thing she could imagine. So sexy that she was sure there was no luckier woman anywhere on the planet right now. They were all alone. The door was locked. Clothes coming off and kissing and touching and lovemaking...they all felt possible now. She squirmed against the bed, goose bumps popping up along the surface of her skin. Her face flushed with dry heat, as if she were basking in the sun. Every inch of her wanted him.

"Have I mentioned how good that feels?" she asked, pleased with how genuinely seductive her voice was.

"It feels good to me, too." His gaze was so intent, eyes dark and focused on her, as if he had nothing on his mind but consuming her.

But he wasn't making a move, and now her brain was searching for the next thing to say. He hadn't left her with an opening. He hadn't led her to the next step. Perhaps he was waiting for her to take charge. Not surprising considering the way things had gone since Wednesday afternoon. She'd put him in his place more than once.

She wiggled her toes, then dug them into the skin of his chest. His hand was on one of the heavenly downward passes. He was mere inches from her center now. Her pajama pants were as bunched up around her upper thigh as they could be. If he wanted to go any farther, he'd have to slip his hand beneath the fabric.

"My pajamas are in the way." She held her breath, waiting for his response.

"I noticed. What do you want to do about that?"

The low rumble in his voice made her back arch again. He wanted her to say it. If she was going to repay the pleasure of the last few minutes, he deserved as much. "I want you to take them off."

His eyebrows bounced, conveying a cockiness he'd earned. "I'm a big fan of that answer." He gently lowered her leg until it was hanging off the edge of the bed like her other.

He towered over her as her vision drifted across his strong shoulders, down his muscled chest and defined stomach. Her eyes dipped lower, and she relished the thought of what would soon be hers, as there was no hiding his current enthusiasm—and readiness—for sex. His warm fingers curled under the waistband of her pajama pants, sending a shiver down her spine as he shimmied the fabric down her legs. She never wore panties under her pj's; it always felt like an unnecessary extra layer of clothes. Aside from her tank top, she was as bare to him as she could possibly be.

They hadn't marked this first moment of vulnerability when they first made love after the reunion. They were both too eager, all action, stopping for few words. At least the first time. There was a stillness to this moment, an anticipation that left her breathless. Perhaps it was because this time they'd arrived by chance, the two of them falling together, as was their natural inclination.

He stepped out of his boxers and she had to shift up

onto her elbows to admire him, all chiseled physique and masculinity. A sly smile crossed his heavenly lips as he stretched out on the bed next to her. He cupped her face and kissed her softly, gently. He took his time. She loved that about sex with Logan. He rarely rushed, and she was always the priority, even when they were both feeling frantic. His tongue wound in languid circles with hers, enough to make her feel dizzy. Their two kisses yesterday had taken hours to shake off. She'd be lucky if she could stand up straight anytime soon after this one.

He flattened his hand against her belly and slipped it underneath her top. She sat up for a second and removed it, then settled next to him again. His hand slowly crept to the flat plane in the center of her chest, fingers smoothing up over the top of one breast; blood rushed to flood her skin, tightening her nipple.

"I don't want to hurt you. You'll have to tell me what's too much." He gently circled the hardened peak with the tip of his finger, teasing and making her crazy in the process.

"It all feels good right now. All of it." She watched as he lowered his head and gave her nipple a soft lick, swirling his tongue around it before drawing it into his mouth. She closed her eyes and reached down between them, wrapping her fingers around his steely length and stroking.

A low groan left his throat and his mouth returned to hers, kissing her with greater vigor than before. He rolled to his back and pulled her with him, inviting her to press her full body weight into his. They fell into a kiss both soft and intense, different from the other kisses this weekend. There was a freeness that hadn't been there before— probably the feeling of setting aside her reservations. She rocked her body against his, craving deeper contact, everything between her legs hungry for him.

Luckily, no birth control was necessary. She straddled

his hips, not giving up on their mind-blowing kiss, their tongues winding in circles as the scruff on his face faintly scratched at her cheeks and chin. He had the most amazing smell in the morning—the faintest traces of woodsy cologne, blended with sleep. It was intoxicating and all his own. She raised her bottom and took his erection in hand, guiding him inside her. Her eyes drifted closed as he filled her perfectly, inch by inch. The sense that she'd reached the promised land was immense, probably because she remembered exactly how good this would be, but it was an odd sensation—her body immersed in quiet jubilation and eager anticipation at the same time.

He took her breasts into his hands, squeezing, then raising his head and sucking on each nipple. The tension inside her had been quickly building already, but that sent her racing for her peak. She kissed him again, wanting to languish in this beautiful moment, knowing that whatever happened this weekend, she would at least have another beautiful memory to stow away in her head. He slipped his hand between their bodies, his thumb finding her apex. He wound it in tiny circles, knowing exactly how to play this, and she luckily could dictate the pressure with her body weight. Still, it was as if he'd been born with the instruction manual for her body inside his head, and he pursued a tempo that perfectly matched the rhythm of his thrusts.

His breaths came shorter now, much like hers, and the muscles of his torso and hips began to coil tighter beneath her. The peak was upon her, her breath hitching in her chest, and everything around her was falling away... everything except Logan. The waves kept coming, and then he cried out with a forceful thrust, his arms reining her in tightly. She collapsed against him as contentment enveloped her. She was exactly where she'd wanted to be from the moment she first saw him two days ago—safe in his embrace.

Logan didn't hesitate to pull her back into their kiss, the motions of his lips helping her savor this blissful moment.

Then Logan's cell phone rang.

It registered as a minor annoyance with Julia, but he ended the kiss, rolling away from her. "No no no," he groaned.

She smiled and smoothed her hand over his stomach. She wasn't about to let technology cut this short. "Let it go to voice mail. We have all morning." She drew a lazy circle in the center of his chest with her finger. "Now where were we?"

He closed his eyes and moved her hand. "I hate to say this, but we're done for the morning." The phone continued its interruption. "That ringtone is literally the only sound that can ruin the mood." He rolled away again and strode across the room.

"Just ignore it. Come back." She patted the mattress, wishing she could transport him back to where he'd just been.

"It's my mom. I have to answer it. She'll just keep calling if I don't. Plus, the mere thought of my mom makes a repeat performance impossible."

Julia sighed and scooted back on the bed, resting her head on the pillow. She pulled the sheet up to her chin. The moment was indeed over.

"Mom, hey. I'm sorry I haven't called. Things have been crazy busy since I got here." He cradled the phone between his ear and shoulder, pulling a pair of basketball shorts out of his suitcase and tugging them on.

And there went my view.

"Oh. Yeah. Right. Jules and me. We should probably talk about that." He shook his head and looked down at the floor. "I know. You're right. I'm sorry you had to find out from the news."

Oh crap. Right there was proof that Logan had put little thought into his plan. Of course his mom would find out about it. She not only lived in town, she was as connected as could be—lifelong resident and a district court judge. The rumor mill had probably started churning the instant Logan told his tale to the reporters. It was a miracle she hadn't called him last night.

"I know. I know." He nodded eagerly. "Hey, Mom, let me put you on speaker for a second." He pressed a button on his phone and placed it on the bureau, then threw a T-shirt over his head and threaded his arms into it.

Logan's mother's voice rang out over the speaker. "I know you're busy with the wedding, but I'd like to see the two of you together before tomorrow. Otherwise I might not get any time alone with you at all."

He closed his eyes, kneading his forehead, clearly wrestling with the conversation. Difficult to explain or not, they were going to have to come clean with his mom as well. "Don't you need to be in court today?"

"As luck would have it, there's a gas leak at the courthouse. I swear it's something new every day. They really need to put some money into that building. Normally I'd complain, but if it means I get to see my handsome son and the girlfriend I'd always hoped he'd find a way to be with, I'm happy. So, no, court is not in session today."

Eight

The press had stayed away. Logan was able to retrieve the car from the valet like a civilized person—no more sneaking around. Whatever his fabrication had done to annoy Julia or infuriate Tracy, it had been worth it. Now he just had to find out how much it would irritate his mother when she, too, learned it was a lie. *Great.*

Only after what had transpired with Julia that morning, he wasn't entirely sure it was a lie. They hadn't had a conversation about it. During his time on the phone with his mom, Julia had received a call from Tracy. He'd hopped in the shower while she talked about lunch plans with her sister, then it had been Julia's turn to commandeer the bathroom. Room service arrived with breakfast; he got a few texts from Carter about the two of them picking up the rings. Julia bustled around the hotel room, Logan did much of the same, and it all just went back to the way it had been twenty-four hours ago. Except now there was sex with Julia fresh in his mind, and he couldn't stop thinking about the surreality of that moment when it was clear she wanted him.

Was Julia experimenting? Was she trying to sound him out? Was she finally coming around to his way of thinking? That they should figure out a way to forgive each other and move forward? He wasn't about to see his child go without a father, no matter how much he worried that Julia might not be capable of loving him, at least not forever.

Unfortunately, Julia was on the phone with her Aunt Judy for the duration of the drive to Logan's mom's. Meaning, yet again, no conversation or clarification. The wedding had taken center stage. And there wasn't a damn thing Logan could do about it.

When they arrived at the house, Logan took Julia in through the side door that led to the kitchen. The room never changed—simple white tile countertops, checkerboard dish towel draped over the oven handle, a ceramic cookie jar shaped like a cupcake, and the picture window above the sink, overlooking the backyard. Coffee was on, also no surprise. His mom was an all-day-long coffee drinker, just as his dad had been. He couldn't imagine his childhood home without it. And that one particular aroma brought back more than memories, good and bad; it transported him to a time when he was a different person, a kid trying to figure out how to be a man.

As much as he loved this house, he never stayed here when he came back into town. Sleeping in his old bed would've invited too much introspection, along with a sore back. Luckily, his mom had converted his room into a sewing and craft space, and the one his brothers had shared still housed their old bunk beds. His mom didn't seem eager to nudge time ahead, and he'd be the last person to push.

His mother waltzed into the kitchen, her chin-length curly dark hair tied back with a colorful scarf. Even with a day off from work, she was the epitome of put-together. Jewelry. Makeup. "I should've known you'd come in through the side door." She beamed as they beelined for each other, arms wide open.

"It just feels weird to go to the front. The mailman and strangers go to the front door." They embraced, both holding on tight. Hugs from his mom always lasted a heartbeat longer than most, a powerful reminder of how much they'd needed each other after his father's death. She'd lost her best friend and husband of fifteen years. Logan and his brothers had lost their hero, mentor and coach. If any family had ever held each other up, they had.

"And here's the lovely Julia." His mother hadn't let go of his shoulders, but she was now looking back and forth between them, a prideful smile on her face. "I always wondered if you two would find a way."

Logan's stomach wobbled at the tone in his mother's voice. It was different from Julia's parents. They were always full of sunny optimism. His mom was an upbeat person, but she also had an unflinching critical eye. She could pick apart any charade. Could she see what was lying beneath the surface between them? That they were drawn to each other, however messed up things happened to get? Or was his mom hinting that she knew what was going on and was simply waiting for him to come out with it?

"Mrs. B. You look amazing. As always." Julia stepped closer, and that was enough to coax his mother from his arms.

"Coming from one of the most beautiful women in the world, I'll take that compliment any day."

He stood back and admired the two of them. Even his mom and Julia looked right together.

"It's all smoke and mirrors, you know," Julia said. "They put me in so much makeup for my movies and photo shoots, it's ridiculous. You have me beat with those high cheekbones."

"Well, thank you. Flattery will get you everywhere." Logan's mom draped her arm across Julia's shoulders. "Can I get you two some coffee? Followed by an explanation of what in the world is going on that I find out from the newspaper that you're a couple after all this time?"

There was his cue to come out with it. "Mom, I had to say that to get the press to go away. To make them stop asking Julia about her costar."

She nodded as if the news was no surprise. "I see. Well, that's a disappointment, but I thought it seemed a little out of the blue." She directed her gaze at Julia. "Coffee?"

His mom pulled two mugs from the cabinet, but Julia had cut way back on coffee because of the pregnancy.

"Oh, no, Mrs. B. I'm good. I had plenty at the hotel. In fact, may I use your powder room?"

"Of course. You know where it is." Logan's mom filled a fresh cup for Logan and topped off her own mug as Julia left to go to the bathroom.

"So?" his mom asked, leaning back against the counter and arching her eyebrows at him. "Anything else you want to share with me?"

There it was—the only invitation she'd extend for him to apologize. "I'm sorry you had to hear the story from the news. It's just complicated. Like most things with Jules."

His mother shook her head. "That's not what I was asking. How far along is she?"

Logan nearly choked on his coffee. "What?"

"One of the most successful actresses in Hollywood is

getting a little thick in the middle? I don't think so. And she's glowing. Good God, if ever a woman glowed, it's her." She sipped from her mug. "Declining the coffee was the final clue. Julia has never turned down a cup of my coffee. Ever. I spent an awful lot of years as a prosecutor. I'm good at figuring things out."

I'll be damned. Logan leaned back and peered through the doorway into the hall. "She's three months along. But it's a secret. Nobody knows." The rest was sitting on his lips. He wasn't keen on saying any of it, but his mother was likely one or two pointed questions away from figuring everything out. He cleared his throat, then came clean—the reunion, the phone call. And the worst of it—her ex.

His mother took another sip of coffee. "So you're telling me there's a chance I'm about to become a grandmother, but you aren't together. Do you love her?"

Just then, Julia ducked into the room. "I didn't want y'all to think I got lost. My sister called and I need to call her back. I'll just be in the living room if that's okay."

"Of course. Feel free to use my office if you need it," his mother replied.

Julia retreated to the other room. Logan was still mulling over his mother's question.

"Well? Do you?" she asked.

He knew the answer, but he wished he didn't have to qualify it. "I do, on some level, but it's not as simple as that. If the baby is mine, we have to get married. I don't see any other way it's going to work. I have to accept my responsibility."

"Of course you do. You've always stepped in and done what was right. You did that when your father passed."

"See? Exactly. Similar situation, but Julia doesn't agree. There comes a time when things happen and you just have to man up and do your job. But she doesn't see my point.

If she'd listen to me and get a paternity test, it would make this much more clear-cut."

His mother shook her head in slow motion, as if she wanted him to feel every bit of condemnation that was coming from her expression. "Please tell me you haven't actually said that to her."

"It's a legitimate request. Any man in the world would ask the question."

"Of course they would, but that doesn't mean I don't expect my son to see the problem. A paternity test does nothing more than give you a free pass to walk away if the answer is that you're not the father, and makes you beholden to her if you are."

"I'm not looking for a free pass. That's not what this is about. But I don't know how I'm supposed to make a decision without that information."

His mother cocked both eyebrows, her lips pursed. She clunked her coffee cup in the porcelain sink. "Logan Brandt, I thought I raised you better than that. How do you think Julia feels?" She then proceeded to say virtually everything Julia had said to him about living with complete uncertainty, all on her own. "Not only that, but her career is on the line here. She's going to have to take time off from films, quite possibly raise a child on her own. It's not easy, Logan. I'm speaking from experience. I had to be a single mom after your dad passed away. Trying to work my way through the prosecutor's office and raise three boys? It was hard."

"I know, Mom. I do. I was there for the whole thing, remember? I did my best to step up to the plate then, too. I'm not going to walk away from her if the baby is mine."

"And I'm telling you right now that if I was Julia, that would not be my misgiving. I'd be far more worried about what you'll do if the baby isn't yours. It would be difficult for any man to step into that role with another man's child. But take your history with her and it's got to be twice as hard. She has prepared herself for you to walk away. Again. That's why she was not particularly enamored of your line about accepting responsibility."

He stared down at the kitchen floor, realizing how much Julia had let her guard down that morning when they'd made love. How would he and Julia ever get past this? It was a catch-22 unlike any he'd ever experienced. "I just don't know what to do anymore. I only want to do what's right, but I feel like I'm damned if I do and damned if I don't."

"It's not just up to you. You both have to arrive at the same decision. That's the only way you both end up happy."

"That's the exact thing we're horrible at."

"What did your daddy always say when he was helping you with your pitching? He told you that practice makes perfect. You have to keep trying."

He kneaded his forehead. Everything going through his mind was starting to give him a headache. "Honestly, I'm not even sure what to try with Julia anymore."

"Something tells me you'll figure it out." She reached out and clasped her hand over his. "Hold on one minute. I want to run upstairs and get you something."

Logan poured out the last of his coffee and rinsed the sink. His mother always kept a spotless kitchen. He stood and looked out at the backyard, exactly the spot where his father had played catcher while Logan perfected his pitch. The mound they'd built with load after load of dirt from the back of the lot was barely visible now, covered in grass and mostly sunken in with the rest of the lawn. Still, the traces remained. Just as the traces of his father remained in his head—James Brandt's proud stance, kind ways and deep voice, which became rough and grumbly as the cancer slowly took him away. Logan could still hear his dad's words—not his final utterance to his son, but the one that made the deepest impression, echoing for years, never shared with anyone until Julia. *You have to be the man of the house now, son. Take care of your mom and your brothers. I can't be here to do it.*

Talk about life's patterns repeating—he had to take care of Julia and the baby. Something deep inside him told him it was the only way. But would Julia let him? And would she want him to stay?

Logan jumped when his mom pressed her hand to his back.

"Logan, hon. You okay?"

He nodded and turned, choking back those memories of his dad. "Yeah. Of course."

She held out a small gray felt drawstring pouch. "This is what I went to get."

Logan was in shock. The last thing he'd expected her to give him today was his grandmother's ring. He'd been told from a young age that he would get it whenever it came time to propose to a woman. He hadn't even asked for the ring with his previous engagement, the one eventually broken, to a woman he'd never bothered to bring home. He'd made every excuse in the book, but the truth was that he'd known his mother would see right through the facade. What he'd had with his former fiancée wasn't real. "Mom. Really?"

She nodded and opened the pouch, revealing the large pale pink diamond in the center, surrounded by white diamonds, all set in platinum. "Yes, really. I have a feeling you're going to need this in the coming days or weeks, or maybe hours. Hard to tell with you two. I don't want you to be unprepared. She'll take you more seriously with a ring." She pulled it from its resting place, turning it in her fingers. "I always forget how beautiful it is. It will look perfect on her hand."

Julia's voice filtered in from the hall. "Okay, Trace. I'll see you in thirty at the boutique."

Logan's mom dropped the ring back into the tiny bag, yanked the drawstring and folded it into his hand. He shoved it into his pocket, still disbelieving that his mother had given it to him, all while wrestling with what would have to happen for Julia to accept it from him.

Julia wandered into the kitchen and tucked her phone into her purse. "It's a modern miracle. My sister doesn't hate me today. Or at least not as much as yesterday."

Logan's mom nodded and stepped closer to Julia, eyeing her belly. He watched in horror as the look on her face changed, as if she was turning into a grandmother before his eyes. "Don't worry, hon. She won't hate you at all once she finds out your little secret."

Julia smiled politely and waved at Logan's mom as they said their goodbyes, but she could only sustain her pleasantness until the side door was closed and Mrs. Brandt was out of earshot. "I can't believe you told her." She should have waited until Sunday to tell Logan. She never should've given in to that little voice inside that said he deserved to know as soon as she'd had her first chance.

"I didn't have to tell her. She guessed."

"What?" Julia stopped at the bottom of the driveway. "How could she guess that I'm pregnant?"

Logan grabbed her hand and pulled her toward the car. "Come on. Let's not have this discussion in the middle of the street. You're worried about keeping your secret, all we need is for some hapless dog walker to wander by and overhear you."

"Okay. Fine," Julia grumbled and got into the car. "I don't understand how she possibly could've guessed."

Logan wasted little time driving away from the curb.

"I'm telling you right now, there's no way you make it through this wedding without everyone figuring it out. The clues are there. Your chest is bigger. You pass up coffee. You're glowing."

"Glowing is such baloney." Julia dismissed the comment with a flip of her hand.

"What? You *are* glowing. I probably could've figured out what was going on if I hadn't been so busy thinking about how hot you look right now."

Heat rushed to her cheeks. Logan and his compliments—so disarming in an argument. "That's not fair. You're flirting so I won't give you a hard time."

"Nope. Just being honest. The only way I can get to you is with total honesty."

She sat back in her seat and wrapped her arms around her waist. Her plan was starting to feel more and more stupid, only it was too late to veer off course. "Thank you. That was nice of you to say."

"If we're being honest, I want to know what happened this morning."

She nearly laughed. "You know what happened. You were there. And I'm pretty sure you enjoyed it."

"That's not what I mean." He quickly cut onto a side street. He put the gearshift into Park beneath the shade of a looming oak tree. "I need to know what's going on. What you're thinking. Last night you insisted you felt nothing when I kissed you and then this morning you change your story. I need to know what you're thinking."

If Logan wanted the truth about her feelings, it would take several hours to unravel it. They were messy. And complicated. And ever-changing. She glanced at the digital clock on the dash. "I'm thinking that if you don't get me to my dress fitting in the next fifteen minutes, my sister is going to blow a gasket."

"I really don't care. I'll deal with your sister if I have to, and I'm tired of the wedding putting everything else on hold. Not talking about this isn't going to help us navigate the maze ahead of us."

She sucked in a deep breath. Dealing with the wedding was a pain, but at least it had afforded her a few moments where she could stop worrying about what the future held. Her mind drifted to those heavenly moments just a few hours ago, when nothing else mattered but the two of them, perfectly in sync. "I wanted you this morning. You touch me and all I want is to give in. And it was wonderful. But that just makes everything more depressing."

Logan blinked in disbelief. "I'm not sure what about that was depressing."

The frustration was building inside her again. "I hate that we can only get our act together in bed. That doesn't feel great."

He sighed, tugging the keys out of the ignition and tossing them down into the cup holder. Apparently they were going to be there for a while. "We do have that problem, don't we?"

She'd been bracing for an argument from him. Instead, he agreed, which felt far worse. "So I don't know where we are, other than at an impasse."

"An impasse with benefits. That's a new one."

"Very funny. You know, even if I forgive you for dumping me after the reunion, that doesn't change the fact that you did it. That's the thing I can't get past right now."

"I said I was sorry. You're the one who doesn't want to accept my apology."

"It's not about that. It's not about saying that you're sorry." *It's that you don't love me. And I can't make you do it.* She blew out a breath, and the quiet felt like it might suffocate her. There were no words she could say aloud to erase the empty feeling he'd left her with the day he took his love—or at least the promise of his love—away.

"Then what is it about?" He turned and reached for her hand, enveloping it in his. "Talk to me. Tell me whatever it is you need to say so we can get past this."

How did she even put this into words? She looked up at him, fighting tears. It felt as though she was about to scratch open her own wounds. "You have to understand, I was so happy when I flew home to California that day after the reunion. I was so thankful that the planets had finally aligned and we were on the same page."

He nodded. "I know. I felt that way, too."

"And then you called and left me a message." She shook her head and closed her eyes, praying for strength. "I remember it so clearly, too. I'd gone outside to get the mail and my phone was inside on the coffee table. You have no idea how my heart leaped when I came inside and saw that you'd called." Just telling the story was making her heart feel impossibly heavy, as if it might fold in on itself from the weight of the past. "And then you told me that I was wrong. That we wouldn't work. That our weekend had been fun, but we had to admit it was over. It felt worse than having the rug pulled out from under me. It felt like the earth had disappeared. One minute I saw a future for us and the next minute it went away. Poof. Disappeared."

"I'm sorry I hurt you. I don't know what else to say. I can't undo what I did."

"And then we talk in your hotel room the other night and you tell me that this all started because of the Derek thing. It's so stupid."

Logan sucked in a deep breath. "It's not just that."

She waited for him to say something else, but he didn't. "Then what?"

"I was a mess walking into that reunion. Feeling sorry

for myself, depressed about my job. And that's the one time, out of all of the reunions that we've seen each other at, that you decide you want to be with me? You didn't want me. You just wanted another project."

She narrowed her stare at him. "I don't even know what that means."

"You're always trying to fix guys. They always have some tragic fault that you seem to think you can fix. And it usually just bites you in the butt at the end. Either that or you actually accomplish what you set out to do and then you're looking for the next person to save. And frankly, I don't care to belong in either of those camps."

"That's so untrue." She crossed her arms and stared out the windshield. Or was that true? Was that really her pattern?

"Just think about it, Jules. When we first started going out, I was a project, wasn't I?"

"That's not the reason I liked you. That's not the reason I wanted to go out with you. I thought you were cute and I couldn't believe that you would even pay attention to me, let alone like me."

"But once you got to know me, you realized just how lost I was. I needed your help. And you did help me. I will always be grateful for that. But once you were sure I'd be fine on my own, you dumped me. I wasn't about to go through that with you again."

Oh. That. All these years later and they'd never, ever, talked about their first breakup. Never.

"I don't want to dredge up the past," he continued. "But it hurt a lot."

"We were kids. Did it really mean that much to you?"

Disbelief and disappointment crossed his face. Julia wasn't sure which one hurt more. "I don't know, Jules. We were in love, weren't we? Did we mean that much to you?"

She nearly choked on the answer. "Of course we meant that much. Of course we did." She stared down at her hands in her lap. "But I thought it was inevitable. You were going off to UCLA, destined to be the famous baseball player. You were going to have every girl in the world you ever wanted. I couldn't compete with that."

He shrugged. "Fair enough. I get that. Maybe we wouldn't have been able to make it work. Very few people do. But it doesn't change the fact that everything bad between us started right then."

They were both quiet, Julia trying to absorb just how badly she'd hurt him. Did it all even out? Was that the way love was supposed to work? "Just so you know, you were not a project. I've never, ever thought of you that way. Not when we were seventeen and not three months ago. You have to believe me when I say that. I just wanted to help you." *Because I love you.* The words were right there, but she couldn't say them. They would go unreturned, and nothing would be more painful than that.

He nodded, but didn't seem entirely convinced. "Okay. That's good to know."

"You know, you said that there was no telling how things would've played out the first time, but can you really say that about this summer, too? What if we'd done well? What if we'd worked it all out? What then? Just think of how different this weekend could be. We wouldn't have to be sitting here wondering what the future held."

Except that the question of paternity would still be hanging over their heads. They might be together, they might even still be in love, but if she'd had the test and taken away the uncertainty, there was a chance that in itself would've been the end.

"Look, I'm sorry if I misread the situation," he said. "I'm sorry that I hurt your feelings. But you have to understand that I did what felt right at the time. It wasn't pleasant for me, either. The summer was hard. I missed you a lot."

"You did?" She looked up at him. Funny how that one tiny admission softened her heart. "Why didn't you call me? I would've talked to you."

"I could ask you the same thing, since you found out you were pregnant with what might be my child."

Well then. The phone *did* work both ways. "Yeah. I see your point."

"So now what?"

Facing him, she scanned his handsome features, wondering if he felt better about any of this. She was still processing. "I don't know. I don't know what to think anymore."

"Okay. Well, let me ask you this. What do you want from me? Let's not even put the question of the baby in the mix. As a man, what do you want from me?"

Talk about a loaded question. It was hard to separate the baby from the equation, but he'd asked her to. That meant she could only go to one place for the answer—the way she'd felt after he'd broken up with her, before she'd found out she was pregnant. "I want you to love me." It was as much a plea to the universe as it was a request of Logan.

"I'll always love you, Jules. There will always be love between us. And you know, I could ask the same of you. I would love it if you could find a way to love me. For real. For the long haul. I realize you were hurt, but you didn't call me when you found out you were pregnant. That doesn't really feel like love."

She felt as if the air had been squeezed out of her. She'd spent an entire summer cursing Logan's existence and a month wishing she didn't have to tell him about the pregnancy. Then she'd spent the last two days thinking he was being nothing but a selfish jerk about the baby. Now who'd been the selfish jerk? She was pretty sure it was her. "You're right and I'm so sorry. That was wrong." *Really, really wrong.* "So now what?"

"Kiss and make up?"

"Yeah, I guess it's time for us to forgive each other. It's not like we don't have other problems to deal with."

"Okay. I forgive you. But they don't just call it kiss and make up. We make up, we kiss."

She dropped her head and hoped to convey admonishment with a single look.

"Think of it as a fact-finding mission. We're both trying to figure out how we feel right now, and we both admit this is the part we always get right. And honestly, I feel like I break through some of your stubbornness every time I kiss you."

"I'm not that stubborn."

"Now you're being stubborn about being stubborn."

Before she could say another word, he clasped the back of her neck and pulled her mouth to his. She insisted on a few seconds of hesitation, but gave in to it quickly, tilting her head as he opened his lips and sent that familiar tingle right through her. She pressed into him. He pushed right back. *Hello, slippery slope.*

She pulled back, her mind buzzing, but he held her head close, their foreheads pressed together, noses touching, both of them breathing heavily. "Logan, we can't. You're going to get me all riled up again. And I'm going to be late."

He blew out an exasperated breath. "Yes. Of course. God forbid we disappoint the bride."

Nine

Julia opened the door for Belle's Bridal Boutique to one of the most unfunny pieces of music she could imagine right now. Electronic chimes played "Here Comes the Bride," announcing her arrival. *Ding ding ding-ding. Here comes the bride. Ha ha ha.*

The woman working behind a tall counter near the entrance looked up and gasped. "Your sister said you would be coming." She hurried out from behind her post and thrust out her hand. "I'm Tiffany. I'm the manager. I told myself I wouldn't get too excited, but I can't believe you're in our little shop."

Julia smiled and nodded. "Well, your little shop is just darling." Her eyes glazed over at the racks of white dresses surrounding them. It was hard to imagine she would ever find herself in this situation of her own accord—picking out a wedding gown. That would mean she'd not only managed to find the right guy, she'd managed to hold on to him, and the entire world knew she was incapable of that.

Her father, sitting in the center of the showroom in a fussy white upholstered armchair, waved her over. He'd been stationed in an area with a carpeted pedestal and three-way mirror. "Hey, Junebug. Where's Mr. Baseball?"

"He went with Carter to pick up the wedding bands. He'll be back in about a half hour." Julia plopped herself down on a love seat, thoughts of her talk with Logan still tumbling around in her head. He'd asked how she felt, but he hadn't offered his own take on much of anything beyond their painful past. She wasn't ready to slap a label on anything, but that kiss had sure given her something to chew on.

"Your mother is in the back with Tracy and the tailor. They should be out any minute."

"Can I get you something to drink?" Tiffany asked. "Your mother and sister are enjoying a glass of champagne."

Not for me. "Water would be wonderful."

"I'll be right back. Surely you remember Ms. Sully from your first fitting." Tiffany's drawl was so thick that the seamstress's name came out as one word—*Mssully.* "She'll bring out your dress as soon as she finishes up with your sister."

Right on cue, a billowing white skirt peeked out from behind the expanse of mirrors. Tracy floated into view. Julia didn't even have a second to process the vision before the tears started. She loved her sister to the very depths of her heart, even when Tracy was being a pain in her backside. Seeing her in a stunning off-the-shoulder gown that would've made Cinderella jealous enough to spit, all she could do was cry. Her mother wasn't doing much better, hand held to her mouth, shaking her head, a blubbering mess.

Julia rose from her seat and went to Tracy as she stepped up onto the platform. "You are the most gorgeous bride I have seen in my entire life."

Tracy gleamed into the mirror, turning side to side and smoothing the dress. She looked down at Julia with pure elation on her face. "Thank you so much. I can't believe this is finally happening." This was what Julia had hoped for this weekend—her sister, blissful and basking in the glory of being the bride. "And honestly, I can't believe that something is actually going right for once. As soon as you got here the other day, I was sure this wedding was going to be a disaster."

And just like that, Julia was thunked back down to earth.

"I really don't think the dress needs any more alterations, Trace," their mother said. "It's perfect. Absolutely perfect."

"I agree." Ms. Sully added as she filed out from behind the mirror with a pincushion on her wrist and a pink measuring tape around her neck. "Now let's get your sister into her dress. This should be quick. It was close to perfect for the first fitting, but I do want to check the length."

Tiffany sidled out from the back room and handed Julia a bottle of water.

"No champagne, Jules?" Tracy asked. "We're celebrating."

She'd worried about this, especially after Logan had made the comment about the secret being impossible to keep. Julia rarely passed up a glass of bubbly, especially not celebratory. "I have a bit of a headache." Not entirely a lie. The summit with Logan in the car had given her more than her head could handle.

"Maybe it'll loosen you up," Tracy countered.

"I'm good." Julia hoped like heck her sister would just drop it.

"Your fitting room is right over here," Tiffany said, thankfully taking the focus off what Julia was and was not willing to drink.

Ms. Sully followed as Tiffany directed Julia to a small room with an upholstered bench. Next to a standing mirror hung Julia's dress, the one she'd tried on the last time she'd been in town. It was pretty, albeit maybe not what Julia would've picked out—pale pink organza with a strapless bodice and puffy skirt—so fluffy that Julia had commented that if the dress were yellow, she'd look like a lemon meringue pie. Tracy had not found that funny.

Julia's mother joined them, closing the door behind her. "The bridesmaids' dresses are so lovely."

"Everyone else had their final fittings weeks ago," Ms. Sully said, unzipping the dress, taking it from its hanger and handing it to Julia. "I would've preferred to have done the same for you."

Julia slipped out of her sundress and into the gown. "I'm sorry. My schedule has been crazy." Stepping in front of the mirror, she tugged up the dress to her armpits, holding it to her chest.

Ms. Sully took the zipper in hand, but judging by the sound of it, and the way the dress had not snugged up around Julia, she didn't get more than a few inches. "It's too small in the bust."

Julia's mother tittered. "That can't be right. The Keys women are blessed with childbearing hips and that's about it. We did not get much in the boob department."

"Look for yourself." Ms. Sully struggled to pull the back of the dress closed, cutting off Julia's oxygen supply in the process.

Julia felt the blood drain from her face. *Oh no no no no no.* She hadn't accounted for this. She'd tried the dress on with a padded bra the first time—a very padded bra. The one she was wearing right now had only a thin lining. She'd been sure that would be enough difference to accommodate her expanded endowments. Apparently not.

Julia's mom let out a snort of frustration. "This doesn't make any sense. I was here when you tried it on the first time. Are you sure this is the same dress? Did you grab one of the other bridesmaids' dresses?"

"The other girls have all taken their dresses home. This is the last one."

A knock came at the door and Tracy walked in, back in her preppy fuchsia-and-lime-green sheath dress, bottle of champagne and three glasses in hand. "I brought the party and I'm not taking a no from Jules this time." The smile on her face didn't last long when she saw the back of Julia's dress.

"Oh no, Jules. What did you do?"

"Me? Why do you immediately blame me?"

Tracy set the bottle down on a small table and hurried over, elbowing Ms. Sully out of the way and yanking on the back of the dress. "Suck it in. Come on." She grunted and tugged, but it wouldn't budge. "What on earth have you been eating?"

"It's not her waist, although that's definitely tighter, too. It's her bust. Her chest is too large for the dress." Ms. Sully pulled the tape measure from around her neck.

Tracy rounded out from behind Julia, confronting her head-on and staring at her bust. "You got a boob job and didn't tell me?" She poked her right in the chest.

"Ow." Julia winced.

Tracy's eyes grew wide. "Oh my God. You *did* get a

boob job. Before my wedding? Now you're trying to steal my thunder by having bigger boobs?"

"I did not get a boob job." Julia wished she would've thought about that answer for even two seconds. That would've given her an out. But it would've been a lie, one that would eventually come to light.

"The only other thing that could make this dramatic a difference is pregnancy," Ms. Sully said nonchalantly, as if she were telling everyone that it might rain next week.

Tracy's eyes practically popped out of her head. "No."

"Pregnant?" Their mother let out a whimper. Julia wasn't sure she'd ever heard a sadder sound.

"Oh. My. God." Tracy's face turned that shade of red again. This was getting to be far too common a sight. "That's why you won't drink any champagne. I *knew* something was up."

Julia's heart was about to pound its way out of her chest, but she wasn't going to deny something she'd have to come clean about in two days. Plus, she was tired. Flat-out exhausted. "Yes, I'm pregnant. I didn't want anyone to know until after the wedding was over. The spotlight is supposed to be Tracy's right now."

Tracy shook her head, practically boring a hole through Julia with her piercing eyes. Her jaw was so tight, it was making the veins in her neck stick out. "You really are trying to ruin my wedding. You knew this was going to happen. You knew your dress wouldn't fit." She turned, poured herself a glass of champagne, and downed it.

"I had no idea it wouldn't fit. I didn't think it was going to be that big of a difference."

"And you just had to orchestrate this to suck the air out of my happiness, didn't you? Right after I'd tried on my dress and we'd all cried together and had such a beautiful moment. The big famous actress had to go for maximum drama." Her voice was ice cold.

Their mother was apparently still catching up. "A baby? I'm going to be a grandmother? Who's the father? Please don't tell me it's that terrible Derek."

"Mom. It's not Derek." At least she had one answer she could give without hesitation.

Ms. Sully leaned over Julia's shoulder. "I've got the measurements I need. I'll do my best to let it out before tomorrow, but no promises. Bring me the dress when you've changed your clothes. I need to get right to work."

Julia grasped the woman's arm. "I'm begging you. Please don't say anything to anyone about this."

"Of course, dear. You can count on my discretion."

"I'm out of here. I can't deal with this." But Tracy wasn't *really* out of there, because she got back in Julia's face. "You make me wish I hadn't made you my maid of honor. I just want you to think about that." A single tear rolled down her cheek, which felt like a knife in Julia's heart.

"Tracy, please don't say things like that. I understand it's a shock. But maybe Julia had a good reason for hiding this from us," their mother said.

"But that's the thing. She wasn't hiding it, really. She was just waiting for the worst possible time to tell us. I'm tired of her grandstanding. Every five minutes there's another fire to put out and it's all her doing."

Julia couldn't have moved if she'd wanted to. Her sister's words were consuming her whole, eating at her from the inside out. Her shoulders drooped; she closed her eyes, part of her wishing she could just psychically beam herself back to her New York apartment or to her house on the beach in Malibu. Anywhere else but here, where everyone was mad at her and her sister despised her very existence. She dared to open her eyes. Staring down, she was mocked by the field of billowy pink. *I'm here.*

Another knock came at the dressing room door. "Is everything okay in there?" Julia's father asked. "There's an awful lot of yelling. And did somebody say something about a baby?"

"I'll be right out, darling," Julia's mother answered, collecting her handbag. "I don't even know what to say," she said to Julia, her voice unsettled. "You know I don't like it when Tracy flies off the handle like this, but she's not wrong this time. You've created so much upheaval since your arrival."

Julia cast her eyes at her mother. The look on her face was difficult to pin a word to, but both *sad* and *disappointed* came to mind.

"I don't know what's going on with you, but I think you'd better get your act together, at least until this weekend is over. Otherwise, it's only going to get worse for all of us."

A puff of air left Julia's lips as she clutched that stupid bridesmaid's dress to her chest. She'd just told her mom that she was going to have a baby. It was a moment she'd thought about many times—one that was meant to be joyous and cheerful. Instead, she was standing in a fitting room, and it had come and gone in as unhappy a fashion as Julia could've imagined. It many ways, it mirrored her future…and her past, for that matter—the ways in which she couldn't stop messing up. "Aren't you going to say anything about the baby?"

Her mother's eyes were watery. "I'm excited for you sweetheart, really I am, but I'm in shock. And this really isn't a good time. I hope that we can talk about it later this weekend. After the wedding is over."

"Exactly why I wanted to keep the secret in the first place."

"How long have you known?"

"Three weeks. Or so."

"Three whole weeks? Oh, Jules. Three weeks?" She shook her head. "And you didn't tell me? Your sister would've been annoyed, but she would've been over it well before her wedding day arrived."

Julia sat down on the bench and buried her head in her hands. Her stomach burned as she realized that her mistake was much worse than she'd thought. "I'm so sorry. Really. I am. I didn't want it to be like this."

"I believe you. I do. Now we just need to wait for your sister to cool down. Speaking of which, let me see if I can find her and talk to her. And somebody's got to get your father up to speed."

"I'm coming with you." She had to fix this. She had to explain.

"It's probably best if you give your sister some space. I'm guessing you're the last person she wants to talk to."

Right now it felt as if there was an insurmountable divide between her Tracy. There was no telling how long it would take for her sister to calm down. When was the next ice age expected? That might be enough time.

"Let me talk to Daddy, then."

Her mother reached for the door. "I'll talk to him. He thinks you can do no wrong. He doesn't want to believe you might ever be untruthful with us. He'll probably be even more disappointed than I am that you kept this from us."

Disappointed. If ever there was a dagger to the heart of a child, that was it. She sat back and knocked her head against the wall as her mother closed the door. If she thought she'd felt alone in all of this when she arrived, she felt that tenfold now. She wrapped her arms around her waist, and the dress gaped in the back. All she wanted was someone on her side. All she wanted was someone who believed she'd had the best of intentions. All she wanted was someone who knew she was trying her best.

All she wanted was Logan.

Ten

After their trip to pick up the wedding bands, Logan and Carter pulled into the parking lot at the bridal boutique. Logan turned off the car and opened his door. Carter, however, seemed content to stay put.

"Everything okay?" Logan asked. "You've been quiet since we left the jeweler."

Carter nodded. "I'm good. Just thinking about everything. To be honest, I keep waiting for the other shoe to drop. When is my luck going to run out?"

Logan closed his door and turned the ignition on in order to roll down the windows. They might be there for a while. "I'm not sure I understand what you're saying. Are you getting cold feet? Because that's perfectly normal." *Hell, I'm the king of cold feet.*

Carter stared straight ahead as if he were pondering the very meaning of life. "When I'm with Tracy, I feel so lucky, especially thinking about the fact that we'd broken up for a whole year. What if she hadn't gotten a flat tire?

What if I hadn't driven by her that day? We might never have gotten back together. My whole life turned around because of dumb luck."

"It's fate. Nothing dumb about it."

"I just think about what I would be doing right now if things hadn't turned out the way they did. I'd be living in my crappy condo, dragging myself to work every day, nothing to look forward to. I look at what that was like and I can't believe I lived through a single day of the year we were apart. It was pathetic."

Wow. Did that sound familiar—that was Logan's life. Sure, swap out the crappy condo for a sprawling home on a wooded lot in Connecticut with a pool and manicured grounds. And yes, he had an array of cars to choose from whenever it was time to head up to the network offices for a production meeting or to the airport to travel to a game, but his life was only a more glamorous version of bachelorhood than Carter's. At its essence, at its core, it was the same. And there was zero indication it was going to get any better. He dated some wonderful women, a pleasure to spend time with, but he never found himself wondering what was next, or even worrying whether they wanted to stick around. Whenever it came to a conclusion, it was almost always the same goodbye. *That was fun. Good luck. I hope you find the right woman someday.*

Logan reached over and grabbed Carter's shoulder. "You know, most guys don't appreciate what they have. Or they don't until it's too late. I'm glad you aren't one of those guys."

"So what about you? What about the stuff you were saying yesterday about not counting out the idea of you and Julia getting back together?"

Now it was Logan's turn to stare anywhere but at his best friend, choosing to fix his eyes on his own hands as he picked at his thumbnail. "I want us to try, but there are a lot of moving parts. I'm not sure it can happen until we resolve one or two things."

"No. Dude. Let me stop you right there. There is no resolving a few things. There are always going to be problems."

"Some problems are bigger than others." *Like having a thing for a woman who might be carrying another man's baby.*

"Listen to me. That day when Tracy got the flat tire? Do you think I was standing on the side of the road thinking about how much we used to fight? Or that she gets up at five and I can't sleep before midnight? Because I wasn't. All I was thinking about was how much I wanted to kiss her. All I was thinking about was how being with her felt right." Carter was clearly worked up about this—his cheeks were flushed and his blue eyes blazed.

"I see your point. You've given me a lot to think about."

"Look. You are my best friend in the whole world. You're the brother I never had. I want you to be happy. And you might have a lot of what most men want, but you don't have it all. I want that for you. If you love her, you have to lock things down with Jules. Otherwise, she gets on a plane on Monday morning and you two just go back to whatever in the heck you've been doing for the last dozen years. Tracy and I call it Olympic flirting. It makes the rest of us crazy to watch you two *not* figure it out."

Olympic flirting. He and Julia *were* really good at that.

Just then, Tracy burst out of the door to the boutique. The instant she saw Logan and Carter, she beelined for them, but she didn't go to her husband-to-be's side of the car. She went straight for Logan. "You. I don't know what your problem is, but I'm tired of this. First you dump her and then you get her pregnant?"

"Well, to be fair, it happened the other way around."
Logan swallowed hard. What in the hell happened in the
last forty-five minutes? And how bad was it going to be
when he walked in there?

"Don't joke around about this. I'm in no mood. I'm
telling you right now that you need to straighten things
out with Julia." She leaned down and looked into the car
at Carter. "Carter, honey. Please get me out of here. I just
want to turn off my phone and eat ice cream and hang out
with you. Everyone else is insane."

Carter practically leaped out of the car, rushing to
Tracy's side, wrapping her up in his arms and kissing
the top of her head. "Everything's going to be fine," he
muttered to her. He then shot Logan the look he'd gotten
far too many times since he'd arrived in North Carolina.
"Pregnant? And you're sitting in the car wondering what
you should do?"

Logan was about to explain, or at least retort that it
wasn't as simple as that, but he and Carter had already had
that conversation. Enough talking in circles. "You two go.
I'll tend to Julia." Logan climbed out of his car as Tracy
and Carter got into hers.

He strode into the boutique. He had to shake his head
when the door chime played "Here Comes the Bride." Mrs.
Keys was standing at a counter, rummaging through her
purse, while Mr. Keys looked on. Neither of them were
pleased. In fact, Logan had never seen either of them look
so unhappy. "Everything okay?" he asked, bracing for the
answer.

"Sounds to me like you and Julia are the ones to answer that question." Mr. Keys's voice was stern and cold,
a complete one-eighty from the way he'd greeted Logan
on Wednesday.

"Logan? Is that you?" Julia stuck her head out from behind a door. She'd been crying. "Come here. We need to talk."

He looked at Julia's parents, desperate to explain. "Can we talk about this in one minute? Jules needs me right now."

"I'd say she needs you now more than anything. And we're on our way out." Mr. Keys ushered his wife out of the shop. She wouldn't even look at Logan.

He headed right over, stepping inside the dressing room. "What happened?"

She blew out an exasperated breath as she latched the door. "My dress didn't fit and now everybody knows. Tracy is furious with me."

"Uh, yeah. I ran into her in the parking lot. I already got on the wrong end of your sister's fury."

"I didn't even have time to explain that I don't know for certain that you're the dad," she whispered. "Plus, I knew it was just going to make it worse. Tracy said the most awful things to me. She said she wished she hadn't asked me to be her maid of honor."

It felt as if ice ran through his veins. That was the worst possible thing Tracy could have said. "What do you want to do? Tell everybody the truth?"

"Surely it's occurred to you how messy the truth is."

"I've been thinking about little else since I first saw you on Wednesday." *And especially in the last ten minutes.*

Tears streamed down her face. "Do you want to know why I didn't do the paternity test? Because I knew that the minute I did, if you weren't the dad, you would never ever want anything to do with me again."

He pulled her into a hug, wishing he could squeeze the sadness out of her. "I would never feel that way." His mother had been absolutely right. This was the real thing holding Julia back. The breakup was one thing, but this was quite another. "We just have to get through the wedding. Tell me what you want to do and I'm on board with whatever it is. Okay?"

"Anything?"

"Anything."

She sucked in a breath and plopped down onto a bench, her dress poofing up around her. She looked as defeated as a person could be. It was no surprise. Her sister, the wedding, her parents…everyone and everything putting pressure on her in their own way. Never mind her worries about the baby. Logan had to give her whatever she wanted right now. It was only fair. He crouched down next to her, pushing aside the mounds of puffy pink dress. She sat straighter and peered into his eyes. Hers were so warm and inviting, sweet and vulnerable. They were like home.

"I just want everything to be okay. I want to feel safe. I want to feel normal. And happy," she said.

Logan reached out and wiped the tears away from her cheek. They were welling in his eyes, too. "I hate seeing you cry, Jules. It kills me."

"I'm sorry."

"I don't want you to be sorry. Please. Stop being sorry."

Again, she sought his eyes. In some ways it felt as if they were having a conversation that was separate from the one that came from their lips. Every part of him wanted to wrap his arms around her and take her away. He took her hand, grasping her delicate fingers. The irony that they were in a bridal boutique while he had his grandmother's ring in his pocket was not lost on him. He would've popped it out and brought her to tears for an entirely different reason if he didn't know that it would take baby steps with Julia. He had to open his heart to her. If he was having a hard time trusting her, she felt the same way.

"Let me keep you safe," he said. "Let me make things

normal. We'll get through the wedding, and then we'll talk about everything when the pressure is off. I think we need to take some of the drama out of your life."

"It's not polite to have the bride kidnapped." A slight smile crossed her face. She pulled up the neckline of her dress, trying to hitch it up. "So you're going to have to tell me what you mean."

"Everyone already thinks we're together. And now your parents and Tracy know about the baby. And between the hotel room this morning and everything that happened in the car this afternoon, you and I both know that staying away from each other never works. Neither one of us is very good at it."

"Yeah. I noticed."

"So let's just try to be together. For two days. Let's be Julia and Logan. Together. A couple. No putting on a show."

"What will we do if people ask us about it? Because you know they're going to. They're going to ask about the baby and whether we're getting married. And I don't think I can pretend about that. I need it to be real."

"We'll just say that we're together and we're focused on Tracy and Carter right now. That's the truth, and if that's not good enough for them, then too bad. We'll just have to walk away or get really good at changing the subject."

"What do we tell everyone later? After the wedding?"

He took her other hand and gripped them together tightly. They were both putting a lot on the line here, willingly creating a tangle that could become an unholy mess to clean up. It didn't matter. Their past was littered with mistakes that couldn't be undone and their future was uncertain at best, but it was theirs. And it was up to the two of them to figure it out. "All we can do is our best right now. If anyone wants to fault us for that after the fact, then that's their problem. And if someone needs to take the heat, I will."

"You don't have to do that. I can take it. I'm used to it."

"You know what? I don't want you to be used to it. Let me shield you from this."

Julia swallowed. "Do you have any idea how many times I've had a guy say he'd stick up for me like that?"

He shrugged. "No idea. You know it's not my favorite subject."

"Zero. Zero times. You're the only one."

"Really?"

"Really. Believe me, I wouldn't lie about that." She stood and hiked up her dress again. "Okay. Let me get out of this silly get-up so we can get it to the seamstress and she can hopefully finish the alterations before tomorrow. I need to get out of this place."

He straightened, now keenly aware of the privacy they had, in a way that hadn't made an impression before. He really wanted to kiss her again. "I don't get to stay?"

She shook her head. "We're in a bridal boutique in the South. Let's not invite more scandal into our lives by being the unmarried pregnant couple making out in the fitting room."

His hand nearly twitched. The ring in his pocket might help to shut everyone up. But he couldn't go there until he knew for certain that she would say yes, and that they were ready. They needed their trial period. They needed to lean on each other again. "Okay, then. Out I go."

Logan quietly exited the dressing room and closed the door behind him. A few steps into the main room of the boutique and the eyes of the women working at the shop were all on him. He was used to women staring at him every now and then, but this was different. There was a whole lot of judgment being aimed at him right now and he didn't like it one bit. Julia thankfully emerged from behind the white door, the pink dress in her hands. One of the women working in the shop rushed over to take it from her.

A fraction of a smile crossed Julia's face as she walked up to him. Relief settled in. As much as she needed reassurance that everything would be okay, he needed it, too. He wasn't going to ask for it, but hopefully that grin from her meant that he could start trusting his instincts again. It was time.

"So? What should we do?" he asked. "We have hours until we need to be at the rehearsal."

"You know what would be awesome?"

Logan hoped she would suggest they go back to the hotel and have sex all afternoon.

"Let's go to the beach."

Eleven

Julia rolled down the car window and leaned against the door frame, letting the wind sweep her hair from her face and the sun warm her skin. Closing her eyes, she breathed in the familiar salty breeze.

"Any particular place you want to stop?" Logan asked.

"Anywhere quiet. I do not want to see people. And if you see a single member of my family, turn around and go in the opposite direction. I don't care how fast you drive."

He laughed, further improving her mood. If ever there was a sound worth listening to, it was Logan's laugh—not as deep as his speaking voice, but close, and it was always unguarded. "If we want privacy, then I think we both know where we need to go."

Privacy. "Yes. Go there."

A short fifteen minutes later, Logan pulled the car over to the side of the road in the perfect spot, right where a long string of rental houses stood between two of the bigger beach hotels. The undertow was particularly strong in this stretch and the sand extra pebbly, making it far less popular with swimmers. With school back in session, it wouldn't be too busy.

Julia kicked off her flats and collected them in her hands while Logan sat on the edge of the public access walkway, taking off his black leather shoes and removing his socks. He rolled up the legs of his jeans. Julia just watched, admiring him. A stunning ocean vista might have been waiting on the other side of the dunes, but the line of Logan's athletic shoulders as he hunched over was more enticing. He stood and gathered his things in one hand, while doing something that she had once taken for granted. He reached for her. Surely he'd done it thousands of times over the years, but it nearly knocked the breath out of her now. So much was expressed in that single gesture—everything she'd wished for, the thing that had left an unimaginable void when it was taken away. She'd felt heartbroken every time she and Logan had ever parted, even when she'd done the walking away.

"Hey, Logan," she said as they advanced over rickety gray wooden slats glazed with sand. Tall beach grass rustled and whipped at their legs. "Can we make a deal?"

"Tentatively, yes."

She stepped ahead of him and came to a stop, taking his other hand and peering up at him. His aviator sunglasses glinted as a curious smile spread slowly across his lips. Between the glare and his grin, it was a wonder she wasn't blind. "No more questions today, okay? Even when it's just the two of us. Let's practice being happy. I think I've forgotten how to do that."

He wrapped an arm around her shoulders, pulling her close and pressing a kiss to the top of her head. At moments like this, his tenderness was unmatched, a gift. "I think we both could use the practice."

Julia sighed, her legs feeling a bit like they were made of rubber. Being in his arms gave her exactly what she'd been craving—a refuge. "Good."

A few dozen steps and they crested the dunes and descended the stairs to the beach. Aside from an older couple sleeping on lounge chairs beneath an umbrella and a man casting a line into the water, the shore was nearly deserted, stretching north for what looked like a mile without another person. Julia let Logan lead the way down to the water. Midafternoon, the tide was low, revealing millions of tiny shells and scattered strands of seaweed.

Julia ventured in to her ankles, but Logan went midcalf, tugging on her hand. "Come on," he insisted. "It's so warm today."

"I don't want to get my dress wet."

He shook his head. "Don't be lame. Just come here."

There was something so sexy about being beckoned by Logan, somewhere between the tempting trouble of a dare and the thrill of an irresistible man wanting you close. She waded deeper. She had to. There was no denying Logan. Not when he was like this. She stood right next to him, the waves indeed threatening to soak the hem of her dress. They both looked off at the horizon, holding hands, leaning into each other as the Atlantic lapped at their legs. His thumb rubbed the back of her hand in a steady rhythm. The sun warmed her shoulders. Between Logan and the rock of the tide, the stress and worry were slipping away.

"Are you ready to give your toast tomorrow?" she asked.

"Yep. I have it all typed on my phone and everything."

"How very efficient of you."

"The best man should be prepared."

"I, of course, went old school and wrote mine on paper.

I'm a little worried it's corny, though. Either that or I'm thinking too hard about it."

"Do you have it with you?" He tugged on her hand.

"I do. It's in my purse. Want to trade?"

"We should probably at least practice."

"On dry land?"

"Yes."

They took their time, Julia kicking at the water as they made their way back up onto shore. They found a dry patch of sand and sat. The wind blew Julia's hair in a million directions as she dug around in her purse for the paper. Amid lip balm, gum and a pack of tissues, she finally found the carefully folded sheet torn from a legal pad. She handed it to Logan as he surrendered his phone to her.

It came as no surprise that Logan's was pure poetry from the first word, but the real curiosity was his subject matter. A few sentences in, she had to say something. "Logan. This is practically the same thing I wrote. Well, I mean, yours is written far better than mine, but that's no shock. You know, you really should write a memoir. I wasn't trying to fix your problems when I suggested it."

"I wouldn't know where to start with that, and I'm not sure anyone would want to read it in the first place."

"But you're an amazing writer. You'd figure it out. I know you'd do a fantastic job."

He returned his sights to the page, which ruffled in the breeze. Forearms resting on his knees, he shook his head and smiled. "Shhh. I'm reading."

Like she was supposed to do the same when he was being so adorable. Still, she returned to what he'd written, just to hear his voice in her head. It only took a few more lines before goose bumps were racing up her bare arms, even in the glow of the fading sun. "Fate returning two souls to each other? Isn't that the exact same thing I said?"

"You said fate *bringing* two souls together."

"Of course. I don't have your flair, Mr. Memoir-Writer. I'm calling you that from now on, just so you know." She went on reading, soon stumbling over another parallel. "We both told the same story, about that night at the beach house when Tracy cut her foot on that rusty old can in the sand. About Carter carrying her inside and how sweet they were to each other."

"Is it really that surprising? It's a great story."

She shrugged. "It is a great story, but it also happened an eon ago. It's still a weird coincidence."

"When you and I are on the same page, we're really on the same page."

Julia's skin tingled with recognition. "It's true. There's not much stopping us when we're in sync." She handed him his phone and tucked her speech back into her purse. "Yours is so good. It's almost too good. I feel like I should change mine. Otherwise people are just going to get bored or say that we copied each other."

"Yours is perfect. Keep it just the way it is. I'll tweak mine. I'm sure I can come up with something else to say."

"See? You can't *not* write." Julia leaned back on her hands, digging her toes into the sand. "You know, I think about that night with Tracy and Carter and I'm still sort of in awe of it. It's still so vivid. It was like watching a movie. We saw them fall in love with each other. It was so romantic."

He reached back for her hand. "Maybe we're watching the same thing."

Warmth rushed to her cheeks. "It's not the same. We're participating. And we're a lot older now. We already fell in love for the first time."

"First off, I think it's better that we're older. It means more. And people can fall in love more than once. My grandmother used to say that the secret to a long marriage was falling in love over and over again. She'd been married to my grandfather for sixty-seven years when he passed away."

Leave it to Logan to break out an especially poignant story, made even better with his impossibly romantic turn of phrase. As competitive as they could be with each other, she'd gladly be outmatched by him when it came to romance. "Yeah? What makes you think things will suddenly work now that it's all so much more complicated?"

He shook his head and raised a finger to her lips. "We aren't asking questions today. No worrying about tomorrow. We only do what makes us happy. We do what feels right." He moved his hand to the side of her face and raked his fingers through her hair. "Like this."

Her heart wouldn't stop fluttering at the anticipation as he rubbed her jaw with his thumb and caressed her neck with his fingers. When his lips finally met hers, the kiss was soft and tender, but passionate. Focused. She sensed a different sweet sentiment with every move of his mouth, which still amazed her, even after all this time. She arched her back, craned her neck, desperate to keep doing the one thing that they knew they couldn't get wrong, no matter how hard they tried. His lips became more insistent, the heat building, his tongue gentle but unsubtle in where this was going. He wasn't kidding about doing what felt right—this was every kind of correct she could imagine. She shut out the bad thoughts that wanted to creep in and went with the moment. Old wounds would take a long time to heal. She couldn't expect it to happen overnight. And the kiss was definitely helping.

Logan really wished they had a blanket, so they could lie back on the sand, roll around a little. But they didn't, which meant he could take this kiss only so far. Not to mention that they were in public, however quiet the beach was that afternoon.

Julia's lips were as sweet now as they'd been every other time he'd kissed her over the last few days, but there was something else behind the kiss now…a promise that they were going to try to find a way. If Julia would just give a little bit, try to understand his hesitation and at least acknowledge that it was okay for him to feel the way he did, he could do the same. Give an inch here, an inch there, until finally they could meet in the middle.

Her hand clutched his biceps, her hair whipped at his face, as they both became more emphatic with the kiss. It was as if they were in their own little world and they were doing nothing but one-upping each other, a familiar part of their dynamic. *I want you. I want you more. I want you the most.* Logan's brain wouldn't stop thinking about what might lie ahead…a continuation of the heavenly fun they'd had that morning. They did, after all, have a hotel room to return to. They did, after all, have several hours until the rehearsal.

Julia's phone started beeping in her purse. She wrenched herself from the kiss and turned away from him, grabbing at her bag and digging in it.

"No, Jules. Let it go." *This is too good.* His eyes were half-open, his breathing labored. Every part of him was poised and ready to have her, make love to her.

"It's not a call. It's the alarm on my phone. We should head back to the hotel to get ready for the rehearsal."

The hotel. Bed. Privacy. "Yes. We should go." Logan grabbed his shoes and stood up, even when it was difficult to fully straighten. Everything below his waist was ready to have her, and it felt as if the blood had left his limbs. Julia scampered up the dunes to the stairs and Logan had no choice but to follow, every step painful, especially as he watched the sway of her hips in that summery dress and the way the wind carried it up to the middle of her thighs.

Logan grabbed a pair of flip-flops he'd left in the back seat and put them on, wanting to hurry as much as Julia did. He started the car and cranked the air-conditioning, needing to cool off. Julia had him way too warmed up. That morning had been wonderful, but it wasn't nearly enough, and everything had been a mystery then. There was far less gray area between them now.

They arrived at the hotel in record time, but Julia didn't seem to notice the liberties he'd taken with the speed limit. She was preoccupied with texting and checking things on her phone. The guy at the valet stand greeted them and took care of the car quickly, and they lucked out when they didn't have to wait for the elevator inside. Down the hall to their room, each step only made Logan's pulse race faster. He would have her. Right now.

He took her into his arms the instant they were inside their room, his hand quickly finding the zipper on the back of her dress and drawing it down. She kissed him back, moaning softly. He loved the sound, until he realized it was a complaint.

"Everything okay?"

"Why did you have to kiss me at the beach that way?" Her gorgeous chest was heaving.

"We were going with it, remember? And being around you is making me crazy, Jules. I want you. Now."

"I know. I want you, too." She kissed him, her tongue winding with his. "But we can't. There's no time. If we're late for the rehearsal, Tracy will literally kill me."

Julia's moans might have conveyed annoyance, but he was about to register a grievance of his own. "Just a quickie. Or a shower. We'll call it multitasking."

She shook her head and kissed his cheek. "You're cute,

but I have to do my hair and makeup from scratch and I haven't shaved my legs."

"See? I'll help."

"Do you really want to rush through this? If we're going to make love do you really want to hurry it? After the day we've had and everything we said to each other?" She pressed her hand flat against his chest. "I want us to be able to take our time with each other." She bit on her lower lip. "I want to be able to be thorough. If you know what I mean."

A low rumble came from the center of his chest. Oh, he knew exactly what she meant. And thinking about it all night was going to make him insane. Still, she was probably right. If they were going to get back to where they used to be, it needed to be more than a quickie. They needed hours to reconnect on every level. "Okay. You shower first. Just be sure to use all of the hot water. Every drop. I want mine ice cold."

"I'm sorry. Really. I am." She popped up onto her tiptoes and kissed his cheek. She flashed a smile and hurried off to the bathroom, shutting the door behind her.

Logan flopped down on the bed, frustration about to eat him alive. *This is going to be a really, really long night.*

Twelve

Logan now knew what it was like to be on the outs with the Keys family. And he didn't like it one bit.

"I have to talk to your dad," he mumbled into Julia's ear as they both stood in the church, waiting for the rehearsal to start.

"Not now," she whispered.

"At dinner."

She shot him a look. "Can we talk about this later?"

He was about to retort that they'd agreed there would be no questions, but the minister had begun delivering orders. Stand here. Stand there. Walk like this. Wait for this. Get out the rings. Wait again. This was going to take forever. All while enduring the cold shoulder from Julia's parents.

Carter and Tracy were wound as tight as he'd seen either of them, but it was seeing Mr. and Mrs. Keys like this that really ate at him. If he and Julia were going to find a future, he couldn't be at odds with them. Surprisingly, the person who seemed somewhat relaxed, or at least comparatively so, was Julia. Whether she'd wanted to admit it or not, keeping the secret of the baby had been a big burden to bear.

By far, the high spot of the rehearsal was standing at the altar with the other groomsmen, watching Julia walk up the aisle. Step by measured step, she was both graceful and statuesque, wearing a gauzy navy blue dress that fluttered at her feet and showed off her gorgeous shoulders. Their gazes connected, and he couldn't have contained his grin if he'd wanted to. Similarly, a smile broke across her face; petal pink washed over her cheeks. She shied away, casting her sights to the red carpet runner. His mind raced with excuses they could use to skip the rehearsal dinner—a horrible headache, a painful splinter. The truth was that he and Julia had shared a roller coaster of a day—from the high points of making love and spending time on the beach, to the low of that moment in the fitting room. They were finally back on track. She knew how he felt about the things that had bothered him for years, and he had begun the process of accepting that he might not be the baby's father. He'd been working hard to see past that possibility. And because of the things they'd patched up today, he craved more togetherness. He longed for them to be alone.

Once the ceremony run-through was done, and the bride and groom had shared their practice kiss, it was time for Logan and Julia to walk down the aisle arm in arm.

"You are so beautiful in that dress," he muttered out of the side of his mouth, pulling her close. "I know I told you at the hotel, but really. It's mind-boggling."

"You told me in the car, too. And don't act like I can even come close to matching the way you look in that suit." She glanced up at him, putting every nerve ending in his body on high alert. "The tie really brings out your eyes. Much better than the ones they put you in on TV."

Damn, it felt good to be admired by her. It was intoxicating enough to be in her presence, but when she was solely focused on him? Forget it. The rest of the world hardly existed. Step by step down that aisle, all eyes on them, he couldn't help but wonder what it would be like to go through this ritual with her. He had some fences to mend with the Keyses, but that would pass. With the ring in his pocket, he was still waiting to find the right moment to ask, the perfect point in time. There'd been twelve years of build-up to a proper proposal. It had to be right, and it had to be romantic.

Would Julia be as much of a wreck for her own wedding as she was for her sister's? He could just see it now—guest list a mile long, a wedding planner buzzing about and bossing everyone around, a big fancy church and an even fancier reception. Between her Hollywood friends and his legion of former teammates, it did seem to call for a grand affair. One rule would have to be strictly adhered to, by both of them—no exes. No exceptions.

Tracy insisted Julia ride with her out to the beach house for dinner, which left Carter and Logan some guy time in Logan's car.

"I can't believe you didn't tell me about the baby," Carter said. "That's huge."

He and Julia didn't enjoy the business of keeping secrets, but they had agreed to keep the question of paternity under wraps for now. They had enough obstacles to overcome, and they didn't need the world weighing in on their future. "I know. I'm sorry. I promised her I wouldn't say anything and I had to keep my word."

"Are you nervous? First-time dad and you have to figure out a way to make things work with the one woman who makes you crazy? That's a big challenge."

Logan felt the corners of his mouth turn down. It was so much more than that, and Carter had no idea. "When you put it like that, yes. I'm nervous."

"I didn't mean to sound all gloom-and-doom. I'm just in awe of you for trying. I think it's awesome. You're going to make an amazing dad."

Logan took the left onto Lumina Avenue toward the Keyses' beach house. Carter's words were still ringing in his ears. Was he really going to make a good dad? He wanted to think so. He wanted to believe he was up to the challenge, even if it meant raising a child who wasn't biologically his. "If I can be half as good of a dad as my father was, I'll be doing pretty well."

"I'm bummed I never had a chance to meet your dad. He sounds like he was such an incredible man."

"He was. I never would've gotten as far in baseball as I did without the things he did for me. I just wish I could've done it all. I still feel like I let him down. Or at least his memory." Logan always missed his dad, but it was especially palpable today. The conversation he'd had with his mom that morning would've been different with his father. Backward or macho or whatever anyone wanted to call it, his dad would've understood Logan's perspective fully. He wanted the baby to be his.

"I don't see any way your dad would've been anything less than totally proud of you."

"I guess. But if we'd won the World Series, I wouldn't have any doubts."

Logan slowed down as they approached the Keyses' beach house, which was all lit up, glowing against the darkening night sky. The parking area under the house was full, so Logan took a spot on the road. He turned off the ignition. "Ready?"

"I want to say one more thing. I know it's only been a year, but you need to find a way to let this go. Stop being so hard on yourself."

It wasn't that Logan needed the affirmation, but he'd take it. "Do I need to start paying you by the hour? Or are you hoping for a future in career counseling for athletes?"

Carter laughed. "I get that you're competitive and that you want it all. But not every ballplayer wins a World Series. Not every dad has a chance to see his child fulfill their dreams. It's sad, but it's life."

I know. Do I ever know.

Tracy pulled up behind them. Logan and Carter quickly hopped outside. Carter walked double-time to Tracy's side of the car, opening her door for her. By the time Logan got to Julia, he was too late to do the same, but he was at least able to close it for her. Tracy and Carter made their way to the house; Logan and Julia lagged behind.

"When do we get to get out of here?" he muttered.

"We haven't even eaten yet. My sister will freak out if we leave early."

"I know, but all I want is to be alone with you."

She stopped just shy of the door. A sly smile crossed her lips. "You're cute when you're desperate for sex."

"I'm not desperate. Just ready." It was about more than the physical urge, though. He needed that connection with her, especially after everything today.

He wrapped his arm around her waist and pulled her forward. Julia kissed him this time and it was so natural, as if they were falling together in perfect sync. It was as if he'd stepped into a dream. She pressed into him, arching her back, hinting at everything he wanted with a welcome side of enthusiasm.

They went inside where everyone was gathering for dinner—aunts, uncles and distant cousins had arrived at the house during the rehearsal, with their Aunt Judy, who lived up the coast in Elizabeth City, in charge. Lined up neatly on the kitchen island were chafing dishes of North Carolina chopped pork barbecue, coleslaw, hush puppies, collard greens and baked beans. Logan's stomach growled, but something else inside him begged for attention as he again exchanged looks with Julia's dad. He had to speak to him.

After dinner and many long toasts, Logan saw Julia's dad step outside onto the deck. Julia was immersed in conversation with her aunt, so he took his chance. He didn't want an argument. He wanted to fix this.

"Mr. Keys," Logan said, closing the sliding glass door behind him. The night air was humid and blustery. "Do you have a minute?"

Mr. Keys was standing at the railing, looking out at the surf. "Always. I always have a minute for you."

Logan finally felt as though he could breathe. "About today. I know this all came as a shock, but I don't want everyone to be too hard on Julia. She really was doing what she felt was right. You know her. She's always worried far more about everyone else than she is about herself."

Mr. Keys let out a quiet laugh. "I do know that about my daughter. That's for sure. She's been like that since she was little. The number of stray animals she brought home over the years would make your head spin. And don't even get me started on the charity lemonade stands."

Now it was Logan's turn to laugh. He loved the image of a young Julia, out there, trying to save the world one project at a time.

"So is this what you were hinting at yesterday?" Mr. Keys asked. "That business of not counting you two out?"

Logan nodded. "You could say that. I know this is unconventional, but things with Julia and I have been rocky over the years. We're doing our best to put it together."

"Unconventional? I'd call it putting the cart before the horse." Mr. Keys's words nearly made Logan's heart seize up. He turned, leaning back against the railing and folding his arms across his chest. He nodded in the direction of the party inside. Julia and Tracy were talking, right on the other side of the sliding glass doors. "You'll understand it much better when you're a dad, but those two girls are my greatest gift. I would do anything to protect them. Keep them safe."

"I understand. I really do."

"But you know, what you and Julia do is none of my darn business. I just want my daughters to be happy." There was an unmistakable wobble to Mr. Keys's voice, underscoring the reasons he'd been testy with Logan.

"I admire you for doing anything to protect your girls."

"I have to admit, I'm more than a little excited by the prospect of being a grandfather." He elbowed Logan in the stomach. "And what if it's a boy? I could have a major leaguer for a grandson."

Logan caught the look in Mr. Keys's eye, a glint of pride. Something about that moment made the baby much more real, far less of an abstract. Would the baby be a boy? A girl? Regardless, he saw ten small fingers and ten small toes, chubby legs and cheeks, a sweet baby face. In his mind, his head, and his heart, the baby looked like both Julia and him. He couldn't see the baby any other way. It might not be the right vision to cling to, but it was an idea firmly planted, and he'd just have to deal with the reality when the time came.

"I want you to know that I won't let Julia down. And I won't shirk my responsibilities. You'll have to trust that we're doing our best to work things out." He watched Julia through the glass—the way she focused intently when someone spoke to her, the way she tossed her head back when she laughed, and the way her smile reflected the light inside her. She was so beautiful, inside and out. Mr. Keys had called her a gift. Logan understood now how true that was. *I love her.* He wasn't sure what he'd done to be lucky enough to have a second chance with her. Or in reality, more like his tenth chance. He only knew that he wouldn't let Julia wonder whether he was there for her. She said she needed to feel safe and like everything was okay. He could do that.

After two plates of food, three lemonades and countless uncomfortable questions about the future, Julia allowed herself to relish the part she'd played in making the rehearsal dinner a success. Tracy had completed the process of softening to her sister, although it had taken some intense conversation during the car ride to the beach, topped off with Tracy downing several glasses of wine. She actually seemed happy with the way things had gone. The food had been wonderful; the cake had arrived on time and exactly as Tracy had wanted it. Everyone raved about the house renovations. Tracy even remarked that the decorations were "perfect." Aside from an uncle from Indiana liberating himself from his pants before heading out for a late-night swim, the evening had been largely free of controversy. Now the final guests were filtering out of the beach house.

Julia was helping clean up the kitchen when Logan came up behind her, wrapping his arms around her waist and kissing her neck. "Mmm. You smell so good." His words and a single kiss sent electricity racing along her spine. And it felt so good to have his broad frame and warm body pressed against hers.

"Thank you. Shouldn't be too long and we can get out of here. Just a few more dishes."

"Can't someone else deal with this? You've worked your butt off today." With that, he gave her bottom a gentle squeeze. "Save some for me, please."

Julia turned around and playfully swatted him on his arm. "You're bad."

"I said please." His eyes scanned her face, amping up the anticipation. Sure, she and Logan had been to bed before. Just that morning, in fact. But not like this. Not when so much was on the line and she was so very well aware of how easily it could fall apart. She decided it was best to celebrate the fragile nature of what was between them. It was new life, just like the baby, and that was to be nurtured and cared for.

"Aunt Judy, do you mind finishing up?" Julia asked.

Her aunt looked up from the living room where she was fluffing couch cushions and picking up plastic cups. "Of course, darling. I'll take care of it. See you in the morning at the church."

"Have I told you how much I adore you, Aunt Judy?" Logan asked.

"You didn't need to. It's all over your face." She smiled wide. "Now shoo, you two."

Julia grabbed her purse and cardigan, took Logan's hand, and out they went into the night. The roar of the ocean was off in the distance, warm breeze sweeping against her skin as Logan took her hand and led her to the car. They climbed inside and Logan went for a kiss instead of turning the key in the ignition.

Julia reared back her head. "If we start here, we'll never be able to leave. And I really don't want Aunt Judy walking by while we're steaming up the windows."

"So true." Logan started the car, and after quickly looking both ways, made a U-turn in the middle of the street and raced off to the hotel. This late at night, they thankfully hit more than their fair share of green lights. Julia hoped it was symbolic of the future—no more stopping. Just moving forward.

By the time they turned the car over to the valet, speed-walked through the lobby, rode the elevator and raced down the hall to their room, they were both laughing. It was a fun and nervous laughter, filled with hope and happiness. Julia couldn't think of a time when things had felt more perfect.

"Before we go in, phones off," he said.

"Yes. You're so smart." She dug hers from her purse and shut the power off. "Good to go."

Logan opened the door and had his hands all over her the instant it closed behind them. "This dress has got to go."

"I thought you liked it."

"I do. I love it. I love it so much I want to see what it looks like on the floor. I think it will go with the carpet quite nicely."

"Just like your suit."

"I feel like we should hang up the suit."

"And not my dress? Talk about a double standard."

He wrapped his hand around her neck and rubbed her jaw with his thumb. "Kiss me and tell me we can worry about laundry later."

"Gladly," she purred, tugging on his necktie as his mouth crashed into hers. He smelled so good—the fragrance she could only describe as Logan, like a good glass of bourbon, warmed in the summer sun.

She took off his tie and he wrestled his way out of his jacket. Her fingers flew over the buttons of his shirt and as soon as that was gone, he turned her around, unzipping the back of her dress. He teased it from her shoulders, pushing it to the floor before pressing his body against hers. She felt the cool metal of his belt buckle in the curve of her back, and lower…a firm declaration of how turned on he was. He took her hair in his hands and swept it back from her neck, kissing her softly with a gentle brush of his tongue. She loved having him stand behind her. There was something so sexy about it, as if he expected no reciprocity, but of course she would be giving.

She reached back, finding his erection, which strained against the front of his pants. She pressed against it with her hand, eliciting a low groan from him. He backed up slightly and unhooked her strapless bra, a double dose of relief—the boning had been digging into her armpits for hours. She hummed with happiness over the reprieve from the torturous garment. Logan turned her in his arms, admiring her breasts with both hands, both eyes and a whole lot of commentary.

"I've always loved your breasts, but I just love how full they are right now."

Heat rushed to her cheeks. "Thanks."

"I meant it. They're stunning. Truly stunning."

"I'm glad you're enjoying them."

He cupped them with his palms, rubbed her nipples with his thumbs, drawing them into tight peaks. A week or so ago, that would've been torture, but the initial tenderness had subsided and between his touch and the pregnancy hormones, she was writhing with anticipation of more. As if he'd heard the wish she'd made in her head, he lowered his head and drew a nipple into his warm mouth, sucking softly and flicking at it with his tongue. She cradled his head in her hands, caressing his temples, leaning down to kiss the top of his head. He switched to the other breast and did the same, ramping up the intensity with licks and hot breath, causing her skin to bead so tightly she already felt as if she might unravel the instant he touched her most intimate parts.

He lowered himself to his knees, clutching her rib cage, then dragging his hands down her sides to her hips. He kissed her lower belly, gazing up at her. The only light in the room came from the nearly full moon, which was low in the sky tonight and cast soft beams through the window sheers. He was unbearably handsome in any light, but she couldn't have imagined him looking any more so than he did at that moment—his eyes and face full of adoration.

"I meant what I said earlier about your current state being a turn-on. Your body is so ripe right now. Every inch of you has a little more to squeeze and I love it. I absolutely love it." He grasped her hips, curving his fingers into the fleshy part of her buttocks, then tucked his fingers into the waist of her black satin panties and dragged them down to her ankles. She stepped out of them, reaching out to the arm of the chair behind her to steady herself. Logan seized the opportunity and backed her up a step, urging her to sit, but making it clear with his hands that he wanted her perched on the edge of the seat. Still on his knees, he coaxed one of her legs outward and hitched the other leg over his shoulder, opening her up to him. "Sit back for me," he said.

She watched his every move as his hand found her center and teased apart the folds. She gasped when he slipped two fingers inside her and rocked his thumb against her apex, slowly but deliberately. Her eyes opened and closed in an unpredictable pattern as her mind warred between wanting to luxuriate in the pleasure and wanting to watch what this incredible man was able to do to her. His fingers continued to glide inside her, and he curled them into the spot that made her arch her back and moan. Every inch of her marveled at how good it all felt, but there was a whole lot of anticipation of the main event going on in her head. "That feels so good," she muttered, feeling as if she might break at any moment. "But I want you inside me, Logan."

He kissed her lower belly. "I love hearing you say that. But we have all night, and I plan to enjoy every inch of you." He then moved his thumb aside from the tender bundle of nerves he'd been working and lowered his mouth to that spot, enveloping her with warmth as he wound his tongue in lazy circles.

Her thoughts were hazy, pleasure coiling tightly in her belly, and all she could do was unwind and let Logan have his way. Her breaths were ragged. Her chest heaved. Her body temperature was climbing steadily, warming her skin. With every pass of his tongue, the release crept closer, until finally she could take the pressure no longer and gave in to the orgasm. She called out his name and grasped his head, as every wave of joy and warmth unraveled her a little more. The minute she got her wits back, she sat up and brought Logan's face to hers, kissing him deeply as the remnants of the release still teased her body. In some ways, he hadn't satisfied her need for him so much as he'd heightened it.

He rose to his feet and stood before her, a tower of defined muscle. She tugged him closer and wrapped her hand around his steely length, rolling her thumb over the tip and watching his reaction. He closed his eyes and his head dropped back as her fingers rode up and down, gripping him until he became impossibly hard.

"Make love to me, Logan," she whispered.

He reached down and took her hand, bringing her to standing. They wrapped their arms around each other, kissing deeply, lips warm and wet. They turned in circles on their way to the bed, an incoherent couple's dance that eventually brought them to their landing spot. They collapsed on the bed in a heap and Logan rolled her to her back. He positioned himself between her legs and pushed himself up with one arm. Julia gasped when he finally came inside, at first only a little, before he flexed his torso and thrust with one strong and fluid movement.

He kissed her passionately, his tongue exploring her mouth and lips, as she wrapped her legs around him and they rocked in a rhythm that was all their own. Julia's mind became a swirl of serene thoughts. Many things in her world had felt wrong lately, but this undoubtedly felt right. It was the one conclusion she could make with zero deliberation. Logan rode in and out of her, lowering his head to her breast and flicking at her nipples with his tongue.

She was already poised for another release, but she focused on relaxing, even when her body was tensing in waves. His breaths were becoming short and labored, and she could tell from the tension in his back that he was close to his own climax. He kissed her again, this time with reckless urgency, his open mouth skating over hers, her cheeks and her neck. His thrusts came faster and more forceful until finally his body froze and a deep groan left his throat. He shuddered in her arms, and that was all it took for her to come undone once more, her body clutching his as he took a few final thrusts.

In utter exhaustion, he collapsed next to her on the bed, not hesitating to pull her against him and kiss her softly. "That was so incredible. Totally worth the wait."

She laughed quietly and shook her head, resting her head on his magnificent chest. "You mean the wait since this morning?"

"This morning was wonderful, don't get me wrong. But this had a lot of build-up. Makes it better." He raked his fingers through her hair. "I want you to know one thing,

Jules. I have always loved you. No matter what happens, I always will."

The confession took her by surprise, but not of a happy nature. It left her with that familiar sinking feeling, mostly because of what he hadn't said recently. Ever since they'd been doing well as a pair, he'd dropped all of his talk of marriage. What did that mean? Was he just trying to get through the weekend? He'd been so insistent about it before, bringing it up whenever he had the chance. Now the subject of marriage, and the future, and the baby were all absent. "You never stopped?"

Logan groaned. "Jules. No questions, remember?"

But she did have a question. More than one, actually. Starting with this—why did "I will always love you" have to sound so much like "goodbye"?

Thirteen

Waking up next to Julia was more spectacular than Logan had remembered. Perhaps because it meant more now. They had managed to reclaim what they had three months ago, only this time he would not mess up.

She stirred in his arms and kissed his chest, bringing his entire body to life. "Good morning," she murmured sweetly.

"It is a very good morning." *Every morning will be good with you.*

"The big day is here."

"It is." The big day was indeed upon them, and not just for Tracy and Carter, although Julia had no idea. Logan had monumental plans for after the wedding—he was finally going to propose. He'd decided last night after Jules fell asleep, spending hours—literally—thinking out every scenario. The way he might feel if the baby wasn't his. The way he would feel if the baby was. What it would feel like to build a family with Julia, the woman he'd never stop loving. He wouldn't take this lightly, as she'd suggested he might. He was ready. They were ready. He would convince her of it. And he was an idiot if he waited even another day. He wasn't about to risk something going wrong. He had to tie up these particular loose strings, ASAP.

"Yep. Won't be long now and it'll all be over. I'll be flying back to LA to finish the movie. You'll be flying home to Connecticut."

He could tease her about this later, right after he'd popped the question. "Back to reality."

She abruptly sat up in bed, turning her back to him. "Have you figured out what you're changing in your toast?"

"Not yet, but I will." With everything else going on, he hadn't had a spare second to think about it. Hopefully something would happen during the ceremony to spark an idea.

She grabbed his T-shirt from the floor and put it on, then made a beeline for the bathroom.

"You aren't leaving me, are you?"

"Gotta hop in the shower. It's my last chance to have an entire day where I don't make my sister mad. I don't want us to be late."

She closed the bathroom door and Logan got up, pulling on a pair of basketball shorts. He began to collect the belongings he would need for the day. He reached inside the pants pocket where the ring was safely tucked away, and gave it a squeeze for good luck. Wouldn't be long until it was on Julia's finger.

Julia had left a tote bag sitting on the floor, which had fallen over, causing several things to slip out, including a book about pregnancy. Curious, he flipped through the pages, quickly becoming immersed and sitting in the chair to read. There was so much to learn. Julia's body was going to do a lot of incredible things over the next six months. As would the baby. Apparently, she'd soon be able to feel the baby kick. *The baby.* It was still difficult to wrap his head around it, but it was getting a little easier with every passing minute, and a kick he could understand.

Julia seemed in a bit of a mood when she got out of the bathroom, but Logan knew the wedding weighed heavily on her mind, so he didn't bother saying anything, preferring instead to keep things light and upbeat. After he showered and dressed, they were off to the church by nine thirty. The ceremony was at eleven, to be followed by lunch and dancing until early evening, which suited Logan just fine. It meant more time for his night with Julia, the one where they finally set their future on the right path.

They ran into the woman from the bridal shop in the church parking lot.

"Everything go okay with the alterations?" Julia asked.

The woman nodded as she handed over a garment bag. "It did. There was enough fabric in the side seams to let it out. Good luck with the pregnancy."

Julia smiled, but Logan knew that particular grin, and it wasn't one she used when she was happy. It was for those moments when she had to fake it. "Uh-huh. Thank you."

The woman left while Logan and Julia walked inside. "You okay?" he asked.

"Doesn't it seem weird that she mentioned the pregnancy out loud?"

Logan shrugged. "I guess. But isn't she the one who figured it out?"

Julia clutched the garment bag to her chest. "We asked the women in the shop not to say anything. Do you think somebody could've said something? I really don't want us to have to deal with the press again."

Logan hated seeing her so on edge, just as much as he

hated the idea of battling the media again. He gripped her elbow and kissed her temple. "Don't be paranoid. It'll be fine."

"Okay." She didn't seem at all convinced. "I have to go get dressed. Then I need to check on the flowers one last time."

"Sounds like a plan. I have to do a few things for Carter, but I'll meet you in the chapel if I can."

"Okay." Her tone was annoyed, but she was worried about the notion of the press returning. Precisely the reason to wait for peace and calm to pop the question.

They parted, Logan finding the room where the groomsmen were camped out. "How's Tracy's future husband?" Logan asked Carter, who was in his tux and pacing, about to wear a path in the carpet.

Carter tugged at the collar. "I already hate this thing. And I can't stop sweating."

Logan clapped him on the shoulder. "Just sit and relax. You're going to do great today. It'll all be fine. I promise." Logan had apparently been put in charge of keeping everyone calm, a job he readily accepted today. For once, he felt as though he could see ahead, to the future. He had a clear course to take. A purpose. "I need to get dressed."

Logan ducked into a small adjacent room to put on his tux. He was putting in his cufflinks when Carter poked his head in. "Julia's out in the hall. She says she needs to talk to you right away. I think she's panicking again."

What now? Please don't let it be the press. "Okay. I'll be right out." He slipped into his jacket and rushed out into the hall.

She knocked the breath right out of him when he saw her. Sure, he'd seen her in the dress at the bridal shop, but this was different and not just because it actually fit her now. Her hair was up in an elegant twist; the morning light from the arched windows that lined the hall cast her in a heavenly glow. She was so gorgeous—so perfect. And his. Now he understood what Carter had been saying about waiting for the other shoe to drop. Logan was damn lucky and he knew it.

"We have a problem," she blurted.

"Just one?" He stepped next to her, inhaling her sweet scent. "Then I'd say we're doing great. You look absolutely gorgeous, by the way."

"Don't be so dismissive."

"I could say the same thing about you. You didn't even acknowledge my compliment." He circled his arms around her waist, wanting her close.

She took a deep breath and forced a smile. "Thank you. Now come with me." She grasped his hand and marched them into the chapel. "Look. It's a complete disaster."

His eyes darted all over the room, searching for evidence of catastrophe. "What is?"

"The peonies. They aren't pale pink. They're pale purple. They're practically lavender." She forged ahead up the aisle, and Logan had to hustle to keep up. "See what I mean?" She pointed to an arrangement attached to the end of the pew as if it were the most repulsive thing she'd ever seen.

She wasn't wrong. They were clearly purple. And who really cared at this point? "Considering everything that has happened over the past few days, this is so unimportant. You did your best, and that's all anyone can ask. In the end, Tracy and Carter will be married, and that's what really matters."

"You don't think she'll freak out?"

"If she does, tell her to freak out at me. You've done so much to make her happy, and that includes keeping a secret that totally backfired on you."

"Please don't say I told you so."

"I won't. I think you know now that it was a bad idea to keep the pregnancy from your family."

She bowed her head. "I do. I messed up. I completely ruined that moment with my mom and there's no getting it back. I think that's my problem. I'm trying to keep any more moments from being ruined."

He put his arm around her and pulled her close. "It will all change when the baby arrives. Your mom will forget all of that. You'll have your moment with her then." All he could think about was the proposal later. He wanted that to be perfect, too. He understood exactly how she felt. "You know, I was reading your pregnancy book this morning while you were in the shower."

"You did?"

"I did. I read all about how big the baby is right now and about how big it's going to get. I read about when you'll be able to feel it kick. That's exciting stuff." *I hope I get to be there.* There was still part of him that knew Julia could panic. Or change her mind. Or say no. And her reaction to something as simple as the color of flowers wasn't doing much to assuage his worry.

She bit into her lower lip, her mouth quivering. "That's so sweet."

"Why are you crying?"

"Because I don't know what to think anymore, Logan, that's why. Two days ago you were all hot to get married and then the minute we start getting along, you drop it. All I can think is that you're just waiting and hoping..." A sob came out of her. "Hoping that the baby is yours."

He pulled her into a hug, holding her close, not wanting to ever go. "Of course I hope that the baby is mine. How could I not hope that?"

Julia's body tensed in such an immediate way that he knew he'd messed up.

He stood back, holding on to her shoulders. The sadness in her eyes had become more profound. "That's probably not the right way to put it. In fact, I know it's not the right way to put it." He couldn't explain himself further. It would ruin his plans for tonight. Guests would be walking into the church any minute now. There was no time.

"No. It's okay. I know what you mean. And you're just being honest."

He breathed a huge sigh of relief. "Exactly."

"You're just saying what's really in your heart. Which is that you only want to be with me if the baby is yours. You've convinced yourself that's the only way this works."

No no no. "That's not what I'm saying. I haven't convinced myself of anything. I love you, Jules, I told you that."

"You told me that you will always love me. It's not the same. And I need you to love the baby, completely. That's the only way this works. Unconditional love. No questions asked."

Visions of Julia's legion of scummy boyfriends shuffled through his mind, the guys who always treated her so badly. Was he strong enough to love a child who was a product of one of those pairings? The pairings that had ripped his heart out, and hers for that matter, over and over again? He wanted to be able to say that he would love the baby unconditionally from his or her very first breath, but the truth was that it might take some getting used to. Not much. But possibly a little. He would get there. He knew he would. But if he was being honest, there was a chance it would take time. "Am I not allowed to have a single doubt?" He took her hand and led her to the far side of the rectory as guests began to file in.

She crossed her arms, the hurt and betrayal radiating off of her. He wasn't doing any better. How had they ended up back at square one again? Neither of them truly trusting that the other would do what they said they were going to do? "No, Logan. You aren't. You aren't allowed to have a single doubt. I don't see any way that two people stay together for the long haul without setting aside every last doubt in their head."

A low grumble escaped Logan's throat. "Love isn't a destination. It takes work. A lot of work. And you're being so stubborn about this."

"I have no choice but to be exactly that, Logan. I can't let you break my heart again. It nearly killed me the first time."

Nearly killed me. "Then we work it out. Again." He couldn't hide his irritation with all of this.

She shook her head, tears welling at the corners of her eyes. "My original plan was the safest. You and I make great friends. We make great lovers. I think we'll make a good mom and dad, but I think those are separate things now. I don't know that we'll make a good husband and wife."

"What are you saying?"

She wrapped her arms around her waist, tears now rolling down her cheek.

"No. No. Jules, don't bail on me." It felt as if his stomach was diving for the floor. This was classic Julia—form an opinion and steamroller ahead, even when her take on things might not be based in reality.

"You know what, Logan? This is part of me correcting my past mistakes. You said you didn't want to be with me when I viewed you as a project. Well, this is me telling you that you're not a project. You don't want me to fix you, fine. I'm done fixing. You figure it out."

"Hoping that the baby will be mine isn't the most selfish thing in the world. It's human. I'm human."

She shook her head. "Do you have any idea how lonely I felt the day I found I was pregnant? That was supposed to be a purely happy day. But all I could do was wonder how I was going to make this work." Her hand went to her belly, cupping the tiny mound that was there. "This child needs love, Logan. Pure and simple. Doesn't matter what color his skin is or how tall she ends up being. In the end, this tiny human being growing inside me is going to need love. If I have to be the only person who gives it, I'll do that. Because I can't sit by and wonder if and when you're going to get with the program. I won't do it. It's one thing when it's my heart on the line, but I won't hurt this child."

"I'm not trying to hurt anyone. I'm just being honest."

Now the tears were really streaming down Julia's face, streaking her makeup and blanching her skin. "You questioned my stance on the paternity test, but this is the exact moment I feared. I knew that the minute I did and we got an answer you weren't going to like, that would be the end of Logan and Julia, forever. I wasn't ready to shut the door on us. But unfortunately, this just makes it feel like you do. I can't let you do it again, Logan. I have to be stronger than that."

"Jules. Come on. Let's just talk. I beg you."

"I can't stay. Not like this." With a swish of her dress, she was gone. Straight down the aisle and right out of his life.

I should've known. I should've known it was too good to be true. Things aren't perfect for Logan and he has to take off. Just like last time.

Julia raced down the hall to the room where her sister was getting ready. She stopped in the doorway, unable to step inside, although she wasn't sure why. Her mom was there, standing by Tracy's side.

"No tears." Tracy looked into the vanity mirror as she adjusted a clip in her hair. "There will be no tears on my wedding day."

"The mother of the bride is entitled to cry, honey. It's practically a tradition." Their mother pulled a tissue from her purse and blew her nose.

Julia stood frozen, sucking in deep breaths as inconspicuously as possible. And to think she'd been worried that flowers or cakes or of course, her pregnancy secret might ruin her sister's wedding. The reality was she was one unkind word away from collapsing into a pathetic pile of pink organza on the floor.

"Hey, Jules. I didn't see you there," Tracy said.

"Yep. Just got here." Julia's lip trembled, but she tried to ignore it.

"Everything good?" Tracy asked.

"Yes. Of course." Her sister would have her perfect day if it killed her. Which meant Julia had to keep her desire to blubber her eyes out to herself.

"Are you okay, darling? Your voice sounds funny. And why are you practically standing out in the hall? Come inside or Carter might try to sneak a peek at the bride."

Julia stepped into the room and closed the door behind her. "I'm fine. Just a little choked up, that's all. It's Tracy's big day and we've been waiting for it for so long. I'm so incredibly happy for her."

Tracy caught her sister's gaze in the reflection of the mirror. She jutted out her lower lip. "Now you're going to make me cry. That's the sweetest thing I think you've ever said to me. Come here." Tracy turned and reached for Julia and good God, Jules couldn't have kept it together if she'd been paid to do it. "I'm so sorry about my behavior over the last few days," Tracy said. "I know I've been hard on you and I'm sorry. Someday, you'll be in my place and you'll understand why I got so caught up in everything. I swear, it'll make you crazy."

In my place. Julia was convinced she would never, ever be in her sister's place. Ever. She wasn't capable of keeping a relationship together. Call it self-sabotage. Call it something else. She messed it up every time, and there was no sign of her changing this pattern any time soon. She and Logan had their breakthrough, the one they'd tried to reach for years. Then it all came tumbling down.

"I'm sorry I caused so many problems. It was never my intention," Julia said.

"I know you didn't do it on purpose. And you'll understand when you're a bride."

A single tear leaked from the corner of Julia's eye and she felt it about to happen—an avalanche of emotion was starting, trembling and quaking, threatening to crush her flimsy composure. "I'm not ever going to be a bride. I'm never going to get married. I'm going to die alone." The crying started. She'd cried more in the last month than she cared to admit. It wasn't a good thing to feel so on edge all the time.

"Don't say that."

"It's true. I get involved with the wrong guys over and over again. I can't help myself."

"Did something happen with Logan? I thought you two were working things out."

"We were, but then he had to go and say something that made me realize he doesn't really love me the way I need him to love me."

"What happened?"

Julia got very quiet, realizing there was a lot more to this explanation than simply recounting what happened.

"The thing is, about the baby, I'm not sure if it's his. It might be the boyfriend I had briefly before him."

"Oh no." Her mother closed her eyes and scratched her temple.

"Please don't freak out. I'm sorry I'm dumping all of this on you right now. We have to walk into that church in a few minutes and everything. I just... I thought he and I had worked it out and that he'd come to terms with the possibility that the baby isn't his, but he clearly still has doubts."

"Well, of course he has doubts. It's okay to have doubts," Tracy said, grabbing a nail file from the vanity and shaping one of her nails. "Carter had all kinds of doubts when we got back together. About whether or not it would work. He was gun-shy, to say the least. I was the one who'd broken up with him, and I think he was afraid I was going to break his heart again."

Many of Logan's words echoed in Julia's head...everything he'd said about the ways in which he'd been sure Julia would break his heart. "But you worked through all of it. You're getting married. Everything is perfect now."

"Everything is not perfect. We worked through enough to say that taking a chance on each other is a good idea. It doesn't mean we don't still have doubts. That's just part of being a couple. If you sit around waiting for the moment when everything is perfect, you're going to miss out on a lot."

Julia couldn't believe what was coming out of Tracy's mouth. "But Logan said that even though he loves me, he's still nervous about how he'll feel if the baby isn't his. And he was dead-set on getting married two days ago. Now that it's a little more real, he hasn't said a word about that. Doesn't that seem like an awfully damning detail?"

Their mother stepped forward and shook her head. "Jules, do you have any idea what you're asking of him?

It takes a big man to accept another man's responsibility, if that's the way this ends up. Of course he's going to have doubts. He's a first-time dad. Being a parent means you doubt everything and most of it comes down to worry that you won't measure up. Look at the relationship he had with his own dad. I'm sure he's worried about filling those shoes. It's not necessarily a reflection of you or the way he feels about you. Logan is a good man with a big heart, and he's wanted to be with you for more than twelve years. I think it's time you finally gave him the benefit of the doubt."

Julia's stomach sank. "So you're saying I messed up. Again."

"Yes. Yes, I am."

Nothing like being real, Mom.

"The good thing about mistakes is they can almost always be fixed."

A knock came at the door. "Five minutes until we're ready for the bride."

"Are you going to be okay, Jules?" Tracy asked.

Once again, totally not okay. Julia composed herself, glancing in the mirror and wiping away a smudge of mascara with her pinkie. "Yes. I'm great. My sister is getting married. That's all I really care about right now."

Fourteen

The ceremony was torture. Standing up there, feet away from Logan, all while the room was filled with the heady scent of flowers and the knowledge that everyone in attendance was witnessing true love. Julia knew they were, and she was happy for her sister, but it only underscored one fact—this was one place she would never be.

When it came to the vows, Julia did everything she could to keep it together, but it was nearly impossible. The gasps and cries coming out of her mother in the front row weren't helping. Then there was Logan. She watched as he listened intently. The man had enough good looks for seven men, but that wasn't what she loved about him. She loved him for his persistence with her; she loved him for the ways he pushed for what he wanted. She loved him for his heart, which she knew from experience was the best place to ever be.

How could one person be everything she ever wanted

and still feel impossible to hold on to? Where was the fairness in that? Nowhere, that's where. But did it really matter? She might not have pushed him away the last time, but she'd pushed him away today, just as she'd pushed him away before. The pushing had to stop. The insecurities inside her, the ones that said she would never be good enough for him, were just going to have to learn to shut up. She had to make things right. She had to find a way to claim her one millionth chance to turn things around.

When it came time to walk down the aisle with him, she didn't waste a second. "We have to talk," she muttered out of the side of her mouth, with a big smile plastered to her face.

Logan smiled, too, but she knew it was for show, not his reaction to her. "Tell me about it."

They stood in the receiving line for a good half hour, shaking hands, kissing cheeks. Then it was time to go in to the reception. Every time Julia thought she'd catch a stray minute, someone would come up to her and start talking. Or they would drag Logan off to chat with someone else. It was a nightmare—no privacy, no alone time, no chance to just talk this out.

When it came time for toasts, she operated on autopilot. She read it exactly as she'd written it, not nearly as well as Logan, the man with the wonderful way with words. All she could think about was being on the beach a mere twenty-four hours ago, the world falling apart and coming together all at the same time. Her entire existence changed with Logan. It was different. It was better. And she was desperate to get back there. Again. Her mother and sister were right. It was horrible of her to hold Logan to such unrealistic standards.

"Let's all raise a glass to Tracy and Carter," she said, lifting her champagne glass, which was full of ginger ale.

The bubbles tickled her nose; tears tickled her eyes. The room was so full of love it nearly made her sick. Would Logan accept hers? What reason did he have aside from the baby? It would be easier on him if he just walked away. There was no doubt in her mind about that.

Logan clinked his fork against the side of his glass and stood. His focus was on Tracy and Carter, exactly as it should have been, but she longed for even a glance, a single flicker of his warm eyes. One look that would tell her that everything would be okay. That he would forgive her. "Just as Julia spoke of fate, I had originally planned to talk about the same thing today. And why wouldn't I? We all look at Tracy and Carter and know that they're meant to be together. It feels like fate that they found each other. Julia said exactly that." His normally strong voice wobbled, and he cleared his throat. "But what I want to talk about and toast to is perfection, or more specifically, the need to cast aside the notion of finding the perfect person. Because the truth is that Carter and Tracy aren't perfect. Neither one of them."

Carter shrugged and slugged back the last of the champagne in his glass, which brought a laugh from the guests and a welcome moment of levity.

"But together, as a couple, Carter and Tracy are perfect. They are there for each other. They don't let each other down. And when they do, they know how to say they're sorry."

Julia's breaths had grown so shallow she thought they might evaporate. Was this Logan's way of telling her that she'd done exactly that? She'd let him down. She would own up to it. She would say she was sorry. If he gave her the chance.

"They know how to forgive and ask for forgiveness,"

he continued. "They know to hold on to each other and not let go, because that is more important than anything."

With that, Logan looked at Julia intently, their gazes connecting, sending a steeplechase of goose bumps over her skin. His expression was difficult to read though and that filled her with familiar doubt. She wanted to think that she saw openness in his incredible eyes. She wanted to believe he would listen to her one more time, and that he wasn't instead holding her up as an example of the ways people don't manage to hold on to each other.

Logan turned his sights to the room of family and friends before them. "I'm not perfect," Logan continued. "I have made every mistake in the book. I have fallen short and I have failed. I've failed some of the most important people in my life. I'm not perfect. We're all imperfect." He glanced over at Julia again, this time looking much more deeply into her eyes. She was hanging on every word, still finding it nearly impossible to breathe. "But the beautiful thing about life is that if you find another person to love, your imperfections aren't important. Two imperfect people can make a perfect pair." He pressed his lips together and looked away. "With that, I want to wish Tracy and Carter a long and happy life together."

Logan sat down after his toast, hoping like hell that had done the trick. What else could he do? If Julia had decided that whatever he had to offer simply wasn't enough, there wasn't much to be done. How many times could he plead his case? It was nearly impossible to convince her of anything, but at least he could say that he'd made a strong argument.

The DJ made an announcement that it was time for Carter and Tracy's first dance. He watched as they made their way out to the dance floor, Tracy in her elegant white

gown and Carter in his charcoal-gray tux. They seemed
as happy as two people could be. *I want what they have.*
His plan to get one step closer to his own wedding now
seemed stupid. He should have given Julia the ring yesterday, when she was happy. He should have remembered
just how tenuous things were between them and been more
mindful of that.

Carter and Tracy started their dance, staring into each
other's eyes, and gracefully swaying back and forth in
each other's arms.

Julia, however, was playing musical chairs. She slid
into the seat her sister had been occupying minutes ago,
one seat closer to him. She patted the empty chair that had
been Carter's. "Come here," she whispered.

He nearly asked if this was a trick, but he couldn't
deny his natural inclination to want to be closer to her.
He obliged. "Yes?"

"I wasn't kidding when I said that we need to talk."

"Okay. When?"

"Now?"

"The bride and groom are having their first dance.
Don't you think we should stay to see that?"

She looked out at the dance floor and bobbed her head
three times. "Okay. We saw it. Time to talk."

He laughed quietly. "For someone who was so concerned with making her sister happy, you don't seem to
care much about it now."

She grasped his arm and squeezed, hard. "I'm more
concerned with making us happy."

His breath caught in his throat. Maybe his speech really had worked. "Okay. Where?"

"Come with me." She took his hand and they made a
careful and quiet exit, going out through the side of the reception hall, outside, and up a set of stairs to a wide stone

balcony with a view of the Cape Fear River running alongside the downtown river walk.

When she stopped, she turned to him and took both hands, squinting into the sun. "I'm an idiot. I'm a total dummy and you're just going to have to find a way to forgive me. Let's get a paternity test right away. I'll do anything I can to have a shot at keeping you for real. We'll put all of it to rest and I'll have to trust that fate will keep us together somehow. We'll just do it. Rip it off like a Band-Aid."

If only she knew the thoughts that had run through his head during the ceremony, about the things he'd said. "We don't have to rely on fate, Jules. I don't want a paternity test. Frankly, you're as much of a test as I can handle."

She smiled softly. "Funny. I could say the same thing about you."

"Believe me, I know." He looked down at his feet, then out at the water, searching for the right words to say. Thoughts of Julia, of the baby, and of his dad had been cycling through his head all day. "I've spent an awful lot of my life hoping to live up to what my dad had wanted for me, the accolades and awards. Trying like hell to win a World Series. But after talking to your father last night, I really realized how much my dad loved his kids. He didn't catch a million pitches for me because he loved baseball. He did it because he loved me. This child deserves the same, and I know I'm capable of giving it. I'm not going to pass up the chance to do that. I don't need a test to prove to myself that I can."

"It's okay to have your reservations. I can live with them. I was being unreasonable and expecting you to conform to everything I wanted. I can trust that it will all work out." She smiled up at him, her face so eager and hopeful. "I can trust that we will work out."

"You don't have to worry about my reservations. There aren't any anymore. The last few hours, thinking about losing you again, all I could think was that I didn't doubt for a second that I wanted this. I wanted us, with the baby. The only hitch is that I need to know that you're on board. I need to know that you're in it for the long haul."

She blew out a breath and her eyes lit up, even out there in the bright sun. "I'm more than in it. I'm so sorry about this morning. I freaked out because it took me right back to that place where I was terrified of seeing you walk away."

He nodded, taking in every word, everything he'd wanted to hear from her. There was no way he was waiting another minute to start their future together. It had to start now. "Before I ask you what I need to ask you, I need to say one thing. No more talk of a paternity test. It's a dead issue."

"Okay…" A quizzical look crossed her face. "I know that's been difficult for you."

Here goes nothing. And everything. He dropped down to his knee, holding her hand.

Her other hand flew to her lips. "No."

"You're saying no already?"

Her head nearly rattled back and forth. "Not what I mean. I'm sorry. Go ahead."

He snickered. "Julia Keys, will you marry me? Will you be my wife? Will you parent with me and live happily ever after with me?"

She nodded, but a word didn't come out of her mouth.

"Marry me and have our baby. Nobody needs to think anything else. I don't care if the baby looks like me. Hell, if we're lucky, the baby will just look like you." He reached into his pocket for his grandmother's ring, something he'd thought about hundreds of times since his mother had given it to him. He slid it out of the pouch and held it up for her.

"Where did you get that?"

"It was my grandmother's. My dad's mom. My mother gave it to me the other day when we were over at the house."

"You've had it all this time?"

"You know, when you first told me that you were pregnant, and I insisted that we get married, that was my way of being a man and taking care of things. That was my way of trying to be a dad. And given that I was only a few minutes into it, I realize now that I wasn't doing that great of a job."

"What does that have to do with the ring?"

"I'm trying to say that I don't give this ring lightly. I've never even thought of putting it on another woman's finger. I think it's because I knew all along that I was waiting for you. I'm dying to put it on your finger. I'm dying to hear you say that you'll be my wife and we can have the happily-ever-after that we've spent more than a dozen years waiting on."

"I love you so much, Logan. Of course I'll marry you."

He stood and slipped the ring onto her finger. It didn't quite fit. "I'm sorry. It's a little tight."

"Bloating." She crammed the ring the rest of the way on to her hand. "Normal pregnancy stuff."

He leaned over and kissed her. "You make it sound so sexy."

She rested her forehead against his and they fell into a snug embrace. "I'm worried about one thing, though."

"No. No worrying. We're done worrying. I don't care if the forecast is for hail and the sky is going to fall. No more worrying."

She bugged her eyes at him. "I was just wondering

whether it's rude to get engaged at someone else's wedding."

"Considering all of the very rude things that have happened at our hand over the last few days, an engagement is the least of our worries. We'll just have to keep it our little secret."

"Oh, because we all know how good we are at doing that."

"This one is different. We're both fully invested in it."

"What about the actual wedding? We should probably talk about that at some point."

Good thing he'd thought about this yesterday during the rehearsal. "Yeah, about that. I guess we should do it here in town. For our parents?"

"Yes. Perfect. How about Monday morning?"

"Monday? But that's the day after tomorrow. There's no time to plan. We have to get the license and you'll have to find a dress. And then we'll have to find someone to officiate."

She shook her head and planted her hands on her hips. "If only we knew a judge…"

"My mom."

"Yes. I don't want to go through what Tracy just went through. I just want to get to the good part. Being with you."

He pulled her against him and gave her another kiss, soft and steamy. "You are so brilliant. I can't wait to get you back to the hotel."

She grabbed his wrist and consulted his watch. "Cake gets cut in fifteen minutes. Everyone should be hammered by a half hour after that. I say we make our escape then." Still holding his arm, she turned to head for the stairs, attempting to pull him along.

"Hey, Jules?" He tugged her back.

"Yes?"

"I think you were right. I should write a memoir."

She smiled the most beautiful smile he'd ever seen, which was saying a lot. "What changed your mind?"

"Now I know it's going to have a happy ending."

Epilogue

Julia stopped in her tracks in the hall outside the master bedroom of Logan's Connecticut estate—*their* estate, now that they had been husband and wife for five and a half crazy, but ridiculously happy, months. She slapped her hands against the wall, pushing her hands into the plaster. The pain was unlike anything she'd experienced, a relentless tightening starting in her back and coiling around her midsection. It left her restless, with a desire to do conflicting things—sit and stand, move and freeze, stay silent and scream.

As she'd learned to do in childbirth class, she tried to visualize anything that felt good. Right now, mental images of their dreamy honeymoon in French Polynesia were the only thing getting her through the contractions. She and Logan had spent two weeks in a thatched-roof villa several hundred yards offshore, on stilts above the clear, emerald-green sea. Their days were filled with exquisite food, skinny-dips in their private pool, lovemaking and a nap every afternoon. At night after dinner, they climbed into the hammock and spent hours talking, snug in each other's arms, warmed by soft ocean breezes, body heat and the deep satisfaction that came with knowing they belonged together. They'd made it. And it was perfect.

"You've got this. A few more seconds." Logan continued to apply counterpressure on her lower back with his hand.

As if his words were magic, the tightening released her and she could move again. "Oh, thank God."

He consulted the stopwatch on his phone. "Still eight minutes apart. About forty-five seconds per contraction. Do you want me to call the hospital again? I feel like this isn't moving very quickly."

"They told us it can take a really long time the first time. I don't want to end up in a hospital bed for hours on end. I'd rather be here with you."

He sweetly brushed her hair away from her face. "I know, hon. I just want to make sure you and the baby are safe and healthy." Approaching from the side to avoid her impressive belly, he wrapped his arms around her shoulders and kissed her temple.

She smiled and took his hand. "And I love you for it. Let's just keep walking and we'll call after a few more contractions."

"Sounds like a deal. Which way are we headed?"

"Kitchen. I need food."

The trip downstairs was slow and deliberate, Logan's arm around her as she gripped the ornate wrought iron banister. She loved this house—it was grand, but homey, and they had all sorts of privacy. She loved being permanently on the same coast as her parents, Logan's mom, and Tracy and Carter. It would be a quick trip for the grandparents to fly up to dote on their grandchild. If Tracy and

Carter decided to have a baby, it would give them more chances to get the cousins together.

Julia toddled from the bottom of the stairs into the kitchen, her belly leading the way. "I just want something simple. Orange juice and an English muffin."

"Good, since that's the extent of my culinary skills." Logan went to work while Julia perched on the edge of a bar stool at the kitchen island, surveying the view through the stretch of multiple French doors overlooking the grounds behind the house. Early March and snow was still on the ground, something she was getting used to. She usually spent this time of year at her beach house in Malibu, just to stay away from the cold. "We need to call about having the pool fence put in as soon as the snow has melted. Otherwise, time will get away from us and the next thing we know, the baby will be walking and we'll both be worried sick about him or her getting outside and falling in."

"I already called this morning. After your first few contractions. I figure we'll have our hands full in the next few weeks. I didn't want to risk forgetting."

"Good thinking."

"That's why you love me." He handed her a glass of juice and smiled that electric Logan smile.

"That's part of it." She grinned back at him. There were days with Logan when she was tempted to wonder if this was all a dream. It was about far more than ending up with the charming, ridiculously handsome athlete. He was her best friend. They made each other whole. She'd spent a dozen years convinced they'd never get on the same page at the same time. But this certainly wasn't a dream—it was better. They hadn't been handed this on a silver platter. She and Logan had worked hard for their life together.

The toaster popped, and Logan buttered the English

muffin, bringing it to her on a small plate. Ravenous, Julia took a huge bite, but that was all she got before her body decided to take over. She leaned against the kitchen counter, bracing herself, dropping her head and breathing through the pain.

Logan was quickly at her side again. "Do you want me to rub your back?"

She shook her head vigorously, the pain nearly impossible to take. "Honestly? Don't. Touch. Me."

He took a step back as if she were a bomb about to go off. "Are they getting more intense?"

She couldn't speak. She nodded.

"I think we should go to the hospital."

Finally, her muscles began to uncoil. Her shoulders dropped in relief, and she caught her breath as warmth rippled down her upper thighs. She wondered for a moment if it was just being around Logan. He did have that effect on her, but as much as she loved him, she was feeling anything but romantic right now. The heat trailed down her leg. Liquid trickled onto the polished wood floor. She stared down as the pool of fluid grew. "Oh my God. My water broke."

"Your hospital bag is already in the car. I'll get your coat. And a towel."

He's so calm and collected in a crisis. "No coat. I'm a human furnace right now. And I'd get two towels if I were you."

"One minute."

He flew up the stairs and she soon heard the slamming of cabinet doors. He was back and ready to go before she could finish her English muffin. Frenetic energy radiated from him as he nervously nodded his head and helped her up from her seat. He was ready to go. He was ready for this to happen. She was ready, too. She was tired of feeling like a human beluga.

* * *

Rushing to the hospital ushered in a chaotic mix of excitement, anticipation and worry. Logan felt too much as if everything was happening *to* them and not because of them. They certainly had no control over the things Julia's body was doing, the immense pain she was having to endure. She suffered through the car ride, but remained quiet and focused. He admired her strength, but was not surprised by her determination to make it seem as if she had everything under control.

Now that he was putting their new minivan through its paces, navigating S-turns and tight corners, Logan was happy to learn just how well it handled. He'd never expected he'd own a car like this, nor did he expect that being behind the wheel of this car would make him feel more like a man than any of the expensive sports cars he owned. It made him feel like a dad.

He got them there in record time and zipped into a parking spot near the emergency entrance. An orderly dashed outside to help Julia into a wheelchair and get her inside. Logan juggled a clipboard a nurse had handed him, along with his phone and Julia's bag. He fielded questions about contractions and Julia's due date as she was wheeled into an exam room.

It didn't take hospital staff long to get her into a gown and up on the exam table. A doctor checked her, then rolled back on a stool and scribbled on Julia's chart. "She's nearly five centimeters. You're lucky you didn't stay at home much longer. You might've been having your baby in the car. Let's get you admitted and up into Labor and Delivery."

Julia's sweet eyes flashed up at Logan. They were filled with both optimism and fear. She seemed to be feeling much as he did—like they were riding a corkscrew roller coaster on Christmas morning.

He leaned down and kissed her forehead. "You're doing such a good job. I'm so proud of you."

"Thanks. I'm nervous."

Yes, darling. Me, too.

They were quickly registered and taken to a Labor and Delivery room. The nurses were a godsend—calm and capable through countless unfamiliar experiences: monitors that beeped, cords that lit up, and a constant parade of people in and out of the room. Julia got something to take the edge off the pain, but it was still very much there, and Logan would've done anything to take it all away from her.

She endured the contractions for hours. Logan did his part, talking her through it, reminding her to breathe, holding a cool washcloth to her forehead and giving her ice chips. Still, he felt so helpless that it had turned into a test of his mental endurance. How long can you watch the person you love most in the world suffer? He was desperate to make this easier for her and there was absolutely nothing he could do.

After nearly six hours, they were both exhausted, but Julia was showing the greatest effects of it. Her face was red and puffy, her eyes tired. They'd been left alone for at least the last forty-five minutes, and he was really starting to worry. Why wasn't anyone helping them? Why wasn't the baby here yet? He was just about to call someone when a nurse they hadn't yet met barged through the door.

"I think you're ready to push, Mom." The nurse bunched up the sleeves of the shirt she was wearing under scrubs and washed her hands. "Baby should be here very soon."

"Um, okay," Julia said, seeming as confused as Logan felt.

"I'm sorry. Who are you?" he asked.

"I'm Maria. I just came on shift about twenty minutes ago." She snapped on a pair of latex gloves. "I've been watching your contractions on the monitor. I think you're ready."

How someone could know it was time for the baby to arrive merely by looking on a television monitor was beyond Logan, but he was in no position to argue. "Okay. What can I do?"

"Help me get her feet in the stirrups."

Logan did as he was asked while Julia moaned with the pain of another contraction.

Maria did the quick examination. "Ten centimeters. Fully dilated. I can see the top of the baby's head, if you want to look, Dad."

Logan was struggling to keep up—holding Julia's hand, wanting to see the baby while also being scared to see the baby. The only logical question sprang from his lips. "The doctor?"

"Should be here any minute. But don't worry. I've caught lots of babies." She blew her curly black hair from her forehead and winked at Logan. "Another contraction, Mom?"

Julia nodded and scrunched up her face.

"Dad, help her sit up to push."

Logan took Julia's arm and again did as he was told.

"Bear down. Push as hard as you can. That's great. You can do it." Maria was a font of encouragement.

"Childbearing hips, my ass," Julia grunted, followed by a low and agonizing groan. When the final sound passed her lips, she collapsed back on the bed and turned to Logan. "Even though I love you, I hate you."

He smiled wide. "So nothing has changed."

"Very funny."

He leaned down and pressed a kiss to her forehead, which was damp with perspiration. "I love you more than you'll ever know."

"The baby is crowning. I think only one or two more

pushes like that last one. Looks like he or she has a pretty impressive head of dark hair.'"

"That's a good sign," Julia muttered.

Indeed, it was, although Logan would've taken a bald baby or a baby with clown hair at this point. He just wanted the little bugger to get here.

Julia pushed like a champ through two more contractions. "I don't want to stop. I can't not push."

"That's good. Just keep going. The baby is almost here," Maria said.

Logan didn't bother to bring up the fact that the doctor hadn't arrived. Maria had more than convinced him she knew what she was doing.

"Here comes the head. One more push and you're home free." Maria stood and kicked the stool out from under her.

Julia folded herself in half, her face turning nearly purple, not a sound coming from her. Instead, a squishing noise came from the end of the bed. Followed by a cry.

"It's a girl," Maria exclaimed, pure joy in her voice.

Another nurse walked in and saw what was happening. She rushed to help Maria clean up the baby and swaddle her.

Logan turned to Julia. Tears were running right down her face, but she was smiling ear to ear. He was in a similar state—consumed by happiness and relief. "A girl. It's a girl."

"I know. Oh my God. It's so amazing. I want to see her." Julia was still catching her breath.

"It'll be just a minute," Maria answered as the baby continued to cry. "Then we'll get her to you."

"You're going to be stuck in a house with two women," Julia said. "How's that going to work for the guy who grew up with only brothers?"

He leaned down and kissed her cheek at least a dozen times, wiping away her tears with his lips. "I think it sounds wonderful."

"Here's Baby Girl Brandt," Maria said, presenting Julia with a tiny bundle of baby tightly wrapped in a striped flannel blanket. "I'll leave you three some time to get acquainted. She's perfect. Congratulations."

Julia held the baby looking like she was born to do this. "Sophie?"

He nodded. "After my grandmother."

"The original owner of my ring."

He reached out and rubbed Sophie's cheek with the back of his hand. Her skin was a bit purple and splotchy, but tender and new. Her lips were sweet and pink and she had the most adorable tiny nose. She was incredibly quiet, eyes wide open and alert. "She's beautiful. Just like her mom." Logan couldn't even comprehend how lucky he was. It was unfathomable. He only knew that he was blessed.

Julia peeked under Sophie's hat. "Looks like some serious curly hair under there."

Logan leaned closer and looked. "So she does."

"A little bit like you had when you were younger."

Logan didn't need to weigh in on it. There was so much better left unsaid. They were a family. And a happy one at that.

* * * * *

Pick up all the flirty and fun Mills & Boon
Desire novels from Karen Booth
THAT NIGHT WITH THE CEO
PREGNANT BY THE RIVAL CEO
THE CEO DADDY NEXT DOOR
Available now!

MILLS & BOON®

PASSIONATE AND DRAMATIC LOVE STORIES

A sneak peek at next month's titles...

In stores from 12th January 2017:

- **The Heir's Unexpected Baby** – Jules Bennett *and*
  From Enemies to Expecting – Kat Cantrell

- **Two-Week Texas Seduction** – Cat Schield *and*
  One Night with the Texan – Lauren Canan

- **The Pregnancy Affair** – Elizabeth Bevarly *and*
  Reining in the Billionaire – Dani Wade

MILLS & BOON®

Why shop at millsandboon.co.uk?

Each year, thousands of romance readers find their perfect read at millsandboon.co.uk. That's because we're passionate about bringing you the very best romantic fiction. Here are some of the advantages of shopping at www.millsandboon.co.uk:

* **Get new books first**—you'll be able to buy your favourite books one month before they hit the shops

* **Get exclusive discounts**—you'll also be able to buy our specially created monthly collections, with up to 50% off the RRP

* **Find your favourite authors**—latest news, interviews and new releases for all your favourite authors and series on our website, plus ideas for what to try next

* **Join in**—once you've bought your favourite books, don't forget to register with us to rate, review and join in the discussions

Visit **www.millsandboon.co.uk**
for all this and more today!